FACE VALUE

Vera Cowie was born in County Durham. She lived and worked in London for some years before giving up full-time work to write, and now lives in Bishop's Stortford. She has always written – her first novel was started when she was twelve – and her first published novel was *The Amazon Summer* in 1978. *Face Value* is her seventh novel.

VERA COWIE

FACE VALUE

Fontana
An Imprint of HarperCollinsPublishers

First published by William Collins Sons & Co. Ltd 1990

A Continental edition first published in Fontana 1990
This edition first issued in 1991 by Fontana,
an imprint of HarperCollins Publishers,
77/85 Fulham Palace Road,
Hammersmith, London W6 8JB.

9 8 7 6 5 4 3 2 1

Printed and bound in Great Britain by
HarperCollins Manufacturing, Glasgow

1

~~~~~~◈◈◈~~~~~~

Cambridge, 1988

When Max enquired for Alex at the Porter's Lodge, he was handed a note. 'Dr Brent said you would be calling, sir, and I was to give you this note and ask you to wait in her rooms. Oriel Court, Staircase B —'

'I know the way,' Max interrupted pleasantly.

The note was brief, in Alex's clear hand. 'Sorry not to be here to meet you, Max, but I have been summoned On High. Make yourself at home. The Jack Daniel's is in the usual place. I've booked a table at Leonardo's as requested. What's the trouble this time? Alex.'

Just like Pavlov's dog, Max thought irritably. Invariably associates me with bad news. Well, it's not what I've done this time, my girl, it's what I want you to do . . .

In Alex's pleasant rooms overlooking the Fellows' Garden she had left the curtains drawn against the damp of the early October evening, and made up the fire. The Jack Daniel's, when he took it from the cupboard, was a fresh bottle. Divesting himself of his Burberry he settled his big frame in the armchair by the fire, stretched his long legs to the warmth and poured himself a much needed drink. The M11 had been clogged with traffic, the result of an accident just before Bishop's Stortford, and getting through Cambridge's one-way system was always a drag, but it was worth it to see Alex. And it had been more than a year. Too long, he thought. Reaching across he pressed the On switch of Alex's compact disc player and sighed beatifically as Erroll Garner's magic fingers wove dreams around 'Misty'. 'Ah . . .' he sighed, 'take your time, Alex, take your time . . .'

He wondered idly why the High Mistress, the name bestowed on the Principal of Beaufort College, Cambridge, where Alex — Dr Alexandra Brent, D.Litt. — was Junior Fellow, had issued her summons. Dame Beatrice Lacey was not one of the 'my door is always open' Principals and any summons from her was not to be taken lightly. He grinned to himself. Not that you could take Alex Brent lightly, there was far too much of her, all to her mother's distaste. He frowned, and his long fingers began to drum on the cracked leather of the chair arm.

He was weighing up the pros and cons of a second drink when the door opened and Alex swept in, not like her at all for she usually moved with the majestic deliberation of a galleon, in keeping with her size. He was also surprised at the colour in her cheeks, whilst her eyes, a true hazel and normally as calm and controlled as the rest of her, had turned quite green with some inner exhilaration.

'Sorry to have kept you, Max. You found the Jack Daniel's I see.' She went across, as he got to his feet, to hug and kiss him. 'It's good to see you again.'

'I was now thinking it's been more than a year this time. Far too long.'

'Never mind, you don't look a day older, though you still need a haircut.' She tugged at the black curls almost brushing his collar. The rest of his thick, curly hair was well salted with grey but it had been like that for as long as she could remember, and she had known him twenty years.

'Neither do you,' Max complimented gallantly.

'Is that why you're here? To see if there's been any improvement?'

Max scowled at her. 'It's a wonder you're not as tilted as the Tower of Pisa considering the size of that chip on your shoulder. You don't have to take attitudes with me, of all people.'

'Sorry –' she sounded meek, '– but since the only time I see you is when you're doing something on Madame's behalf –'

'This visit is in my own behalf.'

'Whatever the reason, I'm always glad to see you. I expect you would like some tea?'

'As many crumpets as I can manage and Indian, not China, if you please.'

Alex's glance was envious. 'How come you can eat like the proverbial horse and never gain an ounce?'

'I work hard.'

'Is she still wielding the whip?'

'Want to see my scars?'

Alex laughed as she went into her small kitchen. 'What news of Chris?' she called. 'Is he being a fractious patient, as usual?'

'No. Not at all.'

'How many bones has he broken this time? All you told me was that he'd smashed up yet another car and himself in the process. How many does that make now – four?'

'Five. This one was a new Porsche he'd only had ten days.'

'Foolish boy.' Alex was frowning with a mixture of concern and irritation as she came back with the tray containing crumpets, toasting fork, knife and butter. 'If only he would realize that not even a thousand miles an hour is enough to escape his mother's hot breath.' Handing Max the crumpets and the fork: 'You've not come to persuade me to go back with you and hold his hand? I know of old what a terrible patient he makes. His boredom threshold is so low it's all but invisible.'

'No, he hasn't sent me.'

Alex's frown deepened as she asked, 'What is it then? Something's up, isn't it? I sense what you Americans so colourfully call bad vibes.'

Max examined the crumpet he was toasting. 'This was a very bad crash. The worst yet.'

Alex sat back on her heels. 'Just how bad is he?' she asked, in a voice that expected the worst. 'A Porsche is a high-performance car. What was he doing – a hundred miles an hour?'

'A hundred and thirty.'

'Oh my God . . .' Alex blanched.

'He's in the clinic,' Max said. 'In intensive care.'

'The clinic? But surely that's for plastic surgery?' Her voice quickened with alarm. 'He's not burned?'

'No. But he is in a coma and on a life-support machine. Clinically he's dead, but your mother won't allow them to turn off the machine. That's why I'm here. To ask you to come back with me and persuade her to let Chris go.'

Alex's face was pale but her voice was steady when she said, 'Since my mother has never had a real conversation with me in my life, what makes you think she'll listen to anything I have to say?'

'Because – in spite of everything, you are her daughter.'

'To her everlasting regret.'

'She's out of her mind, Alex. You know how she worshipped

Chris. She's had the clinic emptied of all other patients; she's flown in every specialist in the business who knows anything about brain injuries and she hasn't left his side since he was taken there. She isn't eating, or sleeping –'

'How long?'

'A week now. They told her he was brain-dead when they put him on the machine, but she refuses to believe them. The thing is –' Max hesitated briefly, '– his face is unmarred apart from bruising. It's the back of his head that is an eggshell. His brain stem is a pulp . . .'

Alex had closed her eyes and Max reached out a hand to squeeze her shoulder. Alex did not go in for openly displayed emotions, the consequence of a childhood where they were wielded as a weapon, invariably to her detriment.

'She has to be made to see reason, and you are the only one who can do it.'

'My mother has avoided the sight of me all my life. How can you expect me to get her to look at me now, at this terrible time? I am the very last person she will want to see.'

'I am asking you to try, for Chris's sake; to end this hideous farce. Your brother is dead. Do you want him to be kept on a machine for years? A living corpse? That isn't good enough for him, and didn't you always urge him to go for the best?'

The compact disc came to an end and the soft sounds of the piano faded, though they had both long since ceased to be aware of them. There was a silence but for the crackle of the applewood fire and the sudden whistle of the kettle as it boiled. Getting to her feet: 'Has she asked for me?' Alex wanted to know.

Max gave it to her straight, as always. 'No.' As Alex turned to go into the kitchen, he added, 'But she is coming apart at the seams. She knows nothing, sees nothing but Chris, her adored son. Eve Czerny is a woman whose *raison d'être* is her appearance but she hasn't so much as glanced in a mirror: there aren't any in Chris's room. If that doesn't indicate how she feels, then I don't know her.'

'Yet you expect her to give her attention to me.'

'I am well aware of the hard time she's given you from the day you were born, but Eve Czerny is an irrational creature; there is just a chance that she might appreciate your going to her now.'

'And pigs might fly.' Alex went into the kitchen to make the tea.

8

'I have to take every chance, and I'm down to the rejects.'

'Exactly,' Alex said, her voice curling.

'I didn't mean you and you know it! That was an unfortunate figure of speech. The truth is that I sometimes think your mother has a grudging admiration for you. You have made yourself what you are, and so did she, even if your methods were entirely different.'

'Yet it's Chris, who never managed to make anything of himself, that she adores, because he was someone she could show off and be proud of. She's made it obvious that she's appalled by me. I must have been quite a blow to her self-esteem. The Empress of Beauty with a child who looks like Dracula's Daughter.'

'That's a crock and you know it!' Max snapped angrily.

Alex came back with a tray bearing crockery and a teapot; Spode Blue Italian. Like her mother she had a deep appreciation of fine things. The tea was darkly amber, the way he liked it. He noticed that as Alex poured it her hand was quite steady. That's my girl, he thought proudly.

'The plain fact is that my mother has no time for me, never has had. I was a mistake, and you know what she does with them.' Alex sipped her tea. 'Why hasn't there been anything in the papers about this?'

'Because she put a clamp on everything, and she spends too much in advertising for them to want to cross her.'

'Then she must indeed be upset. I've never known her to refuse free publicity.'

'It's when you say things like that that you make it plain you are your mother's daughter.'

'Which she will not accept. And you want me to go and persuade her to allow her adored son to die? You know how she feels about Chris, so handsome, so attractive to women. She even went so far as to name her range of men's toiletries after him – Krystos, one of her most successful lines. Me she has always relegated to the cupboard. She won't want to see me, Max. Not now. It won't work.'

'My God, but you *are* like her! She never forgives or forgets either.'

'Even I am not big enough to do that.' Alex's voice was dry as dust.

'For God's sake, Alex! The world is full of women who stand five feet ten in their stockinged feet.'

'But who weigh fifty pounds less than I do.' Sweetly: 'And how is Mora, by the way?'

'Doing a spread in the Seychelles – her last.' Max reached for another crumpet. 'Your mother has decided she has been around too long so we're on the hunt for another Face – or we were until all this happened. Now everything is at a standstill, that's what worries me. Nobody can get any decisions on anything. Eve Czerny Cosmetics is dead in the water.'

'That's what you get when you run a one-woman company. Can't you do anything? You usually do.'

'Only so much. I have a lot of clout but the final say-so is always your mother's and God help anyone who usurps her authority. But something has to be done. I've got to get her back on the tracks.'

'I knew there had to be more to it than personal concern.'

'I am concerned, damned concerned. If Chris had ever had the chance to get right out from under your mother's smothering he might have made something of himself; he was beginning to, that's the tragedy, but all that's down the tubes. I'm a realist, as you should know. I deal in facts, and the one I can't get round is that a billion-dollar company is at a standstill, waiting on one woman's whim. We do what we have to do. Isn't that what you say in your book? Isn't that why Jane Eyre left Mr Rochester? She had no choice, was her reasoning. She acted on her powerful instinct for self-preservation. Maggie Tulliver, on the other hand, didn't do anything except accept whatever came her way with resignation. You made it quite clear which woman was right, was being true to herself. Well, I'm being true to myself by doing what your mother pays me for. I'll be damned if I'll stand by and see a highly successful and vastly profitable company allowed to run aground because of one woman's wilfulness. I am prepared to use any means to hand to get through to her, and if that means shoving you in her face, then so be it.' Having delivered himself of that little lecture, Max finished his crumpet.

'I didn't know you had read my book,' Alex said after a moment, sounding deeply pleased.

'I finished it on the plane coming over. It deserves all the praise it has received. I had never before seen those two particular literary ladies in the light you shone on them. Better still, I couldn't put it down.'

Alex's pale, clotted-cream skin had turned quite pink with pleasure.

'I hope it sells and sells.' Max held out his cup for more tea. 'Did you send a copy to your mother?'

'You must be joking! You know her creed. A woman doesn't need brains but she absolutely must have beauty, since that is far more powerful and will get her everything she wants because men will give it to her.'

'Eve has her own brains.'

'Which she is careful to play down.'

'That's because she has something which will always have the edge on brains where men are concerned. Your mother is a sexpot. What Marilyn Monroe would have become had she lived; living proof that Shakespeare was right: age cannot wither nor custom stale . . .'

'It is stale to me,' Alex said distastefully, 'even though it's profitable. I despise everything my mother stands for. Behind the sugar-fondant exterior is nothing more than a complex arrangement of nuts and bolts. I accept that she is distraught; I know how much Chris meant to her, but only as a possession. Had she truly loved him she would have let him go. My mother is incapable of loving anyone but herself.'

'It's because I'm pretty fond of myself that I'm calling in my markers. You owe me, kid. For all the times I went to bat for you. For getting together with Patsy to shoe-horn you out from under; for persuading Eve to allow you to go away to school; for twisting her arm to set up that Trust Fund which kept you while you learned; for helping put you right where you are now. I have all your IOUs and I have no option but to call them in. Twenty years is long enough to have held them, in my book.' He raised a big hand to still Alex's protest. 'And don't tell me I don't know what I'm asking because I do. Just as I know that you are up to it.' He paused. 'And, even if it makes you embarrassed, I know how you really felt about Chris. Deep down, he was your kid brother and you thought the world of him, right?'

'He accepted me for what I was.'

'And didn't hesitate to make use of you when the going got tough. If you were prepared to take on your mother for him when he was alive, why the hell won't you do it for him now, when he's

11

brain-dead? I'm not asking you to sacrifice yourself, you made it plain what you think of that Victorian womanly ideal. Just give a little of your time to help me get round a tricky situation. Is that so much to ask?'

'At this particular time, yes.'

He contemplated her from under his heavy lids. 'Something has happened, hasn't it? I thought you looked a bit hectic when you came in. The summons from On High – good news, was it?'

'Dame Beatrice wanted to tell me that the College is putting me forward as a candidate for the Revesby Prize.'

'Your book?'

'Yes. *A Study in Contrasts* has put me on the map. If I win it, it's the stepping stone to the Mallory Chair. I'll be a Professor, Max!' Alex sounded breathless with delighted surprise.

'And a sock in the eye for your mother.'

'She doesn't know or give a damn about academic prizes. I want it for me, not for her.'

'Liar,' Max said, unmoved. 'Everything you do is to prove something or other to her.' He smiled. 'Congratulations,' he said sincerely. 'But I still don't see that it makes any difference.'

'Of course it does! Here, I'm Dr Alexandra Brent. Nobody knows I'm Eve Czerny's daughter, a woman who has had five husbands and God knows how many lovers! Her world and mine are in different galaxies and I prefer to keep it that way.'

Max was silent. Not surprising, he thought. A university demanded probity, decency and a reputation untouched by scandal, and what was Eve Czerny if not notorious, in a glamorous, tabloid sort of way. He thought of Eve, contrasted her to the daughter she had never publicly acknowledged. The one so dazzlingly beautiful, so sexually alluring, never for a moment doubting her power over men and the world they controlled or her ability to manipulate that control to her own advantage. The other crushed by her lack of looks, her Edwardian-ideal size in a later world where slenderness was everything, her self-confidence as a woman crushed under the weight of the inferiority complex created by her mother.

The first time he had seen Alex she had been ten years old; plain, heavy, with straight brown hair tied in a long plait and a wary expression, shut away on the top floor of her mother's huge villa some ten kilometres from Geneva like some poor relation, never having any communication with the woman who was her mother. He had not even known she existed until, prompted by his own curiosity, he had come across the little world hidden under the eaves where Alex lived with her governess, Miss Patterson, known as Patsy. Something about the child – and he loved children – had touched his sentimental Italian heart, and applying his considerable charm he had eventually opened her up, brought her out, soon becoming aware that behind the unprepossessing appearance there was a treasure house. At ten years old she was already formidably intelligent, but piercingly lonely. Her middle-aged governess was her only companion; her only source of love and affection, which were returned in full measure, yet she was already painfully aware that her half-brother, the golden child Christopher, was the adored centre of their mother's life.

Eve had been besotted with him from birth. 'Isn't he exquisite? Did you ever see such a flawless skin? And those eyes? Isn't he just the most beautiful thing you ever saw?' she would ask anyone within hearing distance, time and time again. 'He is so perfect I could eat him up,' and she would hug him and nibble small kisses all over his face until he squirmed to escape. And she did eat him up, Max thought now. She chewed him to pieces. And all the while Alex lived the life of a reject, becoming convinced that the reason for her rejection was her lack of beauty. 'I would rather be beautiful than anything else in the world,' Eve was wont to say, and frequently, 'In the religion of beauty, I am its High Priestess.' And its object of worship. Her self-dedication was total. Even Christopher had never been allowed to touch, only look, when she was dressed and made-up ready to go out; when she was not, he was the one who was allowed to crawl all over his mother's silk sheets to be fed titbits from her breakfast tray.

Once, in bed, for his duties early on had included that of lover, Max had asked, knowing he was secure enough to be able to do so: 'What is it you have against Alex? Is it her lack of looks? OK, so she's a plain Jane, but she's as bright as a button and she has a distinct and memorable personality. You can hold the most fascinating conversations with her.'

'That is all plain women are fit for: conversations.'

'But it's not just that, is it? There's something more . . .'

Eve had turned to him imperiously. 'We will not talk of this. It is none of your business. Understand me, Max. You will not raise this subject again.'

'OK, whatever you say,' he had agreed peaceably. But it had not stopped him thinking about it. There's a Bluebeard's locked room here all right, he'd decided. Like who was the kid's father? What did he do that his daughter should become the kid without the iron mask — leave her mother? Eve would never allow that. Her vanity did not permit of any man leaving her. She had to dump them. But when he tried to find out he discovered that Eve had covered her tracks too carefully. He could find nothing earlier than 1960, when she had been the protégée of one Henri Beyle, a Swiss industrialist whose millions had provided her first capital, with which she had set up what eventually became Eve Czerny Cosmetics, a billion-dollar corporation.

It was in sifting through the verbiage — and there were tons of it — that he discovered there was a marked shortage of facts. Like where she was born, to whom, when, and in what stratum of life. She *said* she was of Austro-Hungarian descent and readily admitted to being a refugee from the 1956 Uprising, but nowhere was there any proof as to her age when she left her native country. By the time Max went to work for her, in late 1967, Henri Beyle had been dead for some years and Eve had been married and widowed when Christopher Bingham IV, the father of her son, had been killed in a freak accident on the polo field. Chris had then been four years old. Nowhere, absolutely nowhere, was there any mention of a ten-year-old daughter. Which was when Max decided to put in his two cents'-worth. Once he was securely established as Eve's right-hand man, he acted as Alex's protector, eventually managed to get her out from under an atmosphere that was slowly but surely choking her.

If only it had been the other way round, he thought for the thousandth time; Alex the beauty and Chris the brains. But when did life ever make things that simple? Alex had not spoken to her mother more than half a dozen times in the first thirteen years of her life; had not even seen her for the past seven. To the world at large Eve Czerny had only one child: her son. When Max had protested she had shrugged, said impatiently: 'How can I produce such a daughter? And now, at this stage in my life? For the Empress

14

of Beauty to be seen to have given birth to such an Ugly Duckling would be a contradiction of all I stand for. I tell women that they will be beautiful if they use my creams and lotions. One look at that girl and they will at once ask: "How is it they haven't worked on her, then?" No, Max. I cannot like the child. I never have. I never wanted her in the first place – and you will repeat that at your peril. I have provided for her, haven't I? She is fed and decently dressed and educated. The Trust you persuaded me to set up provides for whatever she needs.'

'Doesn't your conscience ever bother you?'

'Why? I repeat, I have provided for her. That is all there is to it. I do not wish to discuss it further.'

Now, Max sighed, and Alex's look was troubled when she said, 'I know I owe you, Max, more than I can ever repay, but what you're asking for *is* that more. I have my own life to live and my mother has never given a damn how I did it. I know what you're after . . . one look at me and all Mother's old antipathy will override her grief. She'll rise up all teeth and claws.' Bitterly: 'Do you want to see *my* scars?'

'I know every one of them. I was the one applied the ointment and wrapped the bandages, remember?'

'Then how can you ask me to go into the lion's den again?'

'Because the sight of you will get her back on her feet, even if it's only slavering at the mouth. There's a lot more at stake here than a mere estrangement. We are talking thousands of jobs, millions in money and a future that will continue to let you live in the style to which you have become accustomed.'

'Give her time,' Alex said callously. 'She'll come round.'

'Too late. Time is what I don't have. Once it gets out that Eve Czerny Cosmetics is becalmed, Eve no longer at the helm, the takeover mob will move in for the kill.'

'How? Mother owns the company outright.'

'They'll offer to buy and she might just agree to sell.'

'Would that be so bad?'

Max looked horrified. 'Bad? Eve Czerny *is* the company. Look what happened when Elizabeth Arden died – and Helena Rubenstein. Do you want that to happen to Eve Czerny?'

'Frankly, my dear, I don't give a damn,' Alex quoted.

'Well I do. The Eve Czerny image is unique; no other company has the glamour, the hold on the market, that we have. We are a class company – our only real rival is Estée Lauder because she's in the same league. I've worked my ass off to push the company to the top and I intend to keep it there. I know your mother is giving a performance – her whole life is a long-running smash hit – but I'd rather not close the show down while she recovers from her bereavement.'

'Nor will I go on as understudy.'

'You'd never get through the auditions! Once it's officially announced that Chris is dead people will expect a natural hiatus, but your mother has imposed a blackout. The newshounds outside the clinic don't know anything but they're speculating like mad. There are rumours that our new cell-renewal cream has turned out to be a disaster; that it has given Eve such a terrible skin rash she dare not show her face. Customers are anxious, everybody wants to know why she's in the clinic, how badly her son is hurt – what the hell is going on! Why the clinic is closed and all the patients sent elsewhere. The situation is serious. Would I be here otherwise? I'm not exaggerating when I say she's mad with grief . . . everything is in a state of chaos and you can't afford that with a company like Eve Czerny Cosmetics. Rumours are the kiss of death in our business.'

'I have nothing to give my mother,' Alex said, 'which is exactly what she gave me.'

'It doesn't concern you that she's sufficiently unhinged to try to kill herself?'

Alex's look poured scorn. 'She's tried before, more than once – all of them calculated failures.'

'You haven't seen her.'

'Nor do I wish to. I won't be set up as an Aunt Sally, used as a goad to bring her out of her self-absorption. Don't you realize what she'll do if it gets out that she has a 31-year-old daughter? Isn't she supposed to be only forty-five? And it won't do *me* any good either. I'm up for a prestigious prize – what will my chances be if it's trumpeted all over the front pages that I am Eve Czerny's bastard!'

'That case is not yet proven.'

'What else can I be? That's what Mary Brent said when she delivered me up to her – "I've brought you your bastard" were the words she used. Picture that spread over every front page and gossip column and then consider my chances of receiving the Revesby Prize. I have to be whiter than white. You know what university faculties are like.'

'Hotbeds of gossip. In which case, how do you explain me?'

'Easily. You are my Trustee.'

'Not your boyfriend?'

Alex's smile was amused. 'You are and always will be my dearest friend, Max, but let's not pretend it could ever be otherwise. Since when have you ever been seen with a woman who wasn't a head-turner?'

'Christ, but your mother has a lot to answer for!'

'Which is why my answer has to be no, since we both know my mother is answerable only to herself. I will not willingly submit myself to more of the same, Max. If Chris was alive, in pain, suffering, you know I would be there like a shot. But this isn't for him; this is for my mother and I'll be damned if I'll lift so much as a finger to help her!' She met his eyes head on, every bit as stubborn as he was persuasive, and Max was second only to Eve Czerny as one of nature's persuaders.

He was a very sexual animal; Alex had not realized this until, on the occasion of his first visit to Cambridge, she had been asked curious and even eager questions about him. It had borne out something she had heard some years earlier when, as a teenager, she was waiting in his outer office for him to take her to see *Madame Butterfly*. There had been a group of stunning models also waiting to see him; up for the superlative chance of becoming the Czerny Face, and talking about Max. Alex had not then understood what they meant when they agreed unanimously that, sexually, Max Fabian was a ten. In her unworldly innocence she had asked him, been surprised when he had first laughed then said on a grin: 'They think I'm pretty smart, I guess.' But she had wondered at the smirk on his face. It was only later, when she had seen him with one gorgeous female after another that she had finally understood, and been proud for him, for their relationship was totally asexual.

To Alex, Max was her best friend, had been since she was ten years old. He had been Uncle Max for years, until he had said she was getting too old and it was about time she called him by his name. She had worshipped him for years until that hero-worship had developed into a deep and abiding love; that of true friendship. Being what she was – or thought she was – she was content with that and never thought to ask for more, even though she had eventually realized that he was a very attractive man. Not handsome, his face was too rough-hewn for that, but he had a pair of remarkable, plain-chocolate eyes with lashes any woman would have killed for, and a voice that reached you as a caress. Dark, as befitted his Italian ancestry – he had been born Massimo Fabiani in New York's Little Italy forty-three years before – he had the smooth, pale-olive skin of the Latin allied with white, perfectly aligned American teeth and a sensual, well-cut mouth. He had a supersonic intelligence and a sardonic tongue, but what women remembered was the eyes, the smile, the big, splendid body: he topped Alex by four inches. But to Alex he was the kind, loving, patient man who had dried her tears, soothed her fears, listened to her woes, surreptitiously bought her the chocolate Patsy had forbidden, given her the occasional handout, taken her to the circus and the pantomime and never, ever forgotten her birthday. She had even managed to overcome the temporary estrangement that had occurred once she discovered he had for a time been her mother's lover. 'I was younger then,' he had explained, 'and like all men I took your mother at her face value and was conned.'

In Alex's eyes, Max could do no wrong, and in all the years she had known him he had been nothing but good to her; still she was under no illusions as to his ambition. Ostensibly her mother's lawyer, he had over the years become her second-in-command. Eve, who trusted no one, trusted Max and he had proved himself worthy of it. Max never lied. Not even to suit your purpose, never mind his own. But he was as dedicated to the onward and upward progress of Eve Czerny Cosmetics as was its owner and founder, and not just because, over the years, he had been rewarded with generous stock options.

Max loved his work, and Alex had never found anything strange in the fact that so masculine a man should work in the claustrophobic, intensely feminine world of manufactured beauty. He had not Eve's flair – no, genius, Alex thought honestly – for colours, every single one of which she mixed and blended herself until her infallible instinct told her that *this* was the one; or her incredible nose for fragrance; or her talent for self-promotion; but he was a superb organizer. Though hers was always the Last Word, Eve left Max pretty much alone when it came to the day-to-day running of the huge company; the melding and meshing of production schedules and deliveries, the tying-up of stores for her spring and autumn promotions, his keeping the factories strife-free and running smoothly, his shrewd lawyer's brain always alert for the over-extravagant claim, the lavish hyperbole to which Eve was given. 'You can't say that,' he would explain to Eve patiently. 'Because it isn't true.'

'But who knows it? I'm selling dreams, Max. When will you understand that?'

'It won't be a dream if a woman takes your word as gospel and doesn't get the results you promise. She'll sue and take you to the cleaners. Bad publicity is what we don't need, now or ever! Don't come right out and say it – hint at it. Let the buyer jump to her own conclusions. Don't give her the chance to say "But your advertising *said* so."' And he would redraft the ad so that though the implication was there, a definite claim wasn't.

Max was clever with words, Alex reminded herself, which was confirmed when he said, 'I'm not asking you to do this for your mother. I'm asking it for Chris. He would do the same for you. It's ghoulish; like those women in India who used to burn themselves on their husband's pyre. Whatever your mother is – and I know as well as you do what that is – you have to agree that it would be a terrible waste. It's bad enough that Chris had to die; don't let your mother follow him.'

'She won't,' Alex said, contempt edging her voice. 'Chris was special to her, I realize that, but in the last analysis the only person she has ever *really* loved is herself. Once she realizes she isn't going to get what she wants she will rewrite the dialogue. Oh, I'll bring it home to her what has happened – she will see me and *know* that she has lost, but I'm not prepared to suffer for it. I've suffered enough, thank you. Mother takes any loss as a personal affront and God help anyone her eye lights on when it happens.'

'You can handle yourself. You aren't a child any more.'

'Where my mother's concerned I'll always be a child.' Then: 'What about Pamela?' she asked. 'I thought she was able to handle Mother.'

'Eve won't let her inside the clinic.'

Alex shook her head disgustedly.

'I told you,' Max said, 'she's crazy with grief. She blames Pamela for encouraging Chris in his passion for fast cars.'

'Of course! Nothing is ever my mother's fault. The fact that she gave Chris his first fast car when he was sixteen will be conveniently forgotten.'

'Pamela is in a bad way, too. She loved Chris very much. She was good for him. He was beginning to stand up to Eve – which is why she's taking her revenge now. Did you know that Eve cut him off high and dry when he went off with Pamela? She thought that would bring him back. What she overlooked was how much money Pamela got when Fritzie Bahlsen dumped her for wife number four. She could have afforded a dozen Chrises.'

'It wasn't the money that made my mother so furious. It was the fact that Pamela put some backbone into Chris. I didn't see him often enough to give him the constant support he needed; Pamela did. She made a man of him. I shall always be grateful to her for that. At least Chris was happy for a few years of his life.'

'And now she can't even get to see him for the last time,' Max said, applying pressure.

Alex's powerful jaw jutted. 'Don't make me out to be the villain of this piece. My mother obeys no laws but her own and she makes them up as she goes along.'

'You aren't the villain,.but you are the key. I need you to unlock a few doors. God knows what will happen when you do, but I know you're a survivor. You have the strength Chris lacked. And I'll back you all the way.'

'You're still asking too much of me, of all people.' Alex had a stubborn streak as deep as the Pacific Trench.

'I am asking no more than you are capable of.'

He was as inflexible as she was. Alex knew she tended to intimidate – she had been warned of that fact – but Max was the one man who could intimidate her. He knew her too well. Better than she did herself, she thought uneasily, and he had performed miracles on her behalf. She did owe him something. Like her present life, for instance.

'I need the peace and tranquillity here,' she said, as much to her own sense of guilt as to him. 'All I will get from her is what I've always had. The frozen mit, as you so elegantly put it. I thought I

20

was done with all that; that I'd never have to go through it again. I have a good life now, one I've worked hard to achieve.'

'Did you ever think that by going as deep as you could get into the Groves of Academe you might not be able to see the wood for the trees? This is no "life" you lead; it's an existence, but you chose it because it was safe. OK, so you didn't have what I would call tenure in your early life; you never knew if you were doing the right thing, or when your mother would take it into her head to sling you out. So you opted for a nice, safe backwater and I don't give a damn about how hung you are with degrees – there's more to life than learning!'

'*I* like it – and since it does no harm to you – or to anyone – I don't see that you have the right to criticize! I'm *happy* here – understand that. I chose to live the way I live and if you don't like it you still don't have the right to tell me it's wrong! I'm doing what *I like*.'

'To what end? To cock a snook at your mother! To say, "I may not have looks but I certainly have brains and I've got the parchments to prove it!" Do you have a large circle of friends? Do you ever go out with men? Do you have anything to do with what life is all about? The hell you do! No wonder you admire E. M. Forster! But at least he saw something of the world before he turned his back on it!'

Alex jumped to her feet, white with rage. 'I think you had better leave.'

'Not until you agree to come back with me.'

'Never!'

'Then I stay. You'll have to call the porter to throw me out.'

Alex knew he meant it. Max did not make idle threats. 'You don't know what you're asking!' she pleaded.

'And you should know me better than that.'

They stared at each other, and it was then that Alex saw the strain in Max's face and it struck her like a blow. His dark eyes were like craters, but they were terrifyingly hard and cold. She was very still and white.

'We do what we have to do, remember?' he said, his voice as hard as his eyes. 'I'm trying to save a company from going down the drain and your mother from committing an enormous idiocy just because she's playing *Medea*, Actors' Studio style. If I didn't think

21

you could do it I wouldn't be wasting my time asking you, but it's a plain fact that you are the one goad which your mother will feel – and I want her hurting, not numb with grief! I want her brought back to life, roaring, despotic life, and you know enough to know when to duck.'

'There was a time when I would have given anything to have her roar at me,' Alex said, much more calmly, 'but whenever she looked at me she never saw me.'

'I'm hoping that when she sees you this time you will hit her right between the eyes.'

'Killing by kindness?' Alex asked with a crooked smile.

'Nobody is going to get killed. That's not what I'm after.' Max held the hurt hazel eyes and said quietly, 'Haven't I always done my best for you?'

Alex nodded.

'So all I'm asking is that you do your best for me. You don't have to hang around. Just get her back on her feet. I'll handle the rest.'

Alex sighed, which was when Max knew he had her. He had counted on her powerful sense of obligation, something that had arisen out of never having received that benefit from her mother.

'I must be back here by Monday.'

'Done. I've got a plane standing by at Stansted and a car downstairs. We can be in Geneva in a couple of hours.'

'So why did you ask me to book a table at Leonardo's?'

Max recognized the olive branch and accepted it. 'I thought I might get you drunk and kidnap you if I had to.' He stood up, one of the few men who could make her feel small. 'I'm obliged, kid. This clears all your markers.'

While Alex went to the telephone Max sat down again, slack with relief. While he had not *really* doubted – he knew Alex far better than she did herself – it was still a relief. He also knew she had every right to be apprehensive. In her present state, there was no telling what Eve might do or say, even though Alex was right when she said that the reaction she had always got from her mother was out of the deep freeze. But right now Eve was somewhere in the fires of hell. All he could do was be there if she directed her flamethrower in Alex's direction.

'Right,' Alex said, returning from the telephone. 'Give me a few minutes to throw a few things in a bag.'

When she came back she had changed into a grey suit – plain and unremarkable – over a matching polo-necked sweater, but her shoes were still flatties with one-inch heels. She dressed like a woman who knew better than to expect a second glance. I've got to have a talk with her, Max resolved. When all this is over and done with . . .

They boarded the company jet just before six o'clock and took off within minutes. Max ordered sandwiches but Alex said she wasn't hungry. They did not talk much; Max busied himself with papers from his briefcase and made several telephone calls while Alex sat and stared out of the window, seeing but not looking at her own reflection.

Allowing for the time difference it was almost 9 p.m. when the car that had met them at the airport turned into specially opened gates of the Czerny Clinic, which catered for the very rich and very vain, offering every known method of retaining eternal youth. Normally it was lit like a Christmas tree; now it was dark, and once inside there was no sound, no bustle. Even the clinic was in mourning, Alex thought as they entered the lift. They did not see a soul.

Max led the way down a long corridor to double doors which had a light behind their glass panels. Hand on the knob: 'Courage,' he said. 'Remember, you are no longer a child.'

Alex nodded, her face expressionless.

'I won't come in. I want her to think this is your idea. But I'll be within hearing distance if you need help.' He put a hand on her broad shoulder. It was like a board. 'OK?'

Alex nodded and Max opened the door.

The room was lit by only the one light, directly above the bed, illuminating the figure lying motionless on it, connected by wires to machines which wheezed, blipped, purred and sighed. The figure sitting hunched in a chair to the right of the bed did not move as the door opened and Alex stood just inside it, waiting. She knew better than to speak first.

But the figure did not move; there was about it an intensity which was almost palpable. Alex could not see them but she knew that her mother's eyes were fixed on the waxen face of her son, willing him to live. There was no sound but the soughing and sighing of the machines.

Alex cleared her throat, for she found it clogged when she tried to speak, then she took a deep breath and used a word she had never used before to the figure by the bed. 'Mother.' No response. She tried again, making her voice firm. 'Mother, it's Alex.'

She saw the figure straighten slumped shoulders, the droop of despair square to a mathematical rigidity. Slowly, as if it was rusty, the still red-gold head turned and in the light of the lamp Alex saw her mother's face.

She had seen it in all its manifestations. The imperious beauty, the artless charmer, the sparkling hostess, the shrewd business-woman, the gracious chatelaine, the icily controlled fiend – her mother had a face to fit whatever occasion arose, but, Alex realized with a shock, what she was seeing now was no mask; this was the real Eve Czerny, almost catatonic with pain. It left Alex totally disconcerted.

She had never seen her mother other than perfectly and exquisitely presented, fresh from the assembly line that was her dressing-table. Not a hair out of place, not a crease to be seen, every effect calculated down to the last, perfectly placed eyelash. To Alex, her mother had always looked the same. She had never seemed to age, and though Alex knew this was the result of face-lifts performed just before they were necessary, thus avoiding any before-and-after syndrome, the resulting state of unchanged perfection had rendered obsolete even the notion of Eve Czerny ageing. Now, what Alex saw was a woman ravaged not only by time but by grief. A woman who was *old*. It was so shocking it rendered her speechless.

'Alex?' The voice too was rusty, abraded to an uncharacteristic rasp by hours of agonized weeping, but it said the name on a rising inflexion not only of disbelieving surprise but also – and it further completed Alex's rout – of hope. 'Alex?' it asked again, and this time there was not only hope but gladness. It was so far from what Alex had expected as to be unbelievable, but she had enough first-hand experience of the lacerating effect of suffering to recognize the real thing when she saw it. As if to confirm it, her mother brought her hands up to her face, bent it into them and burst into desperate, hopeless tears.

A wrench of pity put the spur to Alex's powerful sense of com-passion but some icy core of reason reined it in. Her mother was a consummate actress with a genius for using emotion to blind or compel. What about the times when I wept? she thought. Did you ever care? This is what I used to pray for; the absolute destruction of your carefully erected barricades of young lovers, miraculous face-lifts and fifty-thousand-dollar dresses.

She became conscious that her mother was repeating certain words over and over and over again, in a voice that was so abject, so raw with pleading, that it shook. 'Forgive me, please . . . forgive me . . .' Alex watched, riveted to the spot by a mixture of shock and disbelief, as her mother groped for the back of the chair, her eyes blind with tears, her haggard face twisted in a rictus of naked pleading before getting shakily to her feet. She took a tottering step forward and stretched both hands in the direction of her mute, utterly confounded daughter and said again, in the same, broken voice: 'Please . . . forgive me . . . I beg of you, forgive me . . .'

Then she crumpled to the floor like a heap of discarded clothing.

2

Hungary, 1932–56

She had been born Anna Farkas, a child of the Hungarian Puszta, that conglomeration of farm buildings, peasant huts, granaries, stables and sheds that occupied the centre of a large estate, often growing to the size of a village, with its own school and church. She was the sixth and last child of Gyorgy Farkas and his wife, also named Anna, descendants of farm servants who had, for generations, belonged to the noble family who owned the estate and the castle which was its core, little more than serfs. The estate lay in the far west of Hungary, in the province of Gyor-Sopron, and the nearest town was Gyor, but Anna was seven years old before she ever set eyes on it. It was not far from the Austrian border; the whole region had once belonged to Austria, as Hungary had once been part of the Austro-Hungarian empire.

She was taken to Gyor along with her brothers and sisters for the wedding of the oldest daughter of her mother's youngest sister, who had married above her station a man who worked on the railways, an unusual event, for the people of the Puszta tended to marry among themselves. Anna was both terrified and exhilarated. All she knew was the endless fields; now the noise, the buildings, the people, came as a revelation. But what changed her life for ever was her first visit to the cinema. It was an Astaire–Rogers musical, and it showed her a world that seemed like a dream. A world of beautiful women, exquisitely dressed, elegant men in black and white, who danced and lived in beautiful houses and drove in big cars and ate delicious food. Anna watched, spellbound, and knew that somehow, some way, she had to enter that world. She wanted it with a hunger that took over and possessed her: nothing else mattered. She wanted it so badly that from then on, everything she did was directed to that end. From then on she haunted the grounds of the castle, stealthily peered through windows ablaze with light at the men and women inside, who confirmed all she had seen on the black and white screen. When the cavalcade of cars came down the road from Budapest she was always there, hidden behind a tree or a bush, watching, listening, learning.

When, later, her mother – who acted as midwife to the Puszta – went back to Gyor to assist at the lying-in of her niece, Anna begged to go with her, promising to be good, to do whatever was required of her, to work, run errands, do anything just so long as she could go to the city. As she was the youngest, and as her prettiness had been much admired on her first visit, her mother agreed. Thus, by dint of begging – though her mother would have beaten her for it – borrowing (a small coin here and there from any purse within reach) and stealing whatever came her way, she managed to acquire the few coins necessary to enter the magic world of the cinema again. When her uncle, jovial at becoming the grandfather of a boy first time, said she had been a good girl and asked what she would like as a reward, she said, round-eyed, 'A visit to the cinema' and he laughed and said she might go with her older cousins. Again she chose a musical, another Fred and Ginger, and again she was transported.

On their return home, to a life she now hated, she would lie in her bed, which she shared with two older sisters, and go over every scene, every song, every dance, and repeat to herself her vow that one day she would live in that world, far away from the hard labour, the poverty, the servile obedience to an authority she hated. She loathed being the child of impoverished labourers, admired her mother's sister for moving up the social ladder, for leaving behind the stigma of being a Puszta dweller, the lowest of the low. She knew she was different, and not only because of her looks. She had nothing in common with her parents – old at forty – and she held her brothers and sisters in contempt for accepting their lot. She hated the work she had to do. It was even worse when the war came, but that was nothing to the way everything changed when the Russians arrived. I am meant for more than this, was her creed. Why has God made me beautiful if not to use that beauty? For she undoubtedly was remarkably beautiful.

Had Gyorgy Farkas not known why his daughter was so different he would have believed his wife had played him false, for whilst they were both dark, as were their other five children, Anna had

27

bright, red-gold hair, a dazzlingly fair complexion and eyes of a turquoise blue so deep, so vivid, that they stopped men in their tracks. Her delicate bones were covered by just the right amount of flesh – puppy fat never ventured near her – all delectably curved. She had tiny hands and feet and a husky, throaty voice as beguiling as her smile. She was also possessed of a sensuality that killed at a thousand yards. And all because her great-grandmother had been seduced by a noble visitor to the castle, an exercise in the *droit de seigneur* that was commonplace in nineteenth-century Hungary. The resultant child had inherited its father's colouring, and had passed its genes on to the peasant who was Anna Farkas, so that she looked like an aristocrat with all sixteen quarterings. She had also inherited her great-grandfather's intelligence and though her education was minimal she never ceased to learn from any and every source. She haunted the wastebins at the back of the castle, took away newspapers and magazines which she hid so as to be able to pore over them in what little leisure time she had. She was also a born mimic; found it easy to copy a voice, a tonal quality, a gesture, an expression.

Her one aim was to escape; to leave Hungary and find that sunlit golden land where she would never be hungry, or have to drudge, where she would be able to lie back in one of those baths full of bubbles and step from it into a warm towel held by a maid. Her mirror told her that her face was her fortune, but she was never going to be able to capitalize on it unless she got away. The one thing she was certain of was that it would be accomplished by a man or men, and when she was seventeen her chance came in the form of a Russian Commissar who came to see why the estate – now a collective – was falling behind in its quotas. Anna spotted him at once; more important, she spotted the way he saw her.

He was at least thirty years older than she was, neither was he particularly attractive, but he arrived in the big black car which indicated high Party rank, and exuded the intoxicating aroma of power. When the big black car returned to Budapest, Anna was in it with him.

That city proved to be something of a disappointment; she had expected another New York, but if the flat in which he installed her was not in that category of luxury to which she was determined to become accustomed, it was a vast improvement on what she had been used to. Best of all, it had a bathroom. Now (and for the rest of her life) she would be able to spend hours luxuriating in hot, fragrant bubbles (for the Russian was able to acquire luxuries of the kind never available to Hungarians) and wrap herself in a warm, fleecy towel. She was also able to release her powerful sexuality, for her protector was a man who liked sex as often as possible, and though he was – she learned by later experience – more greedy than generous, he was better than nothing.

She was apprehensive when, after almost two years, he was promoted to East Germany, but his successor, a very different man, was happy to take her over, and it was from him that she learned what was to stand her in so much good stead in the future.

He was a cultured man, in his early forties, and had served abroad in various Russian embassies; he spoke English, French and Italian, and he had been demoted to Hungary because of some punishable infringement of Party dogma. He liked music – he was an excellent pianist – and it was from him that she acquired the name under which she became famous. He used to call her teasingly 'the eternal Eve' and so she adopted that as her new Christian name, added Czerny from a sheet of music she found on the piano. Eve Czerny. She used to say it aloud in front of her mirror, holding out an imperious hand to be kissed. It sounded right. When the time came, she thought, nodding at her reflection, that is who I will be. That will be my name in the West. Who will connect that with Anna Farkas? She told no one, but she resolved that when she knew how to do it – and who could do it for her – she would acquire a new set of papers in that name.

From her cultured Russian she also acquired a knowledge of good food and wine; he had spent several years in Paris, ostensibly a Russian businessman, in reality a spy. He was able to obtain Western magazines for her, and indulgently agreed to teach her a few words of English. While he was out, she spent her time learning the language, poring over the grammar, practising her pronunciation, although with him she was careful to speak it in a way that made him laugh. He had no idea that the exquisitely lovely young girl who was so childishly eager to learn had a mind that was every bit as keen as his own. It was enough that when he returned at the end of the day she was there, waiting for him, freshly bathed and wearing one of the dresses he was able to obtain, of the kind that never appeared in any Hungarian shop; that she was always ready for sex, was quite content to occupy herself when he had things to do, but equally happy to sit and listen to music with him, or to his telling her about his years in the West. He was proud to show her off, to know that he was envied, and proud of the way she flowered, unfurling her loveliness to him as the sun who had brought her to life. He taught her much, but there was a certain knowledge she had been born with.

She had innate taste; she knew exactly what looked right. She also had style. She endowed the simple dresses he bought her with that indefinable something the French called 'chic'. She could have worn a floursack and still turned every head.

She also had a remarkable pair of hands. Her mother had suffered from intense headaches, her father from muscle strain in the shoulders, but Anna's long, strong fingers had always been able to massage the pain away. She had been taught this by her paternal grandmother, who had died when Anna was fourteen, and who had been taught it by her own mother. Now, Anna was able to put those hands to good use, for her Russian protector suffered from severe muscle spasms, the result of a nervous constitution. Once Anna had persuaded him to let her massage the iron-hard shoulders and rigid neck, he was both astounded and grateful at the ease with which she smoothed and kneaded the stiffness away. 'Truly,' he told her, 'you have healing hands. I have spent time in clinics in the Crimea that has not given me the benefit those hands of yours have bestowed in fifteen minutes.'

Which gave her an idea. Her aim in life was still to be rich and powerful, and while she enjoyed the life of a kept woman there were times – and enough of them for her to take them seriously – when she wished *she* was the one with the money and the power. If she could ally them to her beauty, she would present a triumvirate that could take on and conquer the world, but in the meantime, she had to make do with what she had, all of which had come through men, and use those same men to get sufficient purchase and a firm grip; *then* she could hoist herself to the top. So she set up in business as a masseuse.

Russians were firm believers in the benefits of massage, and once the virtues of her 'healing hands' had been extolled to the circle in which her protector moved, she soon found that she had enough clients to keep her busy six days a week. She visited them in their apartments – in some cases large houses – and kept both her eyes and her ears open. She also made money, because her Russian good-naturedly allowed her to keep all she made.

She found a chemist – who was actually a biochemist – willing to make up the herbal oils she used, her grandmother having taught her how to mix them. He was a Hungarian, and at first never more than frigidly polite to her because she was a Hungarian girl being kept by a servant of their Russian masters, but when she asked him if he would be interested in the information she picked up during her visits, his attitude changed. She knew, from that same gossip, that there were underground elements in the city dedicated to the eventual overthrow of those they regarded as oppressors, and she had shrewdly surmised, from Laszlo Kovacs' attitude to her, that he sympathized with their aims. From there, it was a simple step to say that she had been planted on the Russian by certain people – she could not name them, of course – in order to learn all she could, that she was taking a risk and asking him not only because she sensed he shared her ideals but because her usual contact had been arrested and had disappeared inside AVO headquarters on Andrássy Street. Few who went in ever came out. 'I learn all sorts of things – some of it may be useful, some not – but I do not know what to do with the information if I cannot pass it on.' She sounded genuinely troubled, so much so that Laszlo reported back to his group, who instructed him to ask certain pertinent questions. If her answers were satisfactory then, perhaps . . .

Eve – as she now thought of herself, though she introduced herself to Laszlo by her real name – was able to supply them with names; names of people she knew had been arrested and were in no position to contradict her story. She knew when they had been arrested and for what, and as a couple of the names were impressive, she was able to convince Laszlo's group that she was not a double agent, especially when she supplied them with certain vital pieces of information. She also seduced Laszlo, though in such a manner as to leave him convinced that he had seduced her. He was an attractive man in a sexily ugly way; tall and well built, with a prow of a nose and a pair of remarkably beautiful hazel eyes. In bed he was a virtuoso. He was also a brilliant chemist. When one of Eve's clients developed a distressing skin rash, he made up a cream that cleared it up in five days.

It was at that time, in 1953, that Imre Nagy came to power, and introduced a much more liberal regime. For the first time in years, cosmetics began to appear in the shops, but they were of inferior quality. Anna herself used Elizabeth Arden, which her Russian brought back for her on his occasional trips to Vienna. And it was as she was comparing those expensive, high-quality products with what was obtainable locally that her idea came to her. It was, she used to say dramatically years later, like a revelation.

'What we have to do,' she told Laszlo excitedly, one afternoon, 'is make our own.' She had gone for a fresh supply of oil – the excuse she always used, but she always went between the hours of one and two, when Laszlo closed his little shop for lunch, and that hour was always spent in bed.

'Make our own!'

'Yes. First you analyse the creams and the lotions of Elizabeth Arden, then we copy them – except I have one or two ideas that will make them even better.'

'And where do we get the ingredients?'

'These are face creams, Laszlo, not complicated scientific formulas. The basic ingredients of lipstick are no more than an oil base of spermaceti, beeswax and lanolin made of fat extracted from the wool of sheep! Is that so difficult?'

'How do you know these things?'

'I have read about it,' Eve answered impatiently. 'Colourings are made from basic earth pigments: iron oxides, charcoals and various ochres – red ochre has been used for centuries!'

He sat in fascinated silence as the flower-face proceeded to talk knowledgeably about cetyl alcohol, sodium sulphate and refined lanolin alcohols, white wax and paraffin, oil of almond and rose-water. He had come to realize that Eve was ambitious; that behind the feminine wiles lay a steely determination to achieve her ends, and that while she was capable of looking as fragile as a feather boa she was in reality as tough as carbon steel. She was looking for a way to get ahead; she knew exactly where she was going and she never took her eyes off the road. She had a nerve that was cold enough to freeze, and walked the tightrope between her life among their Russian rulers and her intelligence activities for Laszlo's group with the ease of a monkey.

'You are a brilliant chemist,' she was saying, 'I know you can make up a simple range to start with. First of all a cream I can massage into the face and thus accomplish two beneficial treatments at the same time. Something very soft and liquid – because it must never stretch the skin and –'

He held up a hand. 'And when do I run my business?'

'Once our creams take off you can give that up! There is no money in dispensing castor oil and pills for constipation and your own hair lotion! There is a fortune to be made in cosmetics. Do you know that Elizabeth Arden is a multi-millionairess and that she started with nothing? The same goes for Helena Rubenstein. I intend to be the third.'

Laszlo looked again at the lovely face, aglow with the light of the fanatic. 'Yes,' he said, 'or die in the attempt. This is Hungary, my love. You have been reading too many of those Western magazines.'

'Which is exactly why we are going to be successful, don't you see? From them I know of colours unobtainable here, of creams and lotions Hungarian women have never even heard of. This is our chance, Laszlo – we must seize it! You make up the products and I sell them – and you know I can sell anybody *anything*!'

'You are the only woman I know,' Laszlo assured her, 'who could get blood out of a stone.'

'And to prove how confident I am, I will sell on commission only.'

'You really are serious?'

Eve stared at him. 'Of course I am. And just think – if I enlarge my clientele, who knows what information I may pick up? As a matter of fact, I have been approached by the wife of a high-ranking French Embassy official who has heard of my "healing hands". Through her I may gain entrée into circles you have only dreamed of and learn things you could never have hoped to know.'

'You know,' Laszlo said thoughtfully, 'I think you may be on to something . . .'

The creams were an instant success. Laszlo knew his business, and at Eve's suggestion – she telling him exactly what she wanted – he improved on the contents of the jars and bottles she brought to him.

'This cream is too heavy,' she would say. 'It drags the skin and can only be patted in; I want it light, light, light – like the whites of eggs, almost a froth. Can you do that?' He did. He produced a herbal tonic, to be applied to the skin after thorough cleansing, which Eve christened her Morning Refresher; it contained no witch-hazel, commonly used then, and did not sting.

Eve sold and sold and sold. At first she offered free samples. 'You are always complimenting me on my skin,' she would say, 'so I have had this sample made up. It is the cream I always use and it is a marvel. I should know because I made it myself. Try it. You will never use anything else again.'

From selling the products she progressed to using them in what she had learned from her magazines were called 'facials'. With her infallible eye for colour, she experimented, added, subtracted, merged, balanced, and came up with a range of lipsticks of a colour and depth unheard of in Hungary and surprising even to her non-Hungarian clients.

'This lipstick of yours is superb,' one British Embassy wife enthused as she examined her lips in her mirror. 'Such colour and depth, and it absolutely glides on; better still, it stays on. I'll take one in every colour you have.'

By 1956, she had once more changed protectors, and though she was genuinely sorry to say goodbye to her cultured Georgian because he had been of such use, she was content to be taken over by a still younger man who was a senior officer in the AVO, the hated Hungarian secret police. Eve soon came to despise him. He was very handsome and equally as vain. And he was a sadist. But he was also arrogantly careless; he talked openly on the telephone in front of her, she ostensibly immersed in one of her magazines, in reality filing away every word. He liked nothing better than to submit to her skilful hands, and taught her things to do with them which later formed the basis of her sexual reputation. He also provided her with a small car, and the petrol to run it, so that she could tool about the city to her clients, arriving full of cheerful gossip and looking adorable. She came to be a well-known figure not only among the Russians and the Hungarian Party members, but among the international community. She was making money which she kept to herself, and through the AVO man was able to provide Laszlo with high calibre information.

But all the time she was only waiting for her moment to arrive; that chance she knew, with a faith that could move mountains, would eventually come her way. And on 23 October 1956 it did so. Hungary rebelled. Her AVO lover dismissed it contemptuously: 'Nothing more than a powerless rabble'; but Laszlo thought differently. 'Our time has come,' he told her exultantly. 'Freedom is within our grasp. I am directed to the Technical University, where my Group has established itself. I want you to come with me.'

'No,' Eve said.

'Don't you realize what is happening? We are creating a revolution! We are going to free ourselves.'

That's what you think, Eve thought, who knew much more than he did. But this is my chance to free *myself*. Which was why she said persuasively, 'I can do more good if I continue to do what I am doing. Pass back information – somebody has to. If you are not here then you must arrange for another contact.'

'But it will be highly dangerous!'

'So will the Technical University.'

'Once the West comes to our aid –'

'Then that will make a difference, of course, but until then, I think it best that I continue as if I have nothing to do with this uprising. I am only little Anna Farkas, with her clever hands and magic potions. Who would suspect me?'

Laszlo saw the merit in her proposals. They needed all the help they could get, but when it came to helping herself, Eve was in a class apart. He had enjoyed their partnership; he had enjoyed her, but unlike other men, he saw beneath the mind-boggling surface to the essential heartlessness beneath. He knew that in the last analysis, her interest lay in herself, not in what happened to Hungary. Whatever happened, whether they won or lost, she would survive. Whatever she had to do, and he knew by now that she was capable of anything, to achieve her ambitions she would stop at nothing. Well, he thought, am I not prepared to kill to achieve mine?

'All right,' he said, 'I will arrange a further contact. Word will be got to you as to who it will be. But be careful. There is no telling what the outcome will be; the only certainty is that it will be bloody.'

'I am always careful,' Eve reminded him, winding her slender arms about his neck. 'Now, let us enjoy each other one last time before we part . . .'

'Hopefully, not for long.'

Your hopes, my intentions, Eve thought. This is our last goodbye. Not only to you, but to Hungary. My destiny calls me.

She continued her work as long as the streets were safe; once they became battlefields, littered with rubble and burning tanks – along with a few burning bodies – she left the flat for the safety of the little shop, ostensibly locked and shuttered. Laszlo had given her the keys for 'safe-keeping'. She had not seen her AVO lover for a week, but since the people now controlled the streets of Budapest, the hated secret police were being hunted without mercy and slaughtered wholesale. Eve's only anxiety where he was concerned was that he would remain a loose end over which she might trip some time in the future. She intended Anna Farkas to vanish, eventually to be counted as dead.

People were being buried where they fell, without time for religious rites or formal observances. The AVO were usually hanged by the neck until they were almost dead, then hanged by the heels and set fire to. It was no worse than they had been doing for years to the thousands of people who had been tortured to death in the dreaded HQ in Andrássy Street. Eve felt no compassion for them; it was her own safety which, as always, was her prime concern. On her rounds, she had been witness to a couple of nasty scenes involving women who had consorted with the AVO; she did not intend to let the mob do that to her. Making daily visits to the shop she had stocked a supply of food in the small back room, taking it in a suitcase she left there because she had a further purpose in mind. There was already a small cot, because Laszlo had often worked late into the night concocting urgently needed supplies of his products, and there was water on tap and a small primus on which to heat it. She also took her small portable radio.

From the outside the shop was closed; and she was very careful to keep the small back window, which overlooked an alley, similarly barred and shuttered.

Once established, she concentrated on making up as much of her preparations as would fill the remaining stock of jars and bottles. She knew exactly how to mix and blend them for she had watched Laszlo carefully, and she only stopped when the suitcase could take no more. It was very heavy, but she was determined to take it with her when she left. It contained her future.

She did not mind her isolation; she saw it as safety. Once, somebody rattled the door but she made no sound and they went away. The most remarkable thing was that there was no looting. She kept her radio tuned to the Freedom Radio frequency and from its broadcasts learned how the situation was rapidly worsening. All she felt was impatience for it to come to a climax. But she was happy to spend hours on her face and hair, manicuring her nails. The one thing she missed was her bath; all she could do was stripwash, but at that, she mused, even hot water in a basin is more than I had for the first seventeen years of my life, and once I reach the West – oh, the baths I will have, the perfumes I will pour into the water, the hot, scented towels I will wrap myself in, the oils I will smooth into my skin. I will have it all; all I have dreamed of for so long, now only – if I am lucky – a matter of days away.

She felt no concern over what might happen to Hungary; she took no interest in politics. No government ever did anything *for* the people it governed, only *to* them, and she had learned enough from her Russian paramours to know that freedom from Russia's grip was a pipedream. It only confirmed the rightness of her decision to leave Gyor-Sopron and come to Budapest. It was all part of the destiny she devoutly believed in, along with the old saw that God helps those who help themselves – to whatever they can lay their hands on. She felt no loyalty to her country or to her fellow-countrymen; her sights had been set on the West since she was a child. Nothing, not even this shambles of an uprising, was going to deflect her aim.

And then, one morning, after listening to the latest news on Freedom Radio, she made her preparations to leave. Pitched battles were taking place the length and breadth of Hungary; there were rumours of massive Soviet intervention, Budapest was in a state of anarchy. 'Time to go,' she said on a satisfied sigh. She spent the day dyeing her hair to a dull mousy brown and altering her appearance. She covered her face with a matt foundation of an unbecoming pasty-white and left off the lipstick, eyeshadow and rouge, not that she ever needed much of that. She did her hair in an untidy bird's-nest, and as a finishing touch added a pair of gold-framed spectacles she had purloined from the house of a client. She had substituted the prescription lenses with plain glass. Then she changed into the clothes she had brought. A drab, ill-fitting dress, thick stockings, ugly lace-up shoes, a shapeless coat of cheap, blanket-type material in a miserable grey. She looked, she thought happily, unrecognizable.

It was verging on midnight when she left the little shop, locking it carefully behind her, having removed all traces of her occupation. She dumped the bags containing empty tins, cartons, papers, in the ruins of various houses, along with the empty bottle of hair-dye and Laszlo's keys. From what she had heard on the radio she doubted if he would ever dispense from his shop again.

Hefting her precious suitcase, she set off towards her destiny, making slow progress because the suitcase weighed a ton and she had to pause frequently to set it down and massage her crimsoned hands. She used a devious route, mostly down backstreets and alleys, but making her way steadily and purposefully. She gave no thought to the bodies she stepped over, the stone barricades, the torn-up tram lines littering the streets, the occasional burned-out tank. Once, when crossing a deserted square, still reeking of gunfire, and echoing to more not far away, she paused to stoop and examine the darkened face of the AVO officer hanging from a tree by his ankles. It was not her lover but, with luck, he was in the same position somewhere else. She had to cut herself entirely free of everything and anyone that could tie her to Hungary.

Of Laszlo she had heard nothing for more than a week, but she felt confident that he too would not prove a threat to her future. All that mattered was that Anna Farkas disappear from the face of the earth. When she came in sight of her destination she waited until she could enter it safely. As she had known, the Duna Hotel was crammed with Western correspondents, whose faces she searched, looking for the one she knew, a man she had met at the house of a State Bank official, whose wife had been one of Eve's first clients. They had flirted lightly, but she had been careful not to get too involved even while casually giving him enough information to establish her as much more than what he called a beautician. Now, she threw herself at him, sobbing hysterically. Not recognizing her he was puzzled until she whispered: 'It is Anna Farkas.'

'Anna! My God, what have you done to yourself?'

'It was necessary . . . you do not know . . . please, let me tell you why.'

Scenting a story he took her into the bar and there she poured out the tale she had put together with much care and deep thought. She was a double agent; her cover as a beautician had been to give her freedom to move around the city picking up information. She had been planted on first the Russian then the AVO man for the same reason, but to the Freedom Fighters she was a Russian-loving whore, and now that Laszlo was missing, thre was no one who could clear her name, tell the truth as to why she had done what, knowing it was dangerous, she had volunteered to do. 'I have seen what they are doing to other women who went with the Russians and the AVO . . . they will do it to me if I am caught. I have no one else to turn to.'

'Who told you to come to me?' the correspondent asked.

'Laszlo. He said you would help me. Perhaps you know what has happened to him?'

A headshake. 'No, sorry. All I know is that things are falling apart. The Russians are coming in force and God help Hungary once they get here. I am waiting my own orders to leave.'

'Take me with you, please . . . I beg of you . . . I am a dead woman otherwise.'

'I'll do what I can but I can't promise anything. You can stay here if you like, though. I've got a double room . . .'

'Oh, thank you, thank you . . .' She seized his hand and kissed it.

When he went back down to the bar: 'Who – or what – was *that*?' he was asked.

'Some poor kid who got in over her head; playing tootsie to the powers that be and passing back as much information as she could. Only goes to prove this uprising is not something that happened as a flash of inspiration.'

'Kid! She's got to be forty if she's a day.'

'She's made herself over – take it from me, out from under that disguise she takes your breath away.'

Eve got her own breath back by staying in his room until such time as he and the other British correspondents removed themselves to the safety of the British Legation. Her presence was explained by the correspondent to a British official and she was allowed to stay, though the Legation was crowded.

And there, once again, destiny gave a nod in her direction. Among the people hiding, working or waiting there she spied a face she knew. That of a Hungarian, employed as a consular clerk concerned with the issue of exit papers. In reality he was a spy working for the Russians. He was also a prominent dealer on the black market: Eve had bought from him many times. Now, she thought, he will buy from me: my silence for a set of brand-new papers in the name of Eve Czerny, including the all-important exit permit. She had no trouble. 'One word from me and you are done for,' she told him. He blustered, sneered that she was no better, but she coldly told him she had been a double agent, that the British knew all about her whereas they had no idea he was a Russian spy or a black marketeer. A word in the right quarter . . .

Four days later, a convoy of four cars and a truck left the Legation, destined for Vienna, where they would stock up with food and return to Budapest. Travelling in the third car were Eve and the correspondent.

Her first act, once on Austrian soil, was to get down on her hands and knees and kiss it. Then she embraced and fervently thanked her rescuers. 'God will repay you for all your kindness . . .' Drawing the correspondent aside she gave him the full benefit of her amazing eyes – without the glasses – and said, 'When you write my story – and I know you will – do not use my name, I beg of you. I shall have to hide for a long time; if they know where I am they will come after me. Tell my story by all means – I want the world to know what has happened to my country – but just say that I was an ordinary Hungarian girl.'

'Hardly,' the correspondent said, touched. 'You are a most extraordinary girl and a very brave one. Yes, I will write your story but I won't use your name. And that's a promise.'

Her story eventually appeared under the heading 'A True Hungarian Heroine' with the correspondent's byline, and he sent her a copy of the issue in which it appeared. Eve read it, smiled with satisfaction and then burned it.

3

Switzerland, 1988

'How is she?' Max asked, as Alex came into the huge living-room of the villa which overlooked Lake Geneva.

'Still sleeping.'

'More to the point – how are *you*?'

'Still shattered. Whatever I expected my mother to say it wasn't "forgive me".'

'I told you she wasn't herself.'

Alex sat down on one of the twin sofas by the big fire. 'Of anyone else I would say they had undergone some kind of religious conversion.'

'Speaking as one who was brought up in the Church, I think your mother was baptized a Catholic. She has a healthy fear of hellfire and eternal damnation. Maybe, while she was sitting in that room alone, all her past sins paraded in front of her.'

'She never went to any church that I know of.'

'There are a lot of things about your mother that nobody knows.'

Alex took the cup of black coffee he handed her, turned it beige with cream.

'Anyway, we got what I brought you for.' Max sounded satisfied as he liberally sweetened his own black coffee.

'Why do I have the feeling that I am going to get a great deal that I am not prepared for?' Alex asked.

'You mean the forgiveness bit?'

'She's up to something,' Alex said. 'When did Eve Czerny doubt the rightness of anything she ever did? How often have we heard her proclaim: "I have a destiny to fulfil and *nothing* – nothing – will prevent me from fulfilling it"?' Alex gave an accurate impersonation of her mother Giving a Performance. 'If she wanted me to forgive her why didn't *she* ask me to come? I had the oddest feeling of –'

'What?'

'Well . . . this may sound bitchy, but of an actress playing a part. It just doesn't gel with her character. She loathes the very thought of my existence, so why should she ask me, of all people, to forgive her? I think she is in one of her dramatic phases. You know she's like a chameleon, though she never showed me anything but an expressionless mask. Anyway, the doctor says she's emotionally dehydrated and will probably have one of what Chris called her sleepathons. The longest one he could remember lasted three days.'

'That's her way of getting herself back together. She uses an awful lot of emotional energy when she's in one of her hyper phases.'

'Have you issued the press release?'

'Yes. Since when the phone has gone mad. I'm not allowing anybody near her. The statement said she was in a state of deep shock.'

'Which is exactly how I feel. Why, Max? It doesn't make sense.'

'And you insist on everything making sense, don't you?'

'There is a reason for everything,' Alex said firmly.

'So what is yours for doubting your mother's sincerity?'

'The fact that remorse isn't something she's capable of. Her belief in the absolute rightness of everything she does is unshakeable.'

'You haven't considered the possibility of a change of heart?'

'I would if she had a heart.'

'Something made her go overboard for a couple of men I could mention.'

'You're confusing her heart with her libido.'

'She loved Chris.'

'She had a funny way of showing it. Her idea of love is to own and dominate.'

'Then think on the fact that she's lost her most prized possession. Death hits people in different ways, and this is the first time in my experience that it has hit her.'

'You didn't see her when Chris's father was killed. That was a full-scale production of *The Trojan Women*. I remember her running from the house screaming like a banshee, tearing her clothes – a very flimsy pink chiffon nightgown as I recall. She tried to throw herself into the lake, and when they prevented her from doing that she tried to cut her wrists. Patsy told me there were terrible scenes.'

'So you think that because there was no grandstanding this time she isn't convincing in the part? Well let me tell you that when she was told about Chris — and it was Jonesy who told her because I wasn't around — she never uttered a word. Jonesy said she was turned to stone, and the only words she spoke were "Take me to my son". Since when even he hasn't been able to get near her.'

'She's twenty years older now. Time — and age — have modified her performance.'

'Christ, but you're a cold-hearted monolith sometimes.'

Alex flushed but she said doggedly, 'Don't insult my intelligence by explaining about deathbed conversions. If you're asking me to believe that my mother has done a St Paul, you're wasting your time.'

'Why not? You know she's the arch manipulator; of people, events, occasions — life — to her own ends, and when it comes to deviousness she wrote the book, but you're overlooking one important fact: not even Eve Czerny can manipulate death. Maybe that fact has brought her up against the inevitability of her own, made her realize she has fences mend. Look at your mother in that different light I mentioned; maybe it will reveal a woman terrified of getting old, terrified of being alone, of having lost the one person with whom she had any sort of a relationship that included love in its component parts; of having been forced, through these things, to confront herself, the life she has lived and the things she has done. Maybe then you won't find it at all strange that she should ask your forgiveness.' Max sat back. 'Besides,' he admonished, 'you have to remember that your mother is a purely emotional creature.'

'Whilst I, of course, am not.'

'Well, are you? You're like that German who, when he heard the word culture, drew his gun. Your keyword is emotion. Ever since you retreated into that mind of yours you've hoarded every last particle of yourself like a miser. Whatever your mother may have done, she never stinted in the giving of herself.'

'Only to get!'

'So? Are you so unselfish, then?'

'Whose side are you on?' Alex asked furiously.

'As always, my own,' Max answered, unruffled. 'My message for today is all about giving the benefit of the doubt — yes, what is it, Jacques?'

The butler had entered after a discreet knock. 'Your call to the Seychelles, sir. It has come through.'

'Switch it through to here, will you? No –' he said to Alex. 'You don't have to leave . . . it's only to tell Mora about the funeral.'

He went down the long room to the beautiful little *bureau de plat* where the telephone stood. Alex heard him say, 'Hi, sweetheart . . .' then his voice lowered to an indistinct murmur.

Alex reached across to pour herself a glass of Armagnac. She felt she needed it. She also eyed the tiny, delectable *petits fours* that always accompanied coffee in any of Eve Czerny's houses, but held back from delving. One would have ended up being half a dozen and the thought of Mora Haynes's lean and elegant length reminded her uncomfortably of her own heft and breadth.

Mora and Max had been living together for several years now. She had once asked him why on earth he didn't marry the girl, and he had said blandly: 'Because I go along with old Sam'l Butler. "A brigand demands your money or your life; a woman demands both."' And Alex had been so bemused at Max quoting Samuel Butler that she had not questioned his reply. Now, she wondered again why Max didn't marry Mora: for almost six years now the Eve Czerny Woman; elegant, rich, assured, moving in her world of money and luxury, with her impeccable taste and matching pedigree. Mora looked the part because that was the world she had been born into. The right schools, the right address, the right husband, a perfect cook and *the* interior decorator. Except Mora's husband had turned out to be very wrong and she had been left penniless when he killed himself after bankrupting the family business. Max had brought her to Eve with the words: 'Here's your Face, Eve', and after one look Eve hadn't argued. Mora had been able to resume her lifestyle, educate her children – one of each sex, naturally – at the right schools and salt away a great deal of money because Max had seen to it that her contract had an escalation clause that tied in her fee with sales. Alex found herself wondering if he stood *in loco parentis* to Mora's children as he had stood for her, though he had been only thirteen years older than she was.

She was lost in thought, Max still talking on the telephone when the door opened and she looked up to see Pamela Bradley come in. She was in black: simple, stunningly elegant black, with a single, opera-length string of pearls. Her Titian hair was swept up and away from her face, revealing her exquisite jaw-line and a profile that belonged on the back of a coin. Alex smiled. 'Coffee?' she asked. 'Or a drink?'

'I think perhaps a little brandy . . .' Alex poured it. As Pamela took the glass she said, 'Thank you.'

'I'm sorry you were kept away so long,' Alex said.

Pamela sipped her brandy. 'His face is unmarred,' she said. 'He looks as though he has just gone to sleep.'

Alex said nothing; there was nothing she could say. She knew that Pamela had loved Chris deeply, in spite of the ten-year age difference, and that, had he lived, he had been working his courage to the sticking point of telling his mother he intended to make Pamela his wife.

'Have you decided on a date for the funeral?' Pamela asked.

'That isn't up to me.'

'How is your mother?'

'Still sleeping.'

'But it's been almost twenty-four hours.'

'Not unusual after one of her *crises de nerfs*.'

'Was that what it was?' Pamela asked. She took out her cigarettes. 'I intend to be at the funeral, you know,' she warned.

'You have every right.'

'I doubt if she will agree.'

'I don't know what she will do,' Alex said truthfully. 'She isn't herself.'

'Which one?'

'All of them.'

'Did you ever see the movie *The Three Faces of Eve*? Your mother has thirty-three.'

'I think you'll find that one more has been added,' Alex murmured.

'The grieving mother?'

'She did love Chris.'

'She loved to dominate him. She hated him when he didn't do as he was told. And she loathed me.' She paused. 'All things considered I think you have behaved marvellously in coming here. I know how the land lies between you and Eve.'

'Mined,' Alex said succinctly.

'Congratulations on your book, by the way. It had a marvellous review in the *Sunday Times*.'

45

'Thank you.'

'Chris was going to write to you . . .' Pamela smiled. 'You know how he was . . .' She bit her lip.

'Yes. Always "going to" but never actually doing.'

'But he was beginning to, you know . . . When your mother married that Argentinian – after she had sworn to Chris she wasn't going to – he said he would never speak to her again. That was why she staged that suicide attempt – I say staged because Noël Coward couldn't have done it better. And do you know what she said when he went to see her once she had been "found" in time? And he only went because I insisted that he did. She said: "I knew you would come crawling back to me, because you need me – you will always need me." I have never seen him so angry . . . he wanted us to go off then and there and get married but I counselled caution . . . I was wrong. I should have said to hell with the consequences, even if they were Eve Czerny's.'

They were sitting in silence when Max came back. 'Mora will be here late tomorrow night,' he said. He bent to kiss Pamela's fragrant cheek. 'Hi. How are you?'

'Held together by string and sealing wax.'

'Well, there's nothing more we can do until Eve comes back from wherever she's been, so I'm going to call it a long, hard day.'

When he'd gone, Pamela said, 'That's probably how it's going to be for me now, from now on.' She drew deeply on her cigarette and Alex saw that her hand was trembling. Pamela was a strong woman, normally a supremely confident one, her beauty having been her armour, but Alex knew that underneath she was shattered.

'I keep thinking – if only,' Pamela went on. 'If only I had done what Chris wanted, married him and got as far away from his mother as we could.' She looked at Alex. 'You did.'

'Only because it suited my mother's purpose.'

'Why doesn't she like you?' Pamela asked, feeling she could ask now.

'I don't fit her specification.'

'Neither do I.'

'She saw you as a threat; she saw me as an affront.'

'But that's ridiculous! You're a Fellow of your College, you've published three books – the latest to universal acclaim – and you're

46

still only thirty! I would have thought that was more than enough to be proud of.'

'It's not what I am, it's how I am,' Alex said.

'You mean not beautiful?' It was a statement, not an accusation.

Alex shrugged.

'She is, shall we say – hipped – on that subject, unreasonably so in my view.'

'Mother's reasons are Holy Writ. Her whole life has been dedicated to beauty, she made a fortune out of it, she *stands* for it. When you see her name anywhere it is always followed by her title, Empress of Beauty, and she takes it very, very seriously.'

'That is still no reason to reject a daughter who doesn't come up to her standards.'

'That's your opinion. It isn't hers.'

Pamela was silent, then: 'Did you know that Chris planned to resume his education?'

'No.'

'He'd been studying for months – I found him a tutor. I suggested he ask you but he said it was safer to have someone not known to his mother. She would have been suspicious had you and Chris got together.'

'True. She regarded me as a bad influence.'

'And me,' Pamela said.

'Who did you get?' Alex asked with interest.

'A Yale Professor named Gavin Craig.'

'The economist? I've heard of him.'

'Yes, Chris liked him and he was doing well. Gavin was pretty confident that Harvard would have accepted him.'

'You were good for Chris,' Alex said warmly.

'He was good for me . . . Oh, I know people raised eyebrows at the age gap, but I didn't care. Chris was right for me; the only man who ever was. I thought, when my ex dumped me for number four, that I'd had enough of men in general; I was very bitter. Chris changed all that. He was so sweet . . .' Her voice broke and she bent her head. Alex saw tears blotch the dull black crêpe. 'If only he hadn't taken that car out . . . I told him the worst thing he could do was drive when he was so angry.'

'Angry?'

'He had just been on the telephone a whole hour with his mother.

47

He was so upset he was shaking . . . I know what he was after; to release his own anger as he never dared to with her unless he felt sure of his ground.'

'What had he done this time?'

'Oh, some little transgression . . . but she threatened dire consequences unless he toed the line and did what she wanted – which was to start learning the business.'

'Chris loathed anything to do with Mother's work.'

'I know. But she wouldn't listen. As always, it was what *she* wanted that mattered.'

'So,' Alex said slowly, 'Chris was angry when he went out in his new Porsche.'

'Furious. White with it . . . and despair. Oh, Alex, sometimes he was filled with such despair . . . "She is consuming me," he used to say. If he managed to do something right he was never praised, but oh, the tirades when he did something wrong . . . He had got to the stage of getting a doctor to write a letter saying he was too ill to travel when he got a summons from his mother, because the end result once she'd put him through another of her Performances *was* actual illness. The only way he could deflect her was to flirt with her.' Pamela shuddered. 'It was horrible . . . sick, almost incestuous.'

'I have often thought,' Alex said dispassionately, 'that the reason Mother chose such young lovers was because they were some sort of substitute for Chris.'

Pamela's topaz eyes met Alex's. 'Of course . . .' she said in a hard, cold voice. 'Lately, they were all around his age.' Still looking at Alex: 'I wonder you came back,' she said.

'I was pressured into it,' Alex admitted.

'Max? You would do anything for him, wouldn't you?'

'I owe him,' Alex replied simply. 'If it hadn't been for him –' She shrugged.

Pamela leaned across to lay a hand on Alex's knee. 'I'm glad you did. That business of Chris and the machine . . . it was horrible, but I couldn't get to him . . . She had left instructions that if I tried, the police were to be called.' Wonderingly: 'What did you say to her?' Pamela asked.

'Nothing. I didn't get the chance. All I said was my name and she turned and saw me and then she collapsed.'

'Strange,' Pamela commented.

Not really, thought Alex, who now had the clue to her mother's desire for forgiveness. Not of me, through me. Guilt. Chris had taken out his latest, suicidally fast toy in order to release his anger the only way he knew how. Perhaps anger had clouded his vision, perhaps his judgement had been faulty. And perhaps he did it deliberately, but that did not go with what Pamela had just told her about Chris resuming his education. Yet something, somewhere, did not fit; and Alex liked to complete crosswords.

She was of a rational turn of mind, having been educated by a woman who possessed one of her own. She also had a profound distrust of the emotions, having expended her own in a fruitless quest most of her life. She absolutely agreed with her heroine George Eliot's dictum that 'it is easier to quell the emotions than incur the consequences of venting them', something her mother had never heard of – or George Eliot, for that matter. People had been known to take tranquillizers before a meeting with Eve Czerny. Until she had been able to cut her mother out of her life and mind, Alex had suffered her own traumas, hiding her feelings behind a stolid demeanour which later became fixed as a cool aloofness. 'Why doesn't my mother like me?' she used to ask Patsy bewilderedly. 'What have I done?'

'Nothing, nothing at all. Your mother is dedicated to beauty. She believes that no matter what you are, how you look is what matters, and we know that to be false, don't we. You remember when we read *Adam Bede*: "There is no direct correlation between eyelashes and morals", and "It is generally the feminine eye that first detects the moral deficiencies hidden under the 'dear deceit' of beauty".'

'Is that why she never looks at me? Because I'm not beautiful? Because I'm not deceitful?'

'Your mother never sees anything but herself, but she overlooks one thing. Beauty doesn't last for ever. One day she will come to realize that and then she will be in terrible trouble.'

Is Max right? Alex wondered, as she prepared for bed later. Has she at last realized she isn't growing any younger, as she tries so hard to do? Was that the reason for the younger and younger lovers, not Chris?

Eve fitted what one of Alex's favourite George Eliot characters, Mrs Poyser from *Adam Bede*, had said of another beauty: 'She's no better than a peacock, as 'ud strut about on the wall and spread its

4

Vienna and London, 1956–7

Once in Vienna, Eve had no intention of becoming just another statistic in one of the many refugee camps. In order to complete the next part of her Grand Design she had to be free to move about the city and to avoid her fellow Hungarians in case one of them recognized her. She went to her correspondent friend.

'I'm afraid to go into a camp,' she told him. 'I know that there are people in them who only pretend to be refugees; in reality they are agents who send word back to Hungary as to who has escaped. The only safe way for me is to lose myself in Vienna; become just another citizen.'

Since, when she turned on her senses-befuddling charm, she could make anyone swear the moon was made of green cheese, she had no difficulty in getting him to eat some of it. 'I have money,' she told him proudly, 'I saved as much as I could because I was going to expand my business: I can pay my way. If you could just find me a room somewhere . . .'

He went to an old friend of university days; a shy, retiring forty-year-old bachelor named John Brent, who taught English at one of the city's many private academies. He lived in a small flat high up in a huge house that had once been the Vienna home of a noble family. It had three rooms in addition to kitchen and bath: a bedroom, a sitting-room and a study which had its own door to the landing. This, the correspondent suggested, would make an ideal hideaway for Eve. John at first demurred. An intensely conventional man, the thought of how it would look – for in 1956 there were still very strict sexual demarcation lines – made him wary. Until he saw how Eve looked.

'She doesn't look like a double agent,' he observed in a mixture of relief and disbelief at the sight of the drab, dumpy figure peering nervously from behind her glasses. No danger there of people talking.

'Isn't that the way it's done?' his friend asked, repressing a grin at the shock John was in for once Eve decided it was safe to come out from behind her disguise.

So Eve moved into the little room, sparsely furnished but that could be remedied. It adjoined the sitting-room, beyond which lay John's bedroom, so they were separated by enough respectability to satisfy his repressed, old-maidish scruples. And Eve had her own key. John need never see her except for collecting her rent.

And for a couple of weeks that was how it was. He had almost forgotten she was there, because she never used the single bathroom until he had left for work, until one afternoon when he came home early, the school having a half-holiday on account of some saint or other. He was shutting his door when he heard that of the bathroom open, and he turned to see a woman he did not recognize; a woman of stunning beauty and all-pervading sexuality, with a heart-stopping face about which a nimbus of glorious red-gold hair glowed. It was only when she said, on one of her gurgling laughs: 'I can see you don't recognize me,' that he knew who it was. She pirouetted before him, the skirt of her calf-length dress flaring about her exquisitely modelled legs, her tiny waist cinched, as was the fashion, by a wide belt, her tight, polo-necked black sweater clinging to her firm, upthrust breasts, her eyes sparkling, her enchanting, throaty laugh curling about him with invisible but unbreakable strands. For the first time in his life, John Brent fell – at first sight – blindly, cataclysmically, besottedly in love. He had never actually met her kind of woman before, only looked at them on the arms of other men. Now, when she said, 'I have shocked you . . . come, let me explain', he let her sit him down on the sofa and tell her story. It only served to compound his capture. He was both amazed and admiring. And when, her head tilted to one side like some bright-eyed bird, she said, 'Let us go out to celebrate my release', he was only too happy. Now, men were looking at him. He found it as heady as the wine she insisted they order.

Over supper, he listened spellbound as she told him of her plans, and on returning to the flat she showed him her cache of beauty preparations.

'Since seeing what can be obtained in Vienna I realize they do not have the instant eye appeal of the other famous brands – I had to make do with what was obtainable – but what is inside is every bit as good, if not better, and once I make enough money I intend to have a whole new range of containers specially designed. So much more is obtainable here in Vienna; it is a different world. I don't think you, who are so used to such abundance, can really understand what that means to me, who has grown up with so little.'

She gave him just enough information to whet his appetite, all of it false. She said she was Budapest born, that her father had been a chemist and his were the formulas on which her products were based. He had died some six months before the Uprising – 'thank God, because it would have broken his heart to see what has become of my unhappy country'. Her mother had died when she was twelve and she had kept house for her father and helped in the shop. It had been her idea, once it became possible, to branch out into cosmetics – 'and we were doing so well . . . now that is all done for, the shop destroyed, everything gone except what I have in this one case. But I believe in these jars and bottles. I know they are every bit as good as any of the other brands and it is my intention that one day, Eve Czerny will be as familiar a name as Elizabeth Arden.'

John was awed by the steely determination, what sounded like big dreams issuing from such a small person, but he recognized ambition when he saw it and by the time she let him go to bed he was as convinced as she was. She had done so much already! Her English, though enchantingly accented, was fluent, and she had announced that she intended to learn German. 'I shall need it, after all.' John, who had taken a First in Modern Languages at the University of London, was impressed.

Her first customers came through him. He took her to a parents' evening at his school where he astounded everyone by being accompanied by a raving beauty; he, who had been dismissed as a 'nice man, a good teacher, but so *dull*!' And there, Eve went to work. The women were prepared to be indulgent after their hackles (bristling at the sight of such glory and its effect on their husbands) had subsided, because Eve paid the stares, the fascination, no heed at all. Her smiles and attention she gave to John, giving the impression that he, and he alone, held her interest, and when she

53

also made it plain that Vienna was but a staging post on her way to her destination – the United States – there was an unspoken agreement amongst the women that it was in their interests to do all they could to see that her departure was sooner rather than later. Besides, she was offering a free first consultation.

Eve had spent her first weeks studying the competition, buying samples and trying them out, visiting beauty salons throughout the city to see what they offered, absorbing for future use whatever could be useful. She had not submitted to any ministrations on account of her disguise, merely timidly enquired as to cost and what she would get for it; thus she had first-hand knowledge of what she could charge.

Now, she visited the women in their homes, carrying the little bag she had bought – of the type doctors carried but of bright red and with her name in gold on the side – and there she put her magic fingers to good use. Her artless eagerness to give of her best, coupled with the results she obtained, soon had her name spreading by word of mouth. It soon became the thing to summon 'that little Hungarian girl' to do one's face before a dinner, a gala performance at the State Opera, a reception given by one of the Four Powers – still a strong presence in the city – and from whose wives she obtained further clients.

By early 1957 she was well established. From the magazines she obtained from her British, American and French clients – she declined to have anything to do with the Russians but not for the reason people automatically assumed – she learned much about the beauty business, and from the houses and sumptuous apartments she learned even more. Since, among her clients, she numbered several women who bore names that were historical as well as highly social, she was able to learn how the Viennese aristocracy lived, careful not to be too pushy but never too abject either. It was her intention, once she got to England – her jumping-off point for the United States – to pass herself off as being of Austro-Hungarian origin, which was why she learned Viennese German, rather than the High German John spoke. He was amazed at her progress. 'You have a natural facility for languages,' he complimented her. 'Some people have, and your accent is incredible.'

That it was because she was a born mimic she forbore to tell him. It was easy for her to copy the women she ministered to; a gesture here, an inflexion there, the natural authority that the right name and an intact fortune bestowed. She would, as she waited in the hall to be summoned, study her surroundings; examine furniture, flowers – always fresh, always beautifully arranged – pictures, carpets. She would even take a peek into a dining-room being prepared for a big dinner party and memorize the way the table was arranged, the number of glasses and knives and forks, the place cards, the *little* things that, when combined, made one, big, absolutely *right* whole. She would listen to a client ordering her maid to do this or that, and afterwards, in the privacy of her shabby little room, practise until she too could issue orders as one born to give them. To questions about her background she pretended a fear of the past that had the power to destroy her present, so successfully that the women came to admire her. 'She is a plucky little thing,' she heard one American wife say to another, 'and those hands of hers work miracles. When I think of the fortune I've spent at Elizabeth Arden . . .'

And when she needed a chemist to make up further supplies, she had no difficulty in finding one, because one of her clients was married to a man who owned a well-known pharmaceutical firm which manufactured drugs and she had only to ask her husband. He, in turn, on seeing 'the little Hungarian refugee' his wife talked about so enthusiastically, was willing not only to offer the name of the chemist, but carte blanche to Eve, which indignantly (she never let him see how regretfully) she declined. One wrong move and the women would gang up on her. Eve always took the long-term view when it came to her ambitions. The chemist knew his business, and willing to play the game of 'you scratch my back and I'll scratch yours' charged Eve for only the ingredients he used, and these she altered to comply with what was available from other houses. Deeper and more lasting colour, an increased fluffy lightness to a certain cream, a silkier feel to a lotion. And these improved products she packaged in specially designed jars, clear enough to show the purity of their contents but subtly and expensively clouded to glow under their little gold tops. Her label was her name – which she got another friend of John's, who was a calligrapher, to write in bold, almost insolently arrogant script – like a signature; stark black on white. It took every penny she had earned but to her way of thinking it was money well spent. She would soon make it back.

And then disaster struck. She was going through her diary one night, checking appointments, when a sudden realization had her flipping in a panic back through the pages. Then she counted. The diary went flying as she flung it away with a foul Hungarian oath. She was pregnant; disastrously, inconveniently, catastrophically pregnant. Her single-minded obsession had rendered her oblivious of her body's warnings. Now, she went into the bathroom and weighed herself. She had gained five pounds. Her breasts were both engorged and tender – worse, her fondant-pink nipples were now pale coffee-coloured. She raged against her lack of morning sickness – the one sign that was missing for she had never felt better in her life – but the fact remained: she was three months pregnant. Idiot! Fool! she raged at herself, what were you thinking of? It was Laszlo's child, of course, but it still should not have happened. I should not have let him have me that one last time . . . but I took the usual precautions (a douche; all that was available in the Hungary of those days). Obviously, this one disastrous time, it had failed. She swore again, foul gutter oaths. The last thing she wanted was a child. She did not like children, had not intended to have any, ever. Now what was she going to do? This could ruin her Plans. To have Laszlo Kovacs' child was unthinkable. She had erased him from her life. She was not about to be faced with a daily reminder of something she no longer cared – or intended – to remember. I will just have to find an abortionist, she thought. But how? And through whom? I shall have to be very, very careful . . . And I need the money it will cost for other things. She fell to punishing her pillow viciously. She was lying there, dry-eyed and coldly calculating, when she heard John come in. He had been to the opera, which bored her, which was why she had refused to accompany him. No use asking him, she thought. He's a sexual innocent and a repressed prude. And then a thought struck her. She sat bolt upright. I wonder . . . she thought. It would mean a change of plan, but she could handle that. And there were certain undeniable advantages to be gained. Eyes alight with concentration she got up from her bed, began to pace her floor, planning, formulating, deciding.

John was making himself a cup of coffee when, through the thin wall which separated the kitchen from Eve's room he heard the sound of desperate, agonized sobbing, muffled in such a way as to bring to mind a picture of a face buried in a pillow. He at once went to tap on her door.

'Eve. Are you all right?'

'Go away . . .' It was a wail.

'But I heard you crying. Is something the matter? Are you unwell?'

Another wail was followed by a fresh bout of frantic sobbing. It had him doing what he had never done; entering her room when she was in it. She was sprawled on her bed, her head buried in the pillow, her slender body making the small bed shake with the passion of her tears.

'Eve!' He went across to her, placed a daring hand on her shoulder. 'What is it? What has happened to make you cry like this?'

'The worst possible thing . . . the worst thing that has ever happened to me!'

He felt his heart stagger. 'Someone has recognized you?'

'No . . . even worse.'

'Worse?' He was nonplussed. Her fear of being taken back to Hungary had been one she could not shake. What could be worse than that? 'I don't understand,' he said helplessly.

'How could you? You are a kind and decent man.'

John in his naïveté still did not twig. 'Have you had a business reversal? Lost some clients?'

'It's not what I have lost, it's what I have gained . . . something I do not want and do not know how to cope with . . . something so terrible that I am ashamed to tell you . . .' The hysterical weeping rose in volume.

'You could never do anything to be ashamed of,' John said stoutly. 'It isn't in your nature.'

'It isn't what *I* have done – it's what was done to me . . .'

'Done to you?' His sexual innocence still had him puzzled.

Eve lifted a ravaged face from the pillow. 'I was *raped*!' she all but screamed at him. 'On the night I was making for the Duna Hotel – an AVO man caught me in an alley and raped me – and now I'm pregnant!' Her sobbing was so wild he began to fear the other tenants would hear; even in the midst of his shock his mother's conditioning had the upper hand.

'I told no one . . . how could I? A thing like that . . . I was so ashamed . . . so – degraded . . . and now everyone will know . . .

57

I am finished, I shall be branded, I know I will . . .' She raised a shaking hand to point at his face: 'You see . . . even you . . .' She hid her own in the pillow again.

'Well – of course – it is a shock, I mean rape . . .' He swallowed. One had heard about such things happening, but rape was something of which he had absolutely no understanding. It was something the Russians had done in Berlin, he knew from German friends, but never had it come so close, so – intimately close. He had, for the first time in his life, fantasized about the experience of making love to Eve, even as he had accepted the fact that he never would. His sexual experience consisted of a single encounter with a prostitute, arranged for him by the men in his barracks during his National Service; the Army had discharged him when they discovered he had severe, psychosomatic asthma. It had been so appalling, so embarrassing, that he had never dared approach a woman afterwards, but as his sexuality had been savagely pruned by the religious fanaticism of his mother, it had not been difficult to accept his enforced celibacy. The fact that he was physically unprepossessing also added to his diffidence. He was far too thin for his six foot height, he had started losing his hair in his early twenties and he was afflicted with a shyness that was also psychological. Eve was the first woman – apart from his mother – with whom he had enjoyed any kind of relationship, and he had been so thrilled and flattered that such a beautiful and sexual being should make a friend of him that he had been off-balance ever since. It had taken all his courage to make his escape to Vienna, even if he had had to sacrifice his original hoped-for three years to a miserable one, at his mother's vicious insistence, but now he found even more courage to say: 'Of course I am – upset, but only at the thought of such a terrible thing happening to you.'

'You don't know what it was like, those last days in Budapest . . . nobody does, what sort of animals were roaming the streets, but I was desperate . . . I had to take the chance of getting away . . . and the bitter thing is that I was not far from my goal when it happened . . . he came up from behind and put his arm about my neck and dragged me into an alley . . . it was hideous . . . degrading, and it hurt, oh, how it hurt . . .'

Which led John to believe, as she intended, that she had been a virgin. He was so appalled that he acted instinctively. He sat down on the bed and picking Eve up, drew her into his arms. Her body was shuddering convulsively but it was soft, oh, so soft and warm, and her hair under his nose smelled so fragrant, felt so silky . . .

'There, there . . .' he soothed. 'It's all right, I'm here . . . don't cry . . . you're not alone . . . you know I will do whatever I can . . .'

'Oh, will you?' She drew back, tears dribbling from her drowned eyes. 'I do not know how to go about these things, you see.'

'What things?'

'Why – how to –' He saw her eyes slide away as if too embarrassed to face his. 'How to – not be pregnant.'

John went rigid. 'An abortion!' All his mother's brainwashing erupted as he thundered: 'But that is murder!'

'Then *I* must die, for there is no way I can have this child. I am unmarried, and who will believe I was raped? They will ask why I said nothing, they will think I am lying because –'

'Because what?' John asked, still hot under the collar.

'Nothing,' Eve said, in a way that had him saying the expected: 'It cannot possibly be nothing. If I am going to help you then I must know everything.'

Eve averted her face. 'Because of my friendship with you,' she whispered.

This time, John was so thunderstruck he was speechless.

'You always believe the best of people,' Eve said brokenly, 'but I know how hateful they can be; how they love to cast the worst possible light on a situation that is in any way – suspicious. Don't you see? You are my dear friend; we live in the same house – we –'

'They wouldn't dare!' John choked, red-faced.

'But they will,' Eve wailed. A swift glance at John's face had her pressing home her dagger to the hilt. 'You do not hear the things I hear when I visit my clients; the malicious gossip, the way they laugh –'

John's face went even redder. The one thing he could not stand was to be laughed at; he had undergone enough of that to last two lifetimes. His childhood had been a nightmare because of it. What other twelve-year-old boy had his mother waiting to collect him from school? What other boy had his mother creating a scene when she learned he was being taught in biology a full explanation of the reproductive process? 'Sinful; sinful and wicked to teach children such filth!' she had ranted. 'I will not have it!' And she had created such a fuss that his life had thereafter been a misery, and earned him the name 'Mummy's Boy'.

His upbringing had been of the kind that associated sex with dirt, and as his mother was an aggressive housekeeper, attacking every speck of dust with the zeal of one who has signed proof that Cleanliness is next to Godliness, so she had been vigilant in the isolation of her son from the filthiness of sex which was, according to her, the ultimate in nastiness. It was beyond her comprehension how the God she quoted at every turn should have arranged things so that an unspeakably obscene act was necessary to ensure the continuity of the species. John, who had as a child wondered why he had no brothers and sisters, wondered as an adult how he had come to be in the first place, given his mother's attitude and his father's browbeaten acceptance of her every edict. He had not been allowed to read any book until his mother had vetted it, if they went to the cinema she took him, after first making sure he would see nothing likely to corrupt, and as he approached puberty gave him such a graphic account of the evils of venereal disease that for many years he went in terror of the opposite sex.

Now, the thought of people giggling behind his back brought a burning feeling that churned his stomach. He thought he had left that behind. Not Vienna too . . .

'I will lose my business,' Eve was sobbing, 'none of my ladies will wish to have me in their houses again, an unmarried girl with an illegitimate baby. That is why I thought of abortion . . . if I do not do something I am ruined!'

'No you are not,' John said calmly, because an idea of staggering audacity had just occurred to him.

'But I am! Even in Hungary a girl who goes with men before she is married is shunned.'

'That is why you will not be ruined,' John said. 'You will be married – to me.'

Eve, whose face was in her hands, drew in a sharp breath, not of the shock he thought he had given her, but of satisfaction. Slowly, she dropped her hands, revealing a face that was radiant with joy. 'Oh, that would be –' Then she slumped and shook her head. 'I could not do that to you. It would be monstrously unfair.'

'You mean – you *would* marry me?' John was so thrilled he was almost stuttering.

'Without hesitation,' Eve swore. 'You are kind, you are gentle, you are patient, you are understanding and you look after me.' Wanly, she sighed: 'It is so long since I had anybody to look after me. Not since my father died . . . but I could not ask it of you.' She took his hand, lifted it to her lips. 'But thank you, oh, *thank you* for asking me.'

'We *will* be married,' John said firmly. 'It is a thing I want very much but never thought I had even the slightest hope of getting. I loved you from the moment I saw you come out of that bathroom, but women who look like you don't even know that men like me exist. Why, you could have any man you wanted . . .' He put his hands on her shoulders. 'I would be proud to have you as my wife, proud and honoured.'

'But – the baby . . .'

'We can deal with that when the time comes.'

Eve looked down at her hands. 'But I do not want it,' she whispered. 'You must understand that . . . I cannot help but hate it . . .'

'You are upset,' John soothed. He had known a couple of men, fellow teachers who, gloomy once they announced their wife was pregnant *again*, had become proud fathers once the baby was a physical fact. How can any woman not love her baby? he thought, confident in his inexperience that once Eve held hers, any hostility caused by the unfortunate circumstances of its conception would soon turn to love. Had he not heard his mother say the same many times? 'It is God's will,' she would say to a woman, at her wits' end as to how she was going to manage with yet another mouth to feed. 'It is the way He has seen fit to arrange things, and it is a consequence of indulging in carnal appetites. Yours is the responsibility and you must shoulder it. The child is innocent, and you must strive all your life to keep it so.'

Yes, he thought now, this child *is* innocent. It is not its fault, and we must see to it that it never knows the truth. 'You will come to love it,' he said confidently now. 'You have a great deal of love in you, Eve. Look how you loved that little dog. You moved heaven and earth to see it got a good home when the landlord would not let you keep it here.'

He had caught her in the act of picking it up to throw it out of the front door, which action she had at once smoothly changed into one of tender concern. She had been glad to be rid of the smelly, yappy thing. But again, she thought, it had been fate that had brought John on the scene.

'If you are sure,' she said, letting hope override the doubt in her voice.

'I am positive.'

By the time John left her room to return to his own, it was on the understanding that they would be married quietly as soon as he could make the necessary arrangements.

Eve leaned back against her door with a satisfied smile. It had all worked out exactly as she had known it would. Now, she would arrive in England as the wife of a British citizen, her name added to his on that precious blue passport. Once she was safely established it would be an easy matter to obtain one of her own. It meant rearranging her timetable but it would not be for long. Just long enough to have the child then, once she was sure John felt for it what he had confidently predicted she would feel, she could leave it with him when she left. 'I had never expected to have children of my own,' he had confessed to her. 'And this one will be ours – no, never mind how it came to be. We will not think of that; we will think only that it is yours and mine. That is what people will think, isn't it?' He had been almost gay, until she had asked, 'But – what about your mother?' She knew he lived with her and was totally under her thumb. 'She will be – surprised,' John admitted cautiously, making the understatement of this or any year, 'but once she sees you . . .' He had felt his smile fixing, try as he might. Once his mother set eyes on Eve he knew exactly what her reaction would be, for Eve fitted exactly Mary Brent's description of the Whore of Babylon.

Except Eve was no whore. She was a lovely young girl who had undergone a horrific experience. She will make a wonderful mother, he thought sentimentally, and who knows, in a year or so she might even be a mother again . . . He found himself blushing at the thought, but he was also conscious of a strange, new feeling. It took him some time to realize that it was happiness.

Eve Czerny became Mrs John Brent in a short civil ceremony.

Pretending ignorance, though she had made sure of the details beforehand, she left everything to him, went along with whatever he suggested in a blaze of eager joy, presenting him with the new set of identity documents her first attempt at blackmail had produced. By the time she and her new husband boarded the British European Airways Viscount that would take them to London, her name had been added to his on that reassuring, solidly unimpeachable British passport. They caught the bus to Victoria and the tube from there to South Wimbledon, where they picked up a taxi. John was tense, nervous, chain-smoking, a sure sign that his nerves were in shreds. As they turned into an unremarkable, tree-lined little cul-de-sac he said, 'My mother doesn't approve of smoking so don't tell her I do, will you?'

'I will do whatever you want,' Eve said, squeezing his hand reassuringly. She had brainwashed him into believing that it was his idea to keep the pregnancy secret for the time being. 'Once we are settled in we can tell her,' Eve had said.

'And as far as Mother is concerned the child is mine,' John had added. Not only your mother, everybody, Eve thought.

'I don't want you to think my mother is a difficult woman,' John said now, making it obvious by his desperation that she was, 'it's just that – well, she sets great store by appearances.' His smile was a plea. 'You will find it is a very British trait.'

But Eve had no doubts. When it came to handling people she had no equal. She took one look at Mary Brent and knew she was going to have her work cut out. She was tall, like her son, cadaverously thin, with a bony face, a ratchet mouth and iron-grey hair worn prison-wardress style. She wore a dowdy print dress in some shade of shrinking violet, and her spider-shanks were encased in thick grey stockings, her feet in sensible lace-ups. It was obvious that in her language fashion was a dirty word. She surveyed Eve's grey flannel suit (a Christian Dior copy) with its still small waist and spreading skirt, eyed the pert hat perched atop the red-gold hair, noticed the pierced ears with their tiny gold studs, and her thin lips tightened. She made no effort to embrace her daughter-in-law after inclining one sallow cheek for her son's nervous peck. She merely nodded and turned to lead the way into what was obviously the 'front room', every item of furniture mathematically placed, every flat surface highly polished. The windows were shrouded in concealing net, and the room smelled of furniture polish and disinfectant. It had all the warmth of a condemned cell. Eve, who had watched her husband dwindle into a guilt-ridden small boy, sat down in one of the four-square, rock-hard armchairs in front of the fire, on which a few small coals were struggling for life and losing the battle. The house was cold as well as cheerless.

'Well, this is a surprise, I must say,' Mary Brent said, as affably as a KGB interrogator. 'Now,' she turned to her son, 'tell me all about it.'

'Vy don't I do that?' Eve interposed cheerfully. She made her accent much more noticeable: 'Vat you vant to know?'

'Where you come from, how you met my son.' And trapped him into marriage remained unsaid.

'I vas a refugee who escaped from Budapest ven my country was overrun by the Russians.'

'You are Hungarian, John says.'

'I vas. Now I am British subject.' Eve quelled John's astonishment with a look.

'But your parents are there?'

'I haff no parents. I only haff John,' Eve said, taking his hand.

'No family at all?' Suspicion glittered like knives.

'None.'

'Eve had to leave everything behind,' John interposed placatingly.

'Except quite a lot of luggage, I see.'

'The two big cases contain my stock,' Eve explained.

'Stock?'

'Eve is a beautician,' John explained. 'A very good one.'

'A beautician!' John might as well have said mortician, because it produced the same horror.

'I had my own business in Vienna,' Eve said proudly.

'Oh, Vienna.' Mrs Brent sniffed, making plain her opinion of that city. 'I can't think why John wanted to go there in the first place. He had a perfectly good job here. I don't hold with Abroad. Nasty food and you don't know where the china and cutlery have been.'

'Speaking of china, a cup of tea wouldn't come amiss,' John said heartily.

Mrs Brent rose. 'Everything is ready. I only have to boil the kettle. Come along.'

They followed her into an equally chilly dining-room, though again there was a fire – one single bar of a four-bar electric fire – where the furniture was just as uncompromisingly uncomfortable. An ugly sideboard on which were set lace mats each with an EPNS candlestick mathematically centred, a square dining-table with four chairs, a glass-fronted cabinet containing a set of china that was obviously never used.

The table was laid with a lace cloth and set for three. As Eve sat down in the chair John drew out for her she saw that there were three slices of bread and butter, cut into halves, three small obviously home-made jam tarts, three pieces of cake that was supposed to be of fruit but in which the sultanas, raisins and currants could be counted. The tea, though hot, was almost colourless. Eve longed for a cup of good coffee while she nibbled at a piece of bread so thin it drooped in the fingers, and spread with margarine, not butter. It tasted, she thought, like cotton wool. Her mother-in-law was a mean woman who ran a mean house.

Their bedroom, once they reached it, was no more welcoming. It was at the back of the house, dim with the nets that shrouded the windows, the carpet dun-coloured. Probably older than me, Eve decided. The bed was a double but, when she sat on it, as hard as her mother-in-law's eyes. The wardrobe with its fly-spotted mirror contained wire hangers, and the windows overlooked a pocket-handkerchief-sized lawn surrounded by aggressively tidy shrubs. Well, Eve thought practically, the one comfort is that it's only temporary.

She met her mother-in-law's open dislike and distrust with sunny indifference, and ignored the mutterings about 'waste of money' when she bought new curtains and a new eiderdown to replace the inch-thick ancient relic that provided no warmth at all. When she went shopping one day and came back with an electric fire, her mother-in-law almost had a heart attack and screeched that they couldn't afford it. 'Once I find my little shop we'll be able to,' Eve said, 'and in the meantime, we're paying our share of household expenses, aren't we?'

'A shop!'

'Of course. I intend to open my own salon.'

'But your first duty is to John. He is your husband and the breadwinner.'

But I want more than bread, Eve thought. 'I intend to be a working wife,' she said.

'Wives do not work!'

'Then I shall establish a precedent. It is 1957, after all.'

'John won't like it.'

'John knows and approves. I am talented – very good at what I do, and I haven't seen a salon such as *I* intend to open anywhere in South Wimbledon.'

'You find that sort of thing in Wimbledon Village,' Mary Brent said on a sniff.

'Where's that?'

'Where the toffee-nosed nobs live.'

Ah, thought Eve, then I must go where the money is. So she made it her business to investigate Wimbledon Village and knew at once that this was where she must establish herself. Here were the big houses, the two-car garages, the expensive shops. This was a different world from South Wimbledon. This was *her* world. She sailed into a nearby estate agent's and ten minutes later, a dazzled negotiator in tow, sailed out again. She spotted what she wanted on the fourth try; a corner site with an exclusive dress shop on one side, a hat shop on the other.

'I'm afraid,' the negotiator said on a headshake, 'that it is only the tag-end of a lease, slightly less than three years. This whole block is down for future redevelopment.'

'In that case, the rent should not be unreasonable,' Eve said shrewdly. 'Why is it empty?'

'It was a hairdresser's but they moved to bigger premises a couple of months ago.'

It was one large salon with a small room at the back. It had a lovely bow front and a very elegant front door. 'The carpet, is it included?' Eve asked. It was high quality pure wool, she realized, and though it was the wrong pink she could still make it tone in with her proposed colour scheme.

'Yes.'

'And there is hot water and all the necessary amenities?'

'Oh, yes.'

'Then let us discuss terms.'

She returned to South Wimbledon having signed the necessary papers and with the promise that she should be able to move in within the next six weeks or so. Her mother-in-law was out, and John was at work, so she went upstairs and, unlocking her case – she knew her mother-in-law snooped because she had laid traps and found them breached – she brought out a small velvet bag. From it she drew a brooch, about the size of half a crown, and entirely composed of first-water diamonds which glittered in the sunlight falling through the now lightly netted windows. She had found it caught up in one of her protective coveralls one day at close of business, and realized that one of her rich Viennese customers had lost it; but when that lady asked about it she denied all knowledge, though she insisted that the customer stand by while she made a thorough search. 'Perhaps it dropped in the street?' she suggested.

'It must have . . . I should have had the catch mended, but I never got round to it. Such a pity, it is a very valuable brooch and I was quite attached to it.'

'Surely it was insured?'

'Oh, yes, but it had sentimental value . . . it was the first piece of jewellery my husband gave to me.'

'What a pity,' Eve commiserated, secure in the knowledge that the brooch lay buried at the bottom of a jar of cream in her red sample case.

Now, she knew her foresight in keeping it had been another pointer from the finger of that fate she so devoutly believed in. She had realized that she would not have enough money to do all that she wanted to do by the time she had fitted up the salon and paid the first quarter's rent, but with what she could realize on the brooch her shortfall would be covered.

Next day, she took the Underground into the West End, made her way to a jeweller's in the Burlington Arcade, where she and John, in perambulations about London, had admired the exquisite modern pieces as well as the window devoted to second-hand jewellery. She wore her good grey suit – the Christian Dior which she had spotted in a pile of clothing consigned by a wealthy Viennese to the charity that helped Hungarian refugees, and she had retrimmed the little hat with fresh veiling. Her shoes were also good, of soft grey suede, and being so small – she took a size three – they had not fitted anyone else. Her handbag, old but of expensive grey calf, she polished to a gleaming softness, and she stopped at Fortnum and Mason on her way to the arcade and invested in a pair of good leather gloves, dropping her old ones into a street litter bin. Her last stop was at the perfume counter where she pretended to be browsing and accepted a spray of *Arpège* from a salesgirl whilst declining to buy. Thus equipped, she sailed into the jeweller's with the brooch and came out fifteen minutes later with a cheque that had her face glowing to such an extent that she turned more heads than usual. She had spun a story about the brooch being the property of her grandmother, one of the few pieces she had managed to bring out of Hungary, and she had used her enchanting accent to good effect. The young man who served her – she had waited until the older one was occupied with another customer – had been putty in her hands, and when he had observed that the diamonds were first water, Eve had said coolly, 'But of course. My grandmother never wore anything else.'

Now, she took the Underground back to Wimbledon and deposited the cheque in the account she had opened in the Wimbledon Village branch of Barclays Bank. Neither John nor his mother knew of its existence. Nor would they ever. By the time she opened her little shop, its façade newly painted a sparkling white, her name *Eve Czerny* – lettered in gold in the same style as her labels – standing out boldly, she was down to a few pounds, but she was confident that they would be increased to hundreds by the time she had been open three months.

She had done her groundwork. She had gone into the West End, visited every major department store and given their cosmetic departments an intensive examination, knew that there was one she had to crack before she could regard herself as a name to be reckoned with. Harrods. She also paid visits to the various beauty salons operated by the big cosmetic houses and her eagle eyes and retentive memory noted details she could incorporate in her own shop. One she liked and decided she had to have was the idea of coffee and a light lunch, served to you on a tray at your chair. She also decided she would have to offer a manicure service, but she was confident that what she offered in the way of beauty culture could compete with the bigger, more expensive salons – and just how much more expensive they were made her determined to adjust her prices accordingly. She found a manufacturing chemist and got him to analyse her competitors' lines, then had him adjust her own formulas when she realized they had the edge. She experimented endlessly with colours, her instinct and unerring eye telling her when she had arrived at not only the right but the perfect balance.

By the time she opened for business she had put into practice every wrinkle she had picked up. She employed a young girl – the daughter of a neighbour who thought Eve was the nearest thing to a film star she would ever meet – to serve coffee, which Eve made herself, and small, delectable sandwiches she also prepared, wrapped in greaseproof paper until needed: wafer-thin brown bread with a filling of smoked salmon or flaked crab or pâté or roast beef, bought from the nearby branch of a very good grocer named Cullen's, and very soon, *Eve Czerny* became *the* place to have one's face and hair done whilst nibbling at a delicious sandwich and drinking superb coffee. The prices she charged more than covered her outlay. Her manicurist she poached, simply by offering her ten per cent more than she was already earning.

Her pregnancy was now (unofficially) in its sixth month, but by wearing her smock on leaving and entering the house, and keeping it on until she and John retired to their bedroom, she was able to hide it until the time was right, helped by the fact that her bulge was small, and that the fashion then was for tent coats which concealed wonderfully.

Mary Brent's suspicions finally being confirmed, though she had hesitated to make them known for she had developed a healthy if loathing respect for her daughter-in-law's hold on her son, she demanded to know why she had not been told from the start.

'Because you would not have approved of me working and I needed to lose no time in becoming established.'

'Oh, you are established all right. An established liar! You seduced and trapped my son into marriage because you wanted a father for your bastard. You are a painted whore and a harlot, and the sooner you go on your way the better!'

'And you are a jealous, vindictive, religious bigot! I warn you, continue to give me trouble and I'll see to it that you never see your precious son again! I can cause you more trouble than you have ever dreamed of. You don't frighten me, and you won't prevent me from doing what must be done. Don't get in my way.'

Mary Brent was under no illusions as to the kind of woman her son had married or how that marriage had come about, but she was still taken aback at the venom with which the exquisite creature spoke to her. Normally, only the hellfire and damnation dogma of her Church had the power to make her afraid, but that was nothing to the fear she felt then. She is possessed, she thought. Some evil spirit is in her. But she felt somewhat reassured by the conviction that it was only a matter of time before her daughter-in-law took herself off to greener pastures; that South Wimbledon was merely a staging post. She said nothing more, but she turned her nagging towards her son. 'This house smells like a brothel!' she whined. 'And what is she doing with the money she's coining?'

'It paid for the central heating, for one thing.'

'Unnecessary extravagance.'

'Not on your part.'

'I should think not!' A sneering sniff. 'I notice she isn't spending on preparations for the baby.'

'Her business is her baby,' John said unthinkingly, only to squirm as his mother pounced; 'That I can believe, but I take leave to tell you that if the child she's carrying is yours, then I don't know my own son. I caught a glimpse of her leaving the bathroom the other night and she's no more four months pregnant than I am. Six is more like it and if that baby isn't here in August instead of October then I need to change my glasses.'

John was silent.

'She trapped you into marriage, didn't she?'

'No, she did not. I was the one who asked her to marry me.'

'Why? In God's name why? Anybody can see what she is, and you, of all people, after all I've taught you and warned you about, should have known.'

'Not everyone sees what your prejudice does.'

'Use your common sense, if you have any left. What is a woman who looks like she does doing with a man like you? I've seen the way men look at her. She's the kind that goes from man to man, each one richer than the last. What is that kind of woman doing married to a teacher? She's not our sort and I knew it the minute I laid eyes on her, but for some reason best known to her she's decided that for the time being we will do. Are you *sure* she didn't trap you?'

'It wasn't like that at all!' John shouted.

'Then just how was it?'

'None of your business!'

His mother gasped. 'I can see her pernicious influence is at work already. I shall pray for you, my boy, for you are headed straight for Eternal Damnation.'

'I won't have you talking about Eve like that.'

'While she lives in my house I'll talk about her any way I like!'

'It may be your house but Eve is now paying most of the expenses.'

'She was the one wanted the central heating, wasn't she? She wanted the telephone, and the fire in your bedroom – sheer, wanton extravagance, if you ask me.'

'I'm *not* asking you, I'm telling you that all Eve has acquired *she* has paid for – including that new television set you watch all the time.'

'You're supposed to be the provider, not her! You're supposed to wear the trousers!'

'Then how come you never let me, before I was married?'

Utterly taken aback, Mary Brent could not find her tongue and John took the opportunity to escape. But up in the bedroom, he lay back on the new, thick, cushiony eiderdown and thought about what his mother had said. It was true that Eve was now making far more money than he was, and though she had spent some on the house it was for her own convenience; it was also true that she had, as yet, bought nothing for the baby. There was no layette, no cot, not so much as a nappy. Well, he thought, that's understandable. I know she doesn't want it. Yes, but what's going to happen when it arrives? Who is going to look after it? Because he knew Eve would not. Her driving ambition did not include motherhood.

'Why don't you let up a bit,' he had suggested. 'The shop's doing well, you're making money hand over fist.'

'Nothing to what I intend to make in the future. One little shop in a London suburb is not what I intend to be content with. I want more, much more.'

'But why?'

She had stared at him as though he was mad. 'Because it's my destiny,' she had said, as though that explained everything.

She really believes she is destined for fame and fortune, he thought now. It is an unshakeable conviction.

Just as he now knew, with equal certainty, that he did not figure in Eve's future; that he never had; that he had been used in the furtherance of her obsessive ambition. Not an ambitious man, he found himself both awed and saddened by his wife's juggernaut drive

71

to obtain – what? Money, power, fame? What about happiness? he wondered. Or was that something Eve thought she could acquire as easily as she acquired everything – and everyone – else? And yet he knew that were he to be offered the chance to go back and decide once more, he would do it all again. Eve was quicksilver, too slippery for him to get a grip on, she could think of three things to his one and she was as fast as he was slow at everything, yet she had given him the only joy his arid life had ever known, and the only physical love. She made him laugh, she had changed this cheerless house into a home, somewhere he enjoyed returning to after a day's work, even if she was not always there to welcome him.

It had been fun at the beginning; he had enjoyed showing her London, relished her delight at the glittering shop windows and stores crammed with goods she could buy at whim. Not that she had been extravagant. But she loved to window shop, to say: 'I will have one of those one day', nodding at the glistening fur of a sable coat, or the gleaming paint of a Rolls-Royce, while he, smiling and nodding, had naïvely thought she was joking. She had loved going to the cinema – she was not so enthusiastic about the theatre, which she said was artificial, but the cinema she adored and he had spent more time watching her rapt face than the screen. She revelled in big MGM musicals with their colour and verve, and he knew that she was learning as well as enjoying. Her English had improved by leaps and bounds. But gradually he came to realize that under the Turkish delight façade was a titanium steel foundation and a brain that never stopped working.

Yes, he thought, Eve will go far; her belief in that destiny she swears by will take her there, but it won't be with me. Their life together would be short, but in spite of everything, he knew it had been filled with Eve's particular kind of sweetness and that he would count himself lucky to have had it. The one unresolved question was the forthcoming child, but he knew better than to make any plans for its future, for that, too, was something Eve, and Eve alone, would decide.

5

Switzerland, 1988

Alex was finishing breakfast with Pamela when Jonesy, her mother's dresser-cum-confidante, minced into the morning-room to say that Madame would appreciate it if her daughter could spare her half an hour or so.

'You haven't learned your lines,' Alex rebuked. 'Madame doesn't request, she orders.'

'I'm only telling you exactly what she told me.'

'How is she?' Pamela asked.

'Not herself, very definitely not herself. The one I know, that is. We had our usual bath but it took a mere ten minutes. Most peculiar. We waved away the masseuse, nor did we linger on our face, nor did we wait for our bed linen to be changed, and you have no idea how fussy she is about that. Something,' he pronounced solemnly, 'is up – and not the sort of thing that is normally up in Madame's bedroom.' He tittered.

Alex regarded him with fascinated curiosity. He was an addition to Eve's entourage acquired since Alex had last seen her, seven years before, and she wondered why on earth a woman with a deep and abiding appreciation of virile masculinity – she'd not left Max unturned, had she? – would employ as her closest companion a rampant queen who did his face with as much care as she did hers. His hair was pink, his eyelids blue, his cheeks rouged and his mouth painted. And yet, according to Max, he was trusted with Eve's innermost secrets. He was the one who cleared away the debris after her emotional rampages, applied fragrant compresses to her fevered brow, soothed her with one of his *tisanes* and held her hand when she was feeling sorry for herself. He was also the one who dared criticize her appearance. 'And she takes it!' Max had told her. 'He purses his lips, shakes his head and she obediently trots off and takes off a diamond bracelet or two.'

'But how and where did she acquire him?' Alex had wanted to know.

'In Hollywood. She had a fling with a current sex symbol and Jonesy was his valet. Only it turned out the stud was bisexual – Eve found him playing Little Fishy in his pool with two fourteen-year-old boys – and as revenge she stole Jonesy.'

What he didn't know was that the little painted elf was a repository of most of the carefully and deeply buried Hollywood scandals of this and any year. He was able to make Eve roar with laughter at his tales of the sexual peccadilloes of many a glittering name, names Eve had worshipped years ago, but she was not above using the information he provided for her own ends. It had been through Jonesy that she had met a former superstar whom age, drink, sex and drugs had toppled. She was vastly rich, having bought real estate when it was ten dollars an empty acre and thirty-five years later sold it for a thousand times that price, but she was desperate at the loss of her career and, as always followed in Hollywood, her status. No longer on the A list. Eve had whisked her away to her health farm on the shores of Lake Tahoe where, for six weeks, she had worked on her remorselessly, to such effect that when she reappeared at the Oscar ceremonies, looking twenty years younger, her bloat siphoned off, her face lifted, her body firmed, she had caused a sensation. So much so that when offered a supporting role in an upcoming epic – she who had always had her name first above the title – she grabbed it and proceeded to waltz away with the following year's Academy Award for Best Supporting Actress. To anyone who asked how she had done it she answered simply: 'Eve Czerny'. At the Garden of Eden, they said, you could get rid of anything from an unwanted pregnancy to a double chin. From then on, there was a waiting list for months ahead. And Eve was grateful.

Now, as Jonesy led the way upstairs, he said chattily to Alex, 'I've heard about you and your mother – that you don't Get On – but if you just remember that your mother writes, produces, directs and stars in all her own productions you'll get along just fine. Whatever you do don't upstage her. Just let her do it her own way.'

'That's the only way she knows,' Alex said.

Jonesy nodded approval. 'The sudden demise of Her One and Only was not in the original script and she can't stand unauthorized

74

changes. So don't make any of your own. She's having enough trouble deciding which role to play as it is.'

'How well you know her,' Alex commented.

'I'm the only one that does – well, apart from you, maybe, and I daresay I've seen a different Madame to the one you know – and there's a full range of them.' He eyed Alex surmisingly. 'They tell me you don't take direction, but if you'll take my advice you'll let her feed you your lines. Just remember she's the star.' He opened a double door, ushered her in.

Alex had never been in her mother's suite; the house had been out-of-bounds to her apart from her own quarters, and the sheer sumptuousness of the furnishings astounded her. Each piece was a genuine antique, French, and exquisitely blended. The sitting-room was all white and gold, even the flowers matched, but the bedroom, when Jonesy opened another set of double doors to allow her to enter, was pink, Czerny First Blush had she known anything about her mother's infinite colour range. The bed was huge, a four-poster swagged and draped in two shades of pink – First Blush and Tender Pink, the one slightly deeper than the other – and two kinds of material, velvet and silk. The carpet had a silvery sheen to it, and the flowers here were all roses, cut this morning from the hot-houses at one side of the house.

Eve was not in bed; she was sitting by the huge window, which was open to give a view of the lake, in a big French *bergère*, her feet propped on a footstool, her legs covered in a light blanket. She was wearing a black silk robe, severely cut, but it gave her skin the luminescent quality of a pearl. She appeared not to be wearing make-up, but Alex knew how skilled she was at wearing everything necessary to give an appearance of wearing nothing, and she put the slight pallor down to the absence of blusher.

Eve looked subdued, drained, but Alex reminded herself that she was in the presence of someone who, had she been an actress, would have been mentioned in the same breath as Bernhardt and Duse. She waited, mindful of Jonesy's warning.

Eve turned her head. 'So . . .' she said. 'It was not a dream. You are here.'

'Large as life and twice as ugly,' Alex said.

She saw a spasm change the empty face but it was so quick she might have imagined it.

'Sit down,' Eve said, indicating a chair that had been drawn up opposite her own.

'Thank you, I prefer to stand. Old habits die hard.'

Eve contemplated her daughter. 'You haven't changed, I see.'

'Were you hoping I had?'

'I hope for nothing,' Eve said, her voice as lifeless as her face. 'I have nothing to hope for – now.'

'I am so very sorry about Chris,' Alex said.

'Yes . . . you continued to see each other in defiance of my orders.'

'I ceased to be responsible to you once I left this house, and you never were responsible for me, so orders don't come into it.'

'Why did you come, then?'

'For Chris. To let him die with some dignity.'

'It was you who gave the order to turn off his machine?'

'Yes. Somebody had to and it was obvious you weren't up to it.'

Eve turned her head back to contemplation of the lake. 'I knew he was dead here –' she touched her forehead, '– but I could not accept it here.' She touched her breast. 'But thank you. You always were the defiant one.' She fell silent once more. Again Alex waited.

'I want you to do something for me,' Eve said.

'Oh? And what might that be?'

'I want you to arrange my son's funeral. I cannot do it.' Eve put a white lawn handkerchief to her lips. 'I want him cremated; the pure bright flame . . . I cannot bear to think of him lying in the cold, hard ground . . . but the rest I leave to you. I want it private. Afterwards I want his ashes placed in a white marble urn and I want that urn buried there – do you see that tree? Under its branches . . . he used to play there as a child. Do you remember?'

'I was never allowed anywhere near Chris,' Alex said.

'Reproaches are not what I need,' Eve said and for a moment the emptiness of her voice was filled with something like pain. 'I had thought,' she said, 'that we might reach some sort of – accommodation.'

'Why?' asked Alex.

'You're hard,' Eve said, and her voice trembled.

'What I am you made me.'

Eve made a gesture with her hand as though to say: What I did I had to do – then. 'So you will not stay for a while? Let me try to – make up for certain – things?'

'For some things there is no forgiveness,' Alex said.

'Ah . . .' It came out on a sigh. 'I see.'

'What never existed cannot be restored. You banished me from your house seven years ago; told me to make my own life because you could never give me what I wanted, be what I wanted. I took you at your word. There was a time when I would have given anything for what you are offering me now; I have wept oceans of tears because it was never forthcoming. I have no tears left, and times have changed. I have changed. It doesn't matter any more.'

Another silence. 'Are you happy?' Eve asked finally.

'Happier than I ever was in your house.'

Eve nodded. 'Yes . . . I can understand that.'

'I will arrange Chris's funeral,' Alex said, 'because he was my brother and it is the last thing I can do for him, but once that is over I shall return to my own world. We have nothing to say to each other, you and I, and I will not be used as a substitute – picked up, brushed off and set in an empty place. You made it abundantly clear seven years ago what you wanted me to do, and I did it. That squares our accounts.' In spite of herself Alex's voice shook with anger.

Eve turned her head, looked at her. 'Yes, you always were the strong one,' she said.

'I had no choice but to rely on myself. I knew from the start that I could never rely on you. Do you realize,' Alex asked, and her voice shook now with passion, 'that this is only the second time in my life that you have ever really looked at me? That seven years ago was the first time you ever spoke to me? You still have no idea what you did to me, have you? *Have you?*'

'I did what I had to do,' her mother said, in a remote yet much stronger voice. 'You do not understand – nobody understands.'

'Oh, I understand, all right. I am to be accepted back into the fold, groomed to take my brother's place. How fortunate that you remembered I existed, because if you had had your way I would have ceased to do that a long time ago.'

'There were reasons –'

'You always have reasons, usually created to suit yourself. Well it doesn't suit me. Neither does forgiveness. I'm not divine. I leave that state to you. Once the funeral is over I shall be leaving this house and I won't be back – ever.'

She turned on her heel, strode to the door. Hand on the knob she paused. 'Max would like to see you,' she said in calmer tones. 'About the company.'

Eve did not turn her head. 'Tell him to do whatever he thinks fit,' she said. 'I cannot think about it now.'

Alex closed the door quietly behind her.

From Max's bedroom window Mora Haynes, wearing his silk dressing-gown and eating a croissant, saw Alex walking at a fast rate in the direction of the lake and said, 'I don't think it was a successful interview.'

Max, still in bed, lowered the *International Herald Tribune* he was reading. 'How do you know?'

'Alex is stalking across the lawn in what my English nanny used to call high dudgeon.'

Max leapt naked from the bed to join Mora at the window, just in time to see Alex's stiff back disappear behind a huge cypress. 'Shit!' he said.

Mora asked curiously, 'What is she doing here anyway? I'd have thought she was the last person to come and offer comfort to the bereaved.'

'Chris was her brother,' Max said with a slight edge to his voice.

'But they were never exactly close.'

'They were a hell of a sight closer than Alex and her mother.'

'Beauty and the Beast,' Mora said, licking apricot jam from under her talon-like nails.

'Alex is no beast,' Max snapped.

'All right, but Chris was certainly a beauty. What a pity it wasn't the other way around.' Mora went to pour herself more coffee. 'Mind you, if she ever did something about herself she might not be so bad.'

'Alex is the last woman to worry about her appearance.'

'I think she does it deliberately. There's something aggressive about her plainness.'

'It's her way of getting back at her mother,' Max said absently, frowning out of the window.

'And much good it has done her.'

'You know nothing about it,' Max said dismissively, leaving the window and striding in the direction of the bathroom.

'Of course,' Mora called after him. 'She's your Good Deed for this and every other day, isn't she?' She followed him into the bathroom, leaned against the doorjamb while he adjusted the shower to a perfect temperature. 'Why *do* you bother with her?'

'Alex and I are old friends. I happen to like her. She has a first-class brain and is a damned good writer. If you ever read anything other than fashion magazines you would realize it.'

'Since when did you ever appreciate a woman for her brains?' Mora asked and, smiling, untied the dressing-gown and joined him in the large shower cubicle. She was as tall as Alex but considerably more slender, fine-boned, with a long back and exquisite shoulders she carried superbly on endless legs. Her face was ineffably well-bred and she fitted the part of the Eve Czerny Woman perfectly, from her ash-blonde hair to her superior smile; that of a woman who knows she is beautiful.

'I appreciated you several times last night,' Max said, his eyes kindling at her long loveliness.

'Appreciate me again,' Mora murmured, 'in your own, inimitable way . . .'

Alex covered the ground at speed, her anger propelling her forward. 'Yet another performance,' she muttered as she walked. 'My mother has so many faces she's spoiled for choice. Forgiveness indeed! Eve Czerny has never been sorry for anything in her life.'

I don't trust her, she thought. She is capable of changing not only her appearance but her substance, and if this new Weeping Madonna is to be the latest role she's welcome to it. Now that Chris is gone she wants me to step into his shoes. Alex's sense of humour got the better of her as she thought wryly: At that, they would fit me.

She came to one of the marble benches Eve had placed at strategic points throughout the gardens, where the views were spectacular. This one gave a vista of the lake and distant mountains, and Alex sank down as a wave of heavy tiredness swept over her, emotional not physical. I shouldn't have come, she thought. I knew it wouldn't work. The only way I can cope with my mother is at a distance. She says she's alone. What else have I been all my life? Who have I ever had to confide in, turn to, rely on? Only myself. No, she thought. Not true. First I had Patsy then I had Max. The thought of her dearly loved governess produced the usual lift of the heart. I shall go and see her, tell her everything. She will understand. She always does.

Then her thoughts returned to her mother. Am I doing her an injustice? Has she really undergone some sort of metamorphosis? Is she genuinely sorry for rejecting me? Max said she was alone with Chris for seven whole days. Who knows what she went through? Solitude to Mother is what sensory deprivation is to others, and you've read what happens to people who undergo that experience. They hallucinate for a start. Mother would have had no recourse but to fall back on herself – and who knows what that is? She's adopted so many disguises her own mother wouldn't recognize her – whoever she was.

Oh God, I don't know, she thought, and I don't like not knowing. I like things cut and dried. I knew where I was when she froze me out; I feel I'm losing my grip in this unexpected thaw . . . everything is suddenly all wet and soggy . . . Maybe Max is right. Maybe she has suddenly come face to face with her own mortality; maybe she sat there in that terrible silence and added up the totals of her life. Alone with a son she couldn't accept was dead; unable, for once, to control and manipulate events.

She sighed, and she was still sitting there, shoulders slumped, when a voice said: 'Want a shoulder to cry on?'

'I'm too angry to cry and besides, I exhausted my supply of tears a long time ago.'

'Well, don't exhaust my patience. What happened?' Max asked.

'I think my mother is auditioning for the lead in *The Miracle*.'

'She's worked many of them in her time.'

'This is more than cosmetic surgery. She wants to fit me into Chris's niche.'

'I don't see you as a statue, only statuesque.'

Alex smiled dutifully. 'I suppose I ought to be grateful that my mother is seeing me at all.'

Max said, 'I think Eve is seeing a lot of things, most of them unpleasant.'

'She's on a repentance kick; asked me if we couldn't reach an "accommodation".'

'She never lacked for nerve, or, as one of her rivals put it, "chutzpah".'

'What is she after, Max? On the one hand I know she's playing another part, yet on the other I keep thinking that at long last, she's playing herself. I know she's suffering but –'

'You didn't think she was capable of it?'

'No. Only of making other people suffer.'

'You could give her the benefit of the doubt.'

'I don't have the emotional wherewithal. Mother uses your doubts to club you senseless.' Alex paused: 'But maybe –'

'Maybe what?'

'Maybe she's suddenly sensitive. Oh, I don't know. I can't seem to think straight.' Angrily: 'You see . . . she's already got me floundering.'

'You and me both.'

Alex sighed. 'No, you're all right. You are to do what you think fit. She says she can't be bothered with the company right now.'

Max whistled. 'Now that *is* serious.'

'And I am to handle the funeral arrangements. She wants Chris to be cremated.'

'Anything I can do to help?'

'You can find out what the legal formalities are for a funeral in Switzerland. I don't even know where the crematorium is.'

'Leave it to me.'

Alex smiled gratefully. 'What would I do without you?'

'You've done very well so far.'

'That's what I thought until I came here. She still has the power to – to get me all worked up.'

'Emotions are a necessary part of the average human being.'

'She left mine for dead – the ones that were left after she'd made me waste them all on wanting what I couldn't have.'

'If you've none left then why are you so angry? Anger is an emotion. I know you like to think of yourself as Medea – "I myself, am enough" – but you aren't. You've got the whole range of emotions inside you, only you've got them under lock and key. Your trouble is that you can't take rejection. Your mother's has made you terrified to try again.'

'I can't help the way I am.'

'Of course you can. If your mother can change, why can't you?'

'*If* she has changed.'

'I think she has. Nothing she's done since Chris crashed his car has been recognizable. She's been seized by the scruff of the neck and made to look at the havoc she's created and I think that even when she closes her eyes she still sees it. It may be that only your forgiveness can put her demons back in their cage.'

'That's only a ploy to get me to take Chris's place.'

'Eve is no fool. She knows you loathe everything she stands for.'

'Then why try for something she knows is impossible?'

'Because she thrives on challenges. She's a risk-taker. I've seen her do things that have had me covering my eyes, but she'd always come up smiling. It's the impossible that intensifies her determination. Nobody and nothing gets the better of her.'

'She doesn't know me,' Alex said. She laughed. 'Ain't it the truth.' Her voice was savage.

Max put a comforting arm around Alex's broad shoulders. 'Look, all you have to do is say, "All right, I forgive you", and then go back to Cambridge.'

'It would be a lie, and besides, give Mother an inch and she takes ten miles. She'll want more. She always does.'

'So don't give it to her.'

'Easier said than done.'

'You know what your trouble is? You're a thirty-year-old woman with the emotions of a ten-year-old. You keep on saying you've made your own life but that silver cord is as tight around your neck as it was around Chris's. We are what our past makes us and no matter how fast you run, emotionally you're on a treadmill. You've got to face her and get to grips with her. You can't do it by remote control; you've got to get in there and get dirty.'

Alex shuddered. 'I don't relish the thought.'

'Relish is something I put on a hot dog. You've got your own demons, kid. Isn't it about time you faced them?' He put a finger under her chin. 'You know I'm in your corner.'

'If I ever manage to get back to it.'

'There's a book you ought to read. It's called *The Power of Positive Thinking*. Make a change from Dante in the original.'

'You were the one who got me started on Italian.'

'So let me get you started on the road to redemption. Use that logical mind of yours. Eve is the most illogical creature alive. She does everything by instinct – and while I have to say they are usually

82

right, I think you could give her a run for her money. Find out what she's after. Don't assume that it's her own protection.'

'Why not? It normally is.'

'And what is it you're sitting wrapped up in?'

'For God's sake, next thing you'll be telling me it's all *my* fault!' Alex's voice rose. Max just looked at her. 'I told her and I'm telling you. I can't forgive her – I can't, and that's all there is to it. I'm not divine, I'm all too human – a thirty-year-old woman with what you say are warped emotions. Well, who warped them – froze them? Did she ever once show me any warmth? Any kind of regard? Did she ever ask you about me? Who was it prevented my own brother from seeing me? And she expects me to say: "Of course I forgive you. I know you didn't mean it" when I know damn well she meant every cold word she said!'

'Then why have you taken on the arrangements for the funeral? It means you will have to stay on, you know. These things can't be arranged in five minutes.'

'I'm doing it for Chris. I will make it as – as dignified as I can. She wants it private – private it shall be. She wants him cremated and she wants his ashes buried under the big chestnut at the back of the house. I'll stay and see to that for him, it's the last I can do, but that is *it*! And if I don't have to see her until then, so much the better.' Alex rose to her feet. 'And now if you will excuse me, I have things to arrange.'

Max sighed. 'Happy days are here again,' he said, and getting up, followed Alex into the house.

6

London, 1957–61

Alexandra Mary Brent was born on a sultry August night just as the oppressive heat of the day was cooled by the bursting of equally pregnant clouds. She was expelled even as the first roll of thunder announced her arrival.

'Four hours from start to finish!' Mary Brent was scandalized. 'For a *first* baby?'

Her son turned his back on her and went back into the bedroom. Eve had shaken him awake, said: 'John, the baby is coming.' She was calm, having first-hand knowledge of the process of birth through assisting her mother, when old enough, at the confinements of the Puszta. The midwife was sent for, John was banished to pace and chain-smoke, his mother ostentatiously opening all the windows and emptying the ashtray every time he crushed out a cigarette. When the midwife came down to the kitchen to ask for a cup of tea she said, 'You won't have long to wait. This is going to be penny-in-the-slot.'

The baby weighed exactly nine pounds. She was long as well as large, and she had eyes like purple velvet. She was wrapped in a blanket and given to Eve who said, 'Not now, please, nurse . . . I am too tired to hold her,' and handed her back.

John was delighted. He had secretly longed for a daughter but said nothing to Eve, who obviously did not care what it was just so long as she did not have to bother with it. When he was invited to hold 'his' daughter he did so with some trepidation, not knowing what to expect considering the way she had been conceived, but to his delighted surprise he saw a porcelain-skinned cherub with a thatch of black hair and eye-lashes every bit as long as her mother's, if fine and thin. She regarded him with grave eyes. Why, John thought on a rush of emotion he had never felt before, she's beautiful . . .

When he visited Eve later, the baby was in a crib by her bed, sucking placidly on two fingers, the fourth and the third. John put out a tentative forefinger of his own to touch her other hand and found it seized and held with surprising strength.

'She's got a grip like pliers!' he exclaimed. His voice was besotted. 'She's absolutely beautiful.'

'Not with that nose,' Eve snapped. It was Laszlo's nose; imperious and powerful. Eve was furious. She was damned if she was going to have a constant reminder of a man she wanted to forget meeting her gaze at every turn. And she was most certainly not going to feed it. The less she had to do with it the better. It was a nuisance. Not what she wanted. The sooner she was rid of it the better. Her plans did not include a child. And they were made. Let him fuss over it, she thought. He's welcome to it. Not only Laszlo's nose but his eyes too. Oh, they might be darkly purple now, but they would, she was sure, turn hazel, like his. It was beyond bearing! Laszlo Kovacs was over and done with and she wanted no relics – *none* – of a past she was preparing to wipe from her life.

It was John's suggestion that they name the child Alexandra Mary – Mary as a sop to his mother. Eve didn't care what the child was called. Her mind was on getting back to work.

'A nanny!' screeched Mary Brent.

'Are you prepared to look after it, then?'

'I am most certainly not. You are the child's mother – though I will never believe my son is her father, not with that nose, and your job is at home, being her mother. And where will this nanny live?'

'She will take care of the child during the day. John and I will look after it at night.' Or rather John will, she thought.

'John comes home tired at the end of the day. He shouldn't have to look after a baby.'

'He wants to.'

'More fool him, considering she's not his daughter.'

But it was John who took the baby for walks to the Common, who spent every minute he had to spare with her, who fed her – for Eve had insisted on bottles – changed her, bathed her, put her to bed. She was a placid child who rarely cried, though when she did she screamed, and she gained weight steadily.

Eve, meanwhile, was gaining customers. The beauty business was booming in the Macmillan years of never having had it so good.

The industry was expanding; there was a market out there easily big enough to sustain her present small effort so she got herself involved in direct mailing, using her unfailing ability to pick the right person to help her at any particular time. While attending antenatal clinic she had met the wife of a man involved in cycle-billing; adding inserts to the bills that were sent out by the nationalized industries. Eve had a flier made up and sent out to the thousands of consumers on their lists. It turned out to be pure gold, resulting in a rush of orders. She put a discreet advertisement in the classified columns of the glossies, and when women began asking for her line in department stores, she was able to tell the buyers that yes, they could stock her creams, but she would do the selling. Their response was to decline her offer. She had not told them that she had no demonstrators; she reckoned she could find them without too much trouble and train them to her exacting standards. Girls thought the beauty business was glamorous; she would not tell them about long hours on aching feet. Let them find out for themselves. But she would find the ones with the best skins and they would get to use her products for nothing.

And then her helpful friend was fired for not seeking permission to insert anything other than officially approved fliers, so Eve promptly offered him a job. His contacts would be of inestimable value and she would pay him by results; that way he would really work hard.

He found her two girls, both of whom had worked for the mail order firm and who had tried and liked Eve's products. Both were eager to accept her offer to become trained in the use of Eve Czerny cosmetics and, equally as important, the art of selling them. One was placed in a local department store, the other – the better one – in another store in Croydon, a major shopping centre surrounded by satellite towns in the Surrey commuter belt.

She also found a factory – which made cosmetics for many of the major houses – willing to make up her products to her stringent requirements, but she soon found that unless she was there, they were not giving her what she wanted. What she needed, she reasoned, was a factory of her very own. Which meant that she needed to find a man with enough money to enable her to do it.

By this time, early 1959, she was doing very well but still not selling in the major West End department stores. Until she could come up with a backer she decided that she could greatly increase her sales by gaining a foothold in that lucrative market. So she sallied forth to see what she could do. She made the rounds of the Oxford Street stores, always asking to see the Head Buyer for Cosmetics. Their usual reaction was 'Eve who?' until she ended up at a shop in the unfashionable end of the street, a long-established if somewhat staid shop named Brandon and Bourne. There, when she was shown into the Head Buyer's office, she took one look at the woman behind the desk and knew she had found her slot, for the woman had an appalling skin, blotched and scaly. She listened to what Eve had to say, examined the bottles and jars, opened them, sniffed their fragrance, smoothed a little onto her hands, but was unimpressed. 'There is no demand for your products,' she told Eve finally. 'Create a demand and I will be happy to give further consideration to your line.'

'If I prove to you, personally, how good my creams are, would you then be interested in giving them a trial?' Eve asked.

'How?'

'Let me treat your face.'

The woman flushed and put up a hand to her cheek. 'I've been to the best dermatologists in the business and if they can't do anything I don't see how you can.'

'I have a cream that was created by a dermatologist of genius,' Eve told her confidently. 'It was specially developed for skin conditions such as yours. If I give you a jar, will you promise to use it faithfully – and in exactly the way I tell you – for one week? If your skin is not immeasurably improved by then, I will not trouble you further.'

Her confidence was such that the woman found herself agreeing. She had tried so many creams; what was one more . . .

But Eve gave her three. One, a pale green lotion – 'herbal', Eve said, 'to clear the skin. Yours is not dry, it is oily.'

'But I have been told the contrary.'

'I don't care what you've been told. Your blotches are the result of blocked pores; this lotion will gently open them. At the same time it will loosen the scaly residue. Once you feel it is loose – and your fingers will tell you – then you wash it away with this soap. Rub – and I mean rub – it in; it will remove the scale. Then rinse with warm – not cold, never hot – water.'

'I was told *never* to use soap.'

'This is a special soap; use it morning and evening *and do not miss a day*. After the soap you smooth in this cream. It heals and revitalizes as well as restores. One week. I can see you do not believe me but I know what these products can do. There is nothing else like them on the market.'

In the face of Eve's proselytizing conviction and her genius for selling, the buyer found herself accepting the challenge.

Eve returned to Wimbledon filled with confidence. She had found her niche; soon she would be selling to a market she would, she resolved, eventually dominate. In the meantime, she would continue with the training of the girl she had chosen – from more than twenty applicants – to take over at the salon, for Eve herself intended to demonstrate and sell her line. Her launch had to be done properly.

One week later, when she was shown into the Head Buyer's office, Eve found her in seventh heaven. Taking her to the window, Eve turned her face this way and that, saw how the blotches had cleared, their unsightly redness now smooth and pink, the angry-looking spots gone. 'You should continue the treatment for at least another week,' she instructed. 'There is still some blockage of the pores . . .'

'But already my skin is incredibly improved! I've never used anything like these products of yours. They are miracle workers.'

'I told you so,' Eve shrugged.

'We will stock them for a three-month trial run. I'll put my best girls –'

'No girls,' Eve said. '*I* will be behind the counter.'

'But we only allow the big Houses to employ their own demonstrators.'

'I may be small now, but one day I shall be the biggest of them all.'

The buyer looked at her. 'Yes,' she said, 'I think you will.'

So Eve took her place behind the counter in the small corner she had been allotted, at the back of the cosmetics hall, where she put her charm and her conviction to good use. She could establish a rapport with a customer in seconds, and once she laid hands on them – 'touch your customer and she is in your power', she used to teach her rapt students years later – they invariably left the shop carrying one of Eve's little carrier bags – glossy white with her name in gold, like her jars – containing her entire range.

She always made it her business to learn the names of her customers, to ask about children, to listen to woes, to murmur and coo and sympathize even as she demonstrated; and always, at least twice a day, she would give a full demonstration, entice a customer into the big chair in front of the mirrors she had persuaded the powers that be to instal, and make her over. It invariably resulted in a rush to buy. To those who didn't – usually because they couldn't afford to, for Eve Czerny products weren't cheap – Eve pressed a sample into their hands. 'Try it,' she would say. 'You will soon find that you cannot do without it.'

Her mail-order acolyte, now in charge of production, used to say: 'We can't afford to give away so much, Madame Czerny. It eats into profits.'

'I am setting a small sprat to catch a very large mackerel,' Eve would tell him. 'A whale, in fact.'

By the time word had got out, and she was approached by the other stores who were being pestered by women asking them why they didn't stock Eve Czerny products, the Head Buyer no longer worked for Brandon and Bourne but for Eve Czerny, as did half a dozen girls from the other Houses. Eve took them all down to Wimbledon for an intensive three-day course in selling her way, before installing them, in the whiter-than-white, clinical-looking, high-collared smocks she designed, behind the Eve Czerny counters.

'The emphasis is on the purity of the product,' she said. 'Always clean – no dirty nails – and no nail varnish, that can hide a multitude of sins. Use only my Tender Pink; it doesn't hide, only exhibits.'

She worked from 8 a.m. till 7 p.m., seven days a week. When she was not at the salon or checking up on the stores – and the girls never knew when they might look up and see her there – she was consulting with her manufacturing chemist, who still made up her trial runs, as to how to improve this cream, or achieve a more subtle blend of colour for that lipstick.

She rarely saw her daughter; she was with the nanny in the morning when Eve left and asleep in her cot when she arrived home. She saw just as little of her husband, who had realized with some resignation that Eve was in her evangelical phase, spreading her gospel of Beauty. She made up even more samples, one of each of her range, and had them, accompanied by fliers, sent out to potential customers, informing them that at such and such a store, a free gift awaited those women who bought one or more of her products. It was not new, but it was done with great flair and her genius for merchandising, and it had her products leaving the shelves almost as soon as they were placed there. She sold, she demonstrated, she taught, she preached, she brought herself to the notice of anyone who could further her purpose, but she had not as yet reached her goal – Harrods. It took her *Essence of Eve* to do that.

She had been trying to find a fragrance for some time – something entirely different, something that did not remind the nose of anything else. She wanted one that was unmistakable, unforgettable and would bring only one name to mind when inhaled: Eve Czerny.

She knew that she would have to diversify into fragrances; Elizabeth Arden had done it with *Blue Grass*, Helena Rubenstein with *Heaven Scent*, Estée Lauder with *Youth Dew*. Now, her ever receptive antennae told her that the time was ripe for a new scent. She knew little of the complex construction of a perfume, but she was aware that it was a hideously expensive exercise. She decided that she would have to go to the top. Which was how she came to meet Henri Beyle, who owned the largest flavour and fragrance company outside the United States. He himself had begun as a *parfumeur*, having been trained by the great François Côty himself. He was sixty, and known as one of the great 'noses' of his time. As he kept abreast of the market, he knew who Eve Czerny was, had marked her onward and upward progress, so that he had no hesitation in seeing her when she wrote to him personally – 'Always go to the top' was her maxim – and sent him one of her sample offers. As she had confidently expected, she received a letter within days asking her to call at his Park Lane offices at a stated date and time.

As always she had done her research. Henri Beyle was a public figure, one of the biggest in the cosmetics industry. Based in Switzerland, where his main factories were, he also had a plant in England, where he did work for most of the major cosmetic companies as well as the huge food conglomerates because he also manufactured food colourings and flavourings.

He had been married to the same wife for twenty-eight years and had two daughters. From his picture, she judged him to be a man who appeared to be a stolid Swiss bourgeois but who hid, behind his benign exterior, an astute mind which exercised total control at all times. His wife was short, fat, homely, and his two daughters took after her. Both were married to men who worked for Beyle Industries. There were four grandchildren. On the surface, Eve surmised, a family man. She would know, once she met him, looked into his eyes, saw their reaction to her, what else he was, but for the first meeting she would play it his way.

She looked her best when she entered his office; he would expect, she reasoned, that a woman who dealt in beauty would be a walking advertisement for her wares. Her dress was of a blue to match her eyes, under a matching tent coat. Her small cloche hat was made entirely of coq feathers whose iridescent blues made a perfect foil for the red-gold hair curling round it. She had spent thirty minutes on her face and she smelled heady: a fragrance of her own concoction, but not quite as special as the one she was about to persuade Henri Beyle to invent for her.

He came from behind the desk to meet her, shake hands, escort her to a chair. In her highest heels she was not much shorter than he was.

He went back behind his desk, smiled and said in excellent English, 'So, Madame Czerny, what is it you want with me?'

Eve had decided months ago that it was time to leave the name Brent and all it stood for, as easily as she had shaken the dust of Hungary from her size threes. It was make or break time, not that she intended it to be anything other than make, and the woman who conceived the perfume she had in mind could be no other than Eve Czerny; the 'Madame' was an afterthought. What was good enough for Helena Rubenstein was good enough for her. Now, she said with quiet confidence, 'First, tell me what you think of my products.'

They were ranged to one side of his desk, and she saw him reach out and draw the bottle of her Skin Vitalizer towards him. Hefting it in his pudgy hand he said, 'I think you must be making a great deal of money.'

It was obvious that he was a man who knew the value of a franc. Her tonic consisted of water, grain alcohol, boric acid and perfume, but all balanced to a delicacy that was easily disturbed by variations of temperature and humidity, which necessitated careful storage.

The basic cost of a single bottle was two shillings and sixpence; it sold for twelve shillings and sixpence. After labour, distribution, packaging and advertising costs were deducted, she was still making a clear 25 per cent profit on each bottle sold.

'Not enough for what I now have in mind,' she said candidly.

'And what is that?'

'A fragrance. Something that will get a stranglehold on the market. I am hoping you will create it for me.'

He regarded her thoughtfully. 'Such a creation is a very expensive operation.'

'That is why I have come to you.'

'Do you have any idea what goes into the creation of a perfume?'

'Jasmine, tuberose, orange blossom, sandalwood, cardamom, bergamot –'

'Jasmine absolute sells for two hundred and fifty pounds for one pound in weight – roses even more, and as for bergamot . . . One single ounce of a great perfume contains the essence of ten thousand jasmine flowers, hundreds of special roses from France, a couple of thousand orange blossoms, hand-scraped peel from more than a dozen oranges, sandalwood and cardamom from India. I do not include the laboratory-made aromatic chemicals, which have to go through a whole series of complicated and time-consuming processes before purity is achieved.'

'The one I have in mind will sell in such quantities as to justify every penny of such costs. I am not afraid to spend, Monsieur Beyle, when I know that every penny spent will result in a pound made.'

He did not smile at her cheeky confidence. 'Tell me about this perfume. Describe it to me if you can.'

'I intend to call it *Essence of Eve*, and that it should bring to mind the eternal woman: mysterious, complex, ultra-feminine but not cloying for this is the latter half of the twentieth century and women no longer need to cling. It will be modern yet as old as time: it will wreathe itself about the consciousness and, though powerful, aggressive even, it will develop to a spellbinding subtlety. No one will ever ask: "What is that perfume you're wearing?" They will recognize it at once.'

'A tall order.'

'Which, again, is why I have come to you.'

He considered the lovely face, its absolute confidence, its serene assumption that she was offering him a ride on a rocket that would take profits to the moon.

'My products are the best of their kind,' she challenged. 'They not only look good – and presentation is all, which is why I have an idea for a specially designed flacon for my perfume – they do good. My customer comes from the top end of the market: a woman who expects the best and is well able to afford it. My perfume will be an absolute necessity.' He still said nothing but she knew by the quality of his silence that she had his entire attention.

'The market is changing. The emphasis is now on skin *care*. I am in the process of creating a revolutionary cream which I shall call Renaissance. It will be sold as having rare ingredients and an equally rare formula.'

'Estée Lauder has already done that with Re-Nutriv.'

'And look how that sold! Mine will go one step further, but it will cost three times as much as my other creams and before I launch it I want my perfume to consolidate Eve Czerny as a household name.'

'And what are these magic ingredients?'

'The formula is secret. It was a cream my grandmother made up; she showed my mother how and she showed me. The formula is in here.' Eve tapped her forehead. 'But the real secret is in the selling, and I have one or two ideas about that.'

'I think,' Henri Beyle said with amusement, 'that you are a lady who has ideas about everything.' He smiled. 'Perhaps we could discuss them some time.'

'Perhaps,' Eve agreed, promising nothing but hope, 'but right now, what interests me is my fragrance.'

Their eyes met and she knew that what interested him was Eve Czerny. Which was exactly as she had intended.

'I think,' Henri Beyle said, 'that you had better meet my chief *parfumeur*.'

Essence of Eve was launched in the spring of 1960 and was an instant, bushfire success. Eve had insisted on it being based on oil rather than alcohol. 'It must *last*,' she insisted. 'It must cling to the skin. I do not want my customers to have to reapply every hour or so. It must wreathe itself around them so as to become part of their

93

persona.' To this end, she spent hours with the *parfumeur*, who blended, mixed, added, subtracted, trying to come up with what Eve knew she wanted but was relying on him to create. 'Close . . .' she would say, sniffing intently, 'but not quite there. Perhaps a little less jasmine?' Or: 'Too assertive. It must insinuate, not wield a blunt instrument. I want an impact but not one that will cause concussion!'

She knew exactly what she wanted and refused to accept what she knew wasn't *right*. As time went on, the costs mounted, but Henri Beyle merely looked at the figures that were presented to him and scribbled his initials on the bottom without a qualm. He had known, within minutes, that Eve Czerny was going places, and not because she carried the one passport that took a woman anywhere and everywhere: her beauty. She captivated him. One minute she was like the bubbles in a glass of champagne, going straight to the head with her combination of gaiety and wit; the next she was the deeply serious, incisive businesswoman, forcibly putting across her ideas with the conviction of the true zealot. She was, he mused, the physical manifestation of her perfume. He found he made more visits to the laboratory than usual; that just to sit and watch her, arguing, explaining, elaborating, was satisfying in a way that he had not experienced in many years. She was a mass of contradictions – again like her perfume. She could charm the heart out of your body with effortless ease then be cuttingly impatient because what she had decided was simple was proving intractably difficult for everyone else. She had the energy of a perpetual motion machine yet she never looked anything but appealingly fragile. She could talk the hind leg off a donkey yet sit, chin on hand, and give you her attention in a way that had you walking on air.

That she was a pirate he had no doubt; or that there were in her past countless men who had walked her particular plank. She was a woman for whom a man would willingly don a blindfold. He enjoyed her company so much that the days when he couldn't share it seemed to have forty-eight hours in place of the usual twenty-four. He could talk business to her in a way he had never done with any woman. His wife took no interest beyond that of approving everything he did. Her daughters and her grandchildren were the mainsprings of her life. He was still very fond of her, but for many years now he had indulged in small affairs that were brief but enjoyable; no more than the scratching of an irritating itch. Eve was a bad case of dermatitis. As the weeks then the months went on, he began to dread the day when she would throw her hands in the air, unleash that dazzling smile, laugh that enchanting laugh and say: '*This* is the one!'

Essence of Eve was what catapulted Eve Czerny Cosmetics into the big time. It sold in such quantities that Harrods actually came to her and asked if she would supply them. She said she would if they also allowed her to sell her entire range of products, and to those women who bought the entire range, she gave a free half-ounce bottle in its distinctive Lalique crystal flacon in the shape of a leaf – from the Garden of Eden.

All this time she had been working on her Renaissance cream, and it was launched that autumn with the biggest advertising campaign she had ever mounted, paid for by the proceeds of her perfume. Henri Beyle's judgement was completely vindicated; it took only nine short months to recoup every penny spent on its creation, and he made a healthy profit into the bargain. He also introduced Eve to people whom she used to further her upward progress. When a new play opened in the West End, starring an actress who was a legendary beauty in spite of being well over forty, Eve – whose customer she had become – persuaded her to have one of the publicity stills used to illustrate an article in a mass-circulation magazine, taken at her dressing-table in the theatre, preparing her make-up. Positioned so that it was reflected in the mirror along with the actress's face, and thus seen twice, was one of the limited edition jars of Renaissance, which retailed at £25 for six ounces. Eve sought and obtained permission to use the photograph in her first, full-page advertisement in *Harper's Bazaar*.

She never ceased her intensive selling, standing behind her counter at Harrods, dazzling and squelching the competition and spellbinding the women who crowded round, folding their hands round a jar or a bottle and saying in her throaty, compelling way: 'It is the best buy you *ever* made. I do not say it will work miracles – I am still looking for that – but it will work wonders. Come back in a month's time and tell me so. If I see that it hasn't lived up to my promise I will refund your money.' Needless to say, she never once had to do so.

Her insistence on quality became legendary. She was capable, on visiting the factory which made her range, of consigning a whole day's production to the dustbin because her infallible eye had caught the minutest straying from the *exact* shade of blue or green or grey or red.

'It will not do,' she told Henri one evening, when they were dining at the Ritz. 'I must have my own factories.'

'Yes,' agreed Henri, 'I think you must. And I think I have the perfect spot.'

'Where?' Her eyes sparkled like sun on water.

'Not far from my own.'

'Switzerland!' She had been thinking in terms of the United States.

'I think that is where your image – that of purity and quality control – should be based. Switzerland is famous for its clinics, its health-giving atmosphere. Mountains, lakes, clean air, apple-pie order, stability – and money. I think you should come and take a look for yourself.'

Their eyes met. 'Yes,' Eve agreed. 'I think it is time I did.'

When she told her husband she was leaving it came as no surprise. He hardly ever saw her. She had distanced herself from him physically immediately after the baby, but he understood that she had left him emotionally even before then.

'All right,' he agreed, 'I see no point in trying to keep alive something that never really drew breath.'

'My lawyers will be in touch with you and they will make all the necessary arrangements.'

'Such as committing adultery? You should have no difficulty there.'

'I will pay all the legal costs,' Eve said ignoring his jibe, 'and I am willing to pay you a reasonable sum in consideration of your . . . compliance.'

'That's collusion in this country,' John said, 'but since it is also the way things are done, why should I be different? But I want more than money. I want Alexandra.'

'You are welcome to her.'

'But I want it done legally. Alex already bears my name and is officially my child, registered as such. For accepting responsibility for her I want the sum of five thousand pounds put in trust, giving me the use of the income for Alex's upbringing and education. She is a bright child and worthy of the best I can afford.'

'You are the teacher,' Eve taunted, 'so pay yourself a salary.' But she was pleasantly relieved that John should want so little considering he had many years of support ahead of him. It was a sum she could easily afford: less than £400 a year averaged overall, still less if, as she surmised, John would want his daughter to have a university education. He can do what he likes with it, and her, she thought, just so long as they both disappear from my life.

'I shall consult my lawyers,' she lied, 'and they will tell me if what you ask is both reasonable and affordable.' She sounded puzzled when she asked, 'You really love the child, don't you?'

'Yes, I do. And she loves me. Fortunately, she's seen so little of you that she regards you as a stranger, and once she's old enough to ask, I shall tell her you died at her birth. It's no more than the truth anyway. You rejected her even when she was in the womb.'

'You know why,' Eve said, turning away.

'I know what you told me. I also know better than to believe blindly, as I once did.'

'Not only this house has changed,' Eve observed sardonically.

'Being married to you has been a further education.'

'I have a destiny to fulfil. You have never understood that.'

'I would like to know why you think life has you marked out for something special.'

'By what I came from, by what I am now, by what I shall become.'

'I wonder what the truth of that is?'

'Truth wears many faces but the only one I recognize is my own. I *am* special, I *am* meant to be famous, I *am* meant to be Somebody. I have known this ever since I was a child. My fate is already mapped out and I cannot – do not – wish to change it. Let others live out their petty little lives, safe in their nonentity, their unwillingness to take risks. I'm not like that; my life is one of those with a Grand Design. I have been given special gifts, I have been guided along my path in life, doors opened, people met, all the time pointed onwards.' Her voice was exalted, like that of a Chosen One, except she was in no way humbled by the notion: to her, it seemed no more than her due. It was because she had been born special that

97

Fate had no choice but to acknowledge her. 'My path has been determined for me and I have no option but to follow wherever it leads.'

'Is that your excuse for always doing what *you* want, as and how and when and where *you* decide?'

'I made up my mind a long time ago that it would be what *I* wanted that mattered; that *I* would control my life, not other people. I had enough of controls in Hungary.'

'Yet you expect to control others. To what end? To replace the Goddess of Beauty? Sit on her throne and be worshipped by legions of adoring women?'

'Yes,' Eve answered without hesitation. 'That is what I want.'

'I see. The power *and* the glory.' John looked at her seriously. 'Be careful, Eve. Playing at being a goddess can be dangerous, especially when you come to believe the fiction is fact.'

'I know what I can do and even you must admit that I do it well.'

'Oh, yes, you do, but don't get too arrogant in your belief that there is nothing and no one you cannot manipulate.'

'You haven't done so badly. In giving me what I wanted I also gave you what you needed. Self-confidence. There was a time when you would not have been able to state your terms to me – to anyone.'

'As I said, knowing you has been a second education,' John told her truthfully. 'I have learned a great deal these past four years. I shall probably never see you again – except in the newspapers or on television – but I shall never forget you. Whatever I felt for you did not live long under your neglect, but I shall always be grateful to you.' Eve smiled. 'You gave me Alex.'

Eve's smile vanished. 'I'm glad I was able to do something right.'

'Come now, when have you ever believed anything else? One day, you will come to realize that merely because *you* believe a thing is right, it isn't automatically so. Other people have rights too.'

'In this world, it's every man or woman for themselves, and if I hadn't been so sure, would I have been so successful? Would I have accomplished so much in four short years? You forget that in providing for myself I have also provided for many others by giving them jobs. What's wrong in that?'

'Nothing, except you never do anything for other people, only for yourself. You pick up, use, then discard. I know why you married me, Eve. I had something you wanted – British citizenship. But in the end, you've given me something I never thought to have, and for that – for her – I am grateful.'

'All in all you're not going to do so badly out of me,' Eve said.

'If it didn't suit your purpose you wouldn't give me anything.'

Eve was struck by the way her husband had changed. Gone was the lovesick fool she had come to despise. She knew that he had long ceased to love her, that the rejection was not really on her part but on his. She had the uncomfortable feeling of having, for the first time in her life, come out of a tedious situation without her usual sense of satisfaction.

'You *have* changed,' she marvelled.

'Thanks to you.'

Eve looked at her soon to be ex-husband for a moment, as if she was searching for something – the right thing – to say. Then she turned and left without saying anything.

7

Switzerland, 1988

Thanks to Max's contacts with the press, the publicity surrounding the death of Eve Czerny's only son was low-key. The obituary was short, but it did not deter reporters and photographers from taking up position outside the gates of the villa. Max had a word with the local police, and since Eve Czerny Cosmetics was one of Switzerland's most prestigious and profitable companies, they saw to it that when Christopher's body was removed from the local mortuary to the little church in the nearby village, it was done unobtrusively. Max dealt with the formalities regarding the cremation while Alex went to search for a stonemason and the white marble urn Eve had specified. The headstone she chose was also of marble: white, pure, unflawed. She would ask Jonesy to find out from Eve what she would like carved on it. All she has to do is order the lettering done in gold leaf and it will be just like one of her jars of cream, Alex thought. She knew Chris would have appreciated the joke.

Eve remained secluded; no one saw her but Jonesy, and when Max asked how she was he did no more than shake his head, tight-lipped. Alex he ignored. It was obvious who was the villain in his eyes.

The funeral was set for the following Thursday at noon, and once Alex had arranged everything, she left it to Pamela – who asked for the privilege – to decorate the small church with flowers.

The weather turned damp and misty, and finding time on her hands, for Max was always out, either in Geneva where the headquarters of Eve Czerny Incorporated was situated, or at the factory on the outskirts, Alex decided to explore the villa, since she had never been inside most of its many rooms. Now, she prowled through them, examining, appraising, oddly disappointed. The furniture was priceless, the pictures genuine, the *objets d'art* valuable, yet the whole thing reminded her of nothing so much as a film set. Any moment she expected Eve to sweep on to it, fresh from the hands of her make-up man and hairdresser, wearing some sumptuous costume and all ready for her next scene. She noticed that there were flowers everywhere, and it was only on encountering a woman in the act of arranging them that she realized they were done every single day.

The only room she really knew was the library, since her mother had once caught her trespassing there, but it was not the books she examined; she already knew them. Now it was the photographs she studied, two in particular, both of people no longer young. One of a woman, her dress and hair in the style of the mid-1930s – a bias-cut evening gown and flat, marcelled waves. She had a high-bred imperious face, and sat with military erectness on an ornate sofa clasping an ostrich-feather fan and wearing a fortune in pearls and diamonds. The other was of a man in a military uniform that was right out of *The Prisoner of Zenda*; he had a fiercely waxed moustache, brilliantined hair and sported a monocle. Picking the photographs up Alex found the same photographer's name in the bottom right-hand corner of the ornate silver frames. Karoly – Budapest. When later she asked the only person who might know who they were, Max said straight-faced: 'Your mother's grandparents: the Count Tibor Czerny and his wife Magda.' The only 'grandparent' Alex had ever known was her father's mother, and remembering certain things that lady had said about her mother, she took the Count and Countess for the fiction they were.

But she encountered not a single photograph album. No treasured family snapshots. No family mementoes either, though there were several stylized art deco statuettes, a couple of Erté drawings, several Lalique pieces of carved rock crystal. The photographs she did find went no further back than 1960, when Eve's star had been in the ascendant. Photographs of Henri Beyle, of other famous faces of the period, of Eve's 'first' husband, Christopher Bingham IV, of Christopher Bingham V – many of him, and of course, umpteen of Eve herself, always glamorous, always smiling.

Well, Alex mused, the absence of anything prior to 1960 can be explained by the Hungarian revolution and the fact that no photographs were allowed before then. I wonder what she had to hide, Alex pondered. 'I lost everything but my identity,' Eve had said, in interview after interview. And I wonder who she stole that from? was Alex's thought.

She herself had a very few treasured snapshots, given to her by her 'father' and concealed from his mother because almost all of them showed John Brent and his daughter, all of them taken on outings of one sort or another. One taken by a beach photographer in Margate, another at the zoo, a third snapped by a street photographer in Trafalgar Square, of Alex feeding the pigeons. 'These are our secret,' he had told her. 'Keep them but don't say a word to anyone.' Anyone being Mary Brent, who would undoubtedly have destroyed them.

Even accounting for the baleful presence of a woman who made no bones about her hatred of a child she regarded as 'a bastard', her first five years were, to Alex, one, long, sunfilled afternoon. Since John Brent's death it had been a case of Stormy Weather. Now, as she searched, she found no trace of the photographs that had been taken while she was at Cheltenham Ladies' College, the class groups which were always sent to parents; although, Alex recalled, Max would have received them, since he had been down in the school records as her 'Trustee'. If he gave them to my mother then she threw them away, Alex thought. Naturally they would be of no interest.

Eve's office held nothing that was not to do with her company, and the pictures lining the walls were mostly magazine covers. None earlier than 1961, when fame began. Who are you? Alex pondered, studying them. Where do you come from? Why are you what you are? What made you?

And then she had her first clue. Eve was not receiving any visitors, though the condolence letters occupied several cardboard filing boxes. But when Jacques came to Alex with a card bearing the name Mrs William Randolph, she turned it over to see the scrawled words: 'Remember Vienna?'

'I will see her, Jacques,' Alex said. 'I think she is an old friend of Madame's.'

'Very good, Miss.'

She was American, in her sixties, very smart, well-preserved, stick-thin and obviously a Lady. Alex explained that Madame was not seeing anyone.

'I don't suppose she would remember me anyway. It is thirty years, after all.'

'You knew her in Vienna then?'

'I was one of her first customers when she was a penniless little refugee. I've followed her career ever since, and as I was in Zurich – my husband is a banker and had business there – I thought I would take the chance, pay my condolences and talk over old times.'

'Did you know her well?'

'Not as friends, exactly, but I was a regular client in those days. I remember how she used to trot about the city with that red bag of hers. I was a convert from the first treatment and I've never used anything but the Eve Czerny line ever since, no matter where I've been, which has been mostly anywhere but home. She has certainly come a long way.' The woman's lips, painted in Eve's Primary Red, curved in a reminiscent smile. Then she sighed. 'So sad about her son. I lost one of mine in Vietnam, so I know how she feels. That's why I came . . . but she was always a courageous little thing, even though she was terrified she would be kidnapped and taken back to Hungary to stand trial.'

'For what?' Alex asked.

'Well, I don't know all the details, but I was told by someone who had it from someone else who had it from the correspondent who got her out of Hungary – he was the one who introduced her to John Brent – that she was some sort of double agent; ostensibly cosying up to the Russians but reporting back to a secret under-ground network. Of course, it could only be gossip. A more unlikely double agent I cannot think of, but then, isn't that how they're supposed to be? And there was always a great deal of gossip about Eve Czerny. A woman as beautiful as she was always causes comment and speculation.'

'Did you know her husband?' Alex asked.

'John Brent? I met him once, I think. Tall, stooped, painfully shy. Nobody could understand what on earth she saw in him because she could have had anybody, but the opinion was that she had married him in order to get that coveted British passport. It was not an unknown thing at the time. We left Vienna shortly after she married him and I never saw her again except once, in New York years later. She was married to Christopher Bingham at the time. It was at the theatre . . . I waved but I don't suppose she saw me and by the time I had pushed through the crowds – it was a first night as I recall – she was gone. We were leaving next day to return to Rome so I never saw her after that except in newspapers and magazines. Do tell her I remember her so well; Eve Czerny is not a woman one forgets.' The woman rose. 'You are her secretary?'

'Yes,' lied Alex.

The woman adjusted her mink coat. 'Perhaps, when she is up to it, we can meet some time. I would so love to talk to her again.'

Alex saw her out, walked back from the front door in a state of shock. Her mother a double agent? Never! The idea was so far out it was ludicrous. Wasn't it? Probably another of her inventions. If only I could find out, she thought. How can I do that? If I could find that correspondent. Who was he? Which paper did he work for? Is he still alive? And how was he a friend of my father? Questions danced and tantalized.

Not many people had ever called at the little semi-detached in South Wimbledon, and those who did were always connected with the severe Pentecostal sect which dominated Mary Brent's life, thoughts and attitudes. But something disturbed the bottom layers of Alex's mind. She tried to grasp it but it eluded her. All day she tried to isolate it, but she went to bed no wiser, lay for a long time going over her treasured memories of the happiest years of her life, finally fell asleep still baffled and uneasy. But during the night she dreamed, and in the morning she awoke and sat up in bed as if she had been poked in the spine. 'Of course!'

It was some months before her father had died; it was a Saturday, and he had taken her on one of their historical explorations. To the City, Alex remembered. The Monument, Pudding Lane where the Great Fire had started, to the old City churches, all the time making history come alive for her. They had ended up in St Paul's, and afterwards had walked down Ludgate Hill into Fleet Street. Alex squeezed her eyes tight shut, conjuring the memory into pictures, like an old film, and it unreeled before her eyes. Her father had been telling her about the great newspaper offices, and it was as they were looking at one of them – the *Daily Express* it had been, that unmistakable glass palace – that a man had hailed her father from across the street. 'John – John Brent,' he had called, come hurrying across the road, dodging taxis and buses. What had his name been . . . her father had said it, she knew. 'Peter!' she said aloud. 'Peter Brewster, by all that's holy.' She could hear her father's voice filled with pleasure. She could not remember anything else. While her father and the man had talked she had pressed her nose against the window of a nearby sweet shop; afterwards, for being so patient, she had been rewarded with a bag of jelly babies.

She sank back against her pillows with a gratified sigh, blessing her beloved father for training her memory. Always, after an outing, he had asked her questions to see if she had remembered what she had learned. Years later, when memories were all she had, how often had she retraced every step of those outings. Peter Brewster. She had his name. Now all she had to do was find him.

8

Switzerland and New York,
1961–3

Once settled in Switzerland, Eve proceeded to establish herself as a Name, a powerful businesswoman and an acclaimed international beauty. She became an early, fully paid-up founder member of the Jet Set. Through Henri Beyle she was invited to parties, receptions, galas, soirées, met the socially prominent people with whom she desired to meld. For them she produced the blurred background she had so carefully invented. When they began to come to the sugar-icing white villa she bought on the shores of Lake Geneva, she showed pictures of her 'paternal grandparents', all she had left of her 'family'. In reality they were a couple of pictures she had picked up in a flea market in Paris, since they were obviously of Hungarians. She had no idea who they were, but she doubted if any of the people she now called friends would either; there were no Hungarians among them. Always, she was very careful to avoid her fellow countrymen.

She painstakingly amassed a selection of small but choice things to add substance to her story, like a Meissen plate, of which she would sigh tremulously: 'All that is left of the hundred-piece dinner service that belonged to my great-great-grandmother.' She had picked it up in the Rastro in Madrid. But she always refused to be drawn on her background. A small shudder, a little wince of obvious pain were all it took to still curious tongues, which were made to feel that they were treading on scar tissue still, even now, unhealed. She was well aware that her self-created history would not bear close scrutiny, that there were too many gaps and *non sequiturs*, and to this end she fudged it, said many conflicting things, deliberately muddied the waters so that nobody would see a thing. But nobody could hint like Eve. 'It is all ancient history,' she would sigh on a little *moue* of regret, knowing that ancient was the last word anyone would apply to her.

She was always ready to give interviews, but always made sure that the impression left with the reporter was of *now*, not *then*. When the photographs had been taken, the tape-recorder switched off, she would dispense tea, and over it she would invariably say: 'You know, my dear' (the reporters were always women), 'I started out as a beautician, and I know my trade. If I may speak bluntly? You are wearing the wrong colours for your skin and eye shade. Let me show you how it should be done.' And she would give the spellbound reporter the complete works, afterwards presenting her – dazed from the impact of seeing a beautiful stranger instead of her usual face in the mirror – with a presentation 'kit' of Eve Czerny products. It was invariably 'what Eve Czerny can do for you' which became the theme of the article, with just enough background to confirm her as the one cosmetics queen who sold to the women who were her equals in social standing. When one befuddled reporter wrote about 'Count and Countess Czerny, the paternal grandparents of cosmetics' latest Queen', Eve did not correct it, and as time went on, like all frequently repeated lies, it soon came to be accepted as fact.

Where there were likely to be émigré aristocratic Hungarians, Eve was always elsewhere, but as there were as many of those as there were White Russian 'Princes' she was not often called upon to miss out. She worked hard to establish her image, and once that was fixed, was careful thereafter to associate only with those people whose social standing was firmly based. On being presented to a Princess of the English Royal Family, she agreed charmingly to give the Princess the benefit of her expertise, and was thereafter always greeted by that lady with a kiss as the friendship developed. This being so, she was just as careful never to be a member of the set that congregated about the Duke and Duchess of Windsor. 'Such tawdry imitations,' she would say, which comment naturally got back to the Duchess who made it a point to never, but *never* use Eve Czerny products. As Eve had no doubt that the Duchess would never have paid for anything in the first place, she was totally indifferent. Besides, she was about to leave that 'not quite', almost-there-and-never-would-be world for the one she had been determined to enter ever since she could remember.

She met Christopher 'Laddie' Bingham IV at a charity gala in New York, where she had made a gift of a huge box of every single one of her products to the tombola. With her usual shrewdness she had timed her visit to coincide with that of her friend the Princess, and when that lady greeted Eve with a kiss and a warm smile, Eve knew her position had been established. When, a few days later, she gave a small, intimate dinner for the Princess – twelve people only – she suddenly found herself on every invitation list of the Old Guard hostesses.

Laddie Bingham was the only son and heir to one of the oldest of the Old Guard fortunes; he had been born to what passed in the United States for the purple. The first Bingham had landed on the shores of Long Island in 1642, and the fact that he had been no more than an indentured servant had been carefully and deliberately obscured during the rise and rise of his descendants. This particular one had been married to a girl chosen for him by his mother, but the arrangement had not lasted on account of his compulsive tom-catting. He had never worked a day in his life, though ostensibly a Vice President of the family bank. His work was improving his seven-goal handicap at polo to ten, and bedding every worthwhile woman who came his way. Eve took one look at his tall splendid body, his wheat-gold hair, his handsome, well-bred if somewhat vacuous face, and knew that here was the man whose specification she had been carrying for years. He was from the same mould as the men she had gazed at worshipfully when a child: rich, handsome, of impeccable social standing. His dinner jacket was faultless and when he took out a cigarette case of discreetly gleaming gold, she knew her quest was over.

He spotted her at once. 'Who's that?' he asked.

'That, my friend, is Eve Czerny, the latest fireball to hit these shores.'

'What kind of name is that?' Twelve years of expensive education – once he was free of his governess – had been wasted on Laddie Bingham.

'Austro-Hungarian. She's from some aristocratic family who lost everything during the war. She herself got out of Hungary just ahead of the Russians in 1956. She owns Eve Czerny Cosmetics and I mean owns, because it's all held tight in those little white hands.'

'Taken?'

'You should be so lucky. They've been standing in line ever since she arrived but nobody's made it to first base yet. She's choosy, but with a face and body like that –' The shrug said it all.

'Do you know her?'

'Not in the way I'd like to, but enough to make the introductions. Go ahead.' Laddie felt his shoulder slapped, hard enough to show annoyance. 'Make your play. If anybody can breach the defences you can.'

Eve, who had likewise spotted him as soon as he came in, had heard the buzz.

'I see Laddie Bingham's back.'

'He can put me on mine any time.'

'Where's Patricia?'

'Oh, that's over. He's on the loose again – but not for long if he runs true to form.'

From the corner of her eye, Eve saw his purposeful advance in her direction, being stopped every now and then – usually by a woman – to whom he was always charming, showing no sign of what Eve, every antenna tuned to high, recognized as impatience. By the time he got to her, her back was turned and she had some half-dozen men standing round her like an honour guard laughing delightedly.

When they were introduced, Eve held out her hand in the European manner, and Laddie found himself bowing over it. He let the admiration in his eyes show openly, but all he got from her was a non-committal, 'How do you do, Mr Bingham,' before she was swept away on to the dance floor.

He didn't get near her again for the rest of the evening, but by the time they next met – she was seated across the table from him at dinner two nights later – she knew all there was to know about him. That he was catnip to the ladies; that his mother had been a de Peyser and was regarded as the last of the *grandes dames* now that Grace Vanderbilt was dead; that he was said to be the most versatile and tireless of lovers who was capable of prolonging a woman's pleasure until she begged for mercy; that his father had regarded him as a wastrel and playboy but had no option other than to leave him the Bingham millions, even if they were so arranged as to prevent him from squandering them wholesale until he was thirty-five. He was tanned from the hot sun of the Caribbean cruise from which he had just returned – without Patricia Lambert, the latest of his many *affaires* – and his dazzlingly white American teeth and hot blue eyes were put to good effect during dinner.

Eve, conscious that she was looking her best in a stunningly simple sheath of palest pink silk from Madame Grès, with no jewellery but ten carat solitaire diamonds in each ear, her superb breasts hinted at rather than indecorously revealed, paid him little attention, devoting it to the men on either side of her. As the table was wide, and a silver bowl containing an arrangement of coral pink pinocchio roses stood between them, she was able to monitor him whenever his attention was diverted by his own dinner companions, constantly and intensely aware of his equally intense awareness of her: of the aureole of red-gold hair, the vivid turquoise eyes, the tempting, glossy, deeply pink mouth.

He managed to get to her after dinner, watching and waiting, and at last managed to sit down beside her on the small gilded Louis XV two-seater sofa she had deliberately chosen; this allowed her to receive court one at a time, in the manner of the queen she knew she was.

'We have to stop meeting like this,' he said gravely.

'Easily arranged. I leave for Europe on Saturday.'

'Can I come with you?'

'The *Queen Mary* is big enough for both of us, I think.'

She returned his grave look from her glorious eyes. Her voice was sexily husky, with just the faintest hint of accent, and she spoke English with the ease and familiarity of one who had learned it when young. Laddie Bingham was fascinated. He had been used to female adoration all his life; first from his mother and three older sisters, then from his English nanny, then from the girls he met at his first dances, then from the women he met everywhere. This one knew exactly the effect she was having on him and didn't give a damn. It was so unusual as to further deepen his excitement. He had no idea that under her coolly amused exterior Eve was feeling her own powerful combination of triumph and excitement. She had to concentrate her attention away from the broad shoulders, the megawatt smile, the long legs – she loved long legs on a man, found them powerfully sexual – the sexuality of a calibre to match her own. With this man, she thought, she could achieve the heights. But first things first.

She rose gracefully, the cunning folds of her dress falling about her body with a faint shuss of silk. 'I must go. I have a day full of meetings tomorrow, starting at nine.'

'Let me see you home.'

Eve lifted one white shoulder. 'If you wish.'

She did not allow him beyond the door of her suite.

'When can I see you again?' he asked.

'My time is fully committed —'

'Please.'

The vibrancy in his voice thrilled her. 'Well . . . I am free for lunch on Thursday.'

'What time shall I pick you up?'

'Shall we say — one o'clock, at the Czerny offices on Park Avenue?'

'I'll be there.'

He kissed her hand before he left, but not the back, the palm. For a moment she felt the tip of his tongue touch her scented skin and she had to forcibly restrain a shudder of pleasure.

She found it difficult to sleep that night. The next morning, a tub containing six dozen long-stemmed American Beauty roses arrived.

On the Thursday, he ushered her into a colour-of-a-new-penny latest model Rolls-Royce, after first saying admiringly, 'You look ravishing.'

Eve laughed her throaty laugh. 'Not in the front of a car,' she murmured.

He did not take her to any of the fashionably 'in' restaurants. Instead they left the city and drove out to Long Island. 'Small, quiet, nobody reading your lips and no bush-telegraph. And the food is good,' he said of the restaurant, an ordinary-looking, every-day place with no more than a dozen tables. 'Being on the shore they specialize in fish.'

Once at their table, Eve knew immediately that the stiff white tablecloths and exquisitely folded napkins indicated French cuisine. Only three other tables were occupied and their waitress was elderly, clad in black with spotless collar, cuffs and apron.

'This reminds me of a little restaurant in Paris, on the rue Savant, where the food is heavenly and they do not serve cocktails.'

'You can have one if you like.'

'No, thank you. The American cocktail is a lethal weapon.'

'But you like fish?'

III

'My chef has an ambrosial way with trout, taken from the waters of Lac Léman.'

'I hope you will invite me some time.'

Eve did not answer, she studied the menu instead. It was short.

'Try the *raie au beurre noir*,' Laddie Bingham recommended. 'They catch it off the coast here.'

Eve closed the menu, laid it down. 'I am in your hands,' she told him.

'I think about that all the time,' Laddie Bingham said.

'I am pleased to know that you think,' Eve murmured.

'Lately, only about you.'

'You will have to do better than that, Mr Bingham.'

'My friends call me Laddie.'

Eve made a face. 'That is the name of a dog. I shall call you Christopher.'

'Like my mother. That makes two of you.' There was a pause. 'She's a strong-minded lady too.'

'I thought this country had the monopoly on them,' Eve said mockingly. The wine came, which Christopher had ordered.

'Are we celebrating?' Eve asked, when she saw that it was Krug '47.

'Of course. Our meeting.'

He set out to charm, to ensnare. He told her about himself, asked her about herself, but she told him only enough to whet his appetite. The skate, when it came, was perfection, and Eve ate with enjoyment. Normally she ate sparingly, conscious always of excess poundage; she had inherited a tendency to put on weight easily. But the fish was so delicious, the black-butter sauce startlingly good. And the portions were generous.

They talked easily and well, so well that when Christopher, high on the intoxication of Eve Czerny and Krug, reached across to pick up her hand and kiss the fingers she saw his watch and exclaimed, 'Heavens! Is that the time? I must get back . . .'

She did not have to at all; she had arranged her appointments so as to leave the afternoon free, just in case. Now, she decided to play him a little longer. If she was going to marry this man she had to have him totally in thrall, because, for the second time, she had found herself a man with a powerful mother, except that Edith de Peyser Bingham was no Mary Brent. Eve had learned enough to know that this lady had arranged her son's first marriage to a girl she considered eminently suitable, in that her family were as old, as rich, as 'right' as her own. Eve knew instinctively that although Christopher was not mother-dominated as John Brent had been, Edith Bingham was nevertheless a force to be reckoned with. Christopher had to be whole-hearted in his insistence on marrying a woman his mother did not know and probably would not want to. It was not that Eve was afraid; she looked forward to crossing swords with Mrs Christopher Bingham III, but she believed in attacking from strength, and that lay in the hold she could establish on her son's emotions.

Right now, she instinctively knew, whatever he felt was concentrated between his legs and that, powerful as it might be, was not powerful enough for her purpose. He had to dive deeper, and Eve was able to survive at depths that could crush the life out of any man.

As she had expected, when the *Queen Mary* sailed, he was on board.

'Who is this woman Christopher is pursuing with such avidity?' Edith Bingham asked her eldest daughter Charlotte. 'Alice Templeton tells me she sells cosmetics.'

'It's her own company, Mama. She is a very rich woman.'

Edith Bingham waved an impatient hand. 'Women of that particular type never have enough. They say she is very beautiful. Is she?'

'Gorgeous,' answered her daughter. 'And sexy with it.'

Edith Bingham compressed her lips. 'Don't be vulgar,' she reprimanded. 'Alice also tells me she's the mistress of Henri Beyle.'

'So they say. He certainly gave her the financial backing she needed to float her company, but he's old enough to be her father.'

'I have met Mr Beyle. He had some business connection with your father years ago. I believe his eldest daughter married into the Montreuil family. Marie-Laure Montreuil was at school with me in Switzerland. I shall make it my business to see what I can find out.'

'Oh, Mama, it's only more wild-oat sowing. You know Christopher and beautiful women.'

'Christopher's wild oats stretch throughout the entire Middle West,' Edith Bingham said tartly. 'What worries me is that he's now met a woman who intends to lay them waste and sow her own particular kind of seed.'

*

By the time Eve had visited her offices in London, Paris and Rome, before returning to Switzerland, she knew without a doubt that her seeds were sprouting the idea of marriage.

She had not let him touch her, beyond a goodnight kiss as their acquaintanceship ripened. She had given him a brief taste of what she was capable of and then put him away firmly, saying, 'No, you distract me, Christopher, more than I care to admit. I need all my concentration for my work.'

'You need distraction; you need fun and games and good times. Let me give them to you.'

'I do not receive without giving in return, and I am not yet sure you are worthy of what I have to give. You have a reputation, you know. For never lasting the course. I am not to be taken lightly, as part of the "fun" you talk of so casually. I am serious about everything, not only my work. You, on the other hand, take nothing seriously. Not even me.'

But by the time they reached Switzerland, she knew he was taking her very seriously indeed.

For his part, Christopher Bingham was utterly possessed by love. The thought of leaving Eve was not to be borne. He could not possibly go back home – go anywhere – without her. What tormented him was the fact that, although he knew she was undoubtedly attracted to him, she did not approve of his lifestyle, thought him a lightweight with no real substance or the necessary emotional foundation to carry the weight of marriage.

He ignored the gossip that said she was Henri Beyle's mistress. He had seen them together; she had taken him with her when she went to visit him, now so ill he was bedridden and unable to walk. Her attitude had been one of deep affection, of admiration and worry when she saw how thin he had become. She was even on excellent terms with his wife. How could that be if it were anything other than the affectionate gratitude of a woman towards a man who had seen her potential and put his money where his mouth was?

But Henri Beyle had known at once. When Eve returned later that day alone, he asked only: 'Him?'

'Him,' agreed Eve.

On a sigh: 'I have always known it was only a matter of time.'

'Have I ever lied to you?' Eve asked.

'No. Not to me.'

Eve smiled.

'I envy him,' Henri Beyle said. 'You are a remarkable woman, Eve. Had I met you twenty years earlier we could have owned the world.'

'We already own a substantial part of it.'

'Oh, you will eventually own much, much more. But nobody will ever own you. You only ever grant leases, and short ones at that, but I would not have missed mine for anything.'

'Nor I,' Eve told him honestly, for of all the men she had known, he had taught her most.

He regarded Eve curiously. 'Why this particular man? He is handsome, but so are many others. He has a reputation as a ladies' man, but again, they are legion. He is rich, but so are you.'

'He is what I promised myself many years ago,' Eve said, telling him what she had never told anyone, since she knew he was going to die and take the knowledge with him. 'When I was a child, I used to see men like him and envy the women with them. Their world was so far removed from mine as to be on another planet, but I knew that I had the means to travel all those light years and that one day, I would be one of those women. It is not enough to be rich and beautiful; one must *belong*, and right now I belong nowhere. As Mrs Christopher Bingham IV I will, because his world will become my world and eventually it will be as if I had never lived anywhere else.'

'And will you be happy there?'

'How could I fail to be?'

'You expect even happiness to do your bidding?'

'I expect to be happy because I will at last have attained my objective.'

Henri Beyle sighed. 'I hope so, my dear Eve, I hope so . . .'

He died ten days later, when the truth of the nature of his illness came out. He had been suffering from bone cancer.

Eve was shocked by her own reaction. A feeling she was unable to label, so strange was it. It took her some time to come up with its source. Loss. It so unbalanced her that she turned to Christopher for comfort, and it was to his credit that he provided it unstintingly. At the funeral he held her hand, but she was dry-eyed, composed, for tears achieved nothing. But she was so disconsolate on their return to her villa, that once she had removed her hat and mourning veil he took her slim figure in his arms and said tenderly, 'Marry me. I will make you happy again.'

He felt her rigidity relax. She put up one hand to his shoulder, nestled her cheek against his shirt front and said meekly, 'Oh, yes, please, I would like that above all things.'

She firmly refused to be rushed into it, though. 'It will be done properly, or not at all.'

'Just so long as it is done,' Christopher agreed happily.

They returned to New York to inform his mother and sisters, and to make the necessary arrangements. When Christopher handed her out of the car in front of a house that resembled nothing so much as a French château, Eve's sense of achievement was such that when they were greeted by a venerable butler she was able to unleash on him a smile so radiant that he felt uplifted by it. The huge entrance hall had a black and white tessellated marble floor and a staircase wide enough to take a London bus. There were portraits on the walls which Eve knew at once were ancestral, and the few pieces of porcelain she recognized as Chinese. Mentally she thanked dear, good Henri for his training. He had been a collector. The chandelier was immense, and the carpet thick. There was also a quality of silence that Eve now knew only pertained to houses that were superbly run and very expensively maintained. It was all – and more – that she had seen when gazing wide-eyed through the windows of the castle. Here at last was her dream coming true.

Edith Bingham was in her sitting-room, as were her three daughters. Eve took that as a good sign; it meant she was being received with something more than strict formality. The room was not too big, and exquisitely furnished in soft, Wedgwood blue, from its silk-hung walls to the blue and white furniture, its upholstery a mixture of blues and pinks. There were flowers everywhere, flawlessly arranged in Chinese porcelain bowls, and the carpet glowed with the colours of a stained-glass window.

The family was seated in front of the fire, and as Christopher walked Eve forward, his hand under her elbow, his mother rose to her feet, held out a hand. She was elegantly dressed in pale-grey silk, a diamond bow pinned to one shoulder, a double strand of pearls about her neck. Her hair was white, short and becomingly dressed. Her look was direct, unsmiling.

'Mama, this is Madame Eve Czerny,' Chris said simply but with great pride.

'How nice to meet you at last, Madame Czerny,' Edith Bingham said. 'I have heard so much about you.'

Her smile was pleasant, her handshake brisk. She introduced Eve to her daughters, and then indicated a chair which Christopher set close to his mother.

Eve sank down on it gracefully, her stiff faille skirt rustling. She opened her sable coat and let it droop negligently from her shoulders, revealing its Paris label.

Tea was served. Eve was asked if she preferred Indian or China. Sandwiches were proffered, cucumber or cress. She was asked if the Atlantic flight had been comfortable. Edith Bingham said she was so used to crossing it by sea that she could not get used to doing it in hours instead of days. They chatted about the new Broadway season, about the latest bestseller, about mutual acquaintances. Not a single question was asked, but Eve was aware of four pairs of eyes studying her, though she gave no indication that she had noticed. She knew she looked right; her suit was Dior, her handbag crocodile, her jewels the real thing. But she also knew that there was a seething curiosity behind the well-bred chatter.

It was Charlotte, the eldest, who put her foot through the façade. 'Why do you call yourself Madame Czerny?' she asked Eve. 'You aren't married, are you?'

'No. I think it is because Madame Czerny sounds better than Miss Czerny. Or so the people who write about me think. They were the ones who first referred to me as such.'

'Like Helena Rubenstein?'

'Ah, she is known only as "Madame".'

'Just as Chanel is known as Mademoiselle?' The implication was that Eve had a nerve classifying herself alongside such luminaries.

'I have travelled a great deal,' Edith Bingham said, with a quelling look at her daughter, 'but somehow or other I never got to Hungary. Vienna many times – you once lived in Vienna, I believe?'

'Yes. When I managed to leave Hungary in 1956.'

'And do you ever go back?'

'No. I have nothing to go back to.'

'You have no family?'

'Not any more.'

'We are a large family. My husband was one of four brothers and I myself had two sisters and two brothers.'

'I was an only child,' Eve said.

'And what did your people do?'

'My father was a doctor who specialized in diseases of the skin. My mother was – his wife.'

'But your grandparents were, I understand, a Count and Countess Czerny?'

'Only minor aristocracy, I'm afraid,' Eve murmured sardonically. 'One has to be able to trace one's ancestors back to Charlemagne to belong to the old nobility. Mine begin much later, only in the fifteenth century.' She met Edith Bingham's eyes, saw them flicker, knew she had scored a hit. The Binghams' went back no further than the seventeenth century and then to an indentured servant. She hoped that her confidence would be enough to convince Edith Bingham and deter her from further research, but as the name Czerny was an ancient one – even if it did not belong to her – with many branches, and with Hungary representing everything that, in 1963, the Americans abhorred, she felt safe enough in issuing the challenge.

She sat under the combined, penetrating inspection with un-flinching hauteur. I am every bit as good as you, her attitude said. Do not try to cow me with your pretensions to aristocracy. There is none in this country, never has been. There is a plutocracy, which is a *very* different thing.

'Do say something in Hungarian,' Susan, the second daughter begged. 'It is not a language I am familiar with.'

Eve looked straight at her. 'You are a consummate snob with the manners of a pig,' she said in her native language.

Susan laughed, clapped her hands together. 'So – totally incom-prehensible,' she crowed.

'I can say the same thing in French, if you like,' Eve said in that language. Susan's smile vanished. 'I also speak German,' Eve went on helpfully in that language.

'Both of them like a native,' Chris said proudly.

Eve shrugged. 'My business is international,' she said. 'It is the least one can do to converse in the language of the country where one is employing thousands of its nationals, don't you agree?'

She checked the little fob watch in her lapel; of gold and enamel in the shape of a rose, *circa* 1820, which she had bought from a woman, also Hungarian, who had approached her one day in Paris and asked her, as a compatriot, to buy it. Eve had discovered that the woman was, like her, a refugee but of good family, reduced to selling her possessions in order to live. 'It belonged to my great-grandmother,' she had said proudly. It was so remarkable as to elicit comments whenever she wore it. Now, Hester, the youngest sister, exclaimed, 'What a darling watch! So unusual!'

'It belonged to my great-grandmother,' Eve said simply. She rose. 'And now I must go. We are dining with the French Ambassador and I have an appointment with my hairdresser.' She did not intend to be dismissed like a servant.

As the door closed behind them: 'Well, and well again!' Charlotte Bingham said.

'Who on earth does she think she is?' Susan asked affrontedly. She had not liked the fluent French or the excellent German, and she was sure that what had been said in Hungarian had been an insult, in spite of the smile with which it was uttered.

'I think she knows,' Hester said. They all looked expectantly at their mother.

'A very clever woman,' she said finally. 'Much too clever for Christopher.' And for me, she thought. The assurance had verged on arrogance but fallen short of contempt. As Hester had said, this woman knew exactly who – and what – she was. What worried Edith Bingham was that her son had not the slightest idea. A woman used to controlling, she realized that in Eve Czerny she had met her match.

'Do you think she really is what she says?'

'I think she is sure that there is nothing we can do to prove otherwise. Hungary! What can be got from that Communist prison cell?' Edith Bingham shook her head. 'I don't like it,' she said. 'I don't like it at all.'

But she was there, along with her daughters, their husbands, and the rafts of uncles, aunts and cousins, when Eve Czerny became Mrs Christopher Bingham IV in a simple ceremony 'performed', Edith Bingham thought bitterly, in the yellow drawing-room. The first time that any Bingham had been married anywhere but in church, but the Episcopalian Church also had its rules, and Christopher was a divorced man.

Eve wore a dress of heavy ivory silk faintly blushed with pink. Her small hat was entirely composed of flowers, which matched the old-fashioned Victorian posy she carried. She said her vows calmly, but in a voice thrillingly passionate, and it was as she raised her face for her husband's kiss before turning to survey the assembled guests that she fell in love with him, for he had given her everything she had ever wanted.

Peter Brewster was retired and living in Barnes. Of course he is, Alex told herself after her first surprise. He's thirty years older, for God's sake. If Daddy was alive he would be seventy; so probably, is Peter Brewster. I hope he has a good memory. He was a foreign correspondent and I would have thought you wouldn't be much good at that without a powerful sense of recall. She toyed with the idea of telephoning him, but some lurking sense of a cover-up made her decide to turn up unexpectedly. After all, she reasoned, he has nothing to hide. Has he?

'London!' Max said when she told him. 'What for?'

'Something I have to do. I'll be out and back in a day, not that there's much to do here. The funeral is arranged, my mother is still in seclusion and I have my own life to get on with!' She was short with him, and wearing that look of obdurate stubbornness he knew of old. 'Oh, and I've arranged to use the company jet. It's only standing idle and you're not going anywhere, are you?'

'Would it make any difference if I was?'

'I could always give you a lift,' Alex offered innocently.

Max frowned after her retreating back. She's up to something, he thought. And five will give you ten it's to do with her mother. She's been prowling the house like Sam Spade and she hasn't been her usual stimulating company. He had caught her several times staring into the distance, her eyes unfocused, seeing only the pictures in her mind. Why London? he wondered. She only goes there under sufferance. To her way of thinking it is today's state-of-the-art Sodom and Gomorrah. Patsy? he wondered. Let's find out. He reached for the telephone.

It was an ordinary, post-war semi-detached behind a neat garden. The man who answered the door was tall, stooped, with a thatch of grey hair and heavy hornrims.

'Mr Peter Brewster?'

'Yes?'

'My name is Alexandra Brent. My father was John Brent; you were at university together, I believe.' This was a guess, assumed from his biography in *Who's Who*, for he too was an author, having written what was generally thought to be the definitive history of the Hungarian revolution.

'Good God, that was a long time ago. I haven't seen John for many years.' His journalist's mind asked: 'You said "was". I presume he is dead?'

'Yes. Not long after you and he met in Fleet Street; I was the little girl with him.'

'Was that the last time we met? Yes, I suppose it was . . . my memory isn't what it used to be.'

He led her into a cluttered sitting-room, dominated by a big desk strewn with papers and overflowing bookshelves. On the desk stood a portable typewriter. 'I still keep my hand in; the occasional political article and book review. Do sit down. What can I do for you?'

Alex went into the story she had prepared. 'I'm writing a biography of my mother, Eve Czerny, and since I believe you knew her in the old days, I hoped you might tell me about her early years; what she was like when she escaped from Hungary.'

Peter Brewster was regarding her intently. 'I thought your name was familiar . . . I always read the book reviews. You are the author of *A Study in Contrasts*.'

'Yes.'

'I haven't read it – not my particular interest, Victorian lady novelists – but the review I read was most enthusiastic. It's nice to meet a fellow author. I don't get many visitors nowadays. A foreign correspondent makes his friends in all four corners of the world. John and I were close at university then we lost touch until we met up in Vienna. I was the one who introduced him to your mother.'

'What was she like then?'

'The most beautiful creature I ever set eyes on. She'd got herself mixed up in a nasty situation in Budapest and had no choice but to flee, like some two hundred and fifty thousand of her fellow-countrymen. Most of them sank without trace into the country of their refuge, but that was never your mother's way. She would always stand out no matter where. I read your brother's obituary in *The Times*. Bad business. I will never understand the mania of today's youth for speed.' He heaved himself upright. 'I was about to make myself a cup of coffee. May I offer you one?'

'Please.'

'I've followed the progress of the young girl I first knew as Anna Farkas with great interest over the years – whenever I was in a country with a free press, and that was not very often, I'm afraid. I spent the years after Hungary in one Communist satellite after another.' He went into the kitchen opening off the living-room.

'How did you meet her?' Alex called.

'In Budapest. I was sent there by my paper. Hungary was liberalizing and my editor thought it was worth a series. He sent me because I spoke the language – I spent a year in Budapest between the wars. It was a lovely city then; as cosmopolitan as Paris. Elegant women, good hotels, pavement cafés and a full cultural life. When I met your mother in 1956 it was not even a shadow of its former self. No longer gay but grey. She was the most beautiful creature I ever saw, and she was doing very well as a beautician, giving treatments in private houses. I met her because the wife of an old friend – a former liberal Hungarian politician – was a client of hers. Then suddenly she didn't come any more and I learned that she had been dropped once it came out that she was under the protection of a Russian who was officially a political Commissar but in reality a high-ranking officer of the KGB. That came as quite a surprise. Not that she should attract such a man – that came as naturally as breathing – but that she should be politically involved at all. She had never struck me as a political animal and I don't think she was. She did what she had to in order to survive. Many women did.'

'I see it comes as a surprise to you,' Peter Brewster understated, coming in with the tray. 'You have to remember that Hungary in those days was a harsh, repressed society thanks to Russian dogmatic stupidity and inefficiency, infiltrated at all levels by a network of security police, informers, detention camps, and seething with discontent. You had to queue for food – in a land that had always produced a surplus – and consumer goods were obtainable only by Party members. It was a dictatorship in its crudest, most vicious form. Thousands of Hungarians were uprooted from their native provinces and dumped elsewhere, and collectivism – the ultimate in Marxist shibboleths – was enforced. And everybody had a secret dossier – a *káder lap*. That was a document which defined your class origins – which meant that your past invariably ruled your future. It was marked *P* for *paraszt* – peasant – *M* for *munkas* – worker – and so on. It was a noose round everyone's neck which could hang him at any time. This is the society your mother grew up in.'

Peter Brewster smiled. 'Even then, she had a driving determination to get her hands on the finer things in life, and an awareness that they lay beyond the borders of Hungary. It is my belief that she made a friend of me for that very reason. I could supply her with Western magazines, I could tell her how people lived in free societies, how much money they earned and how free they were to flock to the shops full of the luxury goods they could buy. Our conversations were always question and answer sessions, many of them conducted over a dish of ice-cream at Gerbeaud's – that was Budapest's best confectioner, which was able to serve such treats only after Imre Nagy liberalized things somewhat. And she wanted to learn English. Fortunately, she was one of those people who have a natural facility for languages, and she worked on her accent with a passion that was almost obsessional. Looking back, I now see why. I think even then she had a dream to which she clung to desperately.'

'Was she Budapest-born?'

Peter Brewster concealed his surprise. 'I don't think so. She was very close-mouthed about her antecedents: I think she wanted to wipe all that from her life, but from little things she said, a knowledge she could only have acquired from experience, it is my belief that she came from one of Hungary's western provinces, near the Hungarian border. She once mentioned how you could see the lights of Austria from the fields near where she lived. That being so, her people were probably peasant – the west is farming country. The fact that she had been able to come to Budapest so easily also told me that she must have had help from the people with the power to do such things. It was later on, when I learned she was living with a Russian, that I understood it all.'

Peter Brewster met Alex's stunned expression with understanding eyes. 'That is why, I think, she changed her name when she left Hungary. A case of necessity and self-protection. Women who consorted with the Russians had a hard time – a very hard time – of it during the Uprising.'

'So that is why Anna Farkas became Eve Czerny.'

'I think so. It could also have to do with the fact that one of the leading Party luminaries was named Michael Farkas; he was the Minister of Defence. No relation to Anna, I'm sure; it was not an uncommon name, and he was Jewish whereas your mother was, I am convinced, a Catholic like the majority of Hungarians. Hungary was a bastion of Catholicism in that part of the world.'

'I see,' Alex said, who was seeing much more than she had bargained for.

'At some time or other the Russian was transferred and his successor was a high-ranking AVO officer. The AVO – the Allam-védelmi Hivatal – the Hungarian Secret Police, were always known by their initials. It was only when she came to me for help in getting out of Hungary that I learned she had been playing a double game; passing back information she collected to a man named Laszlo Kovacs. He was a chemist – and a brilliant one – and it was his creams Anna had been peddling round Budapest.'

'What happened to him?'

'Disappeared after the Russians crushed the Uprising, along with thousands of others. Either dead or taken into Russia. It was because she did not know if he was alive or dead that she came to me – he had told her to, so she must have told him about me. I did what I could for her. She hid in my hotel room for a few days then I got her into the British Legation as my girlfriend. When the time came to leave she produced a brand-new set of papers in the name she is now known by. How she got them I have no idea but it may have been through the combined efforts of her two protectors. I think she had been planning all along – Uprising or not – to leave Hungary. The events of October the twenty-third and subsequently gave her the necessary leverage. Anyway, I got her to Vienna and rather than leave her in one of the refugee camps – they had informers planted there too – I asked John, who was teaching at a school in Vienna, if he would put her up for a while.'

Peter Brewster handed Alex the cup of coffee he had poured her. 'She had very cleverly disguised herself – she knew just how – so that she looked twenty years older and thirty pounds heavier. I remember John being utterly confounded that such a drab, unprepossessing creature could have been a spy.' A smile. 'He was so unworldly that it never occurred to him to wonder how such an unattractive woman could have been a beautician. Not until she took off her disguise, anyway. And the sight of the real Anna floored him. I doubt he had ever met such a woman in his life.' A pause. 'John had a very – circumscribed upbringing –'

'You knew his mother?'

Their eyes met. 'I met her once,' Peter Brewster said drily. It conveyed volumes. 'Eve, therefore, was completely outside his experience, which where women were concerned was minimal anyway. At forty – which he was then – he had the emotional responses of a twenty-year-old, and every one of them was floored by Eve.' Peter Brewster eyed Alex over the rim of his cup. 'But then, Eve Czerny is, as the Americans say, an experience, period.'

'Anna Farkas . . .' Alex said slowly. She looked across at the old man. 'Dead in the revolution?'

'I think that is what she intended. That it comes as a surprise to you, her own daughter, makes it plain.' As one thought connected with what followed naturally: 'You do not look like her at all,' Peter Brewster said. 'Nor John, come to that, except you have his height, of course – and his mind,' he added gallantly. 'According to the critics you write very well.'

'Thank you.'

'So, has your biography been commissioned?'

'No. But it will come as a surprise to my mother. She doesn't know anything about it yet.'

'It should make for fascinating reading,' Peter Brewster said tactfully. 'And it goes back far enough – and leaves her powerful enough – to be able to stand the resulting publicity. Good for sales,' he added with a twinkle. 'Of your book *and* your mother's products.'

'Tell me about Laszlo Kovacs.'

'I don't know much. Clever man, violently anti-Communist, took his stand with the students at the Technological University. They were the ones who laid down the official revolutionary policy – that the Russians quit Hungary as laid down in the Peace Treaty, that Nagy be Prime Minister, that elections be held by secret ballot with all parties participating, that political prisoners be freed – that sort of thing. It was the student delegation to the radio station that began the Uprising. An army major volunteered to present the students' demands. He was shot down at the main entrance by the police. That was Hungary's signal to rise – another "shot heard round the world" except, of course, the world put its fingers in its ears.' His voice was bitter.

'Would you say Anna Farkas was religious in those days?'

'No,' Peter Brewster said. 'Her belief was in herself, always.'

There was a silence. 'And Laszlo Kovacs disappeared?'

'As far as I know. The Russians began the deportations almost as soon as the revolution was over; I went back to Budapest with food once I left your mother in Vienna and I myself saw lorryloads of men being driven to Russian-occupied barracks. They were later loaded onto trains and taken into Russia. Some of them dropped notes from the carriages and they lay along the railway lines. If he wasn't dead, Laszlo Kovacs would certainly have been on one of those trains.'

There was another silence. Peter Brewster knew enough to wait, let her get over the shock of what he had told her. Eve had covered her tracks, all right. There was probably a lot more that nobody knew except Eve Czerny herself and she would never tell.

'Were you at the wedding?' Alex asked next.

'No. I was in Egypt, but I called on them a couple of months afterwards on my way back to London. By then, Eve had re-established her business, but this time most of her clients were the wives of the officers stationed in Vienna, the British, Americans and French. She left the Russians severely alone, naturally. She did very well, and Vienna was a very different city from Budapest. Eve loved every minute of it. She was radiant, as I remember. Very happy and newly pregnant. I remember her telling me that if it was a boy she would call him Peter.' A smile. 'But you were a girl.'

'And you have never met her since?'

'No. Just followed her career with interest.'

'And her – lovers. What do you think happened to them?'

'Well, there was a general – cleaning up – once the Russians re-established their control. If Eve's protector was found wanting then I doubt he will be found either. The AVO man . . .' A shrug. 'So many of them were killed I could not say. As neither of them has been heard of in thirty years I think we must assume they will never be heard from again.'

Accident or design? Alex wondered. 'Is Farkas an aristocratic name?' she asked next.

'No. Had she been connected with the once-ruling class her card would have been marked with an *X* – the worst of all the classifications. Eve had an *M*. No doubt because of her Russian. Had it not been for his power she would never have been allowed to do what she did – a parasitic trade in Communist eyes, even in the easier Nagy days. Obviously she shrewdly spotted the opening and plugged it. I know of nobody else who was doing what she did then.'

'And Czerny?'

Amusedly: 'Also the name of the man who wrote those fiendishly difficult piano studies, but a much – shall we say classier? – name than Farkas, and again, not uncommon.'

'Do you think her Russian brought her to Budapest?'

'Probably. Hungarians were not allowed to travel in the way we take for granted. But a powerful member of the occupying power . . . he would be able to arrange it.'

He saw that the hand that raised the coffee cup to her lips trembled slightly. Obviously, Alexandra Brent had been totally ignorant of her mother's past. Which brought him up against the fact that until now, he had never seen any mention of Eve Czerny's daughter in all the thousands of words that had been written about her. Her son, yes. Her daughter – nothing. Why? he wondered. 'I hope I have been of help,' he probed.

'Yes, very much so.'

But not in the way you had expected, he surmised. 'Don't judge your mother too harshly,' he counselled kindly. 'You are a product of a society that has no conception of one that is rigorously – and rigidly – controlled at every level.'

'She never talks about Hungary,' Alex said slowly.

'Not surprising. I never thought of your mother as passionately patriotic. Her sights were set on another world; the one I told her about. Hungary, alas, has always been too small to contain its native talent. It is mostly its émigrés who have left their mark on the world.' His smile was mischievous. 'Look at Zsa Zsa Gabor.'

'I was thinking of Bartók, Kodály and Molnár,' Alex said forbiddingly.

'But your mother is a creative artist in her own way. Has she not created a vast commercial empire from a few creams invented by Laszlo Kovacs?'

'Who has, unfortunately, never been able to profit from that fact.'

Ah, thought Peter Brewster, she doesn't approve of her mother's business. Her father's daughter rather than her mother's. He couldn't handle Eve either. His mother gave him a fear of women and their sexuality. Brewster's journalist's memory brought forth what he knew of Alexandra Brent. A Fellow of her College, regarded as a comer, author of three serious works of non-fiction. He smiled inwardly. Oh, yes, in direct contrast to her mother, whose whole life was a work of fiction. Are you determined to write the truth and shame the devil?

He studied her face, deep in thought. No beauty, too strong of feature, and from the way she had talked, the words she had used, a mind to match. Well, he thought, her paternal grandmother was also a strong character, even if that was all bent and twisted by her own virulent form of religion. Funny, he thought, how strength can bypass the males but concentrate in the female. And even little Anna Farkas had a whim of iron. How else has she gone so far, achieved so much? Yes, he thought, Margaret Thatcher *and* Zsa Zsa Gabor. A formidable – and inflammable – mixture. Hungarians were a volatile, passionate people. He doubted if this controlled young woman knew anything about passion except for its dictionary definition.

As if she had marshalled her facts and come to a conclusion: 'Are there any other people who were in Vienna in 1957, and knew my mother, to whom I could talk?'

Peter Brewster scratched a cheek. 'Well, it is thirty years ago . . . and as I told you, in my job one tends to lose touch with friends as one continually moves on.' He levered himself from his chair to cross to the desk, where he pawed through its disorder, finally bringing out a thick, leather-bound notebook. 'I don't even know if they are still at the address I have, but you could try. A woman named Marion Gilchrist; her husband was stationed in Vienna with the Four Power Commission. She was one of your mother's clients. I could give her a ring, I suppose.'

Mrs Gilchrist was astonished and delighted to hear from an old friend after so long. Alex could hear a loud, confident voice issuing from the receiver which Peter Brewster held away from his ear with a grimace. She readily agreed to see Alex (in the guise of a journalist) and talk about Eve Czerny.

'She's an opinionated woman who ran her husband as I run my car, but she's also an arch gossip. You might learn things I couldn't possibly tell you. Your mother's relationship with her clients would be an important, perhaps even intimate one. I am told it is with hairdressers.'

Alex rose, held out a hand, not smiling at his gentle jibe. 'You have been very helpful,' she said truthfully. 'Thank you.'

'Good luck with the book.'

He offered to ring for a taxi to take her to Barnet, where Marion Gilchrist now lived, and as he closed the garden gate on her said, 'Tell your mother —' Here he spoke some words in a language Alex recognized as Hungarian, but which she had to repeat phonetically. 'She will know what it means,' Peter Brewster said on a secretive smile.

The Gilchrist house was large, imposing, detached, with brutally neat lawns and spartan shrubs. Almost before Alex rang the bell the glossy front door opened and a plump, blue-rinsed lady eyed her up and down before saying, 'You must be Alexandra Brent. I don't usually see journalists' – this was Alex's cover – 'but as it's about Eve Czerny I am willing to make an exception. Come in.'

She led the way into an imposing drawing-room, all Maples walnut and family silver, sat down before an imitation Regency gas fire turned high. 'I lived most of my life in hot climates,' Marion Gilchrist said, very much a daughter of the Raj, 'and I cannot get used to the damp cold of England.'

She was tightly corseted, with the high colour of one whose breath is constricted, dressed in a smart, soft green dress with a small brooch of genuine emeralds pinned to one shoulder. She reminded Alex of the ladies who came to Speech Day at Cheltenham Ladies' College.

'So, you're writing a book about Eve Czerny,' Marion Gilchrist sniffed. 'It's about time somebody told the truth about that woman. Oh, I know what they write about her, but *I* know what she really is. A very clever adventuress. Especially clever with men.'

Her high colour deepened, and Alex guessed that Brigadier Gilchrist had been one of Eve's victims.

'It's about her early years I particularly want to know,' Alex prompted. 'Prior to 1960.'

'I knew her in 1957 when she was a penniless refugee, but she revealed very little about her past. She said it was for safety's sake, always hinting at dark and dramatic mysteries.' Another sniff, of obvious disbelief. 'I've followed her career with both disbelief and amusement. She has come a long way since she used to visit me and give me facials and a massage, a very long way, but it was obvious from the start what she was after. Everything she could lay her hands on, including the husbands of several friends of mine.' The rancour was old but still deep.

'I gather you were one of her first clients in Vienna.'

'Only because Peter Brewster told me about this poor little Hungarian refugee who had clever hands and a way with faces who was trying to make her way and I told him to send her along. We had a lot of functions to attend in those days and one had to look one's best. I must say she knew her business. She despaired of my skin, I remember – we spent many years in India – and she used to lecture me about too much sun and how it was ageing and persuade me to use this cream and that lotion. They were expensive then and cost the earth now, but I must say they do what they claim to do.' Look at me, was the unspoken claim.

'What was she like in those days?'

'Very beautiful, very – charming, but in what I thought was a calculatingly artless way. Men fell for it, of course. I soon noticed how my husband always made it his business to be around when she came for my treatments. She was a very skilled saleswoman. It didn't surprise me when I opened a magazine – oh, years later – to see a picture of her at the top of a long article about her success. She was very ambitious from the start. She wanted things – oh, how she wanted things. I saw the way she looked at my clothes, my jewels – such as I had then – nothing to what I have seen her wearing since.'

'Did she ever mention a man named Laszlo Kovacs?'

Marion Gilchrist shook her head. 'Not to my knowledge. But she knew an awful lot of men, so many that I – all of us – were very surprised when she up and married that teacher. We thought she was after a much bigger fish.' A thin smile. 'She caught them later.'

Alex perceived a virulent streak of jealousy running through the well-preserved face and figure. It was not done for penniless little Hungarians, to whom one could condescend kindly, not only to overtake but to outstrip. Eve Czerny, Empress of Beauty, towered over the wife of Brigadier Alastair Gilchrist and it was obvious that the change was not to Mrs Gilchrist's liking. She was the kind of woman who believed in 'knowing one's place'. Obviously, Eve had not thought twice about assuming this didn't apply to her.

Alex soon decided that there was little to be learned here that would be of any use. All Marion Gilchrist had was gossip, again well leavened by jealousy. It was obvious that, in her opinion, Eve Czerny was nothing more than a common little tart who had made her way upwards by lying back, always under some man, and, from the questions she asked, she was much more interested in learning about Eve Czerny than giving information about her. Alex made her excuses and left.

Well, she thought in the taxi on the way back to Heathrow. The trip was worth it if only to see Peter Brewster. I now know for certain that Eve Czerny is a figment of the imagination; that my mother is probably the daughter of a peasant farmer and that she was not above giving comfort and succour to the enemy if it suited her purpose. If only I could talk to the Russian, she thought in frustration. He could tell me so much more. And Laszlo Kovacs? What had he been to her mother? How had she got her hands on his formulas? How convenient that he should have vanished, for all that Eve Czerny was, she owed to him. 'My father the doctor,' Alex muttered scathingly. More lies. But with what she had to hide is it any wonder? And why had she married the kind, patient man who had been the only father to a daughter she despised – or had done until her recent change of heart. They were so utterly different. No wonder she had taken herself off as soon as she could. She must have been bored out of her mind. And loathed by her mother-in-law. As a child, Alex had been aware that her father's mother regarded her with obsessive hatred, but it was not until John Brent had died that she had understood why.

Alex had been devastated, unable to understand what had happened. She had grieved so deeply that she had become ill, aggravated by a serious attack of the measles. She had been carted off to hospital, where her grandmother had never visited her, and on her return to the grim house in Acacia Avenue had found her grandmother preparing to leave it, taking her with her.

'Where are we going?' the cowed child had asked timidly.

'To see your mother.'

Alex could still feel, at a distance of twenty-five years, the shock of that announcement. Her father had told her – sadly – that her mother had died, which meant she had gone to God. For one panic-stricken moment she had thought her grandmother meant that she too was being taken to God, and she burst into tears.

'And you can stop that crying. I am taking you to your mother and that's final.'

'But my mother is dead,' Alex had sobbed.

'That was the lie my son told you. Your mother is alive and well and flourishing like the wicked always do. She never wanted you and she dumped you on my son when she went off with her fancy man. And that's another thing you need to know the truth of.' She had bent down, thrust her impassioned face into that of the terrified and bewildered child, gripping one arm so tightly that for days afterwards Alex had bruises. 'My son was *not* your father. Do you understand me? You had no right to call him Daddy because he never fathered you. God and your mother are the only ones who know who did. Your mother was a harlot who tricked my son into marrying her when she found she was carrying another man's child. You are the bastard spawn of an evil woman and who knows what evil man, and I'll not have you in my house a minute longer. You are going to your mother and that is all there is to it. You are her responsibility, not mine. Let her assume it. It's about time, and she can afford it. I can't.'

Alex stared blindly out of the window of her mother's Learjet, high over France, still able to feel her five-year-old fear and confusion. Her father was not her father and her mother was not dead and this witch of a woman hated her . . . Never in her life had she felt so alone, so abandoned, so filled with grief.

'Will you stop that crying!' Her grandmother – except she was not her grandmother – had slapped her hard. 'And there'll be another unless you shut up.'

Fearful of a woman she knew hated her, Alex had stopped crying outwardly, begun the first of her many lessons in hiding how she felt. The memory of that nightmare journey was one from which she had awoken screaming for a long time afterwards.

Now, she wondered who her father had been. The Russian? The AVO man? Laszlo Kovacs? One of the many men Marion Gilchrist had hinted at? For many years she had refused to accept that it had been any other than John Brent. He *had* been her father. He had loved her, cared for her, taught her, spent most of his time with her, protected her, mainly from his mother. 'If I see you hit or hear you shout at her one more time I am leaving this house and taking her with me.' Alex could still hear his voice, quiet but very angry. Thereafter her grandmother had ignored her, but Alex had never ceased to feel the virulence of her hatred.

'Why does Grandma say that I am evil and wicked?' she had asked her father.

'Because she is a bitter and twisted woman. You must not believe what she says. You are a child, and children are innocent victims.'

'She says I am a Spawn of the Devil and I bear his mark.'

'That is nonsense. You are my dear little Alex, my Best Girl. Take no notice of anything she says.' But later events were to reinforce everything Mary Brent had said.

There is only one way I'm going to find out who my father is, Alex decided, and that is to ask my mother. If she wants forgiveness then I'm willing to trade that for information. If she's a Catholic, as Peter Brewster said, then it's time she went to confession. It suddenly occurred to her now that perhaps Mary Brent's virulent hatred had been because Eve was a member of the Church of Rome. Oh there's so much I don't know, Alex thought, feeling thwarted. Well, it's time to stop wondering. I want an explanation, Mother. It's not enough to say you're sorry for what you did to me; for the rejection, the unhappiness, the fear, the untold misery. I want to know why you couldn't bear to so much as look at me, why your face always turned into an icy mask when I was in your presence, why you treated me as a burden you couldn't wait to shed. Is it me? Is it because I turned out to be everything you're not? Big, plain, unattractive? Beauty is your creed and I am an Unbeliever. Is that it? Or is it to do with the man who fathered me? Did you hate him? Did he hurt you? If you'll only tell me what led you to reject me then maybe I'll understand and find I can forgive you. Perhaps you did it for the best?

Yes, Alex thought bitterly, *your* best. Whatever, why ever, it's time you told me, once and for all.

10

——◈◈◈——

The Seychelles and Switzerland,
1963–5

Eve demonstrated the length and breadth and height of her passionately grateful love for her husband on their honeymoon, the first week of which was spent on a tiny island in the Seychelles, where the sugar-almond pink house in which they stayed was the only habitation. On the night they arrived, a hot and humid one, he had his first taste of the sublimity to come.

Eve, who hated feeling hot and sticky, wanted nothing more than one of her cool, scented baths, time to prepare herself for what would be, she had vowed, a night to remember, but Christopher had other ideas.

'Let's swim,' he said, already shrugging off his lightweight jacket, hastily unbuttoning his shirt, kicking off his shoes, unzipping his trousers as he progressed towards the floor-to-ceiling windows. At the touch of a button they slid back to reveal a spectacular swimming pool in the shape of a figure eight, lit from the bottom by cunningly placed spots, revealing the intricate mosaic – copied from a Byzantine temple – which showed Neptune in a chariot drawn by dolphins, crown gleaming, trident lifting in exhortation as he breasted the foaming waves. The water shimmered in seemingly multicoloured invitation, and by the time Eve stepped out onto the cool marble of the tiled surround it was in time to see her husband take a running jump ending in a clean dive into the depths. When he came up, streaming water, he called, 'Come on in!'

Eve could see his body quite clearly. It was smooth and hairless but for the blond bush at his crotch, and his penis waved languidly like some blind, hungry worm.

'Come on . . .' he urged. 'Don't tell me you haven't swum naked before?'

'No,' said Eve. 'I haven't.'

'Why on earth not?'

'I can't swim.'

He was astounded. In his world you were taught to swim just as you were taught to dance, ride and play tennis.

Seeing his astonishment: 'I never had time to learn,' Eve said in a meek little voice. 'I was always working . . .'

She looked, Christopher thought tenderly, for all the world like a disconsolate child, in spite of the almost forbiddingly chic Balenciaga cool green sheath, the stiletto heels, the flawlessly coiffed hair. She had more facets than a brilliant-cut diamond, he thought. He had seen the fabled beauty, the flirtatious coquette, the senuous *femme fatale*, even the awesomely capable businesswoman, but this small-voiced, almost shamefaced little girl was yet another of the many faces of Eve.

'I'll teach you,' he soothed tenderly. 'It's easy . . .'

'Will you?' Her face lit as though the child had been offered a long-desired toy.

'Of course I will . . . take off your clothes and we'll start right now.' The peasant in Eve looked round. 'There's nobody here,' Christopher laughed. 'It's a cold supper and we'll serve ourselves. The couple who look after the house are probably back in their own cottage having their own supper. In any case, they're servants; they see yet they don't see, if you know what I mean.'

He had the rich boy's attitude to servants, one Eve determined to copy. Without another word she unhooked her dress, pulled down its concealed zip and let it drop to the ground before picking it up and laying it carefully over the back of one of the luxuriously-cushioned loungers. Underneath she wore a lacy half-bra, a pair of minuscule lace briefs and a matching suspender belt. As if doing a striptease, conscious of her husband's riveted gaze, she proceeded to undo the suspenders, roll down the silk stockings – she had not gone over to tights, now all the rage, because while they might be convenient they were not nearly so sexually arousing – and unclip her bra, finally pulling down the briefs, turning her back so that he caught a glimpse of her rounded, perfectly-formed bottom. Then, as if presenting herself to his gaze somewhat shyly yet proud at the same time, she turned to face him.

Christopher felt his heart leap in his chest at the same time as his penis rose with alacrity to the momentousness of the occasion.

Without her clothes, she was unbelievably voluptuous; the breasts full, high and firm, the nipples, crisping in the cool air, a mouth-watering dusky pink, her belly softly rounded, the hips fuller than her clothes hinted, the thighs surprisingly long for her height, and, at their junction, a perfect triangle of candy-floss the exact same flame gold as her hair.

'Oh, darling . . .' He was at once ravenously and achingly aroused. 'Oh, God, you are so beautiful . . .' He swam towards her and stopped before her, gazing up. He held out his arms. 'Jump,' he said, 'I'll catch you . . .'

With perfect trust, Eve did so, and as his hands grasped her, brought her right up against him, he felt the warmth of her body through the coolness of the water, only the tips of her breasts cool against his chest.

'Oh, but it's so warm!' Eve laughed delightedly, scooping water with her palms and sluicing it over her body so that it glittered with drops and rivulets, making her look as if she was festooned in brilliance.

'Jesus . . .' groaned Christopher, feeling his erection pulsating against her, already nuzzling her blindly, seeking entry. 'The swimming lesson is going to have to wait,' he said thickly, 'because I can't . . . I have to do this . . . feel me . . . feel what you do to me . . .'

His penis against her belly was insistently hard. It was not what she had planned but she was never slow to adjust her priorities, and she knew instinctively that this was the moment to assume command. In one smooth movement, a tiny jump, she had her arms about his neck, her legs scissored behind his hips and she slid him up inside her like a key entering a lock.

He gasped at the heat of her, the strength of her clasping, enclosing, enfolding him, then as excitement took over he began to thrust, his eyes glazing, his hands gripping her wet breasts, his concentration total. As Eve felt his first violent thrusts she steadied herself by taking her arms from around his neck and stretching them to either side of her along the rounded edge of the pool, the water cushioning the pounding she knew she was in for. There had been no preparation, no slow, delicious foreplay culminating in the simultaneous realization that *now* was the right, the perfect time. Christopher was blind to everything but the burning need for friction, for assuagement; conscious of nothing but his own greedy desire and in far too much of a hurry to do anything but gain his own satisfaction. It was nevertheless erotically thrilling to feel the water lap and caress her skin while the hardness and heat of Christopher created electric currents deep within her which sizzled along her nerve-ends before exploding in little jolts which had the effect of rendering her almost liquid. She felt molten, wide open, yet opened herself wider as if to draw him ever deeper into her very self. The little shocks gathered together and became a wave which grew only to be swamped by a bigger one which in turn gathered itself into a roller which picked her up and swept her with it. 'Aaaahhh . . .' Her head went back as her first orgasm rippled through her, spreading outward and upward to every extremity even as her second was gathering itself.

Christopher, whose experience of multi-orgasmic women was not wide, was by now all but mindless with pleasure because Eve's inner muscles were working on his incredibly sensitized penis, squeezing and massaging, stroking and enfolding. His thigh muscles were fluttering and as she began a circular movement of her hips, now squeezing, now releasing, his thrusts increased and he went wild, growling unintelligibly, driving himself into her like a piston, she meeting his every thrust with one of her own while squeezing him as he withdrew for yet another. He felt his own orgasm apply pressure to the base of his spine even as Eve shook with her third, and as it gathered momentum his voice rose to an agonized shriek: 'Oh, God . . . God . . . God . . .' spiralling to a gabbled, 'OhsweetJesusChrist . . .' as he stiffened and came like a geyser, with such force and intense pleasure that for a moment he lost consciousness. His legs gave way; he sagged, his weight pulling him out of Eve's body as he fell back into the water, where he floated, breath rasping in his heaving chest, eyes closed, arms outstretched, for all the world like some drifting piece of flotsam.

Eve lay back against the side of the pool, her own heart racing, though she was by no means as spent as Christopher. She had at least another two or three orgasms in her but never mind, she thought. He has much to learn; he has great virility but he has no idea how to employ it to best effect. He thinks, as do all Americans, that it is the notches on the gun that count, not how they came to be there. I will teach him, she thought pleasurably. I will show him how it is done, how to prolong pleasure to the unendurable and beyond.

Having regained his breath, Christopher duckdived and came up beside her, where he placed a grateful kiss on her receptive mouth. 'That,' he said reverently, 'was something else. *You* are something else, my darling. You made me feel like a lion . . . I've never had an orgasm that went on and on and on . . . I thought I was going to die of pleasure. How do you do it?'

Eve smiled. 'We will teach each other,' she promised, smoothing the wet blond hair back from his forehead. 'You will teach me to swim and I – I will teach you how to please a woman until she begs for release . . .'

For a moment male pride surfaced as jealousy when Christopher asked, 'Did you beg from the man who taught you?'

Eve placed a forefinger over his lips. 'Once I'm done with you it won't matter who taught me, but what I've taught you . . .'

His mother took one look at him on their return to New York six weeks later, after having progressed from the Seychelles to Australia's Gold Coast, to Bali to Baja California back to their starting point, and saw all the signs of a man who was well and truly under a spell. She has bewitched him, she thought on a pang. I have lost him, really lost him. 'You are happy, then?' she asked him, trying to suppress her stab of jealousy and failing.

Her son looked at her before replying seriously, 'I had no idea what happiness was, Mama, before Eve. She's all a man could want. She's companion, friend, lover – she's all women and one very special woman.' His laugh rang. 'She is perfectly named. Eve . . .'

And as she had promised, he was not in the least jealous of the nameless man who had taught her about sex, only grateful that she had passed on her knowledge to him. He had not realized that sex could be so emotionally as well as physically satisfying, though he knew that in enlarging his experience she had somehow also managed to enlarge him as a man. He had come to know that she did not live by what he thought of as the normal rules; she obeyed only what she called her destiny, and at first inclined to laugh when she told him something of her life, he had to admit that the many and varied happenings in it did seem predestined. He had no idea, of course, that what he had been told was the official version of Eve

Czerny's life, with the addition of a detail or two not known to the general public; he only knew that when she told him she made it seem as though he was the only one who knew it *all*.

And she was marvellously without jealousy herself. Naturally, they had run across people he knew; his circle tended to frequent the same places, and quite a few of them were women with whom he had had what he thought of as 'flings', some brief, some lengthy – which to him meant a month or more. Not once did Eve give him a hard time, and not once did he fail to notice that the women knew – and resented her confidence.

'So . . .' JoJo Harrington had asked him waspishly, 'Is she as good as they say she is?'

'As who says?'

'Oh, come now, my dear Laddie, you must be aware that she came to these shores trailing – well, if not exactly clouds of glory, then a few clearly identifiable vapour trails; the kind left by very hot stuff.'

Christopher had levelled a look at her. 'Eve is everything I hoped she was – and more. You have no idea how nice it is to have every one of your expectations fulfilled, JoJo, especially when one has been disappointed time after time after time.'

He had left her white-faced with fury. You don't even know the half of it, he had thought. They told me you were as hot as five-alarm chilli but you were yesterday's cold cuts. Eve can tune my body like an engine, to a pitch where I'm capable of an ecstasy that is like dying . . . only to find myself miraculously reborn and ready to go on. She does things that you would probably shudder at but when Eve does them there is no shame, in her or in me. 'Nothing that gives pleasure is wrong,' she had said to him, 'unless at the same time it gives pain – and there is no pain with us, is there? It is those who fear pleasure who castigate its power, and if God had not meant such pleasure to be experienced, why did he equip us to feel it in the first place? Enjoy what I bring to you, bring you to, my darling . . . it is my gift to you, for haven't you given me everything?'

I'm lucky, he thought, not a little awed, for luck was something he had come to expect as of right. It had taken this extra share of Eve to show him that with all his good fortune, he might still have missed this particular pot of gold. There was nothing more he wanted, or so he thought until, after visiting her doctor, his wife told him that she was pregnant. Exultantly, he seized her, whirled her round, lifting her off the ground in his joy.

'But . . .' said his mother delicately, 'whilst I am delighted – you know that I have longed to see your children – I have to admit that I am somewhat worried. Eve is not exactly a young girl, and a first child at her age . . .'

'Eve is thirty, Mother,' Christopher said impatiently, 'and you had me at thirty-four.'

'You were my last child; I already had three others.'

'Even so. Eve is in the best of health. I had them go over her from stem to stern. I am as aware of the risks as you are, but she's got a clean bill of health.'

'She will give up working, of course.'

'Eve isn't the type to sit around doing nothing. She will work as long as she can. Don't fuss, Mother,' Christopher said, in the light voice she knew meant heavy feelings, so she turned the conversation to other things. What neither he nor his mother ever knew, because Eve had given both her obstetrician and her gynaecologist good reason not to say so, was that the eagerly awaited child was not her first, but her second.

She willed their child to be a son, for as she had loathed the thought of her first child, so she gloried in the prospect of her second, because it would be Christopher's. It would also consolidate her position. She was aware that Edith Bingham was not entirely happy with her son's second marriage; would have preferred his first – empty shell that it was – to have continued because, as she told her daughters, 'at least Barbara was one of *us*'. But she was pleased to learn she was to become a grandmother because this time, surely, it would be an heir.

'There is no surely about it,' Charlotte told her mother spitefully. 'That woman can arrange *anything*.'

Eve was in the sixth month of her pregnancy, spending a long weekend at the Villa Paradis above Lake Geneva, resting in her suite, because during this pregnancy she was not working full-time; this time the child came first. Christopher had left early that morning for Paris, where he was due to play in a charity polo match. When her butler came to tell her that there was a woman in the hall demanding to see her and creating all sorts of commotion until she did, Eve said irritably, 'Who is she? What does she want?' Some ex-employee with a grievance, perhaps. Or one of Christopher's ex-girlfriends. She was in no mood to deal with either of them. When she rested she did just that; thinking beautiful thoughts, always about a son.

'She will not say, Madame, only that she must see you and that it is important.' He paused. 'She has a child with her.'

'A child!' One of Christopher's wild oats? 'Send her away,' Eve said in a cold, hard voice.

'We have tried, Madame. She says if you do not see her she will tell her story to the press.'

She wants money, Eve thought. They always do. And I certainly don't want publicity. 'Very well,' she said irritably. 'Bring her up.'

When she saw who it was she knew a moment's rage so terrible, so fiendish, that her hand instinctively reached for the vase of white roses on the draped table by her *chaise-longue*. Now, of all times, a past she had erased was coming back to spoil everything. Then her hand dropped, curled into a fist which she hid under the light silk coverlet covering her knees as she said icily, 'I might have known.' She spoke to Mary Brent; she did not look at the child she was holding by the hand, as if not to look would deny it existence.

'Oh yes, it's time,' Mary Brent hissed. 'Time you accepted your responsibility. I've brought you your bastard!' Releasing the child's hand she put a hand in the small of its back and pushed, sending the little girl stumbling. From her knees, she stared dumbly from one face to the other; the one twisted by hatred, the other – the most beautiful one she had ever seen – an icy mask which still did not look at her.

'We have an agreement,' the mask said at last.

'Had an agreement. That died with my son. Your bastard is nothing to do with me and I'll not have her in my house a moment longer. She's yours. She always was yours and she always will be. You are her mother but my son was not her father. She belongs here, with you, and here she'll stay.' Mary Brent smiled. It made the child shut her eyes. 'And I mean stay. No shoving her off into some home. I've made arrangements to forestall that. I went to see a certain gentleman before we came here. He is a minister of the Lutheran Church affiliated to my own. I have told him all about you and your child. He will call on you from time to time – at his own discretion – and if the child is not produced, alive and well, he will tell me and I will go to the press. And you wouldn't like that, would you?'

The mask was silent.

'You will accept your responsibility, my fine-feathered whore, or you will suffer the consequences. I have left certain papers with the Pastor, and if you do not do as you are told he will see that you find yourself all over the front pages. Think what that will do to your present marriage, not to say the image you present to the world, every bit of it as false and wicked as the faces you paint. No more throwing away what you no longer want. I've made quite sure you can't, because I know you; how devious and deceitful you are. If you don't produce that child every time the good Pastor calls – and you will never know when that will be – the worse for you.'

'Be careful,' the mask warned sibilantly. 'I am no longer the penniless refugee.'

'I know what you are! You are the whore who married my son and dumped your bastard spawn on him. You used my son, you trapped him into marriage and then paid him off, but don't think you've got any money coming back. That's been spent.'

'Liar,' the mask said.

'Try and get it back! Take me to court!'

The silent, terrified child stared at the carpet, unable to bear the hatred that crackled between the two women. She wept soundlessly, her tears dampening her coat, aware of only one monstrously hurtful thing: she had been brought by one woman who hated her to another who did not want her. Daddy, she keened silently, Daddy, where are you?

She saw the black-laced shoes turn and stump towards the door. At once she was on her feet. 'Don't leave me here, please . . . I don't like it here. Please, take me back home . . . I'll be good, I promise . . . I won't cry . . . please, please don't leave me here . . .'

'Go to the whore, your mother!' Mary Brent cruelly prised the child's clutching fingers from her skirts. 'You are her responsibility. Let her look after you.'

'She doesn't want me, I know she doesn't. Please . . . don't leave me.' The unhappiness she knew was infinitely preferable to the unknown terrors to come. Her crying was panic-stricken, her sobs a wail of bewildered terror. She couldn't understand why nobody wanted her, nobody liked her. What had she done that they should only want to be rid of her? She had tried to be good; she hadn't cried except in bed at night; she had kept out of sight. Why, oh why did nobody love her? Why did they talk about her as if she was a *thing*? Something that did not hear and did not feel.

'You'll stay here and that's that!' Mary Brent shouted. Hand on the door she turned for one last word. 'I'll be watching,' she said. The door closed behind her.

Calm, Eve told herself, placing her hands protectively over her distended belly. Calm . . . She closed her eyes, took deep, regular breaths, finally felt her racing heart subside. Then, still not looking at the sobbing child huddled by the door, she stretched out a hand to the bellpush on the table and stabbed it with a finger.

'Come away from the door,' she commanded in a voice that had the child scuttling back to huddle against the wall.

When the butler came in: 'The child is staying here for a while,' she said, still not looking at her. 'Take it upstairs, get someone to feed it, arrange a room. One of those at the top of the house. Then send Hélène to me.'

'Very good, Madame.'

The butler bent to the child, who shrank back.

'Go with him,' the mask commanded again. 'Now!' The voice rose only slightly but in such a way as to make the child scramble to her feet and take the hand he was holding out.

Eve heard the sobs dwindling away along the corridor until there was silence. She lay there, forcibly controlling herself, until Hélène, her housekeeper, an elderly Swiss, came in.

'There is a child,' Eve said at last. 'She will be staying here for a while. She will need someone to look after her. Who can you spare?'

Doubtfully: 'There is Ursula . . . she is one of a large family and good with children.'

'Put her in charge then. Arrange quarters for them both. Somewhere where I will not be disturbed, at the top of the house. I will see about a proper nurse later. Liaise with Jacques. He knows.'

'Very good, Madame.' She looked round. 'Has the child any luggage?'

'I don't know,' Eve said irritably. 'If she hasn't then see she has what she needs. Just keep her out of my sight, do you understand?'

'Yes, Madame.' Hesitantly: 'What is the child's name?'

Eve did not answer at once then she said tonelessly: 'Brent, Alexandra Brent.'

She said nothing to her husband. She knew him well enough by now to know that he took no interest in the household; other people had always run things like that in his world. He took for granted the spotless bedlinen, the always freshly ironed shirts, the exquisitely prepared meals. She also knew that nobody would tell him what had happened. Eve ran her house like her business. Her standards were of the highest but she paid well provided they were met. Let them wonder, she thought. While I decide. This was a huge house: the top floor – and there were four – was foreign territory not only to her but to Christopher. He probably wasn't even aware that there was a fourth floor. The child would be out of sight and hearing. Once she could think about it calmly she would decide on its future. Right now, all that concerned her was the future of her son. She must not get upset by this unexpected turn of events. She must remain calm and tranquil. There would be a way around the difficulty. There always was if you searched long enough. That done, she dismissed the episode from her mind.

It was several days later when Ursula, the fresh-faced young girl who had been told to look after Alexandra, approached the house-keeper. 'I am worried about the little girl,' she said. 'She will not eat, she will not speak. She just sits, but at night she cries. All the time. I have never seen such an unhappy child.'

'Has she toys to play with?'

'Yes. I bought her a doll and some puzzles and crayons to draw with. She has not looked at them.'

'I had better take a look at her.'

Alex was sitting on a chair by one of the porthole windows, staring out. She was wearing one of the dresses that had been newly bought, a pretty smocked cotton, and her brown hair was neatly braided. She was pale, but to the housekeeper she seemed unnaturally calm. Her forehead, when the housekeeper managed to lay her palm on it without the child flinching away, wasn't hot.

'Come now,' Hélène chided, but kindly. 'You haven't eaten your

146

nice breakfast. Don't you like muesli? Is there something else you would prefer? Nobody's going to hurt you, I promise. Ursula is here to look after you.'

The child was staring at the floor. The two women looked at each other. 'She should have fresh air,' Ursula said truculently. 'It isn't good for her to be cooped up all the time. Why isn't she allowed to go into the gardens?'

'Madame gives the orders,' Hélène reminded her sharply, 'and your duty is to carry them out.'

'But why is she imprisoned up here? And who is she anyway?'

'Do not pry into what isn't your business. You have a good job here, don't you? Which you wish to keep?' Ursula nodded. 'Then keep your curiosity to yourself.' As much as to reassure herself as the maid, the housekeeper said, 'She's probably some poor relation of Madame; somebody without parents.' She looked at Ursula. 'Has she said anything, asked for anyone?'

'No. I can't get a word out of her.'

'Well, your English isn't very good, is it? She probably doesn't understand you.' Once again the housekeeper bent to the child. 'Is there anything you want?' she asked in the same kind tone as before.

'I want to go home,' the child said in a small voice.

'And where is home?'

'Twenty-seven Acacia Avenue, South Wimbledon.'

'Who lives there?'

'My daddy's mummy.'

'And where is your daddy?'

'Dead . . .' The child began to sob. 'She told me my daddy was dead and that she didn't want me and that I had to come here with her. I want to go home, I don't like it here.'

'And your mother – where is your mother?'

'Daddy told me she went to heaven but –'

'But what?'

The child shook her head. She was afraid that if she mentioned the woman downstairs, who so obviously did not like her, she would be punished for it.

'You see,' the housekeeper said, straightening. 'She is an orphan, poor little thing.' She looked at the forlorn face, wet with silent tears, and made a decision. 'Would you like to come down to the kitchen with me? If we ask nicely, Mrs Bünschli will make you some lovely hot toast and you can have some warm milk. But you must be quiet. Madame is resting so we must not disturb her.'

'I know how to be quiet,' the child said. 'Daddy taught me not to disturb anybody.'

'Then come along.'

They went down the backstairs, which led to the kitchen, where Alex seemed comforted by the warmth, the bustle, the smells. Mrs Bünschli, the cook, a plump, motherly woman, fussed over her and made her some hot, crunchy toast spread with butter and honey made from the nectar of Alpine flowers. Alex ate two large slices.

'Ach, she is lonely for people,' the cook said. 'A little company, eh, *liebchen*?'

The child nodded shyly, drinking her milk thirstily. She was happy to sit at the big wooden table and feel not only the warmth from the big stove but from Mrs Bünschli's small bright eyes and comforting voice. From then on, she spent a good portion of each day in the kitchen. Mrs Bünschli would let her have a little mound of dough with which to make gingerbread men, and it would absorb her happily. Or she would painstakingly scrape tiny carrots and shell peas. The household entered into the conspiracy and at the first signs of any activity on the part of the mistress of the house she would be whisked up the backstairs again. She liked Ursula, who, happy to be relieved of her household duties, cheerfully joined in making jigsaw puzzles and drawing pictures. But it was when she brought the child some books – no longer used by her brothers and sisters – that she discovered the way to keep her happy.

'Already she reads!' Ursula told the rest of the servants. 'Her father taught her.'

'She is a bright child,' Mrs Bünschli said, 'who learns very quickly.' They endlessly discussed the whys and wherefores of her presence at the villa, but as its mistress never asked after her, Hélène's opinion that little Alex was a poor relation came to be accepted as the truth.

And then, one day, Alex was aware of great excitement, all centring on the woman she never saw but whose presence dominated her life. Kneeling on the window seat under the huge round window that overlooked the front of the house, Alex saw a big white van draw up, and then its big doors at the back were opened and two men carrying something long and narrow ran into the house. When they came out again it was being wheeled and there was a figure wrapped in blankets lying on it. Catching a glimpse of red-gold hair Alex quickly drew back, but nobody bothered to look up, and the van roared away, making a wailing noise.

In a little while, Ursula came up to take her downstairs, and she found great excitement prevailing. Jacques, the butler, who was kind if distant, let her go down with him into a big cold cellar where he took several bottles from the racks that lined the walls.

To Alex's shy question he replied that the bottles contained wine – a special wine called champagne – and that they were needed for a celebration later that day.

'Is it somebody's birthday?' Alex asked.

'Yes, that is exactly what it is, and if you are a good girl you may have a sip of this wonderful wine. It's a vintage champagne – Dom Perignon.'

Alex wondered if she should tell him that it had been her birthday just two weeks ago then decided not to. She was afraid to do anything that would call attention to her. Always, before, she had had a cake with candles and presents. This time there had been nothing to mark the fact that she was now six years old.

She was happy sitting carefully stripping parsley when the kitchen door opened and a big blond man came in, looking flushed and excited. 'I have a son!' he told them all. 'A seven-pound two-ounce son!'

There was a babble of congratulations. Christopher Bingham looked round delightedly; he had to tell someone, even if it was only the servants. Eve was well, his son was vigorously healthy and his mother, when he had called her, had been heartfelt in her congratulations, for the Bingham line was now secure.

Life had truly begun, he thought, dizzy with happiness, the day he met Eve. When his eye fell on Alex, staring wide-eyed, he asked jocularly, 'And who have we here?' not caring particularly but wanting everyone to share in his delight.

There was a brief, stricken silence then Jacques said smoothly, 'One of Ursula's young sisters, sir. Just paying a brief visit.'

'Ursula?' Jacques indicated the nervous maid. 'Oh, yes . . .' Christopher vaguely remembered seeing her about the place. 'Well, she must drink to my son too . . . everybody must drink to my son, eh, Jacques?'

'The champagne is already on ice, sir.'

'Good, good . . . bring a couple of bottles upstairs for later, but open another couple now. I want everyone to mark this splendid day.'

Alex was given a tiny glassful but the bubbles got up her nose and made her sneeze, which had Christopher Bingham roaring with laughter. When he had gone: 'Do you think he will mention the child?' Ursula asked fearfully.

'I doubt it,' Jacques said calmly, preparing to take his tray upstairs. 'His mind is solely on his good fortune.'

'If he does, then we shall tell Madame what we told the master,' Mrs Bünschli shrugged. 'Madame has given him a son; she will be too proud to take notice of anything else. Besides, by the time she comes home from the hospital he will have forgotten.'

But it was not to be. When Eve came home with her son, to the specially prepared suite of rooms that contained everything any child could want or need, as well as a nurse and a nanny, Christopher innocently let the cat out of the bag.

'Did you ever see such a beautiful child?' he enthused, hanging over his son's bedraped and beruffled crib. 'I've never seen such a beautiful child.'

'All children are beautiful to their parents,' Eve said, amused, secure in the knowledge that her son was the Bingham heir, that her own position was now unassailable. Passionately as she adored her husband, because he had realized her dream, raised her that last, final step to the winner's dais, it was still eminently reassuring to know that she was the woman who had given Christopher what he had longed for, been nagged for by his mother.

'No, Christopher is beautiful to everybody,' his father was saying besottedly. 'You only have to look at him to know, and looks are important, no matter how much money you've got. If you haven't got any money it's even worse, as that plain little scrap downstairs is going to find out one day.'

'Which little scrap?'

'Oh, some kid who was in the kitchen the day Junior was born. All eyes and a masterful nose. Ursula's sister.'

Eve, who recognized the description at once, carefully overrode it. 'What kind of a name is Junior?' she asked mechanically, her mind busy.

'I was Junior for years until I became Laddie. There has always been a Junior Bingham.'

'Not this time,' Eve said. 'Our son's name is *Christopher* Bingham Jr, and that is how he will be known.'

'OK,' her husband said peaceably. 'How soon can we take him home to show Mother?'

'As soon as I'm up to making the journey.'

'He'll wear the Bingham christening robe, of course – we all do – and Dr Kimberly will perform the ceremony –'

'Whatever you want, darling,' Eve agreed.

What *she* wanted was carried out with her usual ruthless dispatch. Not only Ursula but Hélène and Mrs Bünschli vanished from Alex's life. There were no more trips to the kitchen, no more happily being wanted, indulged. Once again people whom she had come to love were removed from her, as if there was a law against her loving anyone. Once again she was on her own. Until Nanny Wilson came. She was a brisk, no-nonsense, Princess Christian-trained fifty-year-old who was used to looking after children whose parents preferred them to be neither seen nor heard. She was much more strict than Ursula and without Mrs Bünschli's twinkling-eyed motherliness. She instituted a regime that was almost martial in its discipline, and while she was not unkind, she was not someone Alex felt she could love. It was not until Miss Patterson, who was to give her lessons, arrived on the scene, that Alex found someone not only to love, but to love her. While Nanny Wilson was always Nanny Wilson, Margaret Patterson soon became Patsy.

One day, when Alex was in her usual place, on the window seat, she noticed a great deal of activity out on the drive; cars being loaded with luggage, people running back and forth. Once again, it seemed, people were leaving her life, but as they were not those with whom she had any daily dealings, she did not feel too nervous, though she still felt uneasy enough to make enquiries.

'Where is everyone going?' she asked Nurse Wilson.

'To America, where Master Christopher is going to be christened.'

'Will I have to go too?'

'No, we are staying here.'

'All by ourselves?'

'A few servants. Someone has to cook our food and wash our clothes.'

'And will Miss Patterson still come?'

'Of course.'

Alex thought that over. 'Will the lady with the red hair ever come back again?'

'Good heavens yes! This is her house.'

'Questions, always questions,' Nanny Wilson commented to Margaret Patterson later, 'but I must admit I would like a few answers myself.' Casually: 'What were you told about the child?'

'Only to see that she was educated, which is a joy because she's so avid to learn.'

'Yes, she's an old-fashioned little thing, unnaturally quiet for a six-year-old.'

'She's also very bright. I never knew a child learn so quickly or love it so much. She's a joy to teach.'

'I got the impression that she's a poor relation of some sort.'

'So did I.'

But it was to Patsy that Alex, once she knew she could trust her, told the story of her arrival at the villa, still, even now, puzzled by confusing stories. How could her father tell her that her mother was dead, yet his mother – Alex now never referred to her as grandmother – had made it quite clear that the red-haired woman (of whom, Patsy noted, Alex was terrified) *was* her mother, not dead but terrifyingly alive.

'You won't tell anyone, will you?' Alex asked. 'I don't think she likes me, you see, and I don't want to be taken away again.'

'Nobody is going to take you away,' Patsy said firmly. 'You are to live here and be looked after by Nanny Wilson and have lessons with me. And I won't tell a soul. It will be our little secret.'

And it was to Patsy that Alex confided the facts about her father, and the nasty lady who was his mother and did not like Alex either. 'Nobody ever likes me,' Alex said wistfully. 'Daddy's mummy said I was a child of sin, is that why? Am I wicked?'

'You are most certainly not. Your father's mother was an old lady who had some odd ideas, that's all. Old people often do, you know.'

'You're not old, are you?' Alex asked lovingly.

'Well, I'm no longer young but no, I'm not old.'

And as the well-ordered days began to run seamlessly together, for the first time since her father's death, Alex knew happiness again.

When, after some four months, the same cavalcade which had left once more returned, Patsy was careful to keep Alex out of sight. They did their lessons from nine until one, as usual, and then they would go down the backstairs and out into the huge gardens, where they would walk, and Patsy would explain the names of the flowers, shrubs and trees, or read, or play hide and seek and Big Bad Wolf. And then, one day, they were summoned downstairs.

'Madame wishes to see you,' Nanny Wilson said importantly. 'You must change into one of your best dresses. Come along, we must not keep Madame waiting.'

Alex looked beseechingly at Patsy, eyes wide, face pale.

'She only wants to know how you are,' Patsy reassured. 'She will see how you have grown and be pleased, I'm sure.'

'Come with me,' Alex begged of her tutor. 'Please.'

Margaret Patterson looked at Nanny Wilson, who nodded. 'It might be best,' she said. 'I've got the feeling that a good impression is called for.'

But it was Nanny Wilson who led her into the great green and gold drawing-room, where the red-haired woman was sitting enthroned in a big gold chair. There was also a man; elderly, dressed in black.

'This is the child,' the red-haired woman said expressionlessly.

The man smiled, held out a hand. 'So this is Alex,' he said. 'Come over here, let me see you.'

Alex looked up at her nurse who urged: 'Go along. Make your curtsey as I have taught you.'

Alex did so.

'Well now,' the man said jocularly. 'You are a big fine girl, aren't you?'

He asked her how old she was, what she was learning, what she liked to do best, was she a good girl and did she say her prayers every night. Alex nodded. He questioned her closely as to her health. Did she eat well, was she happy, who looked after her.

'Nanny Wilson and Patsy,' Alex said.

'I can see Nanny Wilson, but who is Patsy?'

On being brought in, Patsy was subjected to probing questioning, as was Nanny Wilson. It did not take long, and Alex was conscious that the red-haired woman, who was staring out of the window, was at the same time listening to everything.

When they were dismissed, Alex scampered ahead, eager to return to the safety of her own territory, but she could hear her nurse and her tutor talking.

'What on earth was all that about?' Nanny Wilson was wondering, avid with curiosity.

'Perhaps he is the child's trustee,' Patsy said non-committally.

'Well, he certainly wanted to know an awful lot.' Irritably: 'I wish somebody would tell me.'

But Patsy was thinking about Eve Czerny. She had never once looked at Alex, never spoken. She had worn the air of someone doing an irksome duty, no more. Well, Patsy thought, perhaps she will send for me later. But there was no further summons. The life of the household went on in its two, strictly segregated parts. It was the other child, the baby boy, who received all the attention. He too had his own nurse and maid, but they were both French and spoke no English, and in the manner of servants it did not take them long to realize that it was their charge who mattered. Patsy, who spoke fluent, idiomatic French, ignored their haughty snubs on the few occasions when, walking with Alex in the garden, they would encounter the baby in its big English perambulator, and see the nurse wheel sharply and take it off in another direction; or the nursery-maid, coming up the stairs to the third floor, which was where the son and heir was cosseted, would brush past without a word.

It was as though they were untouchables. Alex was well cared for, her clothes – their choice left entirely to Nanny Wilson – of good quality, her food wholesome, her rooms pleasant, but of parental care there was a total lack. Nanny Wilson was kind, in her brisk, spare-the-rod-and-spoil-the-child manner, but it was Patsy to whom Alex turned for the love and affection she craved, and from Patsy, fortyish, spinsterish, academically brilliant, that she received it.

The best times were when they had the house to themselves, and as Eve travelled a great deal, and where she went so did her son, those times were frequent. Then Alex could make as much noise as she liked, clump up and down the wooden stairs to the third floor and below, which were carpeted, go in and out of the kitchen as she pleased, steal titbits from the cook, laugh as she ran around the gardens, often with Curro, the Pyrrenean mountain dog who belonged to Léon the head gardener, who was never brought when Madame was in residence.

And then, there was a sudden surge of excitement. The entourage had returned, bringing the news that Madame was once more *enceinte* and that Monsieur was like a dog with two tails. There was a big party, the house was lit, an orchestra played, voices carried up to the top floor. Madame's laugh was heard more often, and the big boom of Monsieur. But Alex was never sent for. Not even when the day came to celebrate her eighth birthday. There was a cake, with candles, and presents to open, but only the three of them to see what they contained. As always, there was nothing from Madame.

But one day it all fell apart. Madame was on her own, Monsieur having left for America where he was to play in some big polo match at Palm Beach. This was not unusual; he commuted back and forth across the Atlantic much as Patsy drove to and from Thonon. Alex was eating her tea, Marmite sandwiches followed by a piece of angel cake, when she heard screams: peal after peal of agonized, frenzied shrieking, like a soul in torment.

'What on earth . . .' Nanny Wilson went to the door, out of it down the corridor to the landing where she leaned over the banisters. The shrieking was so penetrating it bounced off the walls, echoing and re-echoing. 'Something is very wrong,' Nanny Wilson said. 'You finish your tea like a good girl while I go down and see what's happening.'

Alex finished her tea, but when there was no sign of Nanny she went and hung over the banisters. The screaming was muffled now, but still continuing. Perhaps somebody has hurt themselves, she thought. She went back into the nursery and picking up a book – she was reading *Swallows and Amazons* for the third time – took it over to her favourite seat by the window. She was absorbed when she heard the screams from directly beneath her; knelt up to look out and saw the red-haired woman, wearing a flimsy pink dress that streamed out behind her, running barefoot over the gravel, shrieking all the time, her arms flailing, her upturned face showing a wide-open mouth, from which the screams were pealing, her expression frenzied, no longer an icy mask. She flew over the gravel and onto the lawns, making in the direction of the lake. Then several people – men, women, one of them Nanny Wilson – erupted from the house after her. 'She's heading for the lake,' somebody shouted. 'For God's sake, somebody cut her off . . .'

One of the footmen, young and fleet of foot, took off at a tangent while the rest followed the banshee that was Eve Czerny.

Alex remained kneeling, wide-eyed and curious, until after a while, she saw a procession coming back. The young, strong footman was carrying the red-haired woman, her arms hanging limply, her face very white under the flame of her hair. There was a babble of talk in several languages which ceased as everyone went into the house and the front door was shut.

Alex knew better than to ask questions when her nanny came back. Curiosity, Nanny Wilson always replied when she asked questions, killed the cat. But she lay awake, once she was put to bed, wondering what had frightened the red-haired lady so.

Next morning, when Patsy came, there was a low-voiced conversation to which Alex, ostensibly bent over a page of long division, listened avidly.

'. . . never saw such a display of hysterics. Darting all over the house, tearing her clothes, throwing things, screaming fit to burst, and only the one word . . . no, no, no . . . over and over. They had to wrestle with her – that young footman Frederic had to more or less tackle her like some footballer and you should see his face; clawed to pieces.'

'She was in shock,' Patsy pointed out.

'So were we by the time we got her back to the house. I know it's a tragedy – such a young man, only thirty-eight – and an unlooked-for accident, but at least he died instantly. His neck was broken, I believe.' From under her lashes Alex saw Nanny Wilson shake her head. 'They career round the field so fast on those horses . . . when I was with the St Justs he cracked a collarbone and broke a shoulder when he fell from his horse, but I heard somebody say that this time the horse's leg struck Mr Bingham's head and that's what broke his neck.' Nanny Wilson tut-tutted. 'And her four months gone too . . . if she loses the baby as well . . .' She pursed her lips, tapped her forehead significantly. 'Too highly strung, these continentals. No backbone, not like us.'

The next day, when Patsy came, there was another murmured exchange. '. . . lost the child last night . . . antics brought on a miscarriage . . . another boy . . . that poor woman . . . husband *and* son, God help her . . .'

Lost the child? Alex felt her heart constrict. Would the red-haired woman want to lose her too? That would mean losing Patsy, losing the sense of permanence that made her feel so safe, losing the quiet, peaceful days her disrupted existence craved.

Patsy noticed at once. 'What is it?' she asked. She saw the constricted throat swallow with difficulty.

'I don't want to be lost too,' Alex whispered. 'I don't want to be sent away again . . .'

'No one is sending you away. What has happened has nothing – nothing, do you understand – to do with you. There has been an accident, that's all. Mr Bingham has been killed and Madame is very, very upset because she was going to have a baby and now that has died.'

'Oh . . .' said Alex in relief. 'I thought she had lost it and would be angry with me because she thought I had taken it.'

Hardly, Patsy thought. She never thinks of you from one day to the next. 'No,' she said, 'Madame is not angry with you, but we must be quiet because she is ill and has to rest.'

'I am good at being quiet,' Alex said anxiously.

Yes, too good, Patsy thought. Too quiet. Well, she pondered later, maybe what has happened will make Eve Czerny aware that she has a daughter too, though knowing her – and that only from what I have heard – I doubt it.

She was right. Eve Czerny and her son were taken back to the United States, where her husband was interred in the Bingham mausoleum. She did not come back to the villa for a long, long time.

11

Switzerland, 1988

Alex's motherlode of newly acquired knowledge was something she found hard to handle. It was not that she was morally shocked. What the young Anna Farkas had done was entirely in keeping with what Alex knew about the mature Eve Czerny, who took singlemindedness to its furthest extreme. Alex's own logical mind saw the necessity even while it appreciated how fortunate the young, inexperienced, unqualified girl had been to have the one qualification that could never be acquired: a rare beauty founded on the bedrock of sex. It is all very well to hold up one's hands in horror and ask 'How could she?' Alex reasoned. She could because, unlike me, she was able to. Were I in the same circumstances I would have to find some other way because neither my face nor my body is a marketable commodity. So, why *am* I shocked? Is it because one of her protectors was a Russian? A member of a feared and hated occupying power? Or that the other was a member of the Hungarian equivalent of the SS? Take away the uniforms and they both had the same basic equipment. It was what they put on with the uniform that mattered to the young Anna Farkas. The power. She had neither money nor friends nor family. Only herself and her God-given gift of beauty through which to get to use that power.

No wonder she can't stand the sight of me, Alex thought. What a sock in the eye I must have been to her. Botticelli's Venus giving birth to a gargoyle. Knowing my mother – and I already know her so much better than I did – she hasn't concealed her past because *she* is ashamed of it, but because she knew other people would be, and she has to sell them her products. That's why her official biography goes no further back than 1960. That's why all enquiries as to what and where she had been before then are met with an airily dismissive: 'I was too young to have any history before then.' No wonder beauty is so important to her: her be-all and end-all.

Hers has brought her everything she has. And one thing she didn't want. Me. How furious she must have been, how trapped she must have felt. In which case, why didn't she get rid of me there and then? Unless she saw me as a means to an end . . . Is it because I remind her of things she prefers to forget? Is her revulsion at the way I look, apparently so powerful that she can't bear to look at me, a cover for something else?

As a child, bewildered, unhappy, afraid, Alex had finally come up with the only explanation for her mother's behaviour that made any sense to her. It was the way she looked. She knew – her grandmother had told her often enough – that she bore the Mark of Satan, and as she had anxiously examined her face and could not find it, she had come to the painful conclusion that the mark was the way she looked. Had she not heard her grandmother say: 'She doesn't take after her mother, does she? Talk about Beauty and the Beast!' And her father had been more angry than she had ever seen him, had shouted at her grandmother that she was never to say such things. But it hadn't stopped her; she had just been careful never to say them in her son's hearing. By the time Mary Brent had dumped her on her mother, Alex had come to believe that she was some sort of changeling, unlovable because she wasn't pretty. Ursula and Hélène and Mrs Bünschli had been sent away because they had befriended her. And Nanny Wilson always scolded if she caught Alex staring into a mirror, telling her that if she didn't stop, one day she would see the Devil there.

Well, Alex thought now, it has certainly bedevilled me all my life. What if I've been barking up the wrong tree? What if she couldn't bear to look at me because I was an unpleasant reminder of things she preferred to forget? She got up agitatedly from her chair to pace her small sitting-room, once the day nursery. The power of the unconscious mind is infinite, she reminded herself. It can blind, paralyse, render deaf, dumb and psychotic. What if I have brainwashed myself into believing that it was my lack of looks she couldn't stand because I was unable to accept that the truth of the matter was that it was me. That she couldn't stand *me*.

She did something she did only when she had to. She went to a mirror, examined her face. Long – horse-faced, she told herself bitterly – strong-boned, high at the cheek, long at the jaw, with a prow of a nose. Her eyes were neither one thing nor the other;

sometimes green, sometimes brown, and speckled like a trout, but her eyebrows were strongly marked and in no need of the tweezers. Her mouth was wide, the lips clean cut – chiselled, she thought encouragingly, but the overall effect was one of melancholy. How often had she been told: 'Cheer up, Alex, it might never happen', when she hadn't been feeling miserable at all? Maybe I don't smile enough, she thought, and put one in place. It was as false as paper flowers. A smile had to be natural or it was no smile at all. And I'm just not one of nature's smilers . . .

Depressed, she went back to her window seat, her 'thinking place' where she had spent so many childhood hours. How enormously, inescapably important was one's personal appearance. It mattered nothing that behind her own plain face there was a quick wit, a cheerful disposition, a good mind, a definite sense of humour and a compassionate understanding. Nobody ever bothered to find out because they took her at her face value. Nil. Her mother, on the other hand, had a face value that was worth a fortune and all her life she had never lacked bidders. I can't even give mine away, Alex thought, and had to laugh. If my mother had looked like me, how different her life would have been. How much harder she would have had to work, how much more difficult it would have been. She would have had to do everything on her own because men wouldn't have been interested. Would she have been so shatteringly self-confident, or would she have been like me, with no self-confidence at all? Not where my work is concerned, but that's because I don't lack confidence in my mental prowess; only in my physical shortcomings. Nothing succeeds like success and I have had an unbroken run of that where my work's concerned. It's in my dealings with men that I fail.

'Your trouble, my dear Alex,' a colleague – a homosexual and one of her few friends – had once told her, 'is that you are unable to see yourself as a woman, only as a person. If you set no value on being a woman yourself, how can you expect others to? I realize that you're not particularly feminine, but then neither am I particularly masculine. The difference is that I accept what I am, and therefore do what I can; you believe that what you are has been decided for you and are therefore unable to do anything. Wrong, wrong, wrong! If you're not happy with yourself, then change it!'

Easier said than done, Alex thought now. Robert had physical promptings and powerful desires to drag him out of the closet. I have none. I have lived my life in the mind; my body is something I feed and clothe and keep clean. It goes in terror of my mind, which has its own terrors of more rejection, and I've had enough of that to last several lifetimes, thank you.

And yet, she thought, I *am* alive. Chris, who had all and more of the love I craved from Mother, is dead, and God knows he had beauty. People used to turn in the street when he was out with her. How she loved that. How she took great care never to be seen with me. All right, so maybe I am misjudging her, but it still *hurts*!

So find out, she told herself. Go on with your researches. The more you know, the better chance you have of finding – recognizing – the truth when you finally do see it.

Her next step – and man – in tracing her mother's onward and upward progress after abandoning her husband and child was Henri Beyle, to whom Eve had – publicly and often – paid tribute as her 'dear friend and mentor'. Such an undistinguished, fat little man, Alex thought, leafing through her mother's cuttings books. Yet by all accounts one of the great 'noses'. Had he created *Essence of Eve*? And if he had, what was his payment? Another barter? It was because Henri Beyle was a great *parfumeur* that Eve Czerny had gone to him in the first place, surely.

To find out more about perfumes, their creation and composition, Alex turned to the many technical books on the shelves in her mother's office, but her attention soon strayed from the complex world of fragrances to the world of beauty itself. Before she realized it she was deeply immersed in a subject she had not even begun to realize was so utterly fascinating. She hadn't known, for instance, that Cleopatra was supposed to have written the very first beauty manual; that Greek courtesans – the *hetaerae* – had used cosmetics as a sign of their profession; that in the Italian Renaissance women had gone so far as to paint their teeth. But it was when she discovered a copy of Ovid's *Ars Amatoria* that she received her first, stunning shock. Not that Eve should possess a copy of a work of erotic verse, but to find it obviously well read, for there were comments scribbled in the margin, a practice abhorrent to Alex, to whom books were like living things. But she had to admit Eve's remarks were succinct.

One of them was beside a passage underlined in pencil, which read: 'Did I not say to thee "Cease to dye thy hair?" And now thou hast no longer any hair to dye.' The marginal comment read: 'She would if she'd used my colourants!'

Alex found herself grinning widely. She had never expected to find Eve Czerny the possessor of a sense of humour. Raising her head from the book she stared blindly out of the window, oblivious to the view. I don't know her at all, she thought. She's my mother but she's also a total stranger.

She became so absorbed in reading about the early Church's belief that the use of cosmetics interfered with man's – and therefore God's – image (shades of Mary Brent, she thought), that the luncheon gong went unheard. When Max came to look for her he took one look and sighed, shaking his head. 'Having your daily fix of the printed word? Still, better that than dope.'

Alex looked up. 'Did you know that Chaucer personified beauty as a woman who used no "peynte" and left her eyebrows unplucked?'

'No, but I do now.'

'I had no idea my mother owned this marvellous collection of books – but since I was never allowed past the door of this room I suppose it isn't surprising. Here's another one; this is from *Delights for Ladies* by Sir Hugh Platt, published in 1602. "To make the face white and fair, wash they face with Rosemary boyled in white wine, and thou shalt be fair." Isn't that delicious?'

'Depends on whether you're going to try it or not.'

He saw the familiar chill ice over the vividly alive expression which always took over when she was enjoying herself, but she shrugged, answered flippantly: 'Why not? If it works.'

It was not often that Max made comments about Alex's lack of looks. She knew that to him, she was Alex, warts and all, and he regarded her face with as much familiarity as his own; he hardly noticed it. Not that he let that stop him from chiding her impatiently about the granite mountain she carried on her shoulder. It had never occurred to him that as a keen appreciator of the beauty of women – and a passionate partaker at all times – it might have hurt Alex that he never considered her in that way. But now, like a thunderflash, she saw, along with the newly acquired knowledge that she might have been labouring under a delusion about Eve, that she was not the gargoyle she had always believed herself to be, and therefore *was* worthy of any man's consideration. Like Max, for instance. She stared at him, and for the first time in her life, saw him in the bright light of that knowledge. Not as her friend Max – dear, familiar, kind Max, who had been Uncle Max until he told her there were only thirteen years between them and he had enough of a reputation as a ladies' man already – but as Max Fabian, personable, attractive, sexual *man*.

'What's the matter? Have I grown another head?'

Alex shook herself. 'No . . . sorry. Just thinking . . .' Heat coursed through her.

'That goes with breathing where you're concerned.' He sauntered over to the desk, went round behind it to lean over her, placing his hands flat on the desk so that he loomed over her. She stared fixedly at his arms; he had his shirtsleeves rolled up to just below the elbow, and for the first time she noticed the fine hairs on skin the colour of pale gold. His hands, though large, were long-fingered and powerful – she had seen him crush a whole orange to pulp many times; it was a party piece which used to awe her, and she could feel the warmth of his body, smell the tangy sharpness of *Krystos*, Eve's bestselling aftershave and cologne.

'Hmmm . . . very interesting,' he said, 'but I came to see if you would keep me company for lunch. Mora's gone into Geneva, Pamela's at the church again, and you know I hate to eat alone. I thought ten at table was normal until I went to college.' His voice, always vibrantly deep, rumbled about her like laughter from Olympus, but Max the God had done one of Zeus's metamorphoses; she would never see him in that way again.

She smiled dutifully but kept her eyes downcast to the printed page. She was suddenly so *aware* of Max that she was uncomfortable; aware that her skin was prickling and her heart thumping. Well, she thought wryly, the instinct to propagate the species is the second most powerful there is after self-preservation. I thought my sexuality safely dead – but it seems it has only been in hibernation.

'We can have lunch in here if you like,' Max offered. 'Like old times, remember? When you were boning up for some exam or other and we used to eat off trays. We haven't done that in a long time.'

'I'm not hungry,' Alex said truthfully. Another first. Food was something she was normally always ready for.

'Well I am. You can sit and watch. Give the bell a ring, will you?'

Unwillingly, Alex did so. She would rather he had taken himself off to sit in lonely state in the dining-room and left her alone to get herself sorted out. One small aberrant thought and look what happens, she thought. The proverbial hole in the dyke. But Max was very observant; if he saw a loose thread he would pull and pull until the whole damned sweater was unravelled. Better to give no sign of anything being out of the ordinary. But Max put the boot to that with his next question.

'How are the researches going? Did Peter Brewster come up with some Eyes Only stuff?'

Alex's head snapped up while her mouth opened in shock. 'You had me followed?'

'Darn tootin' I did. Part of my brief is to see that Eve Czerny and/or her company are protected from anything – shall I say untoward? Your researches and the way you're handling them make you about as untoward as a bull in a china shop. Of course I had you followed! People who ride always forget that somebody has to deal with the manure!'

Alex's eyes blazed at him.

Max blinked. 'Good God!' he exclaimed. 'Your eyes have gone green as grass!'

'My eyes maybe, me no! I'm not as green as you'd like me to be. Whatever rights you have over Eve Czerny and her company do not obtain where I'm concerned. I'm nothing to do with either of them! Where I go and what I do is my business, and I'll thank you to keep your nose out of it!'

Her voice had risen and she slammed her hand down on the desk top so that the books jumped.

'Eve Czerny is *my* client, I am *her* lawyer, I protect *her* interests!'

'Not to mention your own!'

'Come off it, kid. This is Max, remember? Ever since you came back from London you've been giving an excellent imitation of a juggler finding he's got five very hot potatoes in the air instead of balls.' In softer tones: 'Me, I've got calluses, see?' He held up his hands, palms out. 'If your fingers are burning then let me juggle for a while. I've got more experience than you.' He smiled and Alex tore her eyes away from the warm, melted-chocolate depths of his.

'You've got a head stuffed with knowledge, but by the line marked "Experience" you would have to write Nil – right?'

'Whose side are you on?' Alex demanded.

'The one on which my bread is buttered, naturally.' Max gave a slight, self-deprecatory shrug.

But Alex was not to be placated. It stung to think that he should have trusted her so little that he had had her tailed.

Reading every nuance in a face that was now anything but melancholy and pink with anger, Max said softly, 'What you do *is* my business, you know. Has been ever since I found you purloining books from the library.' He laughed. 'I never saw anybody look so terrified.'

'I thought you were my mother.'

'We made a pact, remember? I said I wouldn't tell on you if you wouldn't tell on me because I'd been borrowing books too – again without permission.'

Alex's smile glimmered. 'Yes, I remember.'

'I looked out for you then, so why shouldn't I look out for you now?'

'I *am* twenty years older,' Alex pointed out.

'So am I. I guess it's like the song says: "You're getting to be a habit with me",' Max sang in his pleasing baritone.

Alex had to laugh. Max could always get round her. Once again the old, cosy-as-an-old-slipper relationship was back. It was only when he reached out to place a hand over one of hers and say: 'Friends?' that Alex felt a jolt travel up her arm and explode in the region of her heart, though she gave no outward sign. Years of practice had made her adept at not showing her true feelings.

'Friends,' she said, withdrawing her hand casually to straighten up the books just as Jacques came in.

'Lunch in here, if you please, Jacques. On the trolley. We'll serve ourselves.'

'Very good, sir.'

'Now then,' Max said, 'to get back to the point: why are you digging so deep into your mother's past?'

'Because it's buried so deeply.'

'That's like George Mallory saying of Everest, "Because it's there." My father kept a German Luger he liberated from some dead fool but I never felt I had to use it to shoot myself.'

'I don't feel I can forgive her unless I know exactly what it is she feels she needs forgiveness for.'

Max considered her. She forced herself to sit calmly under his gaze, acutely aware of their glossy brown, the thicket of eyelashes any woman would have killed for, the keen penetration as they probed hers.

'OK,' he nodded finally, 'I can go along with that because it's the way you travel anyway. But you realize that however bitter the end may be, you are the one who will have to swallow it?'

'Yes.'

'OK. So where do you go from here? Better, tell me where you've got to. I may not be of much help prior to 1967, but I'm a mine of information about what comes after that. Once you reach that point you'll be coming to me anyway, right? All I did, in having you tailed, was to make sure that you didn't blow any holes in the wall your mother's erected round her early life. I was as aware of that as you were, maybe more, because the few times I tried to drill a hole I got my tools confiscated, and if she built that wall there had to be a damned good reason. Now, be a good girl and satisfy my curiosity. Once we get to my slide area I'll give you unrestricted access to all my classified information.' His smile was completely understanding. 'Pass the hot potatoes, OK?'

But it was delicately smoked trout, accompanied by a creamy horseradish sauce that they ate, and as they did so, Alex told Max all that Peter Brewster had told her. He did not interrupt, only listened intently, and when she had finished he sat silently for a while, sipping his pale gold Montrachet.

'So,' he said finally, 'all you've told me I find entirely in keeping with your mother's character as I know it, except for one bit – the part about her being a double agent. I detect the ring of brass right there. No way is your mother a political animal. She doesn't give a damn about Hungary now and she didn't then, if you ask me. All Eve Czerny cared about was herself. In that sense she is a true internationalist, a citizen of the world rather than one particular country. And she was, then as now, a realist. She used what she had to get what she wanted. Nor is she the first person to steal somebody else's ideas and pass them off as her own.' His glance was shrewd. 'But that's not what bothers you, is it? Nor the fact that she was the mistress of both a communist and a secret policeman. What's bugging you is that you don't know which one of them was your father, right?'

'If he was one of those three.'

'To know that you'll have to ask her.'

'I intend to – once I'm in possession of all the facts.'

There was a second of silence then Max said, 'Well, that's something you'll have to handle on your own, kid. All I can say is it doesn't matter a damn to me who your father was. You are you and that's all that counts.'

'I still think of John Brent as my father,' Alex said, when she could. 'In every sense except the biological one he was – is – my father and I shall always regard him as such. Finding out who impregnated my mother won't change anything.'

Max said nothing. That's what you think, he thought. But he resolved to be around when she did. Alex thought she had every last emotion incarcerated under the implacable security of reason, but he knew her far better than she did herself, and he didn't give a damn how many degrees she had. He would put common sense above every academic qualification there was in existence, because no matter if you had a dozen of them, if you had no common sense you were a fool, and though Alex's own common sense was robust enough, she still tended not to use enough of it where her feelings for her mother were concerned. And if she didn't have any she wouldn't be wasting her time on this particular witchhunt, he thought.

'Right,' he said briskly, 'so where do we go from here?'

'The next couple of years are what I call the Henri Beyle years: the time *Essence of Eve* was created.'

'Around 1961–3 – he died a few years before I joined the company,' Max said. 'Your mother had a picture of him on the wall of her office at that time. A few years later it vanished.'

'Do you know anything about those years?'

'Only what your mother has leaked, but I know someone who does.' He smiled in the face of Alex's quick flare of interest which just as quickly turned into a 'I might have known' smile of resignation.

'Henri Beyle's chief *parfumeur*. An old man named Jean Vernier. A Swiss, like Beyle, now living in honourable retirement in his native village somewhere in the Jura.'

'How do you know?'

'Your mother pays him a pension.'

Now he shook his head at Alex's stunned surprise. 'You see . . . you were sure she would have buried him too, weren't you? Instead of which she's been paying him a pension for the past twenty some years – and a good one too. Out of her own pocket because Vernier officially worked for the Beyle Corporation, which also pays him a pension. I think it was old Vernier who created *Essence of Eve*, and his pension is your mother's way of showing her gratitude. She's made more millions than could pay out twice ten thousand pensions from the sales of that fragrance.'

'When can I see him?' Alex asked.

'As soon as I can set it up. How – er – or should I say who are you supposed to be when we meet him? I doubt if he knows about you.'

'I told Marion Gilchrist I was researching a biography – the authorized one.'

'Good, good. And with me along that will make it even more official.'

'The Jura!' Mora said, annoyed. 'What on earth for?'

'Business,' Max said blandly.

'Since when has Alex Brent had anything to do with the real world?'

'Every bit as long as you have,' Max told her cheerfully. He dropped a swift kiss on her sulky mouth. 'Keep a light in the window.'

'Why do I get a feeling those two are up to something?' Moya said broodingly to Pamela, as they watched the bright red Mercedes Sports roar off down the drive.

'Max and Alex? Oh, they're twin souls, as close as you can get in a platonic relationship.'

'What other kind could any man have with Alex Brent?' Mora asked contemptuously. 'She's built like a percheron and has the looks to match.'

'There's much more to Alex than her looks,' Pamela said coldly, 'and if she does nothing with them it's because her mother's brainwashed her into thinking there's nothing that *can* be done.'

'Well, Eve should know.'

'Alex has lovely eyes,' Pamela said, 'and her skin is flawless.'

'And colourless.'

'Because it only ever sees soap and water. If only she'd use blusher it would make all the difference, because she's got beautiful bones.'

'Obliterated by that nose. I think,' Mora said, from her position as acknowledged beauty, 'that a woman owes it to herself to make the most of everything she's got. I have, you have, and we haven't done so badly.'

'I doubt if what we've done would be considered worthwhile by Alex.'

'Oh, she measures everything by the brainstick. To be honest, I can't think why she came over here in the first place. I've spent more time with Eve than she ever has.'

'Chris was her brother –'

'– half-brother.'

'Eve is mother to both of them. I happen to know that Alex was deeply fond of Chris, as he was of her, and he admired her too.'

'What on earth for?'

'If you don't know it would be a waste of my time telling you.'

Pamela left the room to return to the little church where Chris's bronze coffin lay, because soon, there wouldn't even be that to sit close to; he would be burned to ashes and she would really be alone. But until then, just being close to him was a kind of comfort. But when she opened the door of the little white-painted church, its flagged floor bathed in multi-coloured lozenges of light from the stained-glass windows, she saw that someone was already there, kneeling on the steps by the flower-piled coffin; a woman in black, heavily veiled. It was only when, her footsteps echoing on the stones no matter how quietly she tried to walk, she reached the steps, bowed, then knelt herself, that she caught the glint of red-gold hair beneath the black lace. As if feeling Pamela's surprised eyes, Eve turned her head, and for a long moment the two women looked deep into each other. Then Eve inclined her head in acknowledgement, as though bestowing on Pamela the right to mourn the young man they had both loved.

Jean Vernier lived in a neat little house, looked after by his eldest daughter, a widow whose children had moved away. He was very old, bent and twisted like a gnarled old tree, and he peered at them with rheumy eyes.

'He doesn't see so well but he hears,' his daughter said. 'His arthritis makes him fractious, so I would ask you not to make him talk too long. He tends to move when he talks and it causes him pain, but he is always pleased to have visitors from Madame.'

'Thank you,' Alex said gratefully. 'We won't keep him long.'

His daughter bent over the old man. 'Here is Mr Fabian from the Company to see you, and a young lady who is writing a biography of Madame. They would like you to tell them about how you created *Essence of Eve*.'

The old man nodded, waved her away irritably. 'I am not deaf,' he said.

The small room on the ground floor where he sat overlooked the street, and although spotlessly tidy, smelled of old age and medication.

'So . . . . you are Monsieur Fabian,' the old man nodded on a smile. 'I know the name from the cheques, of course. I hope you haven't come to tell me there will be no more. I don't know what I would do without them.' The faded eyes peered keenly at Max.

'No, I haven't come to tell you that. The cheques will continue as long as you do.'

The old man nodded. 'I did not think Madame would treat me unfairly. And who is this?'

Max introduced Alex by her real name, which elicited no recognition, and then explained that she was researching the life of Eve Czerny preparatory to writing the authorized biography of her life. 'She would be most interested to hear anything you have to tell her about the creation of *Essence of Eve*,' Max said.

'Ah . . . yes, such a perfume! I created many but that one – that one took me the most time and gave me the most trouble. So difficult!'

'But so sublime,' Max praised encouragingly. 'It is still, even now, the company's bestselling perfume.'

'I am glad to hear it, for it cost a great deal of money to create. A fortune was spent on it, a fortune . . . but Monsieur Beyle told me that I was to do as Madame Czerny wanted and so – I did.'

'Was it her idea, then?' Alex asked.

'Oh, yes, the *idea* was hers . . . everything about that particular fragrance was in her mind. She had no idea of the complexities of a perfume, no idea at all – nor did she care. She knew – here –' the old man lifted a claw of a hand to his forehead – 'that it existed, and all I had to go on were the words she used to describe it. You can imagine the difficulties with which I was faced! A *parfumeur* too has an idea, but he knows on what it is based. She did not. Oh, she knew of what a perfume consisted, but nothing of proportions, blending, top notes, base notes. She was no scientist; she was instinctive, with a genius for spotting what was absolutely *right*. And for months all I did was wrong. Every fragrance I came up with was "almost, but not quite". She would lose her patience, I my temper. A difficult woman . . .' The old man shook his head. 'A most demanding woman, but what she wanted, she said, was a crystallized essence of all that was female. I ask you! I could not make a perfume with words!' The old man smiled reminiscently. 'But that is how it was made . . . each time I created something, she would smell it, apply it, walk about, sit with her eyes closed and then she would say: "Too aggressive. This demands to be noticed. What I am after is something that wreathes itself around you so that before you know it – you are captive." And I would go away and change a proportion, or exchange bergamot for jasmine or vice versa and then try again. Twenty-seven fragrances I created before she found what she wanted. Twenty-seven!'

'At least six of which we are selling right now,' Max said.

'Of course,' the old man said simply. 'A Vernier fragrance is a great fragrance.'

'Yet it is Madame Czerny whose name – the only name – is associated with *Essence of Eve*,' Alex pointed out.

'Of course. Can you tell me the name of the man who created *Chanel No. 5*? Or *Arpège*? Besides, it was really hers. I invented it but using her inspiration; her infallible sense of what was absolutely *right*. And all it took, when I brought her the stiletto with a drop of the fragrance on its bulb, was one sniff . . . if you had seen her face, heard her cry of joy . . .' The old man sighed. 'That was a day . . . a great day . . . She danced, she sang, she kissed and hugged me –'

'And Monsieur Beyle,' Alex asked after allowing the old man to wallow in his memories for a while. 'What was his part in all this?'

'To provide the money. He knew what she was, you see.'

'And what was that?' Alex asked.

'Why, a shooting star, of course, a veritable comet! Once in a generation such a woman comes along and when Monsieur Beyle recognized her he at once hitched his wagon. He was enormously proud of her; she was his protégée.'

'And his mistress?'

'So they said, but I do not believe it. Monsieur Beyle loved her like a daughter. Madame shared his dreams. His own children did not care about what he did – but Madame had the vision, the daring, the dreams, and he saw in her himself when young, for he was thirty years older when they met and knew he was dying.'

'Dying!' Alex had never imagined this.

'He had bone cancer. That is why *I* was chosen to create *Essence of Eve*. His powers were failing; for the last year of his life he was bedridden, and had it not been for Madame I do not think he would have lasted that long. Which Madame Beyle knew. She not only allowed, she encouraged Madame to visit, for it was her success, her fame, what she did with what he had helped create, that made him want to live as long as he could to see it. When he died, it was her hand he was holding.'

Max was watching Alex's face. It was stunned with surprise.

'And afterwards, when I retired, she made – arrangements. Every year there is a hamper from Maxim's – she remembers how fond I was of good food and wine – and every month, a cheque. Creating *Essence of Eve* took many months and a deal of hard work, but I cannot deny that I have been well rewarded.'

The old man nodded, satisfied with himself and his grateful *patronne*.

On their way back to Geneva Max asked: 'Another of the faces of Eve?'

'How many are there?'

'A word of advice, kid. You tend to see things either in black or in white. Your mother's whole life is in glorious technicolour. Either change the film or get a new camera.'

'I can only see her as she was with me. Did you hear what that old man said about her hugging and kissing him once he had come up with what she wanted? Well, let me tell you something. My mother has never so much as touched me in my entire life. Did you

172

know that? Not one hug, not one kiss, not so much as a handshake! Now tell me about all that glorious colour!'

Ah, Christ! Max thought. That bloody mountain of hurt is still blocking her view. How the hell do I get enough dynamite to level that? 'Look, kid,' he said patiently. 'Your mother has gone to some pains to conceal her early years. Her Hungarian beginnings are a period she obviously wants to erase. You were conceived in Hungary, remember? And whoever your father was he must have played a vital part in those early years. You are – unfortunately – a reminder of something she would rather forget. So much so that she has been trying to forget you since the day you were born.'

'Then why is she asking for my forgiveness now?'

'I can't tell you. That's something you have to ask her. And the sooner the better. The funeral is the day after tomorrow. Time, my girl, is of the essence.'

'*Essence of Eve*,' Alex said bitterly. 'It stinks!'

12

———❧❧❧———

New York, 1965–7

As soon as Edith Bingham heard of Eve's frenzied reaction to her husband's death, she acted immediately to forestall any unwelcome publicity. Fortunately, her eldest daughter Charlotte was in Paris buying clothes, and Edith called her at once to instruct her to leave for Switzerland and take over.

'There must be no exhibitions, Charlotte. I am told she is sedated, and that was necessary because it seems she tried to kill herself.'

'Good God!'

'Exactly. I will not have my son's death turned into a three-ring circus due to the kind of woman he married. I am sending Edwin Morris over to take charge of her physical well-being. He has been my doctor for thirty-five years and he can be trusted.' To keep his mouth shut, remained unsaid. 'Edwin will decide whether she is fit to travel to the funeral. If she has to come in a state of drugged unconsciousness so be it: I would rather have her here, where we can take care of things, than three thousand miles away where anything might happen. I am relying on you, Charlotte, to see that things are done in the right manner. You understand what I mean.'

'Only too well.'

'I know you don't like her, but we must allow for the fact that she is obviously devastated by what has happened.'

'Aren't we all?'

'Yes, but we know how to act under such circumstances. We have to remember that she isn't one of Us. I believe the Hungarian people tend to be somewhat emotional. I will arrange for a plane to bring you all back. In the meantime I will make all the arrangements here. Oh, and Charlotte –'

'Yes, Mother?'

'See that her black is our kind of mourning.'

When Charlotte arrived at the villa it was to find that Eve was deeply sedated and her own doctor, a Swiss, in charge. When Charlotte told him that her own family doctor was coming to escort the widow back to the United States for the funeral he pursed his lips in a way that said he would not wish that ordeal on anybody.

'She will be fit to travel?' Charlotte asked.

'That depends on how soon you wish her to leave.'

'No later than the day after tomorrow. My brother's funeral is on Friday. Now, may I see her?'

'If you wish.'

Eve was deeply unconscious in the enormous double bed she had shared with her husband; her face was waxy white, its bloom dulled, and her wrists were bandaged.

'I thought she tried to throw herself into the lake?' Charlotte observed.

'She did. When that didn't work she smashed a glass in her bathroom and slashed her wrists. Fortunately, the noise was heard and she was saved.'

Charlotte regarded her sister-in-law with some curiosity. She hadn't believed that Eve Czerny had married for love, though she knew that her brother had. Now it seemed she must revise that opinion. Except that she does tend to the melodramatic, she thought, distastefully. Let's hope she remains sedated until Christopher is safe in the Bingham tomb. It really will be better all round. The thought of what she might do otherwise hardly bears thinking about.

'Now,' she said, turning away, 'I should like to see my nephew.'

Eve made the journey to New York so deeply sedated that ever afterwards she remembered nothing about it. Only Eve, Dr Morris, Charlotte, Christopher and his nanny, together with a nurse Dr Morris had brought along just in case, travelled in the first-class compartment of the private jet, and at JFK they were met by a private ambulance which transferred Eve to the Bingham House in the upper Seventies between Madison and Fifth Avenues, where she was left in the care of her nurse in a suite that had once been the only residence of a Bingham daughter who had, around the time of the First World War, been born retarded. It had only one door to the rest of the house, and was on the third floor, at the back, where the barred windows aroused no comment.

She was carried up the magnificent staircase on a stretcher, past the masses of flowers which turned the great marble entrance hall into a king-sized florist's. Just off it, in the main reception room, her husband's casket was lying, also completely covered in flowers. On the day of the funeral, she was still preventatively sedated, and it was Mrs Bingham Senior who led the mourners, erect and commanding in her black mourning veils, followed by her daughters, their husbands and their elder children, the myriad uncles, aunts and cousins following behind.

It was a big funeral. 'But then, old Chris was well liked,' one old schoolfriend from Groton days commented to another.

'Especially by women.' They both looked round the packed church.

'But where's his wife?'

'I hear she's drugged to the eyeballs. Billy Hampshire told me that he had it from Dolly Talbot, whose cousin is married to a Swiss and lives in Geneva, that Eve Czerny tried to commit suicide when they told her what had happened.'

'Really! Edith Bingham wouldn't like that. She's a stickler for the proprieties.'

'And always thought her son married beneath him.'

'Well, a look round these pews tells me they are filled with women Chris had beneath him at one time or another.'

The organ began to play and, with a rustle, the congregation rose to its feet.

'Not an empty seat in the house,' the schoolfriend said. 'And they couldn't get all the flowers in, I hear.'

'Not to mention the population of the North Shore.'

Through all this, Eve lay oblivious in the big bedroom overlooking the Bingham garden, deep in dreamless stupefaction.

Three days later, she was awake when her mother-in-law entered her bedroom.

'How are you, Eve?' she asked. She was in black, very simple, very expensive black, a twenty-inch rope of pearls and matching earrings her only jewellery.

Eve said nothing. Her face was that of someone struggling to understand. 'Why?' she asked.

'Why what?'

'Why did Christopher have to die?'

'It was a tragic accident. Polo is a dangerous game. We must be thankful that he didn't suffer. His neck was broken instantly.' Her voice was calm, steady. Her tears had been shed in the solitude of her bedroom.

'But why?' Eve asked again.

Obviously, her mother-in-law thought, she is not yet out of her fog. 'Life does not always give us reasons,' she said.

'Well *I* want one,' Eve said. For a minute it was the old Eve; arrogant, insufferably sure of herself. 'There is always a reason,' she said, 'for everything.'

'His horse stumbled,' Edith Bingham said, 'and he fell under the hooves of another one. One of them struck his head and broke his neck. That is the reason my son is dead.' The measured calm with which she spoke was all part of her upbringing. One did not expose one's feelings to the embarrassment of others. Losing her son was a devastating blow but something deeply private. Nor had she ever really regarded her son's second wife as part of the family.

'If you wish, when you feel up to it, we will go together to visit his grave,' she said. 'Would you like to know about the funeral?'

'No,' Eve said. 'I do not wish to know about death. I do not accept this death. There was no reason!'

She could make no sense of it, try as she might, and ever since she had opened her eyes, realized where she was, what had happened, she had been doing her best. Why, after leading her so carefully through the highways and byways of high risk and low cunning, to the man she knew she would eventually find, who would give her all the things she had decided she would have at the age of seven, had Fate allowed her only four short years with him? What was the point of that? She had been meant to live happily ever after. There had been no mention of death in the script she had read. Had there been she would have insisted it be changed. There had to be some reason for all this. If only she could find it.

'It has all been a terrible shock,' Edith Bingham said, 'and you are still upset.'

Of her own terrible sense of loss she said nothing. 'And you have your son to live for.' While I no longer have mine, she thought.

'Where is he?' Eve asked.

'Upstairs, in the nursery. He has company. Hester's two youngest are with him. He is quite happy.' She paused. 'I am so sorry you lost your baby.' Which would have been another Bingham male. *Your* fault, Edith Bingham thought.

Eve turned her head away.

'Life must go on,' Edith Bingham said. She herself had been receiving condolences for what seemed like for ever, and explaining away her daughter-in-law's non-appearance. 'She is terribly shocked,' she had said so many times, 'and as an – emotional – person, she is finding it very difficult to accept her husband's death.'

Now, she saw that she had spoken no more than the truth. She herself had buried deep within her, as was the way she had been taught, her sense of loss, her grief, her own feeling of the senselessness of it all, but something about her daughter-in-law made her uneasy. She had the feeling that Eve wanted answers, and that if she didn't get them, heads would roll. Eve Czerny, she understood, was not a woman to accept anything without questioning why, but she had her own questions and they had to be answered before Eve returned to her own life, the one that had nothing to do with the Binghams and theirs.

'You have a company to run,' she said. 'Christopher told me that it is growing more and more successful and takes a great deal of your time.'

'I always had time for Christopher.'

'I am aware of that.' Edith Bingham was a just woman and she had to admit that her son had been happy in his second marriage. For that reason alone she had been prepared to accept Eve, in spite of not being able either to like or trust her. A woman with the powerful weapon of beauty was always dangerous. 'He was very proud of your success, and I am glad to think that you will have something to – occupy you. That being so, would it not be for the best if you left young Christopher with me? He is, after all, a Bingham.'

Eve turned her head so that she could look her mother-in-law straight in the eyes. 'No,' she said. 'My son stays with me.'

'You could visit him whenever you wished.'

'No.'

Edith Bingham was silent. The thought of Eve Czerny, widow, rich from the profits her company made, even richer because of the

Bingham money left her by her husband, living what Edith knew would be anything but a retiring widowhood she found disturbing. The thought of her grandson – now *the* Bingham, the only Bingham male in a line that had come down through more than three hundred years – being presented, as she knew with absolute certainty that he would be, with a succession of stepfathers was one she found utterly abhorrent. But she decided not to press. It had been too much to hope, she thought wearily, that her daughter-in-law would sail out of her life, like a liner slipping its cables, leaving Christopher Bingham V where he belonged.

Well, she thought, for the foreseeable future at least, Eve is Mrs Christopher Bingham, and her son is heir to the name and its fortune. I owe it to both to see that neither is dishonoured.

'I will leave you to rest,' she said, rising.

'I want to see my son,' Eve said. 'Please have him brought to me.'

Edith recognized the command. 'Of course. I will give the necessary instructions.'

She had to go and receive yet more condolence calls. Perhaps it was as well that Eve occupied herself elsewhere. She wanted no repeat of what had taken place in Switzerland, of which Charlotte had told her in sickening detail, but of which nobody else knew. Or ever would know. Edith had arranged for the family lawyers to talk to those who knew what had happened and ensure that all loose tongues were tied. Thank God it was in Switzerland, she thought, as she went to give orders regarding her grandson. Nobody is ever there at this time of year.

Eve's return to the world was as carefully stage-managed as everything else in her life which concerned the public. She remained in seclusion for a further week after her husband's funeral and then, clad in unrelieved black, she made a supposedly unannounced and solitary visit to his grave. When her mother-in-law saw the pictures in the newspapers the next day, she went at once to Eve to ask how on earth they could have been taken.

'It's my fault, I'm afraid,' Eve said. 'I mentioned the visit to my lawyer and I can only assume that he tipped off the press. He is, of course, no longer my lawyer.' Only because he was retiring, to her annoyance; he was very good at what he did, which was watching out for her interests at all times. All he had done was casually mention the fact to someone whom he knew was 'feeder' to a well known columnist, and the rest all came about as he knew it would.

'Call it my swansong,' he had said, when Eve called to thank him. 'Great publicity and it sets up your new image a treat.'

'What am I going to do without you, Jerry?' Eve asked.

'Manage. I'm not doing this because I want to, you know. I'm doing it because my doctors tell me that if I don't I'm going to be doing nothing at all because I'll be dead. I'm sixty-seven years old and I've been working since I was twelve. I should have had this bypass done years ago but I always had a client who needed me . . . Isn't it enough to be mourning a husband? I don't want you should be mourning a lawyer too.'

Eve looked at the front pages of the tabloids, at the picture of herself, head up, shoulders back, her veils drifting out behind her in the brisk breeze, 'Winged Victory in Black', one headline said. 'The majesty of grief,' said another, 'as Empress of Beauty mourns her tragic loss'. It established her new image firmly in the public's mind. It also angered her mother-in-law.

'What did you want with your lawyer?' Edith demanded icily of Eve.

'I wanted his advice about Christopher's will.'

'That is in the hands of the family's lawyers, Sloane, Ransom, who have been handling our affairs for several generations. Your own lawyer is not concerned in any way.' Edith paused. 'However, I would like to talk to you about what my son has done.'

The will had been read a few days previously. Christopher Bingham IV had left his entire estate to his son, in trust until his twenty-fifth birthday should he inherit before then. His mother was his sole Trustee and would receive unconditional use of the income until Christopher came of age.

'My grandson is now heir to a great fortune,' Edith Bingham said, 'the Bingham fortune, and as a Bingham I think he should remain with me so that he can be prepared, in the proper manner, for his great responsibilities.'

'My son's place is with me,' Eve said. 'I will see that he learns his responsibilities, for Christopher is also heir to my own not inconsiderable fortune, *and* my company.'

'I do not think the two can be compared.'

'Why not? What was Matthew Bingham but a lawyer's clerk when he arrived in New York? He made his money because he was shrewd enough to buy land when he was given the tip-off through his employer's clients. His descendants sold that land at vast profit which they invested in other, even more profitable enterprises. My own business is every bit as profitable. Helena Rubenstein is dead and so, now, is Elizabeth Arden. A vacancy has arisen which I intend to fill. In time, Christopher too will occupy that position.'

'A Bingham running a cosmetics company? When there is a bank, a railroad, several newspapers, a whole string of television and radio stations, not to mention a shipping line!'

'Did you know,' Eve asked, 'that the cosmetics industry is a multi-billion-dollar business? That American women alone spend two of those billions in a year, and that I have a high percentage of that market?'

Edith Bingham was staggered. The total worth of the entire Bingham fortune was less than what was spent on cosmetics in twelve short months, and it had taken three hundred years to build. For the first time, she began to perceive the vastness of her daughter-in-law's undertaking.

'Christopher will be an enormously rich man one day,' Eve said, twisting the knife, 'but it will not be because of what his father left him. It will be because of what his mother *made*.'

She left her mother-in-law too stunned to speak.

She returned to Europe on the *Queen Mary*, spending her days playing with her son in the suite on A Deck, her nights pondering over the pieces on her own particular chessboard. Her best therapy, she knew instinctively, was work. Christopher was dead, and although she missed him desperately, there was nothing she could do to bring him back. She, on the other hand, was very much alive, for had not Fate stepped in twice to keep her so? She had been utterly shocked, on coming out from under her trauma, to learn that she had twice tried to kill herself. She had no recollection of either time, and had it not been for the bandages on her wrists, the healing wounds which were already forming ridges of scar tissue under her fingertips, she would not have believed it possible for her to do so stupid a thing, not once but twice! She could vaguely recall feelings of rage, grief, pain and a frantic desire to follow Christopher to wherever he had gone – to demand to know what the hell he was playing at and bring him back – but now that she was back to herself again she was at a loss to account for these feelings, for after all, even if Christopher was dead, she was still his widow, still Mrs Christopher Bingham IV. All that he had given her, all that he had brought her to, all that she had loved him for, were still hers.

Yet she found she missed his presence, did not sleep as deeply or as well as she was used to, because she had become accustomed, after four years, to sleeping with him. These mornings she awoke early, just as dawn was beginning to lighten the sky, and though at first she had tried to go back to sleep, she had soon realized there was no point and so now used the time to work on her plans. She also missed the sex; more than anything she missed the sex. Her body hungered for him, and she was loath to avail herself of either of the remedies: a lover or self-release. The first was out in these early days of widowhood because it was too dangerous; men liked to boast, and to brag about having slept with Eve Czerny was something a man would never be able to resist. Masturbation, on the other hand, was something she regarded with distaste. It was something she associated with women who were unable to obtain sexual fulfilment in any other way. She had neither time nor patience for the feminists who said it was the only *true* way.

No, she thought, this is something I will have to dominate, that's all. I concentrated on Christopher too much and look what happened to him. I must never make that mistake again. I have a destiny to fulfil, and what *I* want comes second, not first. Why else have I just been taught this particular lesson? Perhaps, she thought, in time, I will marry again. The trouble is that I cannot marry just anybody. He has to be on a level with what I have already had or even better. Well, she thought, it's fruitless to speculate now, when I am only just a widow. Time will tell, and that time must be used wisely. She drew a pad and pencil towards her and began to make a rough schedule of her movements over the next six months.

She did not return to Geneva; she went instead to Paris, where she had a permanent suite at the Georges V and the name of a very good plastic surgeon. He erased all traces of the scars on her wrists, so well that she offered him an exorbitant amount of money and undreamed-of facilities in a purpose-built clinic she intended to build in the hills above Geneva where he could put nips and tucks in the sagging flesh of very rich, no longer young ladies who went in morbid fear of looking old.

That done, she summoned her head *visagiste* and consulted him as to the way Eve Czerny, widow, should be presented to the world. It would be three months exactly, on the day she planned to return to the working world, and she wanted her appearance to be in keeping. He advised a change of hairstyle. Christopher had liked her hair long, so she had grown it for him, he used to like to wrap it around his throat . . . Now, it was long enough to coil into a heavy chignon, and though it was a more severe hairstyle than she usually wore, it was in direct contrast to the eggbeater school of hairdressing then in vogue, and it showed off the classic oval of her face, the flawless line of her jaw, the deep-set jewelled eyes, the luscious mouth, to perfection. She asked Hubert de Givenchy to design her a series of little black suits, each one with only the merest hint of colour in a button, a jacket lining, a sleeve trim, worn with shiny alligator shoes and matching handbag. Eve rarely wore hats unless they were called for.

Again, the press was discreetly salted with photographs and articles. She gave no interviews, posed for no photographs, but she always, somehow, managed to make an appearance in at least one newspaper every week. All the time she stayed in Paris, driving to her office in that city every day, spending time in her factory in Neuilly, conferring with her executives. She went to no parties, attended no dinners and did not entertain. Her seclusion resulted, as she had known it would, in a brushfire of gossip. 'Poor Eve,' they said, 'too shattered to go back to Geneva. Can't face it without him.' But it was amazing how a widow, working quietly, living in seclusion, managed to get so much newspaper coverage.

'Perhaps she has a lover on *Le Matin*,' somebody said.

'Or gives his wife free facials.'

'I think you are being unfair,' somebody else said. 'Whatever she is –'

'Autocratic –'

'Ruthless –'

'Ambitious –'

'Vain –'

'All of those and more, all right, but what she isn't is a Merry

Widow, and what I would like to know is why the newspapers keep on reminding us of that fact? What is she up to?'

It was June before Eve could bring herself to return to Geneva, and even then it was a spur of the moment thing. She sent a telegram announcing her arrival – or gave instructions for such a telegram to be sent – but when she arrived it was to find the villa shuttered and quiet, sleeping away the hot afternoon. Her face, when Jacques opened the front door, was thunderous.

'Faugh!' she spat, as her nose sniffed stale air. 'This place smells like it's been buried! Open the windows, let some fresh air in. Why is nothing ready? Did you not receive my instructions to open up the house? Why is everything shrouded and shuttered?'

'We have received no instructions, Madame,' Jacques said stiffly.

'No telegram from Paris?'

'Nothing, Madame.'

Eve drew a deep breath. 'We will soon find out why,' she said, and strode towards the library, whose double-doors Giacomo, the little Italian houseman, had just flung open wide before scurrying to fold back the shutters and open the windows.

Once Eve had fired the secretary who had failed to send the telegram she had relieved her edgy irritation somewhat, but her mood was such that the staff hurried about their various tasks in silence, stripping off dust sheets, polishing, dusting, airing. Eve sat in the library once Christopher had been taken upstairs to his nursery by his nanny, and issued orders like a teleprinter. There was a pile of mail, but most of it was unimportant: all that mattered had been sent on long ago.

She felt irritable, scratchy, could not bring herself to go upstairs and take one of her cool, scented baths. The weather was humid. Not long out of black, she was wearing a cool linen sheath of palest lilac, but she felt sticky and hot. I should not have come back, she thought; too many memories, too much emptiness . . . Oh, Christopher, I miss you so . . . She rested her head on her propped hands. Suddenly she heard a noise, as of something dropping, and instinctively looked upwards. On top of the sliding ladder, which was used to reach the topmost shelves, a child was crouched, eyes wide, face pale, trying to merge with the bookshelves, her eyes, round and stricken, enlarged by the glasses she wore. For a long moment their eyes met, then Eve turned away to pick up the house telephone and stab viciously at one of the buttons.

'Miss Patterson? I want to see you at once. In the library.' She slammed down the receiver and stalked, stiff-legged, over to the open windows, where she stood breathing deeply, inhaling the scent of the crowded bushes of Malmaison roses which grew just below them.

When Miss Patterson came in she said, 'You wanted me, Madame?'

'What is that child doing here?' Eve asked in an icy voice.

Margaret Patterson instinctively looked up and saw Alex. Damn! she thought. 'Come down, Alex,' she said quietly.

Quickly the child scrambled down the ladder, scuttled to where Miss Patterson stood and tried to hide behind her.

'I'm sorry, Madame,' Margaret Patterson said. 'While you are not in residence Alex borrows books to read.'

'Who gave her permission to do that?'

'No one, Madame. I took it upon myself . . . She has read and re-read all her own books – she reads quickly and widely, and there are so many in here. Now you are back I will, of course, see that she keeps to her own floor.'

There was a silence. Governess and child waited.

Margaret Patterson felt a small hand take hold of hers and hold it tightly. She looked down, smiled reassuringly. 'It's all right,' she mouthed.

'Tell me,' Eve said, 'does that clergyman still call?'

'Yes, Madame. He was here only last week, and the week before that.'

'He comes often?'

'It varies. Sometimes three weeks on the trot then not for a month or so. We never know when he is coming.'

Damned old man, Eve thought. That means that Mary Brent is still alive. Why doesn't she die? She must be near it, surely. Until she realized that even now, Mary Brent could not be more than seventy. She could live for years yet.

'Very well,' Eve said, 'but I do not wish to see either of you in this part of the house, do I make myself clear? You have a whole floor to yourselves. Use it.' She swung to face Margaret Patterson. She did not look at the child. 'I give you a free hand, Miss Patterson.

185

You are in sole charge. Whatever you need, buy it. I do not want these books used by anyone. Some of them are very valuable.'

'Alex has a great respect for, as well as love of, books,' Margaret Patterson said evenly.

'I do not care what she has, those are my orders. Now take her away.' Margaret turned, and taking Alex by the hand, led her out of the room, closing the door quietly behind them.

Eve turned back to the window, but her breathing was shallow and her cheeks were flushed. With a sound that was almost a shriek she reached out to the china cupid – Meissen – which stood on a small table near the window and hurled it, with all her strength, against one of the bookcases. It struck, shattered musically, and fell in shards to the floor. Eve drew in then released a quivering breath. Then she buried her face in her hands.

A month later she left on a trip around the world, during which she would visit every salon, every outlet, every factory, every warehouse, every laboratory. It would take her the rest of the year. With her she took her current secretary – they never lasted long because they could not stand the pace or the workload – and the lawyer she had hired to replace Jerry Spiers, now recovering from his triple bypass. She did not take her son. Her heart longed to, her head told her it would not be fair on him. He was only three and a bit, after all. She left him with his grandmother. It would do him no harm to learn that he was also a Bingham, and with his father's family he would learn all about the man his father had been, for Edith Bingham's sitting-room was now filled with photographs of her son. Eve promised she would call from every city and bring him a present from every country.

Her first stop was California, where she went through her salons in Los Angeles and San Francisco like a forest fire, leaving them frantically replanting. From there she flew to Tokyo, where she was not yet established. By the time she left, she was. From there she went to Hong Kong where, over ten days, she inspected, negotiated and bought a site for a new factory. She had been shipping to the colony from London; her shrewd brain soon appreciated the fact that she could save money by manufacturing *in situ* for the entire Far Eastern market.

From Hong Kong she flew to Sydney, where the leathery skins of the sunbaked Australian women had her exhorting them to use her Renaissance Cream and her new Revitalizer, which replaced essential oils. 'I swear to you . . .' she would say to them seriously, fixing them with her extraordinary eyes, 'if I live to be a hundred, there is no better cream on the market than this one! Try it and see . . . I will give you your money back if I am not proved right.' Her success in Sydney was repeated in Melbourne, in Adelaide, in Perth.

Then, from Australia, they flew to Madrid. They arrived on a Saturday, and the salon was due to be opened the following Monday. She was proudly led around by the manager she had appointed, who extolled the subtle colours, the delicate shadings.

'Wrong!' Eve said. 'Wrong, wrong, WRONG! It has to be changed – now!'

'Changed!'

'The colours are not what is needed here. This is a southern country, a hot country! These are pastel, northern shades! The colours I sell here are not the colours I sell in Scandinavia, you fool, where the women are of entirely different colouring and skin composition! This has to be changed by Monday morning. The painters must start at once and work through tomorrow.'

'But – but Madame. Tomorrow is *Sunday*!'

'So?'

Her hard stare had the manager scurrying off to do as he was bid. When the painters arrived next day, Eve was waiting for them. They were surly, but being Spaniards, lubriciously appreciative of her face and figure, even in the painter's overalls she was wearing. Eve recognized the look and smiled. Child's play . . . By the time lunch – a superb Spanish lunch with great wines – was served, she had them utterly fascinated as she told them how she formulated the colours for her lipsticks and proceeded to do the same with paint: she beat in the yolks of a dozen eggs to get the perfect shade of sunshine yellow. 'For you, Señora,' they promised, much impressed, 'anything.' And they laboured right through Sunday and all through the night, so that by the time Eve returned for the opening reception, this time wearing a Balenciaga suit which elicited an appreciative chorus of '¡Ayie, que mujer!' and '¡Mire la belleza!', they were quite unprepared for the five thousand peseta bonus they shared among them.

That night, squired by the manager who had told his furious wife: 'When La Señora says you go – you go; when she says come

– you come. And that is all there is to it', she attended a ball given in one of the staterooms of the Palacio Real, where she wore a fabulous gown – again Balenciaga, of smoke-grey pure silk chiffon - and hogged all the press notices.

She flew on to Rome where she was so infuriated by her regional manager that she struck him hard enough to floor him. Her secretary, exhausted to the point of a nervous breakdown, collapsed with a temperature of 104° and was carted away to hospital. 'Is there nobody I can rely on?' Eve shouted. 'Why am I surrounded by fools and weaklings!'

Somebody coughed. She swung on him. 'What's the matter with you?'

'Nothing, Madame, I just thought – if you need help. I know somebody who might be of use to you . . . He speaks Italian – he is of Italian stock although he was born in America and –'

'Get him!'

Eve was at her desk, sipping from a glass of champagne – she always drank champagne because she claimed it never made her drunk or sleepy as ordinary wine did, since she drank it so cold it numbed the teeth – and looked at the man standing in front of her. Far too young, she thought. She asked him how old.

'Twenty-three.'

'Do you work?'

'I will when I get back home. I'm a lawyer. I intend to hang out my shingle once I get myself the right office.'

'Why are you in Rome?'

'Visiting my mother's family. They run a garment factory out in Trastevere.'

'Can you work under pressure?'

Massimo Fabiani grinned. 'I've been doing that for the past seven weeks.'

'Do you know anything about the cosmetics business?'

'I can tell one shade of lipstick from another but that's about all.'

The phone rang. Eve picked it up, listened. 'No I will not,' Max heard her say, in a voice that would have crushed granite. 'He ordered that consignment and he is going to keep it. I have his signed order and if he tries to weasel out of it I'll sue. Tell him that!' She slammed the phone down.

'So you are a lawyer,' Eve said thoughtfully. She was anything but satisfied with the one she had. To begin with, he was of a nervous disposition and tended to stutter whenever he spoke to her. It undermined her confidence in him and tried her patience.

'Do you take dictation?' she asked.

'Yes. I was a court reporter during vacations.'

'You're hired.'

He was a godsend. He was one of the few people who ever understood Eve Czerny, and because he understood her he never underestimated her. He was the only one who could persuade her to do what deep down she knew was the right thing to do even if, as she was wont to do now and again, she said she was against it. He realized she was more quixotic than the Don himself, and always made allowances for that fact. By the time they left Rome for Milan, he was already indispensable, because in just two short weeks she had learned that if she told him to do a thing it would be done, and done properly. He was quick to learn, an astute wheeler-dealer and, being Italian, up to every trick in the book.

Max found Eve to be an exhausting travelling companion. She worked on average an eighteen-hour day and was up with the sun, but she could do it because she was able to take catnaps at any time and in any situation. She even slept on cab rides from one part of the city to another. She could be riding in the back seat with Max, close her eyes and be asleep at once. She slept all the way in the train to Milan, where she was to stay with her friend, and oldest client in that city, Mina Riringhetti, the wife of the man who made most of the shoes Italians wore.

Max, who had expected a couple of days off because Milan was a social rather than business trip, was taking a well-earned rest on the bed in his single room in the hotel to which he had been consigned, when the phone rang. It was Eve.

'Have you a dinner jacket with you?'

'No.'

'Then go out and buy one. A good one. You are escorting me to La Scala tonight.'

'My God . . .' Max had told Alex, years later. 'It was December the seventh, Opening Night of the Season; *the* night, and they were doing a new production of *Otello*. I'd enquired about seats as soon as I knew I would accompany her to Milan and they told me they hadn't had a seat for any money for a whole month! I tell you, I was on cloud nine! La Scala! I'd been in every opera house I could get into; the Met – the old Met not the new Lincoln Center – Covent Garden, the Paris Opéra, La Fenice – but La Scala! That's the one – *the* one – if you are an opera buff.'

'Like you,' Alex said.

'Like me. Just imagine that George Eliot was alive today and she had asked you, Alex Brent, to listen to her read the as yet unpublished manuscript of her new novel which nobody but herself had either seen or knew about. *That* is your equivalent of opening night at La Scala.' Max shook his head. 'And in a box, yet. Me with the Riringhettis, me whose old man runs an Italian restaurant on Mulberry Street. I tell you it was historic! Added to which, when I get to the Riringhetti house – which by the way is a *palazzo* the like of which has to be seen to be believed – your mother takes me aside and hands me a Cartier watch, a gold cigarette case and a gold Dunhill lighter. "Props," she tells me. "For tonight you are Max Fabian – American, a business associate of mine. You don't speak the Italian of the Italians you normally speak. You have a good command of the language – which is why you are going with me – but you make a mistake here and there. They like that. It shows you really trying. You will be attentive but not overly so. The relationship – our relationship – is to be seen as briskly businesslike."

'"Why?" I ask.

'"That," she says, "is my business," and more to the general meaning of "either put up or shut up". So I shut up. I thought, I may be just along for the ride but it *is* first class and I aim to lie back and enjoy it.'

'And did you?'

'Is the Pope a Catholic?' Max sighed. 'What a performance – and I don't mean the opera. That was the night your mother met her third husband.'

Eve was not a lover of opera, but in Milan, on this night, it was *de rigueur*, and Mina had been responsible for recommending Eve's salon to her friends, who had in turn recommended it to theirs so that its success had snowballed. One always put business first, so Eve regarded it as a business outing. She asked young Fabiani along because she suspected that Mina, an unabashed matchmaker, was probably concealing 'the perfect man' somewhere behind a curtain, and also because Eve Czerny never went anywhere without an escort. With the Riringhettis and their friends the Ranieris was old Dottoro Mancini who, Eve knew, could and probably would recount past performances of *Otello* in tedious detail. No way was she being paired off with that old man, all set to have Mina spring some handsome jack-in-the-box on her once people had seen who she was with and pursed their lips in sympathy. It was nine months now since Christopher had died. Time to really dazzle them again. Time to show them that she had merely been taking a sabbatical. Time to show them what real competition was.

She had just the dress. A liquefaction of black satin trimmed with white, full-skirted, shushing softly when she moved. With it, the filigree diamond necklace that had been made for Abigail Bingham in 1816 on the occasion of the birth of her eldest son. It lay on the skin like separate drops of pure morning dew, each stone seemingly unconnected and set *en tremblant*, so that as it quivered it caught the light. From her ears, matching pendants swung with the movement of her head. Her hair was swept smoothly from her forehead and coiled behind her head, caught with small diamond stars, and about her head and shoulders, instead of a fur, as every other woman would be wearing, she braved the Milanese winter and wore only a cobwebby mantilla of the finest Spanish lace. Both dress and mantilla were the inspiration of a little-known Spanish designer named Emiliano, whom Eve had put under exclusive contract to design for her, and her alone. She intended to go into the fashion business. The reaction to this dress, tonight, would tell her if she had made a wise decision.

As she followed Mina into the Riringhetti box, she stood for a moment while Guido Riringhetti took her mantilla from her; for a moment, she knew that every eye was fixed on her because there was a break in the chatter; a split-second of stunned silence, like a hiccup, then the noise began again. She sank down onto her white and gold chair, smiled over her shoulder at Max, just behind and to one side of her, who smiled back, leaned forward and murmured: 'Not a dry eye in the house; they are all weeping – tears of rage.' Eve laughed, throwing back her head to reveal her long, swanlike throat, making the diamonds dance and shimmer with light. Max felt light-headed. This was all a dream anyway, and once Eve Czerny left Milan and went back to the States that was it. He would follow because he was expected home for Christmas; this extended vacation had been by way of a last fling before he settled down to hard work and the struggle to get that foot on the first rung of the ladder. Eve might fire him for being too familiar but he found he didn't care. As long as it was afterwards and not before . . .

The house lights faded, the audience ceased its rustle, throats were cleared, the *maschere*, all in black but for white gloves, had solemnly conducted the flustered latecomers to their seats, the red silk interiors of the boxes glowed like jewels as the last lights sank into darkness, the conductor was received with a polite smattering of applause and then he lifted his baton and the first crashing chords coincided with the parting of the curtains. And Max was lost. Eve noted the fact with amusement. He was quite a character, this young Massimo Fabiani, but a real find. He had a way of cutting through what he called the flim-flam and exposing the true state of affairs which lay underneath. He could shout and scream and gesticulate with the best of them, yet he could switch to savagely cutting, Lower East Side invective without missing a beat. He was obviously clever – he had worked his way through Columbia and had been a court reporter as well as done a stint as Judge's clerk, and he knew his way around Italian law, as well as the *mille feuille* layers of Italian bureaucracy, yet he was sitting there utterly lost in what was being sung on the stage, totally oblivious of his surroundings, leaning forward intently, elbow on knee, chin on hand. It had been pure inspiration to bring him with her tonight. He was young enough to cause a first reaction of 'My God but she's cradle-snatching now' to be instantly followed by the realization that he was no more than she said he was: a business associate, along for the ride because he knew Italy, spoke the language and was being well-paid for his efforts. Her manner to him was brisk, verging on the brusque, and always with an underlying note of command. His to her was deferential without being obsequious, and the way he spoke only when spoken to added to the unmistakable impression that he was there only because she had told him to be. A clever young man, Eve mused. One who could be very useful to me.

When the house lights went up at the end of the first act, Mina turned to Eve to ask, 'Well, do we promenade or do we sit?'

It was the custom for the younger women to go to the Ridotto, to parade their finery and size up the competition, to smoke and gossip and see who was with whom or pretending not to be. The dowagers kept to the old custom of receiving visitors in their boxes.

'I think Madame Czerny must give our Milanese *cognoscenti* a glimpse of her beauty,' Guido Riringhetti said gallantly.

Max rose to his feet. 'Madame, will you walk?' he asked Eve gravely.

Her mouth twitched. Really, he was too impudent. But she laid her hand on his arm and he led her out of the box to join the crowd drifting along the corridor and up the stairs to the glittering white and crystal Ridotto, where people turned to stare at Eve, who outshone every woman there.

As soon as Eve heard Mina say, with a brightness as artificial as the wig Desdemona had worn, 'Dino, but what a lovely surprise. I did not know you were back from St Moritz? How was the ski-ing?' she knew this was the one.

'Well enough . . .' The voice was deep, oddly vibrating, and Max, standing by and watching everything, saw the way Eve's head came up, though she had her back to the speaker, like a dog sniffing a scent. He watched as the tall, black-haired, deeply tanned man bent over her hand, watched him make a swift assessment of the diamonds and the eyes – black as onyx – take on a glow as if somebody had just lit a lamp behind them. On the make, Max thought, and he's just made those diamonds to the last dollar. All Max got when he was introduced was a short bow and a brief handshake, but he got the same X-ray treatment before being dismissed as being of no consequence. How do they do it? Max wondered. My dinner jacket is every bit as good as his, my cufflinks are gold, I could live for a week on what it cost to buy this shirt, yet he knew I was not in the offing. Watch and learn, he told himself. What is going on here tonight you won't find in anything William Blackstone ever wrote.

At first glance, Rinaldo 'Dino' di Marchesi appeared to be all that Eve found attractive in a man: dark, Italianate good looks, not as tall as Max but well built, not an ounce of surplus flesh and all of it, Eve was sure, the same deep tan as his face, the whole burnished with a sensuality which hummed, and embellished with a title that went back to the Borgias.

Gee, Max thought savagely, a real life Prince. Probably the one Machiavelli had in mind when he wrote his book. 'I do not like thee, Dr Fell, the reason why I cannot tell, but I do not like thee, Dr Fell,' he said under his breath, but as he was only the hired help it was none of his business.

Dino di Marchesi, however, set out to make Eve his. Max was dropped at his hotel, the others went on to who knows where after a 'Nine o'clock tomorrow morning, in my office', from Eve.

'Yes, ma'am, no, ma'am, three bags full, ma'am,' Max said as the red lights of the enormous limousine disappeared down the street. But he went up to his seventh-floor room whistling the theme of the love duet.

He was awakened by the telephone. Picking up his watch, which had a luminous dial, he saw it was 3 a.m.

'Wrong number,' he mumbled into the receiver, preparing to put it down again.

'Mr Fabiani?'

Max sat bolt upright. 'Yes, Madame.'

'The Prince Rinaldo di Marchesi. Find out about him for me. All about him.' He heard the click as she hung up.

'He's forty, first-rank Roman nobility and flat broke,' Max reported to Eve two days later. 'He's the fifteenth Prince of his line, his father is dead and his mother lives in the faded relic that once was the glory of the Palazzo Marchesi in Rome. He's a widower. His wife died four years ago of an overdose of sleeping pills. She was Adriana Lucarelli. Her old man owns Italy's equivalent of General Motors. She married him at nineteen, couldn't cope and was dead by the time she was twenty-six. No children. She couldn't have any. That's why she got depressed and they gave her pills, which became a habit and she took a handful too many one night. He's gone through the money she brought him. She was also crazy in love with him. Her father wanted the title though he didn't care for Dino, but Adriana wanted him, and what she wanted she usually got. She was spoiled rotten. What she hadn't counted on was that he was the same way . . .' Max paused. 'I think that's about it. Oh, except he has never missed a beauty in his life, but he is known to have perfect taste so I guess you could say it is flattering.'

'What does he do?'

'He skis, he shoots – very well; he's got more cups than a full coffee service, he rides, he drives fast cars and he lays women.'

Eve bit her lip. Really, she thought, he is outrageous. I ought to reprimand him, but he is so clever . . .

'I have a proposition to make to you,' she said, changing the subject.

'Your place or mine?' Max asked hopefully.

Eve froze him with a glance though she was laughing inwardly. 'Really, Mr Fabiani, you have no respect for anything or anybody. You will have to adjust your attitude if you want to be a famous lawyer.'

'I'd rather be a rich one.'

'Then come and work for me.'

'You want *me* to be your lawyer?'

'No. But if you learn well, do as you're told and guard my interests as if they were your own then, perhaps, you might, one day . . .'

'I plan to live a long time.' Max looked at Eve. 'Where would this be?'

'Wherever I am. To begin with you would continue to do what you have been doing for me these past few weeks.'

'Oh, a gofer,' Max said dejectedly.

'You would — find out things for me, keep an eye on others, advise me of the legality of certain — ventures, double check all contracts —'

'Be your hit man,' Max said.

Eve frowned.

'Never mind,' Max said. 'Just say I'm the senior partner of Beck and Call.'

Eve threw back her head and laughed her rich, rolling laugh. 'And keep me amused,' she said.

'I'm glad somebody thinks it's funny.'

'I will pay you twenty-five thousand dollars a year,' Eve said.

'Just to keep you amused? Lady, I'll be the best stand-up comic in the business!'

'Which was how I came to be where I am today,' Max told Alex now. 'And sometimes I have to stop and think where that is.'

But he had soon found out that Eve Czerny always knew exactly where she was at all times, and for a while, after Milan, that was New York, where she disappeared into the imitation French château

195

that was the Bingham town house on East 78th while Max went down to Mulberry Street to the little Italian restaurant his father owned, above which he had been born, the youngest of a family of six, three girls, three boys, to tell them of his sudden elevation to the Upper East Side.

When he reported to the New York offices of Eve Czerny Inc. he was given a small office – 'more your actual hall closet' was how he described it to the family over *risotto al salto* that night, 'but it has a telephone and an ashtray, only Madame doesn't approve of smoking – bad for the skin – so I have to lean out of the window, and as I'm forty floors above the pavement I have to be careful not to fall out when the bell goes.'

'The bell?' his eldest sister Graziella asked.

'The doorman rings it when she enters the building. It means it's time for hut inspection.'

'Sounds like the army,' his father commented.

'I hope to get my commission at the end of basic training,' Max said.

'I hope she's paying you well,' said his mother.

'Well enough,' said Max, non-committally.

'But what about your own law office?' she asked.

'If I can stick at this for a couple of years I'll be able to afford a better one.'

He had no idea that his couple of years would extend to twenty, but he knew the moment Prince Dino di Marchesi turned up in New York that he was looking for his own kind of tenure.

Eve found the Prince to be the perfect escort. He was attentive and amusing, if not as amusing as Max; he danced divinely, he was always charming, always at her service. He invariably obtained the best tables, the best seats, and he never pressed his attentions when he sensed they were not wanted at any particular time, not that Eve let him get any further than the sitting-room of her triplex on Central Park South. With Dino di Marchesi she felt no sexual stirrings, which she found rather strange, because she had – did – definitely feel them around the 23-year-old Max Fabiani. But Dino did make her feel cosseted; he was very good at *being there*. If she did not wish to go out, he was content to stay in. If she wanted gaiety, noise, he would provide both. He anticipated her every want and seemed to know the moment a thought crossed her mind and before she could express the wish. And yet, according to Max, he was 'a prime example of that old Italian pastime *la bella figura*'.

And yet – why not? Eve thought. It would soon be a year, and she was not meant to live alone. Besides, Dino would provide the perfect cover. And she would not be stepping down, but up. The Binghams might consider themselves Old New York, but Dino di Marchesi could trace his ancestors back seven hundred years and numbered a Pope and two cardinals among them. As Max had said: 'That's like having George Washington for your many times great-grandfather, Thomas Jefferson as your now distant cousin and Benjamin Franklin as a dear old uncle on your mother's side.' And she would be a Princess. Principessa di Marchesi. It would look terribly chic on a label. Why not? she thought again. Helena Rubenstein did it, Elizabeth Arden did it. He would be expensive, of course, but she could afford him, and she would control him. No settlement he could run through as if dollar bills were a field of daisies. He would have an allowance, a generous one, but there would be conditions.

He could have – would have if Max was right, and he will be, she thought, he will be – his women, but it would be so discreet that there would be no gossip. The slightest hint and not only his allowance would be cut off. Yes, he would earn his very expensive keep, but with his name, she could make a hundred times what his total cost would be. But first, she would have to see how determined he was.

After Christmas they flew to Rio, where Eve opened a salon. The Prince tagged along, but before he could get to grips with the dark-eyed beauty he saw having her nails manicured, they were off to Buenos Aires, where he got little sleep and caught a bug that confined him to his bedroom (within easy reach of the bathroom) for several days. Eve made sure that word got back to him of the attentions of a certain ten-goal polo player. That night, pale and hollow-eyed, the Prince was up and about. He was there when she went to Mexico City, still tagging along when she returned to New York to collect her son, did not wince when that son kicked him in the shins and announced he didn't like him, and was still hanging in there when Eve took off with her son, his nanny, Max and

13

Switzerland, 1988

To those who thought that only Max Fabian had the inside track where Eve Czerny was concerned, he would say, 'Any time you want to be squeezed up against the rails just let me know.' But there was no denying that he was the only one who could handle her, her capriciousness, her pig-headedness, her unpredictability, with both tact and seemingly inexhaustible good humour. He was the only one she never pushed too far, as she did others. Max had early learned that the only way to survive was to make himself indispensable. Also, he was not afraid of her. Soon, she relied on him utterly, trusted him absolutely. He knew things – and kept them to himself – which no one else knew; besides which, Eve's innate sense of self-protection always warned her when she was going too far. If he argued and was told icily, 'I am sole owner of this company and mine are the only orders around here,' he would bow deeply, say sardonically, 'Yes, Your Imperial Majesty, no, Your Imperial Majesty, kiss my ass, Your Imperial Majesty' and she would invariably giggle and the danger would pass.

He also managed things brilliantly. As much for his own peace of mind as the good of the company, over the years he had trained a dozen men to handle things he needed to delegate as his own power grew. Men who policed the outposts of the far-flung empire, and he defended them staunchly. When Eve would scream, of one of them who had made some minor error, 'Get rid of him!' he would advise the culprit to remove himself to a distant part of the company and bide his time. When, as he knew she would, Eve would say, 'This is no improvement. Why did you get rid of whatshisname? You should have consulted me first!' he would rescue whatshisname from the boondocks and everything would go back to the way it had been before. Eve came to regard Max Fabian as her own, personal miracle-maker, and neither knew nor cared about the hard work and long hours it took to bring those miracles about. But she was the one who changed his name. 'Massimo? It sounds like a wrestler. I shall call you Max — Max Fabian.' And so it was from then on.

When she went on her trips he was always along to watch, listen and learn, until he was so experienced she felt able to go away for weeks at a time and know that everything back at the ranch was under control. He was the one who found the prime factory and outlet sites, the one who soothed the treatment girls when she lost her temper with them, who dried their tears and — if they were pretty enough — kissed them better.

Eve trusted him because, like her, he was ambitious, and his belief in the onward and upward progress of Eve Czerny Cosmetics was as profound as her own. If he brought someone to her — as he had Mora — and said, 'Hire them,' she would not hesitate. On the other hand, he was the one who, should she read about some new genius employed by a rival company and order 'Get him!', had to do so. Usually the women. Eve handled the men.

By the beginning of the 1970s there were Czerny salons world-wide, ten of them in the United States. She had twenty factories and a dozen vast distribution centres, always centralized near her biggest outlets. It was Max's job to conduct the legal manoeuvres that would allow her to maximize profits and minimize tax. To this end he had set up dummy corporations owned by natives of the country concerned, but so incorporated that Eve was in control and should anything happen to the owners they would revert to her.

When the tax authorities came to inspect her books she was always able to produce them with a toffee-nosed flourish because she knew Max had introduced a fiscal system which worked like a charm, ensuring that no matter where or when Eve demanded an accounting *as of that day*, the figures could be produced. It took him months to find the right Comptroller, and he finally winkled him out from under the noses of Peat, Marwick, Mitchell at twice his current salary. When Eve screamed at the cost he told her what it would cost in taxes if she said no. There was no corner of Eve Czerny's empire that Max had not dusted with his own broom, but there were certain areas where Eve, and only Eve, had the ultimate yes or no. The final composition of a formula, any shade of any particular colour, the names of her products, and the design of the bottles, jars and flacons they came in. Which was why, with Eve still prostrated with grief for her son, he was currently in a fix.

The Easter free gift promotion was in hand; a box of sample-sized products given free with the purchase of two items from the range. It was done by most of the big Houses, but Eve's were something else. Always beautifully designed, the box was not something to be thrown away when the contents had been used, and the contents themselves were sumptuous. It was always white – her colour – and gold, with her slashing black signature, and what went into the box was what she, and only she, decided would go into it. Here they were in October, and she had not given her decision as to what her Easter box would contain. It had to be decided now, because production had to get under way, the stores courted and lobbied, the advertising approved. Now he was being assailed on all sides by people wanting to know what they were to do. Nobody was willing to usurp Eve's authority, non-existent though it presently was. Max went to Paolo, her famous *visagiste* and the man most likely to know. 'Never!' Paolo had told him flatly. 'You are asking me to risk not only my job but my life! I would not do this if you were to offer me a statue in the cosmetics Hall of Fame, and anybody who does is either a fool or a dead man.'

Max went to Mora and Pamela. Both used Czerny cosmetics, both, as models – Pamela a former one but with years of experience – and well able to advise. Both refused.

'You must be joking!' Mora told him, scandalized, while Pamela shook her head and said, 'I am the last person you should ask. I'm on her shit-list as it is.'

'Then give me your opinion. *If* you were the one who had the say-so, which five Eve Czerny products would you give away?'

'Well . . . the Renaissance Cream, that's a must and it's always chosen anyway. A lipstick, and my choice would be Red Tape; Morning Starter because that's what I use every morning, and I think the Eyes Right palette, finishing off with the Hand Restorer.'

'Great,' Max said happily. 'How about you, Mora?'

'I don't use the Morning Starter so I wouldn't want that; I use the Simply Perfect Soap, so I'd want that. Red Tape isn't my colour; I'd choose Perfectly Pink. I agree about the Eyes Right palette but I'd rather have nail varnish than hand cream – to match the lipstick.'

'All suggestions gratefully accepted,' Max told them, but when he went back he was told that the Eyes Right had been used in the last promotion, as had the Hand Restorer. It was Madame's policy never to repeat herself. 'Shit!' Max said violently.

'I don't know what the hell to do,' he complained gloomily to Alex. 'I'm not the colour or product expert, that's your mother's province and she's always guarded it very jealously. Her promotions are vitally important because if women are pleased with what they try, they buy. If I make a mess of this one they won't buy, sales will suffer and in the end, so will I. She'll nail me to the nearest cross.'

'Is this what you propose to give away?' Alex looked at the elegant box, its scaled-down gifts nestling in the gold velvet interior. The box itself cost a bomb but Eve had steadfastly refused to use cheaper materials. 'You do not decorate a flagship with second-hand materials,' she had argued.

'Yes, except nobody can agree on the lipstick colour and we used Morning Starter and the hand cream back in the spring,' Max said morosely.

'Well, I'm no expert,' Alex said, 'but I assume that these gifts are to entice women who do not usually buy Czerny products to try and then buy?'

'Right!'

'And Eve Czerny products are at the top end of the market which makes them expensive to the average woman.'

'They are not intended for the average woman.'

'Then why are you giving away the products that potential Czerny clients might well afford to buy in the first place?'

Max looked at her, mouth open. 'My God, I never looked at it that way ... Not my area of expertise, you see,' he went on apologetically. 'This is your mother's baby.'

'Then obviously she is trying to attract more customers. Why else continue with a custom that, if I'm right, she began *before* she became what she is today?'

'Right!' Max said again. 'We did our first one back in 1968 ... yes, Christmas 1968. The idea wasn't new, but Eve was never slow to climb on somebody else's bandwagon, and it does have an effect on sales, no doubt about it.'

'Then the market has to be women who can't necessarily afford to splash out on the most expensive products without knowing what they're like.'

'Right!' Max repeated. He looked at Alex with a mixture of pride, awe and resignation. 'Why didn't I come to you in the first place?' he wanted to know. 'So,' he went on enthusiastically, 'what would you put in the box?'

'A sample of everything that is top of the range and way beyond the average woman's pocket, including a sample of the latest fragrance.'

'*Enchanté*! Christ, do you know how much that costs? And we don't have time to make the bottles now and –' Max pulled at his nose as he had a habit of doing when he was thinking hard. 'I wonder . . .' He cocked an eye. 'Have you smelled *Enchanté*?'

'Yes. Mora wears it.'

'And?'

'Very – sensuous,' Alex said. 'Ultra chic. A very modern, Eighties sort of scent.'

'Which is why it's been such a success since its launch. Your mother has never put a fragrance in the gift box unless it was one which was no longer top of the range – which *Enchanté* is, right now. She did it with *Essence of Eve*, and *L'Amoureuse* a few years ago . . . I suppose we could put it in a plain glass bottle but with a label – there isn't one on the standard sizes, it's the shape that tells you what the fragrance is.'

'Don't spoil the ship for a ha'porth of tar,' Alex said. 'If you give away a miniature replica of a bottle that won a prize for design, you will attract more new customers than the same perfume in a plain bottle. You asked for my opinion, and I would go for the replica every time. You just said that *Enchanté* is recognized by its distinctive bottle, so . . . if a woman can flourish it she will.' Her voice tailed off. 'Why are you looking at me like that?' she asked uncomfortably.

'I'm not used to being confounded.' Max laughed. 'My God, why didn't I realize it? You *are* your mother's daughter after all.'

'If you're comparing me to her –'

'Damn right I am. Why didn't I think of it! *You* are the one who has inherited that instinct of hers; she hoped it was Chris but he neither knew nor cared. What you've been telling me, in your reasoned, logical way, is what your mother does by instinct. The only difference is that I don't think she would go so far as to give away her newest fragrance, which retails at three hundred dollars

203

the ounce. I think she would have used *Always Roses*. It's two years old but still our bestseller after *Essence of Eve*. Using *Enchanté* will be a gamble, but what the hell, Eve has always played for high stakes.' He put his hands on her shoulders. 'Alex, you're a godsend.'

He bent his head and kissed her, not on the cheek, as he always did, but on her mouth. His own was warm, firm, and to Alex, intensely aware of him as she was nowadays, it felt like an electric shock, sizzling away to explode in a shower of sparks at her nerve-endings. Without knowing what she did she kissed him back. For a moment, Max's arms tightened then he put her away from him with a jerk. 'Well,' he said lightly, 'it shall be as you suggest. One each from the top of the range plus – and that will make the difference – *Enchanté*. Let me just write it down . . . Renaissance II, Blooming Cheek with brush, Night Revitalizer Complex, a Sealed Lips-stick, choice of three colours, and last but not least, *Enchanté*. If that doesn't break sales records I know nothing about this business.'

'And if it doesn't?'

'Then it's all your fault. See you later.'

When he told them what the promotion was to be there was a stricken silence, then uproar.

'Are you mad? *Enchanté* in a give-away promotion already?'

'We can't possibly produce a replica miniature in time.'

'Have you thought how much all this is going to *cost*?'

'We will never make the sales to justify the expense.'

'Oh, yes we will,' Max said, unmoved. 'If we don't – then I'll quit.'

This produced further uproar.

'Why don't we give the Easter promotion a miss next year,' somebody suggested. 'In view of the circumstances people will understand.'

'That would be disaster,' Max snapped. 'A lost sale is a lost soul, as Madame is always saying. It goes to the Devil, in this case one of our rivals. We *must* maintain momentum, and there's enough gossip hanging from the grapevine right now. We cannot afford to be seen faltering without Madame's hand on the helm. It's daring, but it's worth the risk.'

'It's not daring, it's nuts,' somebody else said.

'It's the biggest gamble the company's ever taken,' said a third.

'I'm the one who's taking it,' Max said. 'So get going.'

And the beauty of it is, he thought, as he drove back to the villa, Alex thought of it. Of all people. I should have known. Don't I keep telling her she's her mother's daughter? I mean, he thought, it's so *simple*. Nobody has ever given away free samples of their latest, millions-of-dollars-in-research latest products. Renaissance II and Night Revitalizer are just on the market and doing very nicely against their competitors, which are many. Women will fall over themselves for it. Renaissance II retails for fifty dollars the small size, a hundred the large, while Night Revitalizer goes for seventy-five a set of three once-only phials. And all free with the purchase of any two products from the Eve Czerny range. It's a positive steal. Except it is going to cost; more than we've ever spent before because every sample is top of the range. Normally there was a comb or a mirror – known as fillers in the trade because they cost next to nothing. He could not remember a free gift of such quality being offered by any cosmetic House, though back in the 1970s Lancôme had sold special presentations of full-size products at 50 per cent off.

He pulled his car to the side of the road, stopped and took out the notebook he carried everywhere since Eve threw off ideas as they occurred to her, and made some rough calculations. If we can improve on the last give-away we are on to a fortune; if we maintain we can still break even, but my nose tells me this could be the big one. How is it? he wondered, as he started his car again, that we don't always see what's right under our noses? If Alex has just a smidgen of her mother's God-given instincts I can use her. God knows how long Eve will act the recluse. She could bounce back tomorrow and she could still be in hiding a month from now. And I can't afford to wait. Another thought occurred and it had him frowning. What if Eve decided to throw in the towel? I can run the company, the nuts and bolts are the ones I fitted, but the inspiration, the bordering on genius know-how about what will sell, that is Eve's, and God help anyone who tries to take her place. No way would she entertain the thought of training a successor, except for Chris, and he had made it plain – not that she took any notice – that following in his mother's footsteps was not the way he wanted to go.

But suppose, Max thought, just suppose her successor is right under that clever nose; the last person she would think about – or want, come to that. But I would. Alex would be a pleasure to work with. After her mother, a positive dream because she doesn't throw tantrums.

Could be we've got our successor, and born, not made, he thought. Alex thinks and reasons things out whereas her mother goes by her instincts, but if they arrive at the same conclusion the method is immaterial. I wonder . : . he thought again. I would have to approach it – her – very carefully, but if I assist her as much as I can to find out what makes her mother tick there's nothing to stop me bringing her in on a thing or two where Eve's decision can't be got. It's worth a try, anyway. As I've always said, if you prepare for the worst it's a nice surprise when what you end up with is the best. And let's face it, he told himself, when it comes to brains Alex *is* the best, but in the cosmetics business you need more than that. You need that little extra, you need to be *driven*, you need to *want* and to be willing to do whatever it takes to get. Alex doesn't have that. Eve has done things from which Alex would recoil in horror. Eve is ruthless, Alex isn't. Yet she had no hesitation in giving her opinion on what the presentation box needed and it's a damned good idea, one that should succeed. If it doesn't then I'm handing Eve the knife, and even after twenty years she won't hesitate to use it. Alex is the kind of person who would be loyal unto death; Eve, on the other hand, expects you to be loyal to her with no *quid pro quo*. But Eve has the imagination, the daring, the flair, plus her incredible eye for colour and nose for fragrance. From what I know of Alex she has neither. And she also has this cockamamie idea that cosmetics are nothing more than a way for men to enslave women, prodding them on to desperate measures in their efforts to appear beautiful.

He also knew that no way could Alex have done what her mother had: start off with three or four home-made, almost primitive products and within five years have a line of fifteen major products with a range of twelve shades in rouges and lipsticks. Now, Eve produced three different lines – the Eve Czerny, the Young Eve for the under twenty-fives, and the Princess di Marchesi – the most expensive, with a market consisting of women over thirty-five. She manufactured more than one hundred separate products and had the largest range of shades of any cosmetic House. Her gross turnover in the United States alone was approaching one billion dollars a year. Well, Max thought, that could be maintained provided the company can continue to come up with its innovative, market-startling, sales-increasing ideas, every one of them emanating from Eve Czerny's fertile imagination. If Eve retired . . . nah, thought Max. What the hell would she do with herself? Work is the only thing that *really* matters to her. But if the unthinkable happened, what then? Cultivate Alex, he answered himself. Test her out, see if she's got what it takes, and if she has, then take it. In this world, he thought, as he turned into the gates of the villa, it's a case of needs must.

14

Switzerland, 1967–71

When the Villa Paradis was opened up once more in the spring of 1968 it was to welcome the return not of Madame, but of Madame la Princesse.

'But I thought you said she was an Empress,' a puzzled Alex asked Patsy.

'That is her, shall we say, working title,' Patsy explained. 'She makes cosmetics and all her press releases call her the Empress of Beauty. She is a Princess because she is now married to a man who is a Prince.'

'Oh,' said Alex.

'Don't worry,' Patsy said. 'I doubt very much if it will make any difference to you.'

It didn't. Eve neither enquired after nor gave any indication that she gave a single thought to her daughter, and bearing in mind what had happened last time, Patsy was very careful to keep Alex out of the way, the more so because Eve had embarked on a season of entertaining the like of which had not been seen before at the villa. Now, the Principessa di Marchesi gave dinners for forty followed by a ball for another two hundred; she graced them with as many titles as she could cram in to either her dining-room or her ballroom, and at weekends there was often a houseful, with the swimming pool, the tennis courts, the croquet lawn, the terraces full of people. Alex used to watch from her window seat, and once the Prince had been pointed out to her, she wondered why he seemed to spend so much time with the prettiest young ladies rather than with his wife; though the staff breathed more easily because when Madame was happy, they were happy. Alex knew this was so because her mother always seemed to be laughing; she was not so impatient or imperious when she had a man at her beck and call. That was what Alex had heard one of her maids say to another. She hoped he would always be there because she was afraid of the other mother, the one with the cutting voice and dead eyes.

And for a while it seemed that the new, softer Madame was here to stay.

As she entered her eleventh year, Alex was growing. She was already as tall as her mother – 5 foot 3 inches – and weighed 115 lb. She outgrew her clothes so rapidly that Patsy was always having to buy new ones, which caused Eve to ask why.

'Alex is growing very fast,' Patsy explained. 'A dress bought one month does not fit as it should within another two.'

'Then buy her a size larger,' Eve said irritably. 'I'm not made of money, Miss Patterson, and nobody ever sees her so it doesn't matter what she looks like.'

It does to her, Patsy thought, but said nothing, and waited. She knew there was one last, all-important question to come.

'Has Pastor Dietrich been lately?' Eve asked.

'Yes. He was here only the week before you arrived.'

Eve's face contorted, but only briefly; frowns led to wrinkles. 'Very well,' she said coldly. 'You may go, Miss Patterson.'

And don't you wish Alex could, Patsy thought, as she went back up to the top floor. That old man and his visits have some hold over you; you don't like them but there's nothing you can do about them. Long may he live and continue to make them.

But it was the irregular activities of the Prince that triggered off the explosion which blew apart his marriage to Eve. She knew he was a compulsive womanizer, but she had not minded his flirtations as long as they went no further than that. She was in the throes of creating her Princess di Marchesi line, and though her husband had been loftily affronted at the thought of his name appearing on the label of a jar of face cream, a reminder that his very generous quarterly allowances came from the sales of such creams soon brought him into line. And as long as he was there when she wanted him to be, to escort her to this reception, that dinner, an opening night, a new restaurant, she was too immersed in her business to pay him much attention. It was not until the new line had been put into production, colours chosen, names decided upon, packaging designed, promotion under way, advertising approved, that she came up for air and a little rest and relaxation, only to find that her husband had had the temerity to engage in amorous dalliance with one of her employees. The rumours had been circulating for ages, but by the time they reached Eve they had enough substance to make her fire the girl on the spot, creating a scene that had the walls of the salon resounding. What did for the Prince once and for all, however, was Eve's discovery some time later that her ex-employee had set herself up as a rival in the beauty business, on money provided by her ex-employer's husband. Eve went berserk.

'How *dare* you do this to me! How *dare* you set up that cheap little slut in *her* own salon using *my* money! This is the last straw! I have put up with your lavish spending, your religious dedication to *bella figura*, but this, *this* is too much! You've made me look ridiculous and that I *never* forgive!' In her eyes it was the ultimate crime. Nobody muscled in on Eve Czerny's personal and private territory. The word went out that any supplier who did business with the new salon would never again supply Eve Czerny cosmetics. When Max warned her she was sailing dangerously close to the wind and risked prosecution, because what she was doing came under the heading of restraint of trade, she refused to listen.

'I will not have that slut using my methods in her cheap little one-room salon!' That she herself had started in such a salon was conveniently forgotten. 'I want that bastard watched.' Since Eve never swore, this was an indication that nothing was bad enough for her soon-to-be-ex-husband. 'I want him investigated. I want to know how much he gave her, when and how. Find out Max – and soon!'

When Max reported back with the information that the Prince had long been taking kickbacks from suppliers anxious to supply Eve Czerny Cosmetics, or charging for introductions – at a rate which had Eve spluttering with rage – the roof was all but blown off in the explosion which ensued. China and glass were flung, furniture was overturned, doors were slammed, she flew at him, talon nails seeking to rend and claw, and actually chased him from the house, after which she gave instructions that he was never to be allowed entrance again. Max sought him out, at Eve's instructions, and informed him that in exchange for an uncontested divorce, he would not be prosecuted. He would be allowed to keep his new suits (two dozen of them), his handmade shoes, his silk shirts, the brand new Ferrari 'Dino' in bright scarlet (after which Eve had named a lipstick in her new Princess range 'Racing Red') and whatever else he had managed to pick up in his fourteen-month tenure. The rival salon likewise closed its doors some six weeks later and its proprietor was never heard from again, The Prince was also warned to keep his mouth shut. How would it look, Eve said to Max bitterly, if the self-styled Empress of Beauty, who dispensed her time and talents helping other women to be beautiful so as to attract men, was seen to be unable to hang on to her own man?

'Look on the bright side,' Max consoled, practical as ever. 'You've got a brand-new line which is selling faster than we can distribute it, and your rival never got off the ground. Chalk it up to experience – a profitable one materially, and let's face it –' he levelled a look at her which she met warily – 'isn't that where your interests *really* lie?'

Eve's face cleared as her laugh bubbled. 'How well you understand me, Max.'

'Well, it's not as though you were in love with him, is it?'

Her head came up in stiff outrage but as she met the all-knowing brown eyes she laughed again. 'No,' she agreed, 'it isn't.' Then her expression sharpened. 'But I'm not giving up the title. It looks well and –'

'– it sells even better?'

Having dispensed with the Prince, Max's attractions struck Eve as more potent than ever. He was very bedworthy, she mused; she always had a glad eye for an authoritative, wholly masculine male. But he would keep. For now, she had too much to do, too much to concentrate on. The Prince had been an investment, no more, and in the long run a worthwhile one. She had got what she wanted. A title, and a new line entitled to carry it. For once she agreed with something Max had said: 'I say there shall be no more marriages . . .' and she went happily off to Cap Ferrat to spend the weekend with her newly made friend, the Duchess of Padua. That was the weekend Max first set eyes on Alex.

He had been told to remain at the villa and was quite happy to do so. He had no objection to being summoned to places like this. He had the run of the house, the pool, the cars, and Geneva's night life was not far away.

The morning after Eve left he was down at the pool early. He liked to eat, but he did not want to get fat, so a couple of dozen laps made him feel virtuously able to consume at least four, plump, morning-fresh croissants liberally spread with good Swiss butter and apricot jam. This morning, when he got there, he found it occupied. A sturdy, broad-shouldered child was doing a determined breaststroke, for all the world like some eager-to-please puppy. When she came up for air, touching the side, and saw him, her expression went from one of happy pride to stricken alarm.

'Hello,' he said. 'Who are you?'

He saw her swallow. 'Alex,' she said in a small voice. Then in a rush: 'You won't tell, will you?'

'Tell who about what?'

'About me using the pool. She doesn't know I do, you see . . . I always come down early when I know she'll be asleep.'

'I promise not to say a word to a living soul,' Max promised solemnly. 'Cross my heart and hope to die.' Probably the kid belonged to one of the servants, who were not allowed to use the pool.

'Do you live here?' he asked.

She nodded, adding hastily, 'I have to go now.' Heaving herself out of the water, she trotted for her robe and towel.

'I'm Max Fabian. I work for Madame, but you don't have to go just because I'm here. There's room for us both.'

'Patsy will be waiting for me with breakfast.'

'Patsy?'

She did not answer, and there was panic in the way she shoved her feet into her thonged flip-flops. 'You really won't tell?' she asked, begging for reassurance.

'How about if we shake on it?' He held out his hand. 'A handshake binds a deal,' he explained. 'You can't go back on it.'

Looking relieved she took his hand. It was surprisingly firm for her age, which was about twelve, he supposed.

'Thank you,' she said, and for the first time she smiled, before she ran off.

What a solemn little oddity, Max thought as he did a racing dive. And at some time or other Eve had obviously put the fear of God into her. He forgot her as he set himself to do his twenty laps.

It was some time before he saw her again, and it was a case of out of sight, out of mind. He was settling in to his new job, and liking it the more he tailored it to fit him. He travelled with Eve – still the senior partner of Beck and Call – but he was taking over more and more of the burden she carried, never offering to shoulder it but doing things that had to be done anyway and so well that she did not feel he was taking on too much too soon. He was always careful never to overstep the thickly drawn mark. Eve was a tiger if she thought her authority was in any way being either undermined or challenged, but where hers was not the final say-so, it soon became his. Nor was he likely to break under the workload she heaped on him, for she soon found he had an appetite for work – and the stamina to go with it – that matched her own all the way. She congratulated herself on her own business acumen. Young Max Fabian was a treasure, and no mistake, and while he had already become aware of this he was still taken by surprise when Eve decided to assert her claim to 'finders keepers'.

He had escorted her to a splashy promotion of her new Princess line, and after she had received the plaudits and the acclaim, escorted her back home again, his mind on the few days R and R coming up which he intended to spend in the bosom of his family. He was therefore – for the first and last time where she was concerned – totally unprepared to find himself, after a seduction the like of which he had had not even the beginnings of an idea, in Eve's huge bed with her own, celebrated bosom only inches away from his bemused eyes. I ought to have known, he thought, when she cosied up to me over the champagne; that was a green light if ever there was one.

She had invited him in, and asked him to open the bottle of Bollinger cooling in its silver bucket, then sat very close to him on the big white suede couch, her perfume eddying like some seductive smog, her hands fluttering about him like butterflies. When he had tried to clear his throat, which felt as if somebody had swabbed it so dry it was dehydrated, she had laid soft fingers over his lips, wordlessly drawn him to his feet, then led him by the hand – he felt as he had when his mother took him to school for the first time – into her bedroom, where only one very dim lamp was lit and the bed looked like some vast, fleecy cloud. There, she had proceeded to undress him; Max (for once in his life unable to say or do anything that might break the spell) now feeling school was still years ahead, unable to look away from her hypnotizing eyes except to the smile on her lips, which seemed to hold secrets of the Universe Einstein had never dreamed of. She stripped him down to babyhood, and when he was naked, prowled around him like some predatory animal who got just as much pleasure out of savouring what was to come as the actual feast itself.

She stroked, smoothed, felt, probed, making him wince as her fingers found sensitive spots she was obviously very familiar with; she ran her palms over his shoulders, down his arms, over his chest, around his waist where they snaked over his back and slid to his buttocks, which she squeezed before inhaling deeply and purring an appreciative 'Mmmmmmm'. She touched him everywhere except the one area that was aching, throbbing, sitting up and begging to feel those long, feather-duster fingers which tormented him exquisitely, and when she did finally touch it, it was not with her fingers, but with her mouth.

Max felt he was being vacuumed. There had been a girl at Columbia who was known as 'The Mouth' and about whom legends were told around the fire on long winter nights, but she was an amateur compared to Eve Czerny. Max's experience with women – though very intensive for a 25-year-old – had been, he now realized, of the common or garden variety; Eve Czerny was a rare, exotic plant for which explorers spent their lives searching, mostly never to find. He had come across it planted squarely in his path, and it was, it seemed, deadly, for it sucked you dry but in such a way as to have you refilling with a speed that was pure magic; a tweak here, a nip there, a gentle fondle ending in a squeeze somewhere else and his potency was not only restored, it was increased. He had ceased to exist as a person; he was only a mighty, rock-hard, swollen unto bursting appendage which, to Eve, seemed like a popsicle which never lost either flavour or solidity, and it was only when his thighs fluttered uncontrollably that she laughed, deep in her throat, and allowed him to collapse, a now limply shrivelled shadow of his former self, onto the bed, feeling six months old. It was the first time in his life that he had been utterly possessed by a woman; reduced to a thing to be toyed with, enjoyed, and used for her own pleasure.

She took off her own clothes then lay down on the bed beside him, her head propped on one hand, regarding him smilingly, amusement in the still predatory eyes and on that incredible mouth.

Eve Czerny spoke several languages, he remembered, but her native tongue was wordless even while it spoke volumes.

'How do you *do* that?' he blurted, when he could.

'Never mind. That I do it is all that matters. And now that I have shown you what *I* can do, why don't you show me what you can do.'

Manfully – miraculously, for she had wrung him drier than a 1200 rpm spin – he managed to rise to the occasion once she had let her fingers dicky-dance – and how, he thought on a grin – over him in a delicious, tantalizing arousal, and when he was ready, proceeded to exceed every one of his adolescent dreams of the ultimate in sexual fulfilment. It was done in silence, but for gasps, moans, sighs and sharply drawn breaths, rising, in Eve's case, to a sound like a snarl when she was about to climax, which she did with the force of a geyser erupting; she clamped her legs, scissored around his waist, so tightly, that she constricted his breathing, but he hung on in there and felt the centrifuge that was her inner muscles relax as her orgasm receded only to gain speed again as the next whirlpool appeared in the distance.

He had no idea how long it went on, only that it seemed like for ever; that he was flagging but that Eve was not, and realizing this, she let him slip from her after a last convulsive ten-on-the-Richter-scale earthquake only to make it clear, once he was back to breathing normally, that she was not yet done with him. Not terribly experienced at that particular skill, Max learned as fast there as he did everywhere else for she told him exactly what to do, where to do it and how, and he obviously did it well because instead of snarls she now uttered screams and Max had visions of her maid calling the police. But finally she climaxed so savagely that she almost decapitated him and he felt her own thigh muscles flap like washing in the breeze before they fell away from him. Max came up for air, from bleary eyes saw at last the look of a sated and satisfied woman, and managed to fall back onto the bed and into sleep at the same time on a last blurred thought of 'Here endeth the first lesson'.

Next day, he hopefully waited to be told to stay after school, but Eve – who had not, by word, look or gesture, indicated the slightest change in their relationship – did no more than bid him a pleasant 'Good night'.

It was not until some time later, after another public triumph, that she took the lead a second time and gave him his head – after she had given him hers – once more, and he quickly realized that Eve was using him by way of celebration. Success, in her mind, was equated with sex, and for a while, dazzled by her expertise and young enough not to know the difference between sex without emotion and sex with emotion, he had been reduced to cold showers and handjobs, for somehow the thought of other women did not appeal. It was when he realized that he was being used, as cold-bloodedly as she used everything and everybody, that the thrill subsided from a molten glow to a shabby chill and his admiration lost its shine, so that when she took up with a new group of friends which included several very attractive men, his only feeling was relief. He did not mind being left alone, knowing with cold certainty that in serving her he had served his purpose. And she had given him a raise, hadn't she? Which, he thought, I earned, no matter how you look at it.

And it was during a weekend when she was off in Paris with her new friends that he finally discovered the private world up on the fourth floor which he found attracted and intrigued him far more than Eve and her sexual olympics.

It was a rainy Saturday. He had worked all morning, eaten lunch at his desk then worked on, until at about four o'clock he stretched, contemplated with smug satisfaction the empty In tray and decided to go for a stroll. But when he looked out it was to find that the rain which had been pouring incessantly all day was still hissing down. He grimaced. He felt like exercise after being bent over his desk all day. Then, as he looked out, his eye lighted on the protruding wings of the house, one on either side of the central block, and he knew what he would do. He would explore. It was big enough to afford him at least an hour's stroll, far too big for one woman, with four floors and a mansard roof that must hide an awful lot of attics.

The ground floor he knew: dining-room, two drawing-rooms and a large library, plus the room Eve used as her office and the small one adjoining that he shared with her secretary. The first floor housed a vast ballroom in the central block, with the left wing containing further reception rooms and the right Eve's own quarters. Strictly off limits, they were all mirrors and silk hangings. Straight out of Hollywood, he thought, disappointed. A small-town girl's idea of how the rich lived, having seen Elizabeth Taylor or some such throwing a tantrum in one just like it. He had expected that Eve, with her innate sense of taste and eye for colour and design, would have been different. On the second floor were the guest suites, six of them, each furnished in a different style: English country house, Spanish hacienda, French Empire, Fifth Avenue glitter, Eighteenth-century elegance and Art Deco. The third was where the staff slept, including himself and Eve's live-in secretary. Comfortable but nothing like the glamour of the floor below, with rugs on polished floors instead of wall to wall carpeting, plastic baths instead of flower-decorated porcelain, mass-produced prints instead of originals hung on the painted rather than silk-hung walls. No need to impress here, he thought drily. But on the way up the wooden staircase to the very top of the house it was poverty alley. The walls were plain, white-painted, some kind of thin drugget laid on bare boards, the round windows he had seen from the window of his office, like gargantuan ship's portholes, now streaming with rain and making quavery patterns on the white walls. A long corridor was lined with doors. He opened one; it was stacked with luggage. A second contained spare furniture, obviously destined for use by the servants. Nothing and nobody here but us wallflowers, he thought, then on turning to go back the way he had come he heard a child laugh. He turned back and made for the door at the end of the corridor, facing it instead of being on the left, for that was where the sound had come from. As he put his hand on the door he heard the laugh again and a voice he recognized say, 'I do love the Duchess, Patsy, especially when the baby turns into a pig.'

Alice! Max thought, recognizing a childhood favourite of his own. He opened the door, saw a large, shabby but comfortable room with the same round windows under which were window seats covered in faded chintz, a large table in the centre covered with a red plush cloth, a large bookcase crammed with too many books for its size, an old-fashioned dresser bearing cheerfully bright china, and a comforting fire in an old-fashioned grate. Sitting in the big easy chair drawn up close to it was a middle-aged woman stitching away at what looked like a torn hem, whilst on the floor, reading aloud from *Alice*, was the girl he had seen down at the pool. As he opened the door they both looked up and their surprise was equally as great as his.

'Well, hello again,' Max said. 'So this is where you hide out . . .'

The girl jumped up and went to stand by the chair as though ready to defend it and its occupant.

'I was exploring,' Max told them cheerfully. 'Nothing else to do on a day like this. I'm Max Fabian,' he said to the woman.

She inclined her head but did not give her own name. Instead, she said warningly if calmly, 'This floor is out of bounds, Mr Fabian.'

'Really! Nobody told me.'

He did not heed the warning. 'Are you in quarantine or something?' he asked disarmingly, and the alacrity with which the woman said, 'Yes. Alex is not quite over measles,' convinced him that she was lying, confirmed when he saw the startled look the child gave her and the warning headshake given in return, so slight as to be unnoticeable except to Max's ultra-sharp eyes. Leave this to me, it said.

Ah . . . Max thought, every sense alert, what have we here? A child with measles shoved away up here, under the eaves, like poor mad Bertha Mason locked away in her tower at Thornfield. This child is in quarantine, all right, but not because of contagion. She was cleanly and neatly dressed but her dress fitted where it touched and her shoes, though polished, were scuffed. Neat but not gaudy. Nothing like the expensive outfits worn by young Christopher, courtesy of The White House in Bond Street. Max paid the bills. A coat for Christopher would have bought him a decent suit and a new pair of shoes. Alex's dress was chain store. A dependent relative? Nah . . . Eve was not given to acts of charity. His instructions where begging letters were concerned was to burn them. Who, then? And why was she here? Why was she never seen? Why was she looking at him with that same distress, an almost dry-mouthed fear, that had been in her face when she had asked him, down at the pool, not to say he had seen her. Eve! he thought. She's scared I'll report her to Eve. They both are . . .

'Well,' he said cheerfully, 'I've had measles so I think I'm safe, but I guess we have to think of young Christopher. Maybe we can visit another time.'

He turned to go but the woman said, 'Mr Fabian . . .' He turned back. 'Please –' Her tongue came out to lick dry lips. 'I would ask you not to mention to anyone that you have been up here.' It was a request, but it was also a warning.

'No problem,' he assured them both. 'Your secret is safe with me.' He flashed another smile before leaving them.

'Oh, dear,' Margaret Patterson murmured. 'That was unfortunate . . .'

'He's nice,' Alex volunteered. 'I like him.'

'He is also, from what I hear, very close to Madame.' Neither of them ever referred to Eve by any other name.

'He won't tell, I'm sure,' Alex defended stoutly. He had shaken hands.

'No . . . I don't think he will, but he will wonder. That is a young man with an enquiring mind.'

But Max did not enquire, he watched instead, saw things he had no doubt already seen but not registered as being of any importance. Like the fact that trays were laid which never appeared at any of the meals he ate; that reference was made, in his hearing but in Switzerdeutsch (which they believed he did not understand but which Max, with his usual thoroughness, already recognized and was able to follow, though he was not so good at speaking it), to 'the child upstairs' who 'gets little enough, God knows' and who 'deserves a little treat now and again'. This from Mrs Gerbler, the cook, as she ladled out an extra helping of her thick ham broth or placed an extra large slice of cake on a plate. Max had made himself at home in the kitchen; servants always had the truth of things in any household, and being a flirt and a tease and not, as they at first feared, Madame's spy, they soon relaxed in front of him. Thus he learned of the separate establishment upstairs, but nothing more. The occupants of the room at the top of the house were fed, their rooms cleaned, but they were never discussed. It was as though the staff knew their jobs depended upon their silence. Why? thought Max. What is Eve afraid of? For he had no doubt that the child was here on sufferance; a responsibility Eve neither wanted nor liked.

A niece? he wondered. A god-daughter? Then there was the business of the elderly man who came at frequent if irregular intervals for the sole purpose, Max found out, of seeing the girl. If Eve was in residence the child was brought down – Max being carefully confined to his desk beforehand on some urgently needed research or a lengthy phone-call – the backstairs. Max soon found out who he was: a clergyman with a parish in Geneva, some strict Lutheran sect. He also noticed that his visits invariably angered Eve, who was always in a bad mood afterwards. He's checking up, Max thought. But why? If only there was someone he could ask . . .

Part of his job was to pay the household staff. It was always in cash, except for Jacques, the butler, and Caesar the chef who got cheques. Always they checked their envelopes in front of Max before signing the book which, when Max looked back over the years, revealed that Jacques had been at the villa longer than anyone; that about five years ago there had been a clean sweep of housekeeper, cook and several maids, but not Jacques. He had been butler to Eve since she had bought the villa back in 1961. Eight years. But there was no mention of a governess. She was not paid through the household.

Max did some checking and discovered that a Margaret Patterson was down as an employee of Eve Czerny Cosmetics and that her salary was paid into the Credit Suisse in Geneva, and had been for the past six years. Nowhere could he find any mention of a child, but there was a Miss Wilson mentioned, with the bracketed notation: (Nanny); not the stiff and starchy Swiss who looked after Christopher, for her name was Keller. The other nanny had stayed only a year and she too had been paid as an employee of the company. Had she looked after Alex? Had the nanny, the governess and the child arrived at the same time? If so, from where? What was she to Eve, apart from an obvious nuisance?

Whoever she was there was no doubt that Alex was a responsibility grudgingly accepted. As to what her full name was, Max discovered by dint of watching out for the child and her governess coming down into the gardens and then taking the stairs to the top floor at the double to look through the books – and there were enough of them for a library – to see if there was a name on a flyleaf somewhere. There was, in a neat childish hand – Alexandra Mary Brent. Another, in an adult hand read, 'To Alex on her tenth birthday, from her loving Patsy', and dated some two years before. So, she is twelve years old and her name is Alexandra Mary Brent, Max thought, satisfied. Now I've got something to go on. But it took him another three months to discover just who Alexandra Mary Brent was.

He and Eve were in London, on a visit not only to the Grosvenor Street salon but the factory in Acton, and as soon as Max found himself with free time he paid a visit to Somerset House, and there, he hit paydirt. Alexandra Mary Brent, according to her birth certificate, had been born on August 18, 1957, the daughter of John Brent, a school teacher, and his wife Eve Brent, formerly Czerny. Max was so flabbergasted, in spite of his growing suspicions, that he sat staring at the document for some time. Eve had been married three times, not twice. She had married Christopher Bingham as Eve Czerny, but that had been in New York. Next time we're in New York, he thought. In the meantime, he noted down the address given as the Brent residence and from Somerset House drove across the river to South Wimbledon and the little semi-detached in Acacia Avenue. He found his admiration for Eve growing as he sat, on the opposite side of the road, and studied the three-up, two-down house, one of a street of clones with its lace curtains, aggressively tidy lawn and firmly shut front door. Nobody went in or out during the hour he sat there, but a study of the electoral roll revealed that No. 27 was occupied by a Mrs Mary Brent.

He was so distracted that evening, when he was 'on duty' as Eve's escort to a cocktail party at the residence of the American Ambassador in Regents Park, that she took him to task. 'Do stop staring into space,' she hissed furiously. 'I don't care if you're bored; you should know better than to show it when you're with me!'

Max pulled himself together and did his duty, but later, when Eve indicated she was to be left alone with the Ambassador, he studied her from across the room. What are you? How come you ignore your daughter but lavish attention on your son? Why do you have her in your house yet keep her in what is, to all intents and purposes, solitary confinement? Are you ashamed of her? Is that why you don't want anybody to know? Who was John Brent? Is she not his child? I thought I was beginning to understand you, now I'm right back at square one.

Poor kid, he thought indignantly. She's bright, eager to please – and scared stiff of you. They both are. That's why I was warned off. There and then he made up his mind. He would make a friend of Alexandra Mary Brent; let her know there was somebody besides a middle-aged governess she could turn to. He liked children, had always intended to have a family of his own. One day, he thought, God willing. He felt his rancour grow as he watched Eve charming her way to some favour or another. You and your secrets. Well,

I'm going to keep one of my very own – and right under your nose.

But it was three months before they went back to Switzerland, by which time Max had discovered that Eve Czerny had married Christopher Bingham as a single woman, thus contravening New York State laws. I'll bet he hadn't so much as an inkling, Max thought. I'll bet I'm the only one who knows, and that's only because I have a long nose. Well, there's that old man, and it's obvious that he comes to check on you and the child. That's why you keep her, he thought, as enlightenment struck. You don't have any choice!

The next time the cat was away, this time in the clinic to undergo a complete overhaul, Max made it his business to seek out, and ask for entrance into, the secret world on the top floor.

'I told Alex I was of the opinion that you had an enquiring mind,' Margaret Patterson told him wryly.

'It has taken me a whole year to satisfy it, though. The secret is well kept.'

'Everyone knows the consequences of a leak.'

'Why?' asked Max.

Patsy shook her head. 'I don't know. I only know that she keeps the child here because she has to, and that it's to do with that old man who calls. Alex has to be produced, as though she were proof of something.'

'Does Alex know that Madame is her mother?'

'Yes, but only the fact of it. There is no – shall we say – filial feeling. Alex is afraid of her. To Alex, Madame is the Wicked Queen in *Snow White*.'

'Yes, she was beautiful too,' Max agreed.

'Not that it's the competition Madame fears. Alex is not going to be the one to provide that, I'm afraid.'

'She probably takes after her father.'

'I know of him only through Alex. In her eyes he was the kindest, the most patient, the most loving; the centre of her universe. His death came as a severe emotional blow. Then she lost the first friends she made when she was brought here –'

'The clean sweep that was made?'

'I don't know much about it except that Madame found out they

222

were not observing the rules and so dismissed them. But to Alex it was a further loss. That is why I have tried to give her some form of continuity . . .'

'So maybe she can look on me as an older brother. I've got two, and three sisters, so I know all about it.'

'How old are you?' Patsy asked.

'Twenty-six.'

'I suppose thirteen years is a conceivable age difference.'

'My Aunt Rosina is twenty years older than my father.'

Patsy regarded him curiously. 'Now it's my turn to ask why,' she said.

'Why not?'

'Because you are – like me – an employee. What we are doing is dangerous, and while I'm aware that you presently occupy a position of some – influence – I am sure you've learned enough by now to know that Madame's favour is a fragile flame.'

'Oh, sure. As long as I keep her happy everything else is fine, but one mistake and I'm out. I know that. I also know Madame. I've made a detailed study of her. That I've lasted this long is proof of that.'

'True. Nobody else has ever got so close so quickly or been trusted so much.'

'And I intend to keep it that way.'

'I have learned never to count on anything in this house,' Patsy said.

'Well we can count on Madame being away for another five days. She's having a few nips and tucks; nothing major, just getting to them before they can get to her. So why don't we take Alex somewhere, or rather, you take her somewhere and I'll join you. A picnic, maybe.'

'She would like that. We sometimes have one when I take her to Thonon, where I have a little house.'

'How come you live in Switzerland? You're English, aren't you?'

'Yes, but I was for many years governess to the son of an important Swiss industrialist. He was a delicate child and not up to going to school. I had him for twelve years and when I left they made me a present of my little house. But I was bored doing nothing so when I was approached by Madame I agreed to come here, on a daily basis at first, then after Nanny Wilson left, living in.'

'But if Alex goes to school, as you say you would like, you'll be out of a job again.'

'I'm sure I can – if I wish – find someone else to teach. If not, then I can really retire. I am fifty, after all.'

'You don't look it.'

'Thank you.' Patsy accepted the compliment with a twinkle. 'I'm afraid I place no great importance on looks.'

Max raised his hands in mock horror. 'Treason in this house!'

'I have taught Alex that what one *is*, will always be much more important than how one looks.'

Just as well, Max thought, because Alex is not going to be looked at in the way her mother is.

'So, where shall we go?' he asked. 'You know this country better than I do . . .'

And so a pattern was set. The outings were widely spaced, for there were long periods when Max was travelling with Madame, but he always sent postcards, and soon Alex had a scrapbook full of them. Patsy gently dissuaded her from pinning them up on a board. 'It is a remote possibility but Madame might, one day, decide to come up here . . . better we have them where she cannot see them.'

For her part, Alex seized on Max's interest and hugged it to her like a comfort blanket. She treasured his cards, read and re-read his occasional letters, thrilled to the presents he brought back, looked forward to his stays at the villa with passionate anticipation and marked her calendar with red crosses on those days when he took her out.

For two years they played their dangerous game, and once the staff knew – and it did not take long for them to realize what was going on since one of the maids saw the three of them in Thonon one day, while she was visiting her family – they connived in it. Alex had a party on her birthdays, complete with cake, candles, presents and guests, for by this time the servants were part of the conspiracy.

Patsy rejoiced to see and hear Alex join in, for by upbringing and nature she was really a loner. It was Max who coaxed her out of her shell, who taught her how to cope with being teased without bursting into tears, who bought her first bicycle and showed her how to ride it, who made her into a first-class swimmer, like himself, who came to loom so large in her life that only with him did she run to greet him, arms wide, face alight, to be caught up and swung round. Only with Max, in addition to her beloved Patsy, did Alex ever relax to such an extent that she forgot to be shy, but whenever her mother returned to the villa it was as though someone had ordered, 'Lights out.'

In late May 1971, Eve was in Beverly Hills, and at a dinner party one night at the house of a friend whose husband was a Hollywood producer, when she met the man who became her third 'official' husband, Rik Stevens, currently Hollywood's number one male sex symbol. He was not very tall, only slightly built, but he had the sort of classically chiselled good looks, combined with a pair of brilliantly blue eyes, a dazzlingly 'white' smile and a lazy sensuality that had made his last three pictures multi-million-dollar grossers at the box office. He always played the same part: the casual, easy-come-easy-go rich boy who only had to stand there for women to grovel, and who turned out, under his careless exterior, to be made of steel.

Eve was not usually attracted by 'little boy' types, no matter how nice their shy smiles, but something about the way this one looked at her under his lashes had the effect of making her libido stretch, yawn and realize it was very hungry. Max had been very satisfying, once she had given him the benefit of her expertise, but she had broken a self-imposed rule in breaking him in, for normally she never got involved with employees: a fatal mistake in her opinion. Had it not been for the fact that he was, by now, invaluable, she would have dispensed with his services, but fortunately, Max was every bit as much a realist as she was and once the *affaire* had run its course, their relationship was able to go back to normal because she knew she could trust him never to publish the fact that it had, for a while, been something other than that.

Rik Stevens was an entirely different matter. He was a Somebody; he had a Name – and in spite of the little-boy-shy charm, a reputation as a stud. When she was introduced to him he ducked his head, seemed to scuffle his feet, yet the hand that held hers was firm and the vividly blue eyes looked at her in a way that held no shyness whatsoever. It was bold, nakedly appraising – and approving. She also found it disturbing. As their eyes met she seemed to see the blue flash of electricity. There was no doubt about it at all: he was interested, said nothing overtly sexual, yet the whole evening was dominated by their intense awareness of each other, and when he drove her back to his house, at the bottom of a canyon deep in the Holmby Hills, where it lay in a secluded hollow shielded from prying eyes by a dense growth of trees, Eve was aroused to a state of avidity.

One look at the erotica hung on the walls, placed on tables, resting on shelves in cabinets – most of them paintings and carvings from the East: India, Japan, China, Indonesia – and she knew she had been right. Sex was anything but perfunctory with this man.

On one wall was a series of paintings – Tibetan, Rik Stevens explained – all variations on a theme. Paradise, populated by gods and goddesses, every one of them engaged in the act of copulation; there were Japanese pillow books, exquisitely drawn and coloured, again illustrating every position that was possible in the physical joining of man and woman; on the glass coffee-table was a carving of a bull god, with three heads and a plethora of arms thrashing the air, standing about eighteen inches high but with a red-tipped phallus at least six inches long, aimed at a woman, lying on her back but with shoulders raised and an imploring, ecstatic look on her face, her legs spread wide, ready to receive him.

'Twelfth-century Indian,' Rik Stevens said, watching her. 'The act of fusion is the centre of everything, don't you think? The very essence of life because it keeps on creating life.'

'Indeed,' Eve murmured, feeling heat flush her face, swell her already moist tissues to a dampness that was beginning to get out of control. But he made her look at his treasures, each of them adding fresh fuel to the fire she was burning, until in desperation she asked where the bathroom was.

He showed her, closed the door with a smile on his face, then whistling soundlessly pulled his black tie loose before making for his bedroom.

When Eve came out of the bathroom she found everything dark but for a glow of light at the end of a long corridor. She followed it, stopped in the doorway with a gasp. Having cooled her wrists, dampened her forehead, forced her mind to dominate her body, she felt her newly restored self-control explode at the sight of him. He sat in the dead centre of a Japanese-type futon, only it was at least eight feet square, and he was stark naked, in the lotus position; feet thrust into the backs of his knees, arms placed at his sides, palms turned out. His eyes were closed but he heard her, said softly: 'Take off your clothes.'

She obeyed him and the rustle as they were shed was the only noise apart from his deep, regular breathing. Naked, Eve stood waiting. For once she was the acolyte, not the celebrant, but she waited obediently, absolutely certain now that she was about to experience something extraordinary. Finally he opened his eyes, looked at her, beckoned her forward. He did not smile. He was deadly serious. As Eve drew nearer – the room was cavern-sized and the bed was its centre – she saw, as if expectantly awaiting her arrival, his penis – of a size that made her gasp again – bobbing gently against his flat belly. She stood before him, a glimmer of pearly flesh in the shadows, awaiting his further instruction, and he beckoned her again. She stepped onto the futon, approached him until she stood immediately in front of him.

'Kneel,' he commanded.

She did so.

He reached out his hands, grasped her by the elbows and, as though she were a doll, lifted her. Instinctively, Eve spread her legs so that when she sank down onto him his enormous penis penetrated her, so deeply she thought it would split her in two. Never in her life had any man filled her so completely. Never had she known one so slight to be so strong, but the muscles that bunched his upper arms were as hard as his penis, and it was obvious from the powerful shoulders that he worked out regularly. As she felt herself enclasp and enclose him, she could not repress a moan of sheer pleasure, and as he arranged her legs – ankles crossed behind him, thighs wrapped about his hips, she felt him inside her, moving as if he was able to direct his penis by will, for his body had not stirred. She felt wholly in his power; impaled, penetrated more deeply and thoroughly than she had ever been, absolutely under his control. Only when he directed her, by the merest touch of his fingertips on her waist, for he held her there, lightly but insistently, did she begin to grind her hips in a circular motion which became in turn a gentle rise and fall before changing yet again – always at the signals from his fingertips – and felt the hot, hard rod within her, flexing, advancing, retreating, now stabbing, now caressing, now touching some deep inner core of her that seemed to open, allowing him to enter where no man ever had before, and with the least effort.

There was nothing frantic, nothing greedy, only a smooth flow as of a calm sea, yet her pleasure peaked, again and again, to almost unbearable ecstasies that had her hips trembling and her head hanging back, mouth open, gulping air. Never had she come so thrillingly, so seemingly endlessly, so many times, yet he sat immovable, his eyes still closed, his hands still light on her heated flesh. Only the sweat pouring from him showed the intense effort he was undergoing – and on her behalf. That was what thrilled her; that he should be doing this incredible thing for her.

She felt he was buried so deeply within her he would take root there; that they would be joined for ever. Her orgasms were so intense, so all-engulfing that she was not conscious of anything but what was happening deep inside her; had somebody emptied a gun next to her ear she would not have heard. Each time she climaxed, he seemed to still, his sensitized penis reading her inner convulsions, and she reached the stage where she felt she was losing consciousness, so unbearably pleasurable were the incredible sensations he was producing inside her. Once more reading her body, she felt him tense as her final climax peaked and for a moment, as she fell into a dizzying spiral, she was aware of a gathering in him. His hands gripped hard for the first time as the rock-like shaft within her gushed its own fulfilment, flowing from him into her, and for the first time she understood what he had meant by his reference to the Essence of Life.

As she sank into the deep sleep of the totally replete she understood that she had been given a taste of a new kind of sexuality that was a revelation, even to her. And that one taste was enough to make her addicted.

They became an 'item' and when they left it was together, and for the Villa Paradis, where the maids went into a frenzy when they saw who Madame's guest was.

'Well, well,' Max said sardonically, as he recognized who it was Eve had in tow. 'Pretty Boy Floyd.'

'I thought he was a gangster,' Alex said. Max had been giving her an insight into recent American history.

'So, if I'm not mistaken, is this particular gentleman.'

'Why do you say that?'

'I know the type,' Max said, withdrawing from the window where they had been watching them arrive. 'Well, I must go and make myself agreeable because something tells me that we're going to be seeing a lot of this particular pretty boy. Lie low, kid. I'll get back to you as and when I can.' He dropped a kiss on her hair and went off whistling blithely.

'Do you think he's pretty?' Alex asked Patsy, puzzled that a man should be so labelled.

'In a way, I suppose he is,' Patsy explained. 'Fair-haired, blue-eyed, not aggressively masculine.'

'Max isn't pretty, is he?'

'No . . .' Patsy laughed. 'Anything but.'

'I think Max is much nicer looking than that pretty boy,' Alex said.

'So do I,' agreed Patsy. 'Now, I suggest we get back to our German lesson.'

Rik Stevens stayed the weekend, and when he had to leave to go back to Hollywood for the preliminaries of his next movie, Eve changed her schedule and instead of spending a couple of weeks at the villa, flew to California with him. Max had booked them both into the Beverly Hills Hotel, but he was soon aware that Eve was not staying in her suite but at the big house in Holmby Hills.

He was the only one not surprised when, one weekend, before leaving for location shots in Arizona, Eve and her pretty boy flew to Las Vegas and were married, but he did see something which disturbed him. Always, wherever she travelled, Eve had taken with her a picture of Christopher Bingham Senior; it had always stood on the table by her bed even during her marriage to the Prince. Now, Max noticed that it was no longer there. Discreet investigation found it at the bottom of a drawer beneath a pile of French satin undies. I think you're making a mistake, Princess, he thought. The only resemblance is the blond hair. He looked at the studio portrait of Rik Stevens, the fourth having replaced the second. Like the old, proverbial, three-dollar bill, he thought, I think you're a phoney, but only time will tell.

Eve remained in America for as long as her husband was shooting his movie, devoting herself to the American end of her business, which was proving to be the most profitable of them all. She opened a new salon in Palm Beach and a new Czerny clinic in Scotsdale, Arizona, but for the most part she lavished her time on her husband, and there was no doubt, to Max's all-seeing eye, that she had the look of a woman well and truly satisfied; that glazed, creamy look which betokens, he thought, one who is having a fucking good time, but as he was tightening his own grip on more and more of Eve's empire, he was the last one to complain. Eve didn't go so far as to give him *carte blanche*, but she sent him where once she would have gone herself, which is why he was several thousand miles away in Australia when the pretty boy took off his mask.

Eve and her husband were in residence at the villa, he having finished his picture and Eve her business. Now, they were going to loaf for a while, soak up some sun, see a few people, but mostly, each other.

Eve's mood was sunny; not a cloud in the sky. The staff breathed more easily, the atmosphere was one of deep contentment, the weather was glorious; hot sunny days which had the lake bluer than ever and still as a glass eye. Even a visit by the old man Dietrich had not ruffled the surface of Eve's own pool of sexual satisfaction and almost smug contentment. Can I pick them or can I pick them, she thought to herself, as she watched her husband's naked body disappear into his dressing-room. He was an early riser from long habit, being used to crack of dawn wakings in order to be at the studio by 6 a.m. Added to which, he thought sleep a waste of time; six hours was plenty for him, and he could get by on four or five easily. Eve, squinting at the clock, saw it was just on 7 a.m. and, turning her head away, pulled up the covers and sighed luxuriously at the thought of another two to three hours' sleep. When not working she was never woken before ten, and these days, her nights were so active that she needed all the sleep she could get; lack of it was a killer where a woman's looks were concerned. But had she not slept alone for two years? Just Max, for a while, anyway, and the occasional, very discreet, ultra-careful indulgence here and there, if the time was right, the man was worth it and could be trusted to keep his mouth shut. The one thing Eve still guarded jealously was her reputation. But even that, she thought drowsily, as she let herself sink back into sleep, could be misleading. Her husband proved that. What he did and what he was reputed to be bore no resemblance at all . . .

*

Alex was sitting on the side of the pool, getting her breath back, when she saw the man in the short towelling robe coming down the steps from the cabanas. She got hastily to her feet but she was too late; he had seen her. 'Hi,' he said, exactly as Max had done. 'Who are you?'

He walked right up to her, uncomfortably close. Alex moved away.

'My name is Alex,' she said, as she had been taught by Max. 'My mother works here.'

'Oh, I see . . . you been in?'

'Yes.'

'How's the water?' He put a foot in, stirred it around.

'Warm. It is always kept at sixty-three degrees.'

'Fine . . .' He put his hands to the belt of his robe, tugged and it fell open. With a shrug of his shoulders it slid to the ground. Underneath he was stark naked. He regarded Alex's hot face with amusement. 'You never seen a naked man before?'

Alex shook her head. 'Then you won't know what this is?' He held out his penis, a rubber truncheon dangling from the brush of blond hair at his crotch.

Alex scrambled to her feet. 'Don't run away . . .' His other arm shot out and its grip on her shoulder hurt as he dug in his fingers. 'I only want to show you. Go on, take a good look; there's women willing to do anything to get a look at this . . . as for what they're willing to do to touch it . . .' He took hold of Alex's hand and placed it on himself. It was warm, flaccid, but under her fingers Alex felt it quiver, as if her touch had bestowed life, and the rubbery consistency harden. 'See, it likes you . . . There's nothing more it likes than a lady's touch – 'cept maybe a lady's mouth . . .'

Alex jerked her hand away convulsively and turned to flee, but he was fast. 'Hold on there . . . no need to take fright! I'm only showing you all the good things in store for you . . . how old are you?'

'Thirteen,' Alex managed.

'Thirteen . . .' His voice caressed the word. 'Why, that's just the age I was when I found out how to get into the promised land. If you're a good girl I'll show you . . . if you're not a good girl, well then I guess I'll have to tell on you usin' this pool . . . that's why you're here so early, isn't it?' He laughed. 'I know because I was once a pool boy myself; always got there early before anybody was up and about so as to use it, have it all to myself, a rich folks' pool, just like this one, a house like this one, rich folks who talked like this . . .' His slow South-western drawl slipped easily into the clipped, prep-school, Ivy League accent he used in his movies. 'I learned how to speak like this from them . . . I learned a lot of things about rich people while I worked for them, especially the women . . . those rich bitches are something else . . . they taught me most all I know, so why don't I return the favour and teach you.' He must have seen Alex recoil because his easy drawl hardened as he went on: 'If you don't want to let me, then I'm going to have to tell on you . . .' His eyes bored into hers and in their vivid blue was a look that said he wasn't fooling around. 'In the meantime,' he said to her silence, which he took for acceptance, 'we won't say anything to anybody. It will be our little secret, OK? Because if you told somebody, why, I would have to tell about you usin' this pool when you're not supposed to and your mommy might lose her job. You wouldn't want that now, would you?' Alex shook her head. 'Right. You run along now, but don't forget – same time tomorrow morning.' He laughed. 'I reckon you've seen enough for one day,' he said, stroking himself lovingly before falling backwards into the pool. Alex ran.

Upstairs, she leaned against the door of the little sitting-room and shook. She did not cry. She had learned to keep her feelings to herself a long time ago, but her eyes burned and she felt sick. She ate no breakfast, which was most unusual, and was so silent all day that Patsy thought she was coming down with something. Alex went to bed that night to toss and turn, knowing that what was coming would be horrible, dreading it yet terrified to tell Patsy because if she did it would end in Patsy being sent away and she would be left alone again; bereft and friendless. She wished Max was here. When she could bear it no longer she buried her head beneath the pillow and wept.

She was there on time next morning, almost paralysed with dread. He showed up five minutes later, sauntering along to a cabana which he opened, beckoning to her. Alex went up the steps as slowly as she could, looking round desperately to see if anyone was about. There was no one. There never was at this time in the morning. She shrank back as she went in and he shut the door behind her, slid the bolt.

'Now, then . . .' he said.

It was the beginning of a progressively terrible nightmare. That first time he made her undress and sit down in one of the deep-bottomed cane chairs with her legs wide open, then staring fixedly at the faint down, the parted pink lips, he masturbated. When he had stiffened, bucked, made mewling sounds and then erupted onto her belly in an arcing stream, Alex bit her lip so hard it bled. She told Patsy later that she had struck it on the side of the pool. Then he let her go.

This went on for several days, then he changed the programme. He made her rub his penis up and down while he fingered her between her legs, causing strange unwelcome feelings which made her thighs go weak and a hotness spread through her.

Then that changed to him probing her, first tentatively with his finger then, finally, commanding her harshly to 'pump good', he rammed his thumb inside her and used it as a piston, his long nail gouging her delicate inner flesh as he growled at her to 'do it harder, faster'. It hurt, and her rhythm faltered and she handled him roughly. He howled and his hand slashed her across the cheek, cutting her lip. 'Little bitch!' He rammed his thumb in so deeply that Alex screamed in agony. He clapped a hand over her mouth. 'Shut your fuckin' mouth!' he hissed. Then when he saw the blood trickling from her mouth he said: 'Not a word to anyone, you hear? Not one, goddam fucking word or you and your mom are done for. You tell a living soul and I'll see you both hounded to hell. Now get!'

Alex scrambled into her clothes and ran as fast as she could, tears mingling with the blood, feeling another trickle down her inner thighs. When she got back upstairs she went in extra quietly and crept into the bathroom where she was appalled and terrified to see the blood already staining her knickers. Patsy would see and know something had happened. She had already started her periods and Patsy had explained what they were and the changes in her and what they meant, but this was not the time of the month. Hastily she took off her white cotton knickers and began to wash them, crying silently all the while, her lower belly aching, her hands shaking, her body shuddering. Patsy, who had not slept much because she was worried at the change in Alex over the past ten days and at a loss to account for it was lying awake, heard the splashing and got up to investigate. Opening the bathroom door she found Alex, sobbing silently, the corner of her mouth torn and oozing blood, frantically scrubbing at her knickers in water that was already pink.

'Oh, dear God!' Patsy made to move forward, hand outstretched in both alarm and concern but she was stopped in her tracks by the frenzied face Alex turned on her. 'No! You mustn't. You mustn't tell anyone. You mustn't, do you hear? If you do he'll tell and you'll be sent away. Please.' Her voice was rising. 'I promised I wouldn't tell, and if you do he'll know I broke my promise and you'll be sent away. Promise you won't tell – promise, *promise*!' It was demanded on a note of growing hysteria that, to Patsy, sounded demented.

'Who will tell?' she asked, as calmly as she could.

But she saw Alex's lips tighten. She continued to stare at Patsy with the sort of gaze that twisted your arm. 'Promise!' she insisted. 'You must *promise*! Promise not to tell *anyone*!'

'I promise,' Patsy said. She saw Alex sway slightly as she was released from her intensity, though the hands that once more frantically began rubbing at the now almost indistinct bloodstain were still trembling. 'Alex, darling . . . let me help.' Patsy's own voice shook as she felt her throat thicken, and her eyes prick. There was something so – so *brave* – about the thirteen-year-old girl, big for her age and already well developed but even so, still a child – scrubbing valiantly so as to conceal the evidence of something so hideous, a crime so monstrous it was never talked about. Who? Patsy thought, her mind skittering. When? How often? No wonder she has been so withdrawn, so far removed from herself of late. Has someone been coming in over the wall? Perhaps from the lake? Oh, God, she thought, how do I find out? Because I have to, even if I can't tell until I discover more.

'It's all right, pet,' she said, still speaking in a calm, matter-of-fact voice, 'let me do it. You take off that dress and I'll run you a nice hot bath, then I'll make you a nice hot drink.' She went to the bath, turned it on, sprinkled in two handfuls of the fragrant salts which one of the maids had brought up from the supplies kept for the guest bathroom. All Alex and Patsy were ever provided with was

Eve Czerny soap. 'Go on,' Patsy said as if it was a normal day, 'get undressed. Give me your frock and I'll wash that too . . .'

As Alex undressed, Patsy watched through the bathroom mirror, saw the dried blood on her inner thighs and bit down hard on her lip. She saw that Alex's hands still shook so much she had difficulty undoing the buttons from neck to waist, that she had to kick her sandals off and had to struggle to unfasten the teen-bra she had recently begun to wear. And as she lowered herself into the water Patsy saw her mouth open in a grimace of pain as the hot water penetrated her inside. A doctor, she thought, I must get her to a doctor . . . what if she's been raped? Oh, dear God, what to do for the best, what to do . . .

But she forced herself to go on rubbing at the stained clothes, knowing they could not be sent down for washing with the rest of the dirty laundry. She used the soap and the nailbrush. They would have to do the job. Drying could be done by placing them on the radiators. She would say Alex had spilt some ink or something if enquiries were made . . . The main thing was to find out who had done this hideous thing and what he had done. All she knew for certain was that he had terrified – blackmailed – Alex into silence by threatening to have Patsy sent away, which meant he knew enough about the household to be able to do so . . . More, he had the power . . . 'Oh my God . . .' Her stomach lurched. No wonder she's terrified . . .

She scrubbed fiercely, keeping an eye on Alex, also scrubbing herself so hard that her skin was already turning red. I have no proof, she thought, not a shred of evidence that points to him, because Alex will never name him and her mother would never believe her. Oh, dear God! she thought again, her skin chilling at the thought of what Madame's reaction would be. Bad enough that he should turn out to be a pervert, but to debauch Alex, of all people . . . Patsy squeezed her eyes shut in fright.

But it has to be him, she reasoned. Alex has been swimming at seven in the morning whenever her mother is in residence for months and months now, and there's never been any trouble, never. The servants know she swims, Max knows, the only one who doesn't is Madame, so if *that man* found Alex there it has to be because he's an early riser. How do I find out? she thought. Spy, her quick wits told her. Get up early tomorrow morning and go and see for yourself. He will probably be expecting Alex to turn up, only she won't. As of today Alex is sickening for – for chickenpox. That will have Madame taking Christopher away or insisting Alex stays quarantined up here until every last shred of infection is gone. Then we'll see what he does . . . Once I know for sure then I can decide where to take the evidence.

'All right, darling?' she turned to Alex, now bright pink and tiring. 'Here, let Patsy do it . . . there's a good girl . . .' Patsy took the brush from Alex's hand and replaced it with the big sponge, plentifully lathered with soap. 'There . . . that's better, isn't it . . . ?'

Alex burst into tears; shattering, gulping, gouts of sobs which came from her inner depths. She flung her arms about Patsy and held on tight.

'There, there . . . it's all right, Patsy's here . . . no one will hurt you any more . . . we will take care of everything . . . Max will know and he will put it all right . . .' Yes! she thought. Max. She felt as if a weight had been lifted from her shoulders. That is what she would do. She would tell Max.

Margaret Patterson was not the kind of woman who fell apart at the first crisis, but this was something she had never had to cope with. During the war she had been an ambulance driver; in the blitz she had seen and dealt with appalling injuries; what had her feeling helpless now was not what Alex might have suffered physically, though that was bad enough, it was what it had done to her mind, for Alex, by virtue of her upbringing, was a worldly innocent. All she knew came from books and Patsy had never censored her reading, giving her free rein to range as far and wide as she wished, since to her way of thinking, an unformed mind would not take in what it did not fully comprehend. She had seen Alex take up a book only to discard it, but a couple of years later it had been read with passionate attention. She knew all about sex, for Patsy had answered her first curious questions with matter-of-fact frankness; once Alex had begun to menstruate Patsy had gone fully into both cause and effect. Alex knew and understood, but she was totally inexperienced, and that her first introduction to sex should be with a pervert not only made her governess feel angry but helpless. Alex needed to know that not all men were like that; that this particular one was an aberrant. That was why Patsy wanted Max to know, because she also knew he, and only he, could set Alex's fears at rest.

Equally important, he was in a position to do something about it. Patsy knew better than to confront Madame. That was why Alex was so terrified, for Madame would not believe it, not from a daughter she preferred not to know about. Her reaction would be to get rid of the nuisance – Patsy – and God knows what would happen to Alex after that. Only one thing was for sure. She would be punished for it – severely punished, for if ever a woman was besotted with a man, Eve Czerny was wholly in thrall to the boyish, shy charmer she had married.

'Now, let's get you dry . . .' Patsy said, helping Alex out of the bath. 'And then you must tell me everything that happened –'

Alex shook her head violently, eyes wild.

'You must, darling, because I have to know if he hurt you and if I need to ask Dr Schuler to come and take a look at you.'

'No!'

'All right, no doctor,' soothed Patsy. 'Just me . . . but I have to know what happened. I promise I won't tell anyone, except Max.'

'No!' Alex's voice was as wild as her eyes. 'You mustn't tell Max, you mustn't! I don't want him to know . . . Please, please, don't tell him, don't tell anybody . . . Max will be angry and he'll want to tell Madame and if he does that you'll be sent away and I shall be left alone again . . . oh, please, please . . . don't tell him . . .' She clutched Patsy's hands desperately, her voice shaking and breaking under the violence of her fear.

Patsy took hold of her shoulders firmly. 'Now listen to me, Alex. That man will not tell *anybody* about you using the pool, because he knows that if he does I will tell Madame what he did to you.'

'But she won't believe you, she'll believe him . . .'

'Not if we get Max on our side. Max is the only one who can speak the truth to Madame, you know that, because she knows he tells it to her for her own good. That evil man is deliberately frightening you into silence because he himself is afraid. He knows what he did is wrong – very wrong. That he can go to prison for it.'

'But she will be so angry . . . she hates me enough already. She will send you away and lock me up, I know she will.'

'She will do no such thing, because I won't allow it. Neither will Max. He will be angry – and you know what Max is like when he's angry.'

Alex's enormous eyes, brimming with tears, seemed to lighten a little. She nodded.

'Max is your good friend, isn't he?'

'Oh, yes.'

'Then he won't let you be punished for something that isn't your fault.'

'But I shouldn't have been there . . . I'm not supposed to use the pool when she's here . . . it's my fault . . .'

'It is *not* your fault! He's the one at fault. He is a foul degenerate who must be stopped. What if he does it to another young girl?' Patsy's voice faded. 'What's the matter? Why do you look like that?'

'If I don't go back tomorrow morning he'll know I've told somebody . . .' Alex's sobs broke out afresh. 'I'll have to go back . . . I must . . .'

'You are never going anywhere near that man again! I am going to let it be known that you are sickening for chickenpox. This floor will be strictly quarantined. You know how Madame is about Christopher. She's paranoid about him catching so much as a cold.'

'But he'll know, he *will*,' Alex said in agony.

'Then let him worry and wonder.' Sharply: 'He doesn't know who you are?'

'He knows my name and I told him what Max said I must say – that my mother works here.'

'So he thinks you're the child of one of the servants. Good,' Patsy said. 'Let him start to pry about you and Madame will be angry indeed! Now then, come along into your bedroom and get into bed and then you must tell me everything he said and did – everything, because if I don't know the whole story we can't do anything.'

She put Alex into a clean nightie and tucked her up in bed and then made her a cup of hot, sweet chocolate into which she crushed one of her own powerful sedatives; she was a migraine sufferer and they always gave her at least three hours of much needed, pain-free sleep.

'Now,' she said, sitting on the side of the bed, 'start at the beginning and tell me everything.'

Afterwards, she examined Alex as best she could, and to her laywoman's eye, though Alex winced when she touched her, it didn't seem as though any serious damage had been done. The blood was the result of his savage thumb action breaking Alex's hymen.

Patsy hid her revulsion behind a concerned expression when Alex told how she had been made to masturbate her mother's husband.

We must be thankful he did not fully rape her, Patsy thought, but had I not discovered her this morning that would no doubt have happened in time, and from what Alex, in her innocence, described of the penis she had been forced to manipulate, its size was considerable, so it would not only have deflowered but damaged.

She sat by Alex's bed till the sedative took effect, and left it only when she heard Marthe, who was the maid who serviced the top floor, come in with the breakfast tray. Her good morning was as cheerful and brisk as ever but Patsy told Marthe – who would relay it to the rest of the staff – that Alex was not at all well and from the spots that were beginning to appear on her skin it looked like she was coming down with chickenpox. 'She must have picked up the virus last time we were in Thonon,' Patsy sighed. 'That means quarantine for a couple of weeks, I'm afraid.'

'Oh, what a pity,' Marthe sympathized. 'And in the middle of such lovely weather. Poor Alex.'

That done, Patsy ate a solitary breakfast and then, moving in her normal quiet way, she went carefully down to the third floor and along to Max's suite where she put in a call to him in Sydney. He always left a copy of his itinerary when he went on a trip, so she knew where he would be, but there was no answer. She would have to try again later.

Next morning, she left Alex sleeping and by seven o'clock she was down at the pool, concealed behind a large rhododendron bush. After about ten minutes, she saw Rik Stevens come down the flight of steps from the terrace, obviously looking for someone. She saw him frown when he registered the empty pool, watched as he investigated every cabana, found them empty. He stood scowling for a moment, looked up at the windows of the house with a threatening glare and then, with a shrug, dropped his robe. He was naked and every bit as big as Alex had described. Patsy had to clench her jaw to suborn her anger. When he had swum to the far end of the pool she quietly retreated and made her way round to the back of the house again.

When finally she got hold of Max she gave him the facts before saying, 'I don't have sufficient clout to tell Madame, added to which she's not likely to believe me even if I challenge her to have Alex examined.'

'How is Alex?'

'Terrified. She thinks that if anything is said to Madame it will end only one way – with me being sent away. That is something she can't handle. She has seen too many people disappear from her life. She has to be sent to school, Max. For her own safety and my peace of mind. I've already made enquiries at my old school, Cheltenham Ladies' College. I'm sure Alex has the ability to win a scholarship if necessary. I'm going to pull strings and make her sit last year's papers to see how she does; if I know Alex she'll walk it. Whatever, she can't stay here, not after this.'

'Tell me everything once again – from the beginning.'

Patsy did so. There was a silence then Max said, 'We have to play this one by ear. If I come home now then the cat is out of the bag and we are the ones who will end up being clawed. You're right when you say Madame will never believe it. What we have to do is prove it to her. For now, do nothing and say nothing. How long can you keep Alex out of the way?'

'Two weeks, perhaps three.'

'Good. I'm due back in Switzerland in two. What's the situation regarding Pretty Boy?'

'I'm told they plan to remain at the villa until the end of the month.'

'Good. Keep your eyes and ears open and your mouth closed. Whatever you find out, phone me and let me know. By the time I get back I will have thought of how we can get Pretty Boy right smack in the centre of the true picture.'

'All right.'

'Is Alex OK? I mean, do you think a doctor is necessary?'

'Not for what that man did, but if Alex is supposed to have chickenpox . . . I should call Dr Schuler.'

'Can you trust him?'

'I think so. He has looked after Alex ever since she came here, seen her through the usual childhood ailments. He only comes to see the servants. He is the staff doctor, not Madame's.'

'Call him. Get him to examine Alex; we may need his statement later.'

'All right,' Patsy agreed, 'but it won't be easy. Alex is dead set against telling anybody.'

'You'll have to make her see that she has no choice. It should be done anyway. He could have done some internal damage.'

'She did bleed a lot,' Patsy said, subdued.

There was another silence then Max said in a tight voice, 'Then get Dr Schuler to go over her – tell him the truth if you are sure he can be trusted –'

'He can.'

'Then get him in right away. Anything else you feel uneasy about, call me, do you hear?'

'I will. Thank you, Max. I don't know what I would have done without you . . .'

'What are friends for?'

Alex put up fierce resistance to the idea of being examined by Dr Schuler, though she both liked and trusted him, but when Patsy explained that it was purely on health grounds, that she had her own duty to see that no internal damage had been done, no infection caused, Alex agreed, since if there was something wrong and it was not attended to, it might have to come out anyway if she fell ill.

'If only I had not gone swimming,' she said desolately. 'It is all my fault . . .'

'It most certainly is *not*!' Patsy said firmly. 'All right, so you were breaking what is, to my mind, a spiteful rule; that doesn't make what he did any less disgraceful. Somehow we have to see that he doesn't do it again.'

'How?' Alex asked hopelessly.

'I don't know yet, but I intend to find out.'

Dr Schuler, for twenty-five years a village doctor, was neither surprised nor revolted by what Patsy told him. He had seen and experienced a great many unusual things during his time as an ordinary village GP. He liked Alex, treated her as a highly intelligent thirteen-year-old should be treated, and explained what he was going to do so that she was as relaxed as she could be during his examination.

'The hymen is torn,' he told Patsy, as he scrubbed his hands, 'and there is internal laceration, but only slight. The nail was obviously in need of cutting. There is no trace of infection but I will give a course of antibiotics just in case. But it is not the physical damage that concerns me as much as the psychological. How has she been since?'

'Withdrawn, not that she is an outgoing child, but much more silent than usual. She broods.'

'And what do you propose to do about what has happened?'

'There is nothing I can do without proof. It is a case of her word against his and while he has power, she – both of us – have none. Madame would not be pleased if I were to point the finger.'

'Madame has little to do with the child?'

'Madame has nothing to do with her,' Patsy said bluntly. 'She gave me sole charge and the responsibility that goes with it. Alex is – tolerated as long as she gives no trouble.'

'There is some – relationship?'

'Through Madame's first husband,' Patsy said obliquely.

'Ah . . . I see.' He took Patsy's discreet explanation to be that Madame was Alex's stepmother, and as it fitted his own theory, accepted it unquestioningly.

'Always a difficult situation,' he said.

'*Very* difficult in this particular case.' Patsy met his keen interest guilelessly.

He nodded. 'I understand.' He went to his case, took out a bottle into which he counted twelve small white tablets. 'Three per day for four days; that should take care of any infection. She is a healthy child – I think this is only the fourth time I have been called upon to treat her.'

'True . . . the other times were for measles, once when she sprained her wrist, and once for a very bad cold.'

'Doctors and teachers must, of necessity, have good memories,' Dr Schuler observed drily, 'and in this case, as it is supposed to be chickenpox, I will remember to call in again in a few days' time to check on the patient's progress.'

'Thank you,' Patsy said gratefully.

From Madame, there was no reaction to the news that Alex had chickenpox, only an order that she be kept strictly away from the rest of the house. But Patsy noticed that one of Geneva's top paediatricians was called in to give Christopher the once over –

which meant, she thought, that they aren't leaving, which can only mean that *he* doesn't want to go, and that she's either unwilling or unable to make him. But if Madame's husband made any enquiries about Alex they were very discreet because Patsy heard nothing, though with Alex so quiet and withdrawn she had other things to think about. Like the fact that Alex spent hours in the bathroom, and whereas this was not unusual because even in the bath she found time to read, it was unusual now in that she took no book with her, and when she came out she was pink from an obvious scrubbing. Patsy was troubled. If Alex began to equate sex with a feeling of being unclean she might run into serious psychological trouble in the future. And though she still sat up on her favourite window seat, it was not to curl up with a book but to sit and stare out of the large porthole window. Patsy tried to get her to talk about it, to examine it and thus understand it, which was how they usually worked, but Alex always changed the subject.

By the time Max came back from his trip Patsy was deeply worried.

Alex was in bed when he finally managed to get upstairs, his first hours being spent closeted with Madame, reporting on his trip.

'But she was happy, that's the main thing,' Max said, accepting a glass of Jack Daniel's from Patsy, to whom he had given a private stock for his consumption when he was visiting. Patsy did not drink alcohol; tea was her tipple. 'Figures are in the jet black, profits are up, ditto sales, and she was in a good mood anyway. Whatever else that son-of-a-bitch gets up to he does his duty by his wife. Now tell me – what's been happening?'

'Nothing. The chickenpox story was accepted without question, though I was wrong about Madame taking fright and removing Christopher from the scene. All she did was have him looked at by that expensive paediatrician. They've shown no sign of moving on. I think *he* likes it here.'

'Has he been enquiring for Alex?'

'Not that I know of. He's too shrewd for that, surely. Why should he show interest in what he thinks is the child of a servant?'

'Do you think he will know about the chickenpox?'

'Only if Madame told him, and you know she never speaks about Alex to anyone.'

'He's probably wondering what's happened to her, then, and also if he's safe.'

'He still swims early in the morning. I've been down several times to check.'

'Good,' Max said. 'I was hoping to hear that.'

'Why?'

'Because that's how I intend to catch him in the act.'

Patsy's face froze. 'You're not suggesting that Alex goes back!'

'How else are we going to nail him?' Max leant forward. 'Look, I've got it all worked out. I go down first, taking with me the camera I bought in Tokyo: absolutely silent, wide-angle lens, any focus you care to name, and I get into position in the middle of one of those enormous rhododendron bushes with my little tape-recorder – right off the latest Japanese drawing-board, fits into my pocket and will pick up any sound within a radius of thirty yards –'

'But he takes her into one of the cabanas.'

'I'm getting to that. It's always the same one, isn't it? And they have louvres which are usually open and through which I can see and introduce my dandy little tape-recorder not to mention my camera. Don't worry, everything will be in place by the time I'm ready to shoot the scene. All I need is for Alex to be there and for him to think he's still got it made.'

'But – surely – I mean, it's two weeks now, I doubt if he'll be expecting her again.'

'I think he will. I think he thinks she's running scared and that if she knows what's good for her she'll turn up. Maybe he knows somebody has chickenpox and with her no-show has put two and two together. Once time went on and nothing was said he'd know she hadn't told on him. So why shouldn't she come back? She's supposed to be afraid for her mother, isn't she? He probably thinks she's been worrying herself sick and can't wait to get back on the job. After all, he *is* Madame's husband, and Alex is only a servant's brat. And he's an arrogant son-of-a-bitch. He acts like this is *his* house. I know, I've seen and heard him. I didn't like him the first time I set eyes on him and now I know why. He made my flesh creep. Little girls – defenceless children – are right up his street, and all that calculated little-boy-lost charm covers as ugly a con-man as ever I saw. Almost as soon as I got into the house I had Jacques complaining about how he'd been mauling one of the maids – that pretty young redhead – comes up here when it's Marthe's day off –'

'Lotte!'

'That's the one. Evidently he's been cornering her in the bedrooms and shoving his hands where he oughtn't and threatening her with the sack if she complains. It was only because Jacques caught her crying that he found out.'

'But she's only just seventeen!'

'He likes them young. I've told Jacques to send her home for a few days and report her as sick. By the time she comes back Pretty Boy should be long gone.'

Patsy shook her head. 'You're taking an enormous risk. Madame will be fit to tie . . . he stands high in her regard.'

'I'm aware of that, but it's a risk I have to take. Alex needs to go to school and there has to be a compelling reason to send her there. Also, I happen to want Madame out from under. Right now she thinks she's married to God's gift and he's beginning to throw his weight around, mostly in my direction. I have enough of a load to carry right now and I'm not having him add to it. He knows I don't like him and he's been telling carefully selected tales about me. I don't know why he married Madame but I know it wasn't for love. He's after bigger game. He wants to control her in and out of bed. What worries me is that she doesn't seem to care what he does as long as he does her – as often as possible. I left here in what I might modestly describe as an impregnable position; I come back to find he's been undermining my foundations.'

Max shook his head. 'No question about it, Patsy, he has to go, and under the darkest cloud I can get to come and rain on his parade. Apart from what he's done to Alex I have my own score to settle.' He paused. 'And I think I can say that once I've told Alex what I propose to do she'll be willing to do her part. You needn't worry that he will actually *do* anything; he won't get that far because I won't allow it. But I want him showing Alex his assets and I want him telling her loud and clear what he wants her to do with them; once I have him on film and tape I'll expose him to Madame.'

'Light the blue touchpaper and retire?' Patsy shivered.

'There's a chance it might blow me out of here, but so long as it blows Alex into a good school I'll take my chances. I'll talk to her as soon as I can. Right now I have repairs to make. If that creep thinks he can get rid of Max Fabian he's got another think coming. I've got an idea but it will take time to set up. In the meantime, keep Alex away from him and don't worry.' He grinned as cheerfully as he could. 'Never fear, Max is here.'

'I never do, when you are.'

But when she told Alex, the usual radiant delight was unforthcoming. 'I haven't time to see him,' Alex said, trying to sound disinterested. 'I should catch up on my work. I haven't been doing much recently, have I?'

'But Max has been away for a whole month.'

'He's been away that long before.'

'And you've always been glad to see him on his return.'

'Well I don't want to see him now.' Alex's voice rose slightly and Patsy let the matter drop.

When Max was able to return Patsy told him of Alex's reaction.

'Where is she?'

'In bed. She says she has a headache. I think she's ashamed.'

'Then I have to put that right. I'm very fond of Alex and I don't want her to be afraid of me just because I'm a man.'

'All she knew of men came from you – until now. That, I think, is what she finds so disturbing. That you aren't all men.'

'Maybe that's my fault, but what with having to be so damned careful all the time it's always a case of easier said than done. Whatever, I have to do the right thing now.'

'It's such a pity that it all happened now, when she was really beginning to come out of her shell. She's not nearly so timid and no longer hides herself away when there are strangers around. She was starting to believe that she's neither unlikeable or unlovable, which was the case for many years. That's why what has happened is so bad for her. She knows – because I have told her – that men who do things such as were done to her do not do them to women because they like them; they do it because they hold women in contempt. She believes that her mother's husband was merely showing his contempt for her – who and what she is, a nothing; confident that she will say nothing because he knows her mother would never believe her. She loathes what he did, but what worries me is that she's coming to loathe herself more. Oh, I know it's an accepted reaction, but in Alex's case it's so much worse because it's only recently – only since you took an interest in her – that she's begun to have any self-esteem at all. This has sent her right back to square one, and it grieves me.'

Max was silent, but Patsy thought he looked rather grim about the mouth. Then he went across to Alex's door and, without knocking, opened the door and went in.

When Patsy went in to say good night, Max had been gone a good half-hour but she had waited, wanting Alex to have time to herself to think about whatever it was Max had said. He had been in with her about twenty minutes, and when he had come out he had given his usual, cheerful good night before going back downstairs. Now, as Patsy opened the door, she saw that Alex was sitting up in bed, knees raised, a book in its usual position propped against her thighs. Patsy breathed a silent prayer of thanks. It was the first time since the incident that Alex had picked up a book of her own volition.

'Time for lights out,' Patsy said.

'Is it? Can't I have another half an hour? Please?'

'Well . . .'

'To celebrate Max's return,' Alex wheedled. 'Look what he brought me, Patsy.'

She held out a wrist. On it was a delicately carved filigree of painted ivory interspersed with tiny beads of coral. 'It's Japanese . . . He got it in Osaka . . .'

'It's very pretty,' Patsy approved. Just the thing for a young girl.

'And this . . .' Alex held up an exquisitely bound book. 'Japanese paintings. Prints, of course, but some of them were painted when we were still in the dark ages!' Her voice, her face, were alight with pleasure of the kind that had been missing of late, and her eyes were no longer opaque and unreadable as they always were when she 'holed up inside herself' as Max put it. They were bright and as shiny as jeweller-polished stones. God bless you, Max, Patsy thought. I don't know what you said but whatever it was, it was what she needed to hear.

With her intuitive, adult-beyond-her-years perception, Alex said, 'Max explained things to me. About men like Madame's husband. He says they're sick, and that I don't have to feel that he owns me or my body. He says I'm still in control of myself and that all I have to do to prove it is to see that man punished.'

Patsy moved uneasily.

'I have to do it, Patsy.' Suddenly, it seemed that Alex was the adult, Patsy the frightened teenager. 'Max will protect me. He won't let that man actually *do* anything, but we have to have proof. It's the only way I'll be believed.'

'If you're sure . . .'

'Max says it will be all right and Max always knows, doesn't he?'

'It would seem so.'

'I *want* him to be found out,' Alex said in a fierce little voice. 'I want *her* to know what he is.'

'It will be – difficult – afterwards.'

'Not if I'm able to go away to school, and I do so want to go. Not to leave you, but –'

'I know,' Patsy said gently. 'I understand.'

'Max says there will never be a better chance because if he can show her, she'll have no choice but to believe, will she? And it's not as though she doesn't hate me enough already, is it?'

Patsy winced at the matter-of-fact acceptance of what was, to her, a terrible aberration. 'Max says she will be glad to get rid of me, but that I'll always have you and him to count on, and I will, won't I?'

'Always,' Patsy said, controlling her wavering voice.

'I can come to you for holidays, can't I?'

'I should like that very much.'

'And you will come to Speech Days and things – Max says he will as often as he can, so I won't be any more alone than I already am, will I?'

'No.' Patsy's throat clogged.

'Don't worry,' Alex said, taking hold of one of Patsy's hands. 'It will be all right. Max says so.'

Two mornings later, when Alex, wearing her swimsuit under her dress, went down to the swimming pool, she appeared to be no different from any other morning. The only difference was that it was some fifteen minutes earlier than usual, and that Max, when she got down to the poolside, was in position in the depths of a huge, spreading rhododendron, tape-recorder and camera at the ready.

'You all right?' he asked in a low voice. 'We can always scrub the whole thing if you feel you can't go through with it.'

'No!' Alex's voice was emphatic, though every bit as low as his.

'I want everybody to know what he is, but most of all I want *her* to know.'

'Right, you know what to say?'

'Yes.'

'And what not to do?'

'Yes.'

'OK. Get into the pool then, but keep to this end when you see him coming.'

Alex undid her button-through dress and dropped it on to a nearby lounger before doing a perfect running dive into the water, reappearing halfway down the pool but turning to do a powerful crawl back in Max's direction. She did several widths before, on shaking the water from her eyes, she saw her mother's husband coming down the terrace steps in her direction, but she pretended she had not seen, and turning, she duck-dived to swim away from him. Through the screening branches, which were uncomfortable and made it not only difficult but imperative that he didn't move, Max saw Alex's current stepfather drop his towelling robe and stand naked right where Alex would see him when she surfaced.

As Alex's head came out of the water Max pressed the button of his recorder so as to capture the actor's natural voice saying, 'So you really do know on which side your bread is buttered, eh?'

'I don't know what you mean,' Alex said nervously.

'Oh yes you do. You're the kid who had chickenpox, aren't you? I heard it mentioned on account of Christopher. His mother gets anxious when there's any kind of sickness around. You OK now?'

'I'm not infectious, if that's what you mean.'

Rik Stevens laughed. 'I've had chickenpox twice,' he said. 'I don't think I'll be catching it again, but I'm glad to see that you don't want your mother to lose her job. One word from me, kid, that's all it will take unless you get out of that pool right now and let me give you another lesson.'

'I don't want to,' Alex said, defiant but shaky of voice.

'But I do, and what I say goes around here. Either you get out of that pool and into that first cabana or I go straight back inside and tell Madame that you've been using the pool against her strict orders. You'll be out of this house -- you and your mother – and on the streets before you've had time to dry off – and I'll personally see to it that there's no reference. *Then* see if your mother can get another job!'

'I don't like what you do to me.' Alex began to cry as Max had told her, although it took no effort at all in her current fragile state of mind.

'What I've done to you up till now has just been a taster. I've had two weeks and a bit to think about it, so today I reckon I should make up for lost time. I've got some real goodies in store for you today, kid. My old man here is rarin' to go . . . look at him, he's already strainin' at the leash.'

Max's finger silently depressed the shutter of the Japanese camera focused unerringly on the film star's erect penis, as thick as a club and obscenely purple-red.

'Don't make me, please . . . don't make me . . .' Alex was sobbing now.

'I like it when they beg,' Rik Stevens said. 'Now get out of that pool and into that cabana — time's awastin'.'

Alex scrambled out of the pool and head bent, shoulders hunched, scurried up the steps to the first cabana. Max waited until the slatted door had shut behind them, heard the bolt shot home, then backed out of the bush, shedding blossoms everywhere, and raced up the steps after him, his feet silent in rubber-soled boat shoes. Round behind the cabin he had placed a bench, onto which he climbed. The louvres he had opened earlier to their fullest extent, and as he had surmised, Alex's latest stepfather was in too much of a hurry to bother to glance up. He was standing threateningly over Alex, who was making a slow and clumsy job — as instructed — of taking off her swimsuit. 'Do it to the slow count of twenty-five,' Max instructed. 'That should give me time to position the camera and the tape-recorder, but keep him talking if you can — get him to spell out what he has in store for you. You don't have to listen; just so long as my recorder catches every word while I literally catch him in the act. Not that he will get to lay a finger on you, OK? If he does — fight! Kick, scratch, bite — scream. I'll be with you in seconds.'

Now, Alex was sobbing as she pleaded. 'Please . . . don't hurt me again . . . you made me bleed before and I had to hide my pants . . . just let me go, please. I won't use the pool again, I promise. That's why I came this morning; to tell you that I won't come back any more . . .'

'Too late; you've used it too many times . . .'

'And every time you use me . . .'

The sex symbol scowled. 'I don't like sassy fast-mouths,' he warned. 'Just remember who I am, little girl. I sit pretty high on the roost around here. One word from me and you're out on your ear. Now strip!'

'What are you going to do to me?' Alex asked fearfully.

'You want to know? Well, I guess anticipation is half the pleasure . . . First . . .' And he began to enumerate what he was going to do, his voice salivating at the prospect, his hand all the time fondling, stroking his erect penis, now pointing straight up like some questing dog, quivering in its intensity. Rapidly, Max pressed the shutter, time after time, the little recorder's tape circling steadily and silently. His rage was such that he had to force his hands to steadiness, and his jaw was clenched so tightly that little bunches of muscle stood out on either side of his mouth.

Finally, Alex stood naked and Rik Stevens smiled, his eyes shining wetly like his mouth. 'Now come over here,' he said softly, 'and get down on your knees.'

Max glanced at his watch. Now! he thought, and right on time, as instructed, Patsy's voice called, 'Alex? Alex, where are you?'

'It's my mother,' Alex cried, loudly.

'Be quiet!' A hand flashed out to clamp itself over Alex's mouth.

'Alex? Where are you . . . are you in a cabana?' The voice came nearer.

'OK, go to her,' the words were hissed furiously, 'but you breathe one word . . . one solitary word, kid, and you and your mother are done for, you hear?'

Alex nodded, feigning terror, though Max's alert eyes saw at once how her rigid tension relaxed. As she opened the door, Rik Stevens flattened himself against the wall behind it.

'I'm coming!' Alex called. 'Just a minute . . .' The swimsuit was on in seconds and she was out of the door and running down to where Patsy stood on the first step.

Seizing Alex's hand she went into her own rehearsed speech. 'I thought I told you not to come here,' she scolded. 'You know Madame's orders . . . now come along quickly before anyone sees us . . .' Their voices faded.

Max snapped a picture of Alex's stepfather listening intently, head cocked, though his mighty weapon was not now cocked but drooping, limp with the fright of a narrow escape.

'Shit!' The expletive was virulent, and the first of a long stream of obscenities which flowed with the ease of long practice. But he still waited a full five minutes before opening the door cautiously and peering out. Then, sure the coast was clear, he sauntered out, down to the pool, plunged in, did two swift lengths before climbing out and shrugging back into his towelling robe. Then he disappeared in the direction of the house.

Max let out a long, shaky breath and stepped down from the stool. His mouth was dry and his hands were trembling but, he thought exultantly, he had the goods on that perverted bastard. It's not exactly in living colour, he thought, as he wound back the tape, unlike his movies, but the sound deserves an Oscar, for the actor's voice was unmistakable if somewhat nasal instead of East Coast crisp. 'Let's see you try and get out of this one,' Max said happily. 'But first, let's see how Alex is . . .'

'Was I all right?' she asked, when Max came in.

'You deserve an Oscar,' Max told her. 'Best Actress. As for you, Patsy, you get Best Supporting Actress. Me, I'll settle for Best Director.'

'I was so nervous,' Patsy confessed. 'I'm sure my voice wobbled.'

'Sounded perfectly OK to me,' Max assured her.

He tipped Alex's chin, looked straight into her eyes. 'You've got guts, kid,' he complimented, in the Humphrey Bogart voice that always made her giggle. Then, soberly and with an almost savage anguish: 'I only wish there had been some other way . . . but we had to get him dead to rights.'

'I know,' Alex said, the child comforting the man.

'You knew I was there all the time – that I wouldn't have let things get out of hand?'

Alex stood on tiptoe to plant a smacker on his lower jaw. 'I knew you would look after me. Don't you always?'

Max turned to Patsy. 'What did I tell you? A –' He was going to say fucking marvel but modified it to '– one in a million.'

'And you *are* going to tell Madame?'

'I'm not only going to tell her, I'm going to show her and make her listen.'

Alex shivered. 'She'll say it's all my fault, I know she will. It always is where I'm concerned.'

'Not the way I tell it.'

Patsy coughed slightly. 'Where – er – how will you get the pictures developed? They're not the kind one usually takes into the chemist's, are they?'

'Never fear. I know someone who will produce a perfect set of eight by sixes and keep his mouth shut.' His grin showed his dimples. 'Anything smaller would not do justice to the – er – magnificent scenery.'

Alex choked on a giggle, which turned into full-throated laughter which ended in tears.

'It's OK, baby . . .' Max enfolded her against his massive chest. 'You came through like a trouper but it was a nasty experience, one that shouldn't be part of any girl's growing up, but he'll get his. You have my word on that – and do I ever lie to you?'

Alex shook her head as she accepted the clean white handkerchief he gave her.

'When will you tell Madame?' Patsy asked.

'When I've got everything set up. There are a couple of things I have to do first . . . I may have to go away for a couple of days but don't worry, I'll be back for the confrontation. First I have to persuade Madame to do something she wasn't keen on when I first told her about it.'

'What's that?' asked Alex.

'I can't say anything about it now, but if it comes off you'll find out.'

'They're staying on here, then?' Patsy asked.

'Yes. Plans are for them to be here until Pretty Boy has to go back to Hollywood to start his next movie, which starts shooting towards the end of next month. All you have to do is sit tight and don't – repeat *don't* – go anywhere near that pool. He won't do anything. He got a sharp fright this morning so my guess is he'll lie low for a while. That's a guy as knows how to protect his own interests.'

A week later, Alex and Patsy were just about to sit down to supper when Marthe came in, eyes huge with excitement, breathless from more than four flights of stairs.

'You're to go downstairs to Madame's sitting-room right away,' she said.

Alex and Patsy looked at each other and Alex swallowed. 'We'll be right down,' Patsy said calmly.

'I'm scared,' Alex said in a small voice. 'She will blame me, I know she will . . .' She bolted from the table and Patsy heard her vomiting in the bathroom.

Following her, Patsy bathed her white face with the damp facecloth. 'I will be there and so will Max,' she said. 'So don't worry.'

'But she hates me, you know she hates me . . . and she loves him, doesn't she? She married him, didn't she?' Alex's voice was strained and high.

'We must go,' Patsy said gently. 'You know she hates to be kept waiting.'

But when Patsy tapped on the white and gold door of Madame's private sitting-room, the voice that bade them enter sounded normal.

Eve was standing in front of the fire, her back to them. She was wearing a favourite Fortuny hostess gown, the sort of dress she wore when dining at home; of bronze silk, intricately and finely pleated. Against it, her hair glowed like newly polished copper. She did not turn. They waited. Alex was clutching Patsy's hand, though she was by now as tall as her governess, and Patsy could feel her body pressing as close as it could for comfort. She squeezed the hand that held hers as if to say, 'It's all right. I won't let her bully you.'

They waited. There was no sound but the soughing of the wind in the trees outside, the ticking of the little rock crystal clock, the crackle of the fire. Alex's wide eyes went round the small but luxurious room in awe. She had never been inside this room before, and its sumptuous decoration – the Aubusson carpet, the old gold silk of the upholstery, the Fantin Latour flower paintings, the porcelain, the eighteenth-century furniture – were so far removed from the attic eyrie as to make it impossible to believe they were both part of the same house.

Her eyes finally came to rest on the portrait above the fireplace; the Annigoni portrait of Madame. He had painted her sheathed in purple velvet as befits an Empress, one bejewelled hand holding the cloth in place at one shoulder, the other bare where the velvet had slipped, revealing the pearly gleam of satin-smooth skin. Her glorious hair was down about her shoulders, and the eyes held an insolent smile which matched the curve of her mouth. You may look, it said, but you go down on your knees first.

'Where's Max?' Alex whispered on a breath. Patsy shook her head. Then the door at the other end of the room opened, and Eve's husband stepped through it. 'OK, honey, where's the fire? Jacques said –' He stopped abruptly as he saw the two figures at the other end of the room.

Eve turned from the fire and Alex saw with fright that her face was the well-remembered mask of old, an exquisitely formed set of features as lifeless as papier mâché, yet Alex sensed – almost felt – the rage that was being kept under ruthless control; it came towards her in waves of heat. Yet the voice was almost indifferently cool when Eve said, 'I won't introduce you to each other since I believe you're already intimately acquainted.'

Eve's husband's stare was as blank as her face. 'Know who?' he asked. Eve said nothing, only looked, but it spurred him to say, 'I don't understand. Who is this kid, and what has she been saying about me?' Then his expression changed, as if his director had said, 'Now I want you to show light dawning as you suddenly realize . . .' His tone was almost indulgently relieved when he said, 'I see what it is . . . I told you about this sort of thing, didn't I honey? About the legions of crazy women who write and say they've had my baby? I'm a sex symbol, remember? The world is full of crazy females who claim I've had sex with them at one time or another. No man with a healthy libido could get through them all in three lifetimes.' He turned to Alex and his tone was reproachful. 'Nice try, kid, but you're out of your league. Try Warren Beatty. He has the reputation, not me.' He turned back to his wife to state earnestly, 'I've never seen this girl in my life.'

'Then how come she's seen you – and I mean all of you.' Eve crossed to her desk and picked up a flat paper envelope which she tossed in his direction. He caught it neatly but he still looked mystified until he opened the flap and drew out the first picture. Alex saw his expression change and for a moment he was stricken silent, but again he obeyed his inner director to say indifferently, 'Pictures can be faked . . .' Yet he still riffled through them and his face tightened. He did not turn to look at Alex, he was too clever for that, but he had no need to. She sensed how he felt.

'So this is not your voice?'

Eve stabbed her forefinger at the little recorder she was now holding. '... likes you, see?' The voice was unmistakable even if the accent was different. 'See how he sits up and begs? He knows he's in for a treat, that you're going to make a fuss of him just like you did those other times ... he liked that. Your mouth is just the right size ... and when you've given him enough head then we'll see how he likes it inside you, OK? He likes them young ... nice and tight and brand new ...'

'No ... please, I don't want to, please ...' Alex's voice was ragged and breathy with panic. 'Please don't make me ... I don't like it ...'

'What you like doesn't matter. It's what *I* like, because around here, what I say goes. Either you do as I say or you're out on your ear. Now come over here and get down on your knees.'

Eve's finger stabbed the recorder to silence.

'I rather think yours is the mouthful,' she said with cold amusement. 'Where do you come from and what were you? A field hand? A cowboy, perhaps, since that common little accent is definitely Western.'

'Oklahoma, as it happens,' her husband said easily, 'and tapes can be faked too. This is not the first time this sort of thing has been tried.'

'No, but it's the last. This is Switzerland, not Hollywood. Your studio has no power here, nor does it have the police in its pocket. If I make them a present of these pictures and this tape they will take the matter very seriously indeed, especially when they're backed up by a signed statement from the doctor who examined the girl and can testify to the fact that her hymen was broken savagely and that there are lacerations in the walls of –'

'All right!' It came out hoarsely.

'I will take you to court,' Eve said in calm, measured tones. 'I will expose you to public disgrace. Your career will be finished –'

'Or?' he interrupted.

'You leave this house now, as you are. Your things will be sent on. You will not contest the divorce. You will do exactly as my lawyers tell you.'

He was staring at her in utter amazement. 'Who the hell do you think you are? Do you know who you're ordering around here?' In jibing tones: 'I'm no two-bit Italian prince down on his luck scrabbling for dimes. I'm Rik Stevens and my movies are box-office dreams! Yes, I have a studio behind me, and if you think they'll stand for this you're out of your skull! I'm worth far too much to them. Do you know how much *The First and The Last* grossed last year? Thirty million dollars . . . you can't push me around like some no-hope extra. Take me on and you'll find out you've bitten off more than even you with your expensively fixed teeth can chew.' He was so confident as to be cocky.

Eve considered him and her smile had his own fading. 'You think so?' She raised her voice. 'Max,' she called.

He came out from behind the heavy swathe of antique brocade curtain. 'You called?' he asked in Jacques' best pompous manner. Alex stifled her giggle in Patsy's side, but she couldn't hide the joy on her face. Patsy, too, let go an unheard sigh of utter relief. She had had the feeling that any minute the situation was going to explode.

'Tell Mr Stevens about the negotiations you have just concluded.'

'With pleasure.' He bowed before turning to a suddenly tense and very wary face. 'As of two o'clock yesterday afternoon – California time – fifty-one per cent of Bercowicz International belongs to Madame Eve Czerny. I signed the papers and concluded the deal, on her behalf and as her proxy, at that time. Mr Bercowicz no longer has any role to play in the company. He has been replaced by a Mr Douglas Hirsch.' Max smiled sunnily. 'It would seem that Mr Bercowicz's cherished dream of making another *Gone With The Wind* has been blown away by reason of the cyclone of disapproval which has greeted his latest epic *All Passion Spent*, which has just caused a big bang throughout Southern California by its colossal flop at the box office. Since it was released three months ago it has failed to recoup even ten per cent of its enormous cost – would you like me to give you the exact figures?'

'You're lying!' The crisp upper-class East Coast accent was gone; in its place the nasal Western twang of his Oklahoma antecedents, as fear burned away the acquired surface gloss.

Max put a hand into his inside pocket, came out with a long, legal-looking document. 'I have here our copy of the contract. I presume you know Mr Bercowicz's signature from your own contract. Do examine it at your leisure.' He walked forward, held the contract under the actor's nose, lifting up the first page to reveal the signatures at the bottom; his own and that of Cyrus L. Bercowicz. 'Your contract, of course, now belongs to Madame, it being part of the deal. As the major shareholder, hers is now the final authority on everything, but you may rest assured that your four-picture deal is not affected. The two remaining pictures will go ahead as planned. Starting date of July twenty-eighth for your next – er –' Max pretended to refer to the document, 'ah, yes . . . here it is, *Second Chance*, co-starring the lovely Lora Welles, to be directed by Sidney Shallert.' Max smiled again. 'Contingent, of course, on your doing exactly what Madame has already told you to do. If you don't, then I'm afraid your contract will be terminated on the grounds of moral turpitude.'

'I don't believe it! Cy Bercowicz would never sell me down the river! He can't afford to –'

'He can't afford not to. He's too deep in debt. He put every penny of his profits into *All Passion Spent*, he sold his yacht and he mortgaged the fake Italian *palazzo* up in Bel Air.' Max sighed. 'Mr Bercowicz, I am afraid, is, not to put too fine a point on it, flat broke. What he made from this deal he will need to pay his creditors, and from what I hear the line stretches to San Diego.'

Rik Stevens's white face swivelled from his wife to Max and back again. 'You set me up! You planted this little bitch! Somebody told you –' He clamped his jaw tight.

'That you like little girls? Yes, I found that out, too. We know how the studio had it all hushed up, how much it cost them to do so.'

Eve's husband was silent, his mind working furiously. 'Cy can't be broke,' he said at last and with confidence. 'My last two pictures grossed more than sixty-five million dollars.'

'Which he has spent with the recklessness of a man under sentence of death – which he was. Apart from the millions – and millions – he sank into *All Passion Spent* he personally produced and directed two other multi-million-dollar turkeys. He also has a very expensive wife. You know her well, I believe. The lovely Sally Barnes? She adores diamonds, big ones. He also spent seven million dollars on that *Queen Mary* he called a yacht before he sold it for three. And he's in hock to not one, but three Las Vegas casinos. The gentlemen who own them are *very* anxious to have their debts paid in full.'

'It can't be . . . *it can't be*,' the actor repeated desperately.

'It is. Mr Bercowicz was forced to sell a fifteen per cent interest in the studio his father built in order to finance *All Passion Spent*, and he'd disposed of ten per cent the year before that. He'd sold bits here, bits there which, when the crunch came, left him somewhat powerless when they took a vote. Oh, and I forgot to mention: he's also being chased by the IRS for two years' back taxes.'

'How come I didn't know? Cy would have told me. We're friends . . .'

'Mr Bercowicz has no friends. Only creditors. He inherited a thriving studio from his father seven years ago, since when he has run it into the ground. He was sick, of course. A sad case of bankruptcy. Had he not accepted Madame's offer he would have gone down the tubes. Cy is great at spending money but when it comes to making it . . .' Max's wolf-grin flashed again, 'he can only do that with women, like you. He was only too glad to save his own skin; yours did not come into it. I guess he knows that one way or another you'll float to the top, even if it's only as a corpse.'

'There's a fix here somewhere . . . you've been against me ever since I came into this house –'

'You bet I have. I knew what you were the moment I set eyes on you; an arrogant, jumped-up son-of-a-bitch who came to believe his own publicity. Hollywood has changed. Louis B. Mayer is dead; the old studio system was buried some time ago. Big stars can no longer get away with murder, even if the moral climate is no longer as strict as it was when they crucified Ingrid Bergman. Men who abuse children are not very popular with fans, be they ever so loyal. This girl is thirteen years old; back home they'd take a dim view and your star would lose its shine. Over here they don't give a damn who you are, only what you've done. Madame now *owns* you, get that through your thick skull if you can. In future you will work for her and do exactly as you're told.'

The handsome face was white with fury, the eyes flickering between Max and the masklike face of his wife. His tongue came out to wet dry lips, and the little-boyish features had sharpened to a foxlike awareness of being trapped. But his rage overcame his fear as he burst out, spitting the words in his wife's direction:

'Work for you! Be owned by you! The hell I will! I owe you two pictures on the contract you've acquired from Cy, but after that we're finished.'

'No. *You* are finished if you don't re-sign because I'll release this evidence to the Swiss police. If you don't work for me, you don't work for anyone. Do I make myself clear?'

He changed from anger to hurt reproach. 'I can't believe you're doing this to me.'

'Then let us have done with it. You are at liberty to leave. Your car should be waiting at the front door. I don't care where you go so long as it's out of this house, but I expect you to report for work on July the twenty-eighth.'

'Look, let me explain –'

'I know what you are, and I no longer have any use for it.'

It was like scrabbling for a handhold on a marble monolith. 'Eve – for God's sake –'

She turned her back on him and rang for the butler. When he came in, she said quietly, 'Mr Stevens is leaving now, Jacques. Is his car outside?'

'Yes, Madame.'

'And you have packed a bag – he has his passport?'

'Yes, Madame.'

'Then there is nothing to keep you,' Eve said to her husband.

'You haven't heard the last of this!' It came out as an animal snarl. 'Nobody railroads me. I'd advise you to watch your rear, lady, because one of these days, somebody is going to kick your ass!'

The door slammed behind him.

Eve turned to walk back to the fire. 'You may go,' she said to them all. Alex tugged at Max's sleeve. 'What about school?' she whispered.

'Not now, sweetheart. Do as she says, go on.' Max's voice was equally soft.

Reluctantly, Alex followed Patsy out.

When they'd gone Max asked, 'Is that all?'

'Yes,' Eve said. He left.

Alone, Eve let out a shaky breath, clutched at a chair. Then she squared her shoulders, picked up the photographs and the recorder, and took them to the little private elevator which ascended to her bedroom. There, she went into her dressing-room, where there was

260

a wall of mirrors. Sliding one back, she pushed aside the rank of plastic-covered evening gowns to reveal a wall-safe. She twirled the combination – the date Eve Czerny Cosmetics was officially established – opened the safe and put the packet and the recorder inside before shutting and locking it again. Then she carefully took off her dress, revealing the single piece of satin and lace that was all she wore beneath it, hung it away, removed her diamond and emerald earrings, carried them back into her bedroom and dropped them into her four-tiered jewellery casket. Going to her dressing-table she opened a drawer, took out a pair of scissors, and carried them through into her husband's dressing-room, where she proceeded to cut, slash, rip, hack, slice every item of his clothing. In a frenzy of ice-cold rage, the only sound her frantic panting.

Only when everything was in tatters did she stop, her breasts heaving. She dropped the scissors onto the pile of rags and staggered back into her bedroom where she fell on the bed, face up, and lay for a moment, staring at the ceiling. Then she turned over and buried her face in the quilted crêpe-de-chine of the bedcover and burst into shattering sobs, her hands gripping the fragile material so hard it tore.

'Why?' It came out muffled. 'Why? Why does this always happen to me?' She cried until all that was left were dry heaves. Finally, her face still buried in the wet silk, she fell asleep.

15

Cambridge and Switzerland, 1978–80

Christopher Bingham was fifteen when he found out he had a half-sister; moreover, that she was twenty-one years old and about to graduate from Cambridge University with a Double First in English.

It was his practice – learned at a very early age as being of vital importance in his never-ending struggle for supremacy with his mother – to eavesdrop whenever he could, especially on her conversations with Max Fabian, whom Christopher both admired and resented. So when he saw Max go into his mother's sitting-room and close the door he knew at once that what they were going to discuss was something he should know about; for he had also learned that knowledge is power, especially where his mother was concerned.

Now, as he very carefully turned the doorknob – which he had previously oiled – and opened the door just wide enough to allow their voices to carry, he heard Max ask angrily, 'Aren't you pleased with Alex's academic success?'

Alex? thought Chris. Who is Alex? He crouched as near to the door as he could.

'Why should I be?' His mother's voice was one he knew; ice cold and deadly.

'Because you're her mother, for God's sake! She's worked her butt off these past seven years and as much to prove herself worthy of your investment than for her own sake. Now that she has, the least you can do is say "congratulations".'

'Since I have no doubt that is what *you* will be doing, I see no need.' Watch it Max, Christopher thought gleefully, you're treading on very thin ice. Oh, how he would love to see that man just once miss his footing and go under.

'She's a good friend of mine, yes, but she's *your* flesh and blood. If you gave her one-tenth of the attention you lavish on Chris –'

'We will not discuss my son.' Icicles hung from his mother's breath.

'What's to discuss?' Christopher's listening face flamed at the contempt. He was well aware that Max regarded him as a spoiled brat. 'I'm not interested in Christopher, but I *am* interested in Alex.'

'That is where we differ,' his mother said. 'Let us be clear once and for all, Max. Do not bring up this subject with me again. I allow you great freedom; be careful not to abuse it. There are limits beyond which even you may not go. Do I make myself clear?'

'Only too well.'

Which was when Christopher made himself scarce because that was a dismissal if ever he heard one. He retreated to his room where he locked the door, took out his forbidden cigarettes and pondered what he had heard. A sister? Twenty-one years old? And obviously *persona non grata* where his mother was concerned. Why? he wondered. Who and what is this Alex? Why have I never heard of her? And who was her father? Mine was Mother's first husband, which means this Alex has to be one of Mother's deliberately erased mistakes. And Alex who? he thought. If I'm going to find her – and I think I must if I'm going to know what to do with this useful piece of information – I have to know her full name. And another thing, if Mother won't even talk about her, why has she paid for her education, because Max mentioned an investment. And my mother never spends money for no reason. And how come Max is involved? He's never bothered himself with me.

Jealousy spurted in Christopher. If he knows then I must find out from him, he decided. He thinks I go behind his back, so for once let it be true.

He waited until both Max and his mother were out of the house before he went up to Max's suite on the third floor, where he carefully – and he knew how because he had been doing it to his mother's for years – searched his desk, coming across a letter addressed ready for posting to a Miss Alexandra Brent, with an address at Beaufort College, Cambridge. Christopher weighed it thoughtfully. He was not above opening letters; he had done that before, too, but only his mother's. Max was different. Christopher had a healthy respect for both his tongue and his vocabulary, not to mention the power he wielded. Except in one respect, Christopher thought on a smile which turned into a frown, because it was obvious, in spite of his mother's disapproval, that Max was consorting with the enemy. I have to find out, Christopher thought. Something tells me this is important. He read the address again. Cambridge. Well, he thought, we are due in London at the end of the month . . .

Alex was in the midst of packing up the accumulated books and files acquired during three years' hard work when there was a knock on her door and she opened it to be confronted by a beautiful, smiling, Murillo-angel teenager, gazing at her with all the confidence of one who knows he will meet no opposition.

'Hello,' he said warmly. 'You're Alex Brent, aren't you?' He held out a hand. 'I'm Christopher Bingham – your half-brother.'

Utterly taken aback, Alex took the proffered hand. 'Good God!' she said faintly.

'Well he's been good to me,' Christopher said easily, stepping past her. 'How's he been to you?'

'Does your mother know you're here?'

Christopher laughed.

Alex's face hardened. 'Look, you're not going to embroil me in any trouble of your making.'

Christopher looked hurt. 'Trouble? I've only just found out about you, and what I learned made me curious to meet you, see you.' He looked Alex up and down; she was a good head taller than he. 'I remember you,' he said, 'you used to be in the gardens sometimes . . .'

'You have a good memory.'

'I never forget *anything*,' Christopher said.

Alex was nonplussed. This assured boy was nothing like the angelic child she remembered. He had all the confidence of someone twice his age, which would be, she calculated, fifteen. Fifteen! He came on like somebody who'd never see fifty again.

'Where are you supposed to be?' she asked finally.

'At the Science Museum.'

'On your own?'

'I gave my "minder" the slip. Don't worry – I do it all the time. I hate being led around on a lead. I took the tube then the train and came straight here. You're about to graduate, aren't you? With a Double First? What are you going to do with it?'

He sat himself down in her only easy chair and took out his cigarettes.

'I don't,' Alex said, when he offered them to her, 'and neither should you at your age.'

'I do lots of things I shouldn't. It makes life bearable.'

Alex bit her lip. 'How is Madame?' she asked drily.

'Is that what you call her too?'

'It's all she's ever been to me.'

'You're lucky,' Christopher said enviously. He regarded her. 'Why has she kept you hidden all these years?'

'She doesn't like me.'

'I gathered *that* – but why?'

'I have no idea.'

'You must have done something?'

'How about being born?'

Alex had changed considerably since her first, strange, bewildered days at school. She had found Cheltenham Ladies' College terrifying at first; had not known how to deal with the sophisticated, boy-mad girls she had encountered there, who, unlike her and one or two others who were academically inclined, regarded school as something to be endured rather than enjoyed. Her clothes had been unfashionable, only serviceable, and she was totally out of touch with the pop music, the mini-skirts, the teenage culture of the 1970s. Her peers were for the most part infinitely more worldly than she was, and they regarded her as a 'swot' and a 'grind' who took no part in the 'pashes' that went on between junior and senior girls. For the most part they had, after enjoying the joke at her expense, left her alone, forming their own cliques and coteries; and as she had been classified, by dint of her academic prowess, as being a year ahead of her age group, she found herself isolated. But that was nothing new, and when she finally made a friend it was not a pupil but a junior mistress, herself a brilliant former student at the College, only ten years older than Alex and instinctively drawn to the lonely intelligent girl who showed all the signs of becoming a blue-stocking, like herself.

From Susan Anstey, Alex had learned a lot and under her encouragement applied herself, winning every prize in her year, while her marks averaged out among the highest the school had ever awarded, but only Max and Patsy had been there to congratulate her, just as, in a few days' time, they would be there to applaud when she was awarded her degree, Susan Anstey having married a Professor at Princeton and now living in New Jersey.

Alex at twenty-one had gained in confidence, aware that she had a superior brain and proud of the fact. In September, she would be returning to Cambridge as a post-graduate, but before then, she was going to visit Patsy at Thonon, where they would spend a couple of weeks before going to Italy. Hopefully, Max would be able to spend a few days with them, depending on his always heavy schedule. From her mother, as always, there had been nothing.

'Where were you born?' Christopher was asking curiously.

'London.'

'And where's your father?'

'Dead.'

'Was Brent his name?'

'Yes.'

'Was he married to our mother?'

It sounded strange yet oddly natural when he said 'our mother'; obviously he had already accepted her as his sister, whole or half.

'Yes.'

'Well, well . . .' Christopher said happily. 'Mother does love her little secrets, doesn't she?' He seemed to gloat over the fact that he, now, was privy to one of them. Then, as if it was nothing more than the kind of thing he was used to: 'She must have hated him – I mean – to keep you at a distance all your life.'

'I know nothing about it,' Alex said cautiously, remembering who and what this boy was.

'But aren't you curious?'

'I know when to leave well enough alone. You, it seems, haven't learned that yet.'

'But I'm your brother! Why should I hate you? I need allies, not enemies. Mother *loves* me – she says – and that's far worse than her keeping her distance. She gets her teeth in and won't let go.'

Yes, thought Alex, fifteen going on fifty. And is it any wonder? 'If you intend to bring me into the bosom of the family you're showing your age,' she remarked.

He regarded her with unshakable confidence. 'I know how to

handle Mother,' he said, 'and if I decide I want to be friends with my sister . . .'

'She'll never allow it.' Alex paused. 'And what makes you want to be friends with me?'

'We're brother and sister!'

Alex read him like the open book he was to become to her. 'And you don't have many friends?' It always took one to recognize one.

He flushed. 'Mother is – over-protective. She never let *me* go away to school. How did you manage it?'

'She wanted me out of her life.'

'Lucky you,' Christopher said bitterly.

'How is Madame?' Alex asked, after a pause.

'More beautiful than ever, richer than ever, and still queening it over everybody. Only Max manages to stand up under it all.'

Alex smiled. 'He always has.'

'*He's* your friend, isn't he?'

'Yes. One of my two best.'

'Who's the other one?'

'My old governess, Miss Patterson.'

'The white-haired lady who used to be in the gardens with you?' He smiled again at Alex's surprise. 'I see a great deal more than Mother thinks I do. I wanted to play with you – I was about seven, I think – and I was told I wasn't allowed. When I asked why I was told it was my mother's instruction, so I asked her if I could – she never refused me anything in those days – and she got very sharp and said I was to do as I was told. Nor would she answer my questions. I got a new bicycle out of that, as I remember . . .'

Alex began to perceive something of the relationship between Eve Czerny and her son. 'Why weren't you allowed to go to school?'

'Oh, Mother couldn't *stand* to be parted from me, miss my childhood and suchlike rubbish. I have tutors. My present one is a man only his mother could love.'

'And where is he?'

'I neither know nor care.'

'How did you manage to get here, then?'

'I filched some notes from his wallet. I used to carry my own money then Mother found out what I was doing with it so now he keeps it. You don't have to worry. I've slipped his leash before many times. I'll just say I went sightseeing – which is true. I've never seen Cambridge.' He waited for Alex to ask what he had been doing with his money – spending it on cigarettes and motor magazines – but she didn't. He felt oddly disappointed. She was looking at him with a chill dispassion that had him squirming. She looks a lot older than she is, he thought. In fact, there's nothing really youthful about her, except her skin. Mother would love that skin. Like ivory and not a line to be seen. Christopher knew a great deal about women's skins.

'What's the matter?' he asked. 'Aren't you pleased to see me?'

'I'm wondering how your mother will react.'

'Our mother,' Christopher corrected.

'She's never been a mother to me.'

'Why not?'

'Ask her.'

Christopher said, 'You must be joking!'

'I never joke about her.'

Christopher realized that he had stumbled into more than he had bargained for. This was not going to be as easy as he had thought. But there was still time. 'They tell me Cambridge is well worth seeing. All those old colleges. Tell you what –' His gold-brown eyes sparkled. 'Would you show me around? I'll buy you lunch.'

Alex shook her head, unable to control her laughter. 'You really don't give a damn, do you?'

'It's the only way I can cope,' he answered matter-of-factly. He jumped up. 'If I get the four-thirty train I can be back at the house by half-past six, so shall we get going?'

'I have things to do –'

'But this is a special day, isn't it? We've only just found each other – well, I found you. I made up my mind to when I learned you existed.'

'And just how did you do that?'

'Oh, I have my ways.'

'I'll bet you have, at that . . .'

She put him on the train at four-thirty, after promising he could come and see her at Thonon, and swearing not to say a word to anyone, not even Max. 'I can deal with Mother if I'm left alone to do it my way,' he said anxiously. 'It's our secret, do you agree? Just between you and me . . . I'm good at keeping secrets. I know lots of things and I've never told anyone.'

Alex felt uneasy. 'Madame doesn't like people doing things behind her back, and I don't want to be dragged into her orbit again.'

'Don't worry, you won't be. Honestly.' He looked up at her and smiled. He had all his mother's beauty and every bit of his father's insouciant charm.

'Well . . .'

'Good. I knew you'd agree. I like you. Mother's a fool – and that's not like her. She's every bit as clever as you are, in a different way. I suppose that's where you get your brains from . . .' His white teeth dazzled. 'They seem to have missed me – or so she's always telling me.'

'Don't worry, you'll do fine with what you've got,' Alex told him. If only he doesn't overdo it, she thought, as she drove herself back to college in her little Mini – an early twenty-first birthday present from Max. He knows more at fifteen than I did, but living in Madame's world, how could he not? He already believed that whatever he wanted he would (not could) have. When she had remonstrated with him about doing the dirty on his tutor he had shrugged and said cynically, 'He won't say anything. Of all of them – and he's the fifth – he's learned quickest that if he does he's only doing himself out of a highly paid and not too onerous job of bodyguarding. Mother will believe me in the end – she always does, providing I tell her what she wants to hear.' Appalled, Alex perceived that he already knew how to handle Eve and her quixotic temperament; that he knew enough to know that he held power over her as nobody else did; that he meant more to her than anything – 'except perhaps her business, of course,' he had said coolly, reaching for his fourth cream cake. 'That is really Mother's baby more than any flesh and blood.'

Alex had been astonished at the perception of one so young. In years, she thought. In experience he can give Methuselah a century or two. He had been endlessly curious about her, asking questions with no trace of shyness, only the confidence of one who had, from a very early age, been exhibited as something extraordinary – and always to adults.

'Have you got a boyfriend?' he had wanted to know.

'No.'

'Why not?'

'It's not my scene,' Alex had returned lightly, using jargon he would understand. Not that I've had the option, she thought. Five foot ten, eleven stone and the invisible woman.

'Mother always has one in residence and several others on the go. I think somebody's made her seek safety in numbers.'

Alex kept her face only mildly interested, but she felt a jolt. Had Rik Stevens left scars? She knew he was still making pictures for the company Eve had bought when she had bought him; still a box office attraction, still a household name.

'What do you like?' he had asked next. 'I mean, do you have any hobbies?'

'No . . . I spend most of my time working.'

'I like to work on engines. Charles – he's Mother's chauffeur – says I'm a natural. I can drive, you know – I learned when I was twelve – but Mother only allows me to drive the car inside the walls of the estate. I have to wait until I'm sixteen before she'll let me have a car of my own.' An expression she was to come to know very well rearranged his features.

'No,' Alex said, 'I won't allow you to drive my Mini.'

He sighed. 'Oh, well, it was worth a try.'

His last words as the train drew out were, 'See you in Thonon . . .'

'Is it wise?' Patsy asked, when Alex told her what to expect. 'Madame won't like it at all.'

'I know, but – well – I feel sorry for him, I suppose. He's a boy without friends; he wants to go to school but his mother won't let him. He told me that his Grandmother Bingham wanted him to attend his father's school – Groton – and then go on to Harvard, but Madame refused. She said she would miss him too much and also not be a party to his growing up.'

'Hmmm . . .' Patsy sniffed.

'I know, but from what he told me she's clearly besotted with him.'

'She always was.'

But when he eventually came – having once more given his tutor the slip – she was as amused and beguiled as Alex had been.

'Poor boy,' she murmured, after an afternoon spent together, and they watched him set off in the direction of the centre of town, 'he is lonely, isn't he? Far too much time spent with adults instead of his peers. Horrendously precocious –'

'But not unpleasantly so.'

'No . . . no, he's not. But I wouldn't like to get on the wrong side of him, all the same. Behind that sunny smile lies his mother's temper, mark my words.' Which Max, when Alex, not wishing to draw Patsy into the danger of Madame's wrath, told him the truth, confirmed.

'That's one mixed-up adolescent,' he said, accepting a cup of Patsy's strong tea and helping himself to one of her hot buttered scones. 'Once he gets over the wall she's never going to get him back, and he's only biding his time.'

'He seems to have a peculiar relationship with his mother,' Patsy remarked.

'He does. She's as jealously possessive of him as she is of any lover. I would go so far as to say it's positively neurotic. Eve hasn't had much luck with the men she chooses – God knows why because she's still a very beautiful woman and could have her pick – but I think she believes he will make up for all that. Five will get you ten he only ends up breaking her heart – or whatever it is she carries inside her ribs. I sometimes think it's a crystal timepiece.'

'She has never married again,' Alex said after a moment.

'No, just had a series of lovers – some live-in, some not. But if I'm right – and am I ever wrong? – number four is about to enter the trap, and that won't do her relationship with her son any good at all because Christopher can't stand him.'

'Would that be Carter Witney?' Patsy asked placidly.

'You said you never read the gossip columns!' Max chided.

'Who is he?' Alex asked.

'Well, seeing as *you* never do read them!' Max said. 'He's currently rated the number one Hollywood boy genius – except he hasn't been a boy since Whistler's mother raised hers, and if he's a genius I'm Albert Einstein. But he makes movies which break every box-office record and he's also currently making Eve somewhat absentminded. Unfortunately, he is pure Hollywood and never moves without his entourage. He has a chorus of yes-men, each with a different tone depending on what kind of a yes he wants at any particular time, and a battery of aides, writers, lawyers, accountants – he's a man who would die of fright should he ever find himself alone. Eve puts up with it because for some reason he appeals to her, but Chris hates him because when Carter and his hangers-on descend, while he hates being smothered by his mother he's also young enough to hate it even more when she neglects him, no matter how slightly. Also, Carter has a son of his own, only eighteen months older than Chris, who sees him as a potential rival. He told his mother in my hearing that if she married "that creep" as he put it, he was leaving her – as though he was her husband. And he will too. He did it once before. She cut off his allowance for some transgression or other and the next thing we knew he turned up in Oyster Bay with his grandmother. It took Eve two months to persuade him to come back.'

'Does she realize this?'

Max shrugged. 'Eve believes that in the last analysis she will always be able to handle Chris. The fact that he took off after you shows how wrong that is.' Max frowned. 'I suspect he found that out by listening at one keyhole too many.'

There was a shocked silence then Alex said, 'What a happy household.'

'You got the best deal, kid. You'll never know how lucky you were to be left alone to develop normally – even if it was in the isolation ward. What Chris needs is a good school and the arrogance knocked out of him by a bunch of kids who won't take any shit no matter who his mother is. What he gets is what I would call the most twisted kind of pampered neglect. He has no friends, do you know that?'

'Neither did I.'

'I mean none at all. You had Patsy and me. He has nobody and nothing. Worse, he has no inner resources to fall back on like you. The one thing he's good at and wants to take up his mother won't hear of.'

'The mechanic business?'

'He told you?'

'I had a hard time changing the subject.'

'He's a natural with any kind of engine but he has an unfortunate yen for speed. He persuaded his mother to buy him a Go-Kart and it ended up faster than my new BMW. He was twelve at the time. His room is plastered with pictures of Porsches and Ferraris and Aston Martins. God help us all once he gets his first car.' Max held out his cup for a refill. 'But let's talk about something interesting. Now that you've got your BA I suppose you want to go for your D.Litt.?'

'Yes.'

'And then what?'

'Let me get my doctorate first.'

'Who can argue with the inevitable?'

Alex laughed. 'Such faith . . . I'm touched.'

'Just so long as it's not in the head.'

But Alex became serious. 'No, I mean it. If I hadn't had you I don't know what would have become of me. Patsy and I would never have been able to obtain our freedom. I'm grateful, Max. More than you can ever know. Getting to know Chris has made me realize that.'

'Just so long as you're happy.'

'That's what disturbs me about Chris. He's not. I could see he was envious; that his relationship with Madame is – well, not to put too fine a point on it – somehow incestuous.'

'Only emotionally,' Max said. 'It's a real love-hate brew. Don't get caught in the fumes, they're lethal.'

'But he looks to me, I know he does. And he *is* my half-brother. You did so much for me and I was nothing to you.'

'You were worth it.'

'That's an awful thing to say.' Alex's voice was angry.

'I know him, you don't. Eve's got a screw loose where he's concerned. Maybe it's to do with his father. Every time another relationship goes wrong, Christopher Bingham IV's photograph comes out of storage.'

'Then why is his son called Christopher Bingham Czerny?'

'That was Eve's way of making it clear that he was *her* son. As it is, whenever he goes to stay with his grandmother he comes back more Bingham than Czerny and his mother erupts. He used to spend his summers there; now he stays no more than a few days and never without Eve. Since the old lady died, though, he doesn't seem as keen as he once was. I don't think his aunts have much use for him, and if they could somehow get their hands on the Bingham millions he's going to inherit when he's twenty-five they'd dump him and his mother.'

'Then he needs a friend.'

Max looked at her. 'Well, you're of age now. Just so long as you're aware of what you're getting into . . . He's a born manipulator, you know, and always to his own advantage. I don't know what he wants with you but you can bet it's to get at his mother in some way. If you should ever find yourself in no man's land between the two, they'll both blow you to bits.' His voice was level, his eyes fixed on hers. 'He is his mother's son.'

Christopher came often to the little house above Thonon that summer, his mother having departed on a month-long cruise with Carter Witney, who wanted to scout locations along the Mediterranean coast for his new production of *The Count of Monte Cristo*. Since Eve was well aware of the friction between her lover and her son, and since her lover had indicated that he would prefer not to have Christopher along – his own son was spending the summer with his mother in Connecticut – Eve agreed when Christopher suggested he remain at the villa, along with his tutor. She could call him every night, he said practically, and he promised not to get into any trouble.

'So I have a whole month of freedom,' he gloated to Alex. 'Why don't you come to the villa for a few days? Nobody will say anything if I tell them not to . . .'

But Alex wouldn't do that. 'Far too dangerous,' she reasoned. 'If you want to spend time with me then it must be at Thonon. I'm already taking quite enough of a risk, thank you.'

Christopher, who learned quickly, knew enough by now to know that Alex was not one to be wheedled or cajoled. Unlike his mother she didn't make emotional judgements or decisions; hers were based on facts and reason, and since he was determined not to lose her from his life, he didn't argue. Time enough to steer things in the direction he wished them to go.

For her part, Alex soon realized that her half-brother had been brought up to regard himself as unique; the son of a remarkable and very rich woman who, being a law unto herself, had raised her son to obey none but hers. But he also believed that he would have to be constantly on guard, because first and foremost what people would always want from him was his money, since he was not only his mother's heir but his father's. When he was twenty-five and inherited the Bingham fortune he would become one of the world's most eligible young men. His attitude to this was ambivalent. On the one hand his sense of his own financial worth made him arrogant, on the other he really had no interest in money *per se*, except insofar as it could get him whatever he wanted.

From what he said – and though his chatter seemed artless and even naïve, Alex shrewdly detected that she was being given an intensive course on The Life and World of Christopher Bingham Czerny – it became apparent that his mother's attitude swung between vicious verbal violence and smothering, over-protective adoration. She either demanded blind obedience and wasn't slow to punish cruelly when it wasn't forthcoming, or looked on indulgently while he ran riot, showering him with expensive gifts which after his initial delight were soon discarded, usually broken because he had an insatiable desire to know how anything and everything *worked*.

But it was also apparent that she believed her son was herself reborn – he was as beautiful in his way as she was in hers – and an heir to be proud of, one who would take over her still expanding empire when she decided the time had come. And in spite of her repeated declarations of devoted 'love' she had no compunction in leaving him in the hands of paid servants; of putting her own concerns first and becoming impatient if he complained. She expected her son to grow up to fit the specifications she had drawn up, and it was when he seemed to be deviating from them that she grew savage. It's no wonder that he's developed his own defences against the constant see-sawing her behaviour towards him has produced, Alex thought. At least to me she was consistent.

It was no wonder either that in her absences he ran wild; to him, servants were just that, people whom his mother paid to look after him but who were never to be obeyed. Alex was different. She soon realized that he was desperate for some kind of relationship that was steady, secure and predictable. She reduced him to white-faced shock after one piece of dangerous folly – taking Patsy's venerable old Renault and tinkering with the engine so that when he took it out for a joy-ride he was apprehended by the police for dangerous driving and excessive speed. Alex had to ask Max to get him out of that, but she was the one who made it plain that if he wanted to continue to see her it was on condition that he gave some consideration to his sister and Patsy, and did as he was told. If he didn't, he was no longer welcome. Alex, Christopher realized, was, unlike his mother, not a woman to say one thing and mean another. She didn't rant and rave and scream, she spoke calmly but so coldly that he felt ashamed, and also frightened. Alex had come to mean a great deal in a very short time; at last he had someone he could really trust, talk to, confide in, as he would have liked to do with Max – he envied to his soul the relationship between Max and his sister – and he got a real fright when he saw that she meant what she said: one more stupid escapade and he was out.

From that moment his respect for his sister took root, and never once, in all the years that followed until his untimely death, did she ever let him down, though he did her, usually when his mother had him in such a state that his only recourse was to lash out at somebody. Alex was not impressed by who he was, what he was, how much money he would inherit. She could not be manipulated, only reasoned with; all you had to do to convince Alex was give her a reasoned argument and a logical conclusion and if it convinced her you were in. If it didn't, it was a waste of time to proceed any further. He was in awe of her brains: the way she had Patsy's *Times* crossword done in under twenty minutes; the way she invariably beat him at backgammon, the speed with which she read, the ease with which she explained things; even more, the speed with which she understood them. She could do three or four things to his one, and in his admiration he did his best to emulate her, soon losing interest when he knew it was impossible. His one area of triumph was his expertise with all things mechanical. When Patsy's little carriage clock stopped for no good reason, he took it apart, found what was wrong – a broken cogwheel – replaced it and put the whole thing together again. Alex, who was hopeless at anything like that, was so impressed that she made him feel ten feet tall. He could mend anything, was never happier than with bits and pieces of something mechanical or electronic strewn about him, ready to be put together in perfect working order. He overhauled Patsy's old Renault so that it ran as if it was new, not twelve years old.

'He's a born mechanic,' Patsy commented to Alex.

'If his mother had any sense she'd set him up in a garage.' But that, Christopher had made clear, was the last thing she would ever do. At the end of two weeks Alex and Patsy left for Italy while Christopher went to join his mother in Nice, preparatory to flying to America, and it was October before they met again, once more in Cambridge where Alex was now doing her postgraduate work.

Over the next couple of years they saw each other as often as time and circumstances permitted. Alex marvelled that Eve had no idea, but this was what Christopher enjoyed most of all. It meant he was ahead on points. He had his first car at sixteen, a Mini, which he souped up and crashed: he was made to do without for a while then got another one, this time an MG. After that he graduated to a Jaguar, which he again upgraded. When he was seventeen he got his first really fast car, an Aston Martin, and it was in that car he had his first, major crash during a race with his step-brother on the Grand Corniche.

Max called Alex to tell her that Chris was in the American Hospital at Nice with two broken legs and cracked ribs; that he was asking for her and working himself up into a state because his mother would not hear of Alex coming. 'But I think you had better,' Max said. 'He's making himself worse than he should be. The breaks are clean – no complications – and the ribs are only cracked, but his temperature is staying sky-high. I've managed to persuade Eve that it's for his own good, not yours. So . . . will you come?'

'She knows, then?' Alex asked, feeling her stomach churn.

'She knows.'

'And?'

'Where you're concerned it's always the same; ice-cold calm. It's odd – she rants and raves at everybody else but where you're concerned it's a case of Greenland's Icy Mountains. Christopher is asking for you – constantly, and the doctors have advised her to let him have his way. I'm sending the jet to Stansted – it's only twenty miles down the M11. Can you get there within the next hour or so?'

Alex took a deep breath. 'All right.'

'That's my girl.'

Christopher was sitting up against a bank of pillows, chest bandaged, legs in splints, and as Alex walked in his face lit up. 'I said you'd come once you knew,' he said. He turned to his mother, who had been sitting by his bedside and now rose to her feet as Alex closed the door behind her. 'Told you so.'

Alex looked at her mother. 'Madame.'

Eve nodded, her face the expressionless mask of old. She seemed no different. The years had not aged her in any way. No lines, no wrinkles, chin and throat taut, skin glowing, hair gleaming, figure as slender yet voluptuous as it had ever been, wearing a stupendously chic sugar-pink Chanel suit with gilt buttons and lots of chains. She smelled of her own, deliciously sensuous *Essence of Eve*, still a bestseller.

'How are you?' Alex asked her brother.

'Much better now that you're here. I told them I would be.'

'What else have you told "them"?' Alex asked.

'The truth. How we've been seeing each other over the past couple of years.' He was a young man now, his voice was deeper, his face no longer beautiful but in the process of becoming handsome, though his blond hair still curled and the brown eyes still glowed under the incredible lashes. 'I've told Mother you're my best friend as well as my sister and I know I'll mend quicker around you.'

Alex did not look at Eve, but she shivered in the icy forcefield emanating from her.

'Will you come and stay with me when they send me home to convalesce?' Christopher wheedled. 'Please?'

'I have my work –'

'You can work at the villa. Please, Alex. There's a huge library and anything not in there can be got for you. It's only broken legs and a rib or two; I'm strong and I'll soon mend but I'll be so *bored* unless you come and cheer me up. I don't know what I'll do if you don't come. Die of misery, I expect.'

'Well . . .'

'I'm anxious for my son to make a complete recovery,' Eve said, in an expressionless voice, 'and it seems he believes he can only do that with your help. If your work permits I shall be happy to have you for as long as you can spare.' It was said with a remote politeness. Eve was adapting herself to circumstances, but she would make sure they never arose again.

For her part, Alex was torn. On the one hand she knew that she meant a great deal to her brother, on the other she was well aware that he was using her to get at Madame. But the plea in his eyes wasn't for show; he really did want her company. And she had become so fond of him, almost against her better judgement; there was something so likeable about Chris under the spoiled-brat surface. He was generous to a fault, he was good-natured when removed from his mother's orbit, he was amusing, affectionate – and lonely. Max had told her that he had developed an alarmingly high temperature when he had first broached the matter of Alex and Eve had flatly refused his request. 'He knows she has a terror of anything happening to him – shades of his father – and he's capitalizing on it, but he genuinely wants you, I'll say that for him.'

Even so she had no desire to return to a place she had thought never to see again. But, and it was a big but, there would be Max.

'Please say you'll come,' Christopher was begging. 'I need you to.' Alex flicked a glance at her mother. Her face, if not quite the familiar mask, was still expressionless. She can't stand the thought, Alex realized and there and then made her decision. 'I'll give you four weeks, no more; absolutely no more.'

'Done!' Christopher's smile obliterated the sun.

'Nothing has changed,' Alex reported to Max later. 'She still looks at me as though I'm invisible.'

'Is that why you agreed to stay? To give her no choice?'

'I'm probably banging my head against a brick wall but I felt so angry!'

'That's a change from feeling miserable, but are you sure you can cope with her? You've never really spent any time with her, and she's a Mother with a capital M. The fact that she's agreed you may stay doesn't mean that she wants you to. Just remember, she won't allow anyone to come between her and Chris, and act accordingly.' Max paused. 'I managed to persuade her that you'd be good for him in the way of tuition. He's almost uneducated, you know.'

'He's nobody's fool.'

'That's not the same. That's self-defence learned so as to do his own coping with Eve. And be careful what you say to him; she can grill him until he's ready to say anything.'

'What a happy household I'm joining.'

Max's look was so serious it was almost grim. 'You don't know the half of it.'

Max drove Alex back to the villa from the airport; Eve had accompanied her son in the ambulance that met the plane. She had ordered a room prepared on the ground floor. To Alex she said, looking straight through her, 'I have had one of the guest suites prepared for you.'

'I would rather stay in my old quarters, if that is all right with you.'

If it wasn't Eve gave no sign. 'As you wish.' Never once had she addressed Alex by her name. It was as if the deliberate 'you' was intended as a reminder of her lack of status.

'I never thought to see these rooms again,' Alex said to Max, looking round her old home. 'Everything seems so much smaller.' She went across to the big porthole window. 'The hours I used to sit here . . .' There was a different bed in the bedroom; bigger, newer, more comfortable, freshly made up with flower-sprigged Pratesi sheets, a match to the flowers on the draped bedside table. Why, she knew all the time . . . Alex thought. I'll never understand that woman. Never in a million years.

'I wonder if I'll be allowed to use the pool this time?' she remarked to Max, who said, 'You're a guest and they always do.' He turned her to face him, his big hands on her broad shoulders. 'You're over that nasty little episode, aren't you?'

'I never think about it,' Alex answered truthfully.

Max nodded, looked relieved. 'Good.'

Patsy was astonished when Alex rang her that night, insisted on a full explanation. 'I think it's very noble of you, considering the circumstances under which you left.'

'The present ones aren't exactly to my liking either, but it's for Chris.'

'You've become very fond of him, haven't you?'

'It's nice to have a relative of one's own.'

'By the way,' Patsy said, 'you'll be interested to know that Pastor Dietrich is dead. There was an item in the paper about him. He was seventy-eight.'

'That means he too is no longer in a position to answer my questions.'

'Well, we did try. I still think he owed you an explanation, in spite of him saying that he couldn't betray Mary Brent's confidence.'

'And by the time I got to her it was too late.'

Just before going up to Cambridge Alex had gone to the address she had never forgotten, intending to face her old enemy and demand answers to questions that had haunted her for a long time.

But the small semi-detached was bright with new paint, and the woman who answered the door knew nothing about Mary Brent. She and her husband had bought the house two years ago from the Pentecostal Church. She gave Alex the name and address of the solicitor who had handled the sale for them, and he confirmed that Mary Brent had succumbed to Parkinson's Disease, leaving all she had to her Church. He knew nothing more. That dead end had left Alex no further forward, and since the old man had firmly, if courteously, refused to say anything about the arrangement between him and Alex's 'grandmother', she was left with her questions unanswered and the knowledge that the one person who knew the answers was unlikely to give them.

As expected, Chris was a fractious patient. Alex arranged her time with him to coincide with when his mother was elsewhere, and insisted that several hours be given over to coaching; badly needed, she rapidly discovered. He could read and write but even simple arithmetic was beyond him. Yet he could understand a mechanical diagram at a glance, and knew the workings of every engine ever invented. The only things he read were magazines such as *Popular Mechanics* and biographies of idols such as Jackie Stewart, and Stirling Moss. But he could reel off the changes in the Aston Martin since its inception, or the design improvements in the Jaguar, and was tolerant of Alex's own lack of education in the mysteries of the torque and engine ratios and the four-wheel drive.

'He's just not interested,' Alex said to Max disbelievingly. 'All he thinks of is engines and speed. Would you believe he wants to be a racing driver?'

'Fat chance,' was Max's comment.

And once he was told, via his mother, that Carter Witney was coming to stay for a while, even what interest he had vanished. 'This ought to be fun,' he told Alex, eyes gleaming with an almost unholy relish.

'You like being with him?'

'I like being without him. The only good thing about him coming here is that it's on his way to the exit. He and Mother fight all the time. He's very tough – I think that's why she fell for him; you know, the masterful "I am the greatest" kind of macho fake – but when she found out that he really does expect to be top dog he was done for. There's only one star and that's Mother. You'll see.'

Alex did see, and she also heard, soon after Carter Witney, all smooth suiting and Hollywood tan, swept up the drive, his car leading a Presidential-type motorcade. He was not very tall, definitely not handsome, with a pug-ugly, coarse face into which a cigar was thrust at all times, but he had an animal magnetism and a personality to match. His voice was rasping, uneducated. 'His real name is Yossel Moisewitch,' Chris had told her gleefully, 'and he was born in the Bronx. After all her top-drawer gentlemen I think Mother took a fancy for a bit of rough.'

To Alex he explained the current state of play between his mother and her fourth – 'no, fifth really' – husband. 'They're in the middle of a decaying orbit. Mother's marriages and affairs always follow the same pattern. The launch is a triumph: the rocket goes straight up and away, heading for the moon. That's when she's full of enthusiasm, starry eyed and soppy with love's no-longer young dream, convinced that this is *the* one. Then something goes wrong, always the same thing. She pulls rank and the crew mutinies. The rocket goes off course, the orbit begins to decay and eventually goes out of control. When it hits the ground there's an almighty explosion and Mother picks her way out of the wreckage with the same excuse: "It wasn't *my* fault. I did *my* best and this is what I get. After all I've done for you . . ." etc, etc.' Christopher's voice, as he recounted this, was entirely matter of fact.

'Carter is very successful, you see. His movies make vast amounts of money. He won't be her courtier, following one step behind, ready to bend the knee. If she is Queen Bee, then he is Top Dog – and his bite is worse than his bark. You wait, they'll be going at it hammer and tongs in no time, and this is supposed to be a last-chance attempt to repair the rocket. They'll have a passionate reconciliation – he's supposed to be fantastic in bed – but it won't last. Mother's men never do.'

He met his sister's appalled gaze. 'I get the impression that all this comes as a shock to you. Why? You spent eight years in this house, didn't you?'

'Yes, in it but not of it. I neither heard nor saw any of the antics you've just described. Well, only once.'

'When was that?'

'When your father was killed.'

'Do tell. I was far too young to remember. I think I remember my father: tall, blond and always laughing. He used to toss me up in the air . . . I hated it.'

'She was very – upset. Very emotional.'

'She tried to kill herself, didn't she?'

'She didn't tell you that!'

'Of course she did! When I was giving her more trouble than usual. She sat me down and solemnly told me that my father had been the love of her life, that she loved me so much because I was his son, all she had left of him. You know the sort of thing. She wanted me to be like him, inherit his mantle, that sort of crap.' Christopher smiled. 'I used to hear an entirely different story when I stayed with my grandmother. She can't stand Mother. She thinks she's an adventuress.'

'In terms of opening up new territory I suppose she is.'

'Not in that sense, stupid! I mean a gold-digger. According to Grandmother it was my father's money and position my mother loved.' Alex saw her brother's face change, become cynical with contempt. 'Love!' he said. 'I'm never going to have anything to do with love. It mucks up everything. It's not love that makes Mother marry so many times or take so many lovers. It's sex, and that has nothing to do with love. She only kids herself it does. You're well out of it,' Christopher said with unconscious brutality. 'And I'm going to follow your example.'

'Don't model yourself on me,' Alex said harshly. 'I'm the last role model you should be emulating. Love is something I've had very little of in my life.'

'You're lucky. I've had too much.'

Is it possible to have too much, Alex wondered later. Of the wrong kind I suppose it is. I was lucky in Patsy and Max; it was from them that I had the only love I've ever known, and if past experience is anything to go by, I expect it's going to remain so.

Her Cambridge years had been entirely devoid of the social pleasures enjoyed by the other girls of her year. The picnics, the May Balls, the punts on the river, the various Societies, the pub crawls. In her first year, she had shared rooms with a devastatingly pretty girl whose sex appeal drew every male within scenting distance, every one of whom had treated Alex as another piece of the furniture. Only once, when a planned foursome for which tickets had already been bought turned into a threesome because one of the girls went down with shingles, had Alex been taken to a performance of a Footlights Review. It was on coming back from the loo in the interval that she inadvertently overheard them discussing how best to avoid taking her on to a late supper. 'I mean,' one of the male undergraduates was saying, 'she's not exactly the life and soul of the party, is she?'

'She's shy,' her pretty room-mate had said.

'And about as attractive as a Sherman tank. She's so *big*. And I can't stand blue-stockings.'

That had done it. Alex had pleaded a headache and retired not only from the evening but from the field. Her mother was right. She was an affront to the eyes. She had retreated as deep as she could get into the Groves of Academe and never come out again.

She never did get to meet Carter Witney. After a screaming and shouting session in which many hard words were exchanged and objects thrown, he fulfilled Chris's prediction and walked away from the crash and out of Eve's life.

When Eve came into her son's room that evening, Chris looked at Alex. See? his look said. What did I tell you?

Eve was in black, as though in mourning. Plain, very Parisian, very expensive black. No jewellery, but wearing a noble, self-sacrificing expression. 'Christopher, my darling boy . . .' Her voice throbbed.

Alex rose, studiously ignoring her brother's frantic if silent plea. She was not going to get caught in the middle.

Next morning, she was informed by Jacques, now very grey but still immensely dignified, that she was at liberty that day. Madame would be spending the day with her son.

Alex needed no second bidding. After breakfast she went to the garage and took out the little red Citroën she had grudgingly been allowed to use, and drove over to Thonon.

'Do you regret coming, then?' Patsy asked, as they sat in the garden later.

'Yes and no. Not for Chris; he's a scamp and shudderingly cynical for a seventeen-year-old, but it's her I don't like being around. I'm there under sufferance and she makes no bones about letting me know. She still doesn't look at me, you know. I just don't exist in her eyes. I've seen her turn from people with a face alight with

284

laughter and a vivid expression, only for it to freeze if her glance happens to alight on me. All the life goes out of her. She wears that mask I first saw the day Mary Brent literally threw me at her.' Alex turned a frustrated face to her beloved governess. 'Why, Patsy? Is it because I affront her? Or is it, as I'm coming to believe, that there's something I don't know about her past; something important which involves me. Something to do with my real father, whoever he is. She was obviously forced to take me. Pastor Dietrich's visits made that plain. But what was it Mary Brent held over her? If only there was some way I could find out, but I don't know where to start. The first five years — my first five years — are buried in an unmarked grave.'

'Would it not be better to leave them there? Some things are better left alone.'

'I *had* left them alone until I came back here, that's the ironic part of it. It's seeing her, being with her; it does it to me every time.'

The next week was impossible. Eve never left her son alone, and Alex saw that what Chris had told her was no exaggeration. She smothered him with her idea of affection, fussing at his pillows, asking him how he felt, was there anything he wanted. She kept hugging and kissing him, ruffling his blond hair, calling him her darling while Alex sat, stone-faced and silent.

'It's her penance period,' Christopher explained on a shrug. 'When she decides she will sacrifice herself for me. It won't last long. It never does. She'll get bored and go off looking for new fields to conquer.'

And on the seventh day, when Alex went into Chris's room she found him looking considerably less hag-ridden. 'She's back to normal,' he announced with relief. 'She's going into Geneva. Probably to have the full works. Open the windows,' he begged, 'let's have some fresh air. *Essence of Eve* gives me a headache.'

Eve was gone for forty-eight hours. 'Business' to attend to. 'I wonder who he is?' Chris mused.

Eve returned remade; glowing with resolution and a febrile gaiety. There was to be a dinner party; full fig, followed by a reception. There was to be music, dancing, lots of people and a good time had by all. Alex and Chris were left alone as Eve bent herself to playing the perfect hostess. She conferred with Caesar as to the food, with

Jacques as to which wines should accompany it; she herself chose the tablecloths from the drawers and drawers of them stacked in the specially fitted linen closet. She decided which china, which glasses, went round with a slide rule measuring the distance between chairs at the dining-table and making sure that the tablecloth hung at exactly the same depth all the way round it.

She harried, she questioned, she criticized, she complained, and rearranged every single hideously expensive, designer-assembled flower arrangement; the entire house was in a state of chaos until, two hours before the guests were to arrive, Madame retired to her suite to prepare for battle.

'She always has to be the centre of attention,' Christopher informed Alex knowledgeably. 'The most beautiful, the best dressed, the finest jewels – and she will be. She always is. Mother never lets her standards slip, only sets them a notch higher every time. The older she gets the more she seems to need to win the gold medal. Still, once she's triumphed she'll be purring like a pussy cat. That's what all this is in aid of; to confirm Mother in her standing as a Great Beauty, a Great Hostess and one of the best dressed women in the world. It's all shoring up the cracks in the foundations.'

But when he learned that his mother planned to turn his sickroom into another reception room by bringing in her guests to see him, he lost his cool. 'I will not be put on exhibition,' he shouted. 'I am not a waxwork and I won't be cooed over and sympathized with or lectured at . . . "Your poor mother, she's so worried about you . . ." Worried enough to give a dinner party for thirty people! It's not me you're worried about,' he shouted at her, 'it's yourself, as usual. You want to show people that you're not one whit disturbed by your latest flop; that you're in control, as always – well I won't let you control me, so you can keep them out of my room. I'm going to have a quiet evening with Alex –'

'You will do as you are told,' his mother said, in a tone of voice Alex had never heard, and which flayed. 'My friends are naturally anxious about you –'

'Curious, you mean! Wanting to see how badly hurt I am – then *you* can receive *your* condolences with quiet dignity. I'm the one who is injured, not you, but you always have to be the centre of attention, don't you?'

Alex, standing silently by, tried to melt into the woodwork, but knew she had failed when Eve said, not bothering to glance in her direction, 'Leave us, if you please.' Issuing instructions to a servant.

'No, stay Alex.'

'Leave us!' The voice rose ever so slightly and Alex heeded the warning.

Outside, she met the nurse, who met Alex's bemused gaze and shrugged. 'What a circus,' she muttered disgustedly. 'It's as well she's paying generously for all this. How can one nurse the boy in such conditions? How am I expected to cope with a patient who's in a highly excitable state most of the time? I will have the devil's own job settling him down tonight; his temperature is probably soaring this very minute.' She shook her head. 'What a mother! I've never seen the like before.'

Alex went up to her rooms, and later, from her old vantagepoint, she watched the guests arrive, emerging from the sleek Mercedes and Rolls-Royces, the women exquisitely dressed and sumptuously bejewelled, the men providing the perfect foil in their distinguished black and white, and as she ate her solitary dinner, she visualized the scene in the dining-room below: softly and flatteringly lit by its shaded wall-lights which cast a romantic glow on the exquisitely embroidered tablecloth, its design and colours exactly matching the pattern of the Sèvres porcelain dinner service, which was also echoed in the porcelain handles of the *vermeil* cutlery. The flower arrangements – low, because Madame did not like her view of her guests obstructed – set in glowing bowls of Chinese porcelain, glittering crystal glasses bearing the monogram of Catherine the Great. Well, doesn't she believe herself to be an Empress? Alex thought, downing her Château Latour 1961 at a great rate, for Caesar, an old friend, had provided her with her own separately cooked share of the dinner. Cold lobster mousse, perfectly roasted quail with creole rice and celery braised in butter flavoured with coriander, a salad comprising six different kinds of lettuce in a tangy orange dressing, followed by a hot raspberry soufflé with peach sauce and ending with a savoury of tiny new potatoes, exactly matched in size and shape, stuffed with caviar and melted butter.

Empress Eve the Great, Alex thought, rather drunkenly, for she was not used to great wine and the claret was a big, headily perfumed vintage, incredibly soft and smooth; rich, ripe and highly intoxicating. Caesar had given her a half-bottle decanted into its own small rock-crystal flacon, and she drank the lot, on top of the perfectly chilled Montrachet which had accompanied the lobster. She'll be sitting at the head of her table, as cold and white as a stalactite. – for Eve's dress was a glittering column of white silk embroidered with crystal, pearls and silver thread in the shape of bees – queen bees, Alex thought. She never misses a chance to shove that down your throat. If she knew I was eating exactly what she is she'd be furious; I'm supposed to be dining off bread and cheese in my garret. What would she do if I was to go downstairs and say, 'Meet Madame's other offspring. I'm her daughter Alex.' She giggled drunkenly. Serve her right. I'm the skeleton in her cupboard, all right, except that I'm anything but a skeleton.

She sat and brooded, the wine rampaging through her veins, mugging her customary rational caution. It's time I demanded to know why she's so unwilling to acknowledge me; why she keeps me hidden like some hideous monster she's ashamed of. Because she *is* ashamed of me. Why else doesn't she look at me, never grant me the courtesy of so much as a smidgeon of her attention? With everybody else she smiles, she laughs, she listens, but not me, oh no, never me. All I get is that mask she puts on in my presence. Even her voice is different. Lifeless. All she has ever done is deny *my* life, *my* existence. Why? *Why?* What is it about me she just can't stand? Who I am? What I am? Why I am? Well, it's about time she gave me some answers. I have a right to know.

Her resolve grew as her state of inebriation increased. I'll confront her tonight, she thought. Face to Face. Why not? she thought, as the wine liberated emotions long confined and they began to demolish their prison. Why should I put up with this unsatisfactory state of affairs? She hit the table with her fist. Unsatisfactory! That's the understatement of this or any year, as Max would say. And I've put up with it for far too many of them – eighteen, to be precise: ever since I first came to this house when I was five years old. The old aching memories rose through the fog of alcohol, their power to hurt undiminished. '*I've brought you your bastard.*' '*She is yours and always will be. You are her mother but my son was not her father.*' '*You will accept your responsibility or you will suffer the consequences.*' Who was my father? Alex seethed drunkenly. Is it his memory she hates? Did he abandon her? Is that why she hates me? Was I conceived in circumstances so awful she can't bear to be reminded of them?

She rose to her feet, swaying slightly. Time to ask some pertinent questions and get some truthful answers.

She went into the bathroom, splashed cold water onto her face, but she still seemed to have acquired a loose-jointed, floating feeling and a recklessness quite foreign to her normal cautious nature.

'You've got a tongue in your head,' she told her reflection, which seemed strange; her eyes were enlarged and her cheeks flushed. 'Use it.'

But sitting on a hard chair behind the pillar on the landing, waiting for dinner to end, the reception to be over, Christopher visited, her head drooped and she lapsed into an alcoholic haze. The sound of many voices awoke her with a start. Eve's guests were leaving. Wraps and furs were being draped over white shoulders, cheeks proffered, hands kissed. She blinked, rubbed her eyes and watched as the last of them went through the front door. When it closed behind them Jacques locked and bolted it as usual. 'A successful evening, Madame,' he offered gravely.

'Yes, as always . . .' Eve sounded eminently self-satisfied. She moved her shoulders as if they were stiff, lifted a hand to rub the back of her neck.

'Will there be anything else, Madame?'

'No, nothing more. I will just go and see my son and then I shall be off to bed.'

'Very good, Madame.'

Jacques disappeared back into the drawing-room. Humming to herself, Eve walked briskly down the corridor to her son's room, opened it slightly and slid inside. When she came out she was tiptoeing and drew the door closed soundlessly. Then she made for the stairs. As she came up them, Alex lurched to her feet. She no longer felt aggressive but rather nauseous, and she had the beginnings of a murderous headache. As the alcohol drained away so had her courage, but as she turned to flee her legs seemed not to support her and she had to clutch at the nearest object, which happened to be a small console table. It went over and it was as she bent to pick it up that she heard Eve's voice, cold and sibilant. 'What are you doing here?'

Alex straightened the table and turned with as much dignity as she could muster. 'I should like to speak to you,' she said.

She saw the mask replaced by an expression of contempt. 'You're drunk!' her mother hissed with disgust.

'No I'm not. But I'm angry. I think it's time I had some answers from you.'

'I owe you nothing, and that includes answers.'

'Oh, yes you do.' Anger fuelled Alex's resolve as the alcohol had done earlier. 'I want straight answers. Are you *really* my mother? If you are, why have you always treated me like a hateful stranger? Why have you never given me anything remotely like the attention you lavish on your son? What have I ever done to you that you should treat me like some distant poor relation? What did Mary Brent have on you to make you keep me when it was the last thing you wanted? Why was I produced to that old man for inspection every now and then? Why –'

'Silence!' Eve's voice curled around Alex like a whiplash. She glanced over her shoulder but the hall was empty.

'Why are you ashamed of me?' Alex demanded, her anger acting as a raising agent to her voice.

Eve took a step forward; her long fingers fastened on Alex's arm and forcibly turned her to the long mirror hanging on the landing wall. 'There is your answer!'

Alex stared at herself; five foot ten and built – as she had heard a male Fellow (from Oxford) who passed for a wit say of her 'like the Royal Albert Hall – a national monument'. Her naturally melancholic cast of countenance – My face is a whole series of downward curves, she thought in anguish – with its prominent nose and powerful chin, framed by ordinary brown hair, as fine and flyaway as cobwebs, stared back at her. She had abnormal colour in her cheeks, a combination of wine and rage, but in her plain white shirt and navy skirt, her flat shoes, though she dwarfed Eve, she was also totally diminished by her.

'I am known as the Empress of Beauty. Take a good look at yourself. How can I possibly acknowledge a daughter like you.'

'Cruel,' Alex whispered.

'No. Honest. My whole reputation would collapse like cards were it to be known that I, Eve Czerny, had given birth to something so ugly.'

Alex closed her eyes. She was beginning to feel sick.

'I did my duty by you; you were fed, clothed, educated,' Eve said.

'But you never loved me.'

'I cannot love what is not beautiful.'

'That isn't natural.'

'Nevertheless, it is my nature.'

Alex frowned at the white figure; it was beginning to blur. 'There's more to it than that, I know there is.'

'You know nothing,' Eve said. 'Nor have I anything to tell you.' She took her hand away from Alex's arm. Her grip left fingerprints.

'Go back to your own world,' Eve said, with absolute finality. 'There's nothing for you here, nor can there ever be. You have money – the trust fund I established was a generous one – you have brains. Use them to do the best you can with what you have. I did.'

'But not with me!'

'I will not be questioned by you.' The mask was settling back into place, the momentary fracture closing. 'I am well aware of my son's motives in bringing you here, but it makes no difference.' Her smile was one of confident contempt. 'There is nothing I do not know about my son.'

'Or want to know about me.'

'Do not ask for what cannot be given.' Eve turned to go. 'I have nothing further to say.'

'You haven't said anything in the first place!'

Eve turned to face her again. 'Because there is nothing I wish to say. Understand that here and now.' Eve paused, and Alex saw a strange brooding look darken the brilliant eyes. 'I had nothing when I started out to become something – *nothing* – and I was even younger than you. I made myself by myself. What is to stop you from doing the same? Why does it matter who you are? What matters is who you wish to become. Shape your life to your own design. I did.' Alex saw the eyes clear, the beautiful face settle back into the normal expression of lifeless formality she knew so well. 'I do not want you here when I come downstairs in the morning.' Then she turned and walked away.

Alex stood staring at the closed doors of her mother's suite long after they had shut with a final click. She felt stunned, bewildered and utterly hopeless. She also felt sick. Clapping a hand to her mouth she ran for the door to the backstairs, only just made it up them and into her bathroom.

*

Patsy told Max what had happened when he called from Paris. He said, 'I have to be in London soon. I'll go up to Cambridge and cast a cold eye.'

'Never cold, Max. Only concerned.'

Something in Patsy's voice had him saying, 'You're worried about her, aren't you?'

'I'm wondering if perhaps I am partly responsible for the way Alex is. I was – am – a spinster. Alex has no experience of normal family life, from which one learns to love.'

'You gave her plenty of that.'

'I did what I could, but her mother's influence was pernicious. Alex is too young to be already thinking of herself as an old maid. She knows nothing of the joys of youth. She has so little *pleasure*, Max. No dances, no parties, no young men. Only work. Amassing degrees and setting herself up for a life of sterility and loneliness –'

'Patsy, Patsy . . . This isn't like you.'

'I don't want Alex to be like me either. I had responsibilities, an invalid mother to support. I was the sole breadwinner, and by the time I was free and able to consider myself it was too late. I don't want that to happen to Alex.'

'Leave it with me, Patsy. I'll do what I can.'

'Haven't you always?' asked Patsy.

16

Switzerland, 1988

On the morning of the funeral Alex was down by seven-thirty. She had not slept; the thought of what was to come had prevented her. She found the kitchen empty but for Jonesy; breakfast was never until 9 a.m., while Eve was never woken until ten. He was sitting at the big table cradling a large bowl of milky coffee. He looked up as Alex entered and said, 'You too? I've never had such a dreadful night, what with worry about today, not to mention the week I've had with Madame . . .' It seemed that his attitude had changed.

Alex helped herself to the coffee he had made. 'How is she?'

'She's a bloody marvel, that's what. As calm as the Med on a hot day. Mind you, that's the tranquillizers. I always slip one into her early-morning cuppa and another into her coffee at night. That fancy doctor of hers left them with me. But she's not eating. Once this is all over and done with I've told her she's to go into the clinic for a complete rest to get her strength back, because she's living on her nerves. Then a nice long cruise . . . she's got offers from everybody – and the letters! She'll be busy for a long time answering them all. I'll go up in a minute and lay out her clothes. I thought that beautiful black *redingote* Hubert de Givenchy made for her ex-ma-in-law's funeral, and the little hat from Jean Berthet; it'll take a veil.'

'I hate black,' Alex said.

'Yes, well, it's not your colour, is it? You have to have colour of your own to dominate it – like Madame. You don't take after her at all, do you? I got the shock of my life when I found out who you were. Never a word in all the seven years I've been with her.'

'It's more than seven years since she and I have seen each other.'

'I don't see my family either. But then, they made it plain they preferred it that way. But it'll be different now, won't it? I mean, she's got nobody else now, has she?'

'Right now, Jonesy, you're closer to my mother than anyone, and you probably know her better, too. Can I paraphrase and say that "no woman is a heroine to her dresser"?'

Jonesy preened modestly. 'Well, I don't deny we do seem to — meld, shall we say. From the moment we met. I don't deny she can be difficult — we have our little tantrums and vent our spleen in no uncertain terms, but is it any wonder? The things that poor woman has to put up with sometimes, and the things she's accomplished!'

'From rags to riches?'

'Well, I never saw the rags — but I'll bet she could wear them and still look gorgeous. Madame is a natural; you have to be born with what she's got. You can't buy it — as a lot of women seem to think they can. Perhaps it's her Hungarian blood.'

'Austro-Hungarian is what I've been told.'

Jonesy sniffed. 'Whatever, wherever. Madame is a true international anyway.'

'Does she ever talk about her early years?'

'Oooh, we never mention years, dear. As we go along they sort of — contract; ten become five, five become one, and so on. I've heard her tell people about how she got started, but I've heard it so many times I don't listen any more.' He pursed his lips. 'As for anything told to me in *confidence* — well, my lips are sealed, as they say.' He sipped his coffee then laying down the cup leaned forward. 'Mind you . . . this week I've heard her say more about her — shall we call them — early years than I ever have. She was going through her jewellery — nothing like a death in the family to start you thinking about your own mortality — and there, at the bottom of the box, was this little brooch in the form of an *A* . . . just cheap, not even gold plated — but I saw the look on her face when she picked it up. I made a joke — something about that not having anything other than sentimental value and she said, in a funny sort of voice — almost wistful — and one thing Madame is not is wistful, "That is the first piece of jewellery I ever owned . . ."

"But why an A?" I asked. "Your name begins with an *E*."

"My middle name", she says. "Anna." As if I don't handle her passport renewals and don't know her name: Eve Czerny Bingham de Marchesi Witney de Barranca.'

'De Barranca!'

'Her last little mistake. Argentinian he was; used to play polo with her first husband . . . well, who she says was her first husband . . . I mean, you had a dad, didn't you? Or is it because you aren't – shall we say kosher – that she don't recognize you?'

'Her first husband was a man named John Brent,' Alex said.

'Ahh . . .' Jonesy accepted that little nugget with almost lip-smacking satisfaction. 'She broke the law, then.'

'Broke –'

'She married her second husband as a single woman, didn't she? There's no mention of anybody named Brent anywhere, anyhow, and I should know. I've seen her marriage lines – all her marriage lines – and on the ones she got when she married poor Chris's dad she's down as Eve Czerny, spinster.' Jonesy nodded, eyes sparkling, his genteel vowels falling like ninepins in his excitement and his South London antecedents showing like rust through peeling paint. He leaned forward. 'And when I saw that little brooch I remembered something she'd obviously forgotten. About – oh . . . six years ago it was. We'd just arrived at JFK and I was seein' to the luggage – always so much of it on any trip – when this woman comes up – smart, she was, a lady, no doubt about that – and she says, "Anna? It is Anna Farkas, isn't it?" Well, if you'd seen your mother's face – but only for a second or two. Then she turns to this woman – oh, real hoity-toity. "You are mistaken, madam," she says, "my name is Eve Czerny." And she hops into the car and I have to scramble to get in before she drives off without me.' Jonesy nodded. 'That's why she keeps that cheap little brooch – her with a fortune in some of the best stones I've clapped eyes on, and I've seen a few in my time.' Jonesy shook his head and sighed. 'I think she's been thinkin' a lot about the past, this week.'

'Has she said anything about me?'

'Not a word. But you saw her, didn't you? I nearly had a heart attack when she told me to go downstairs and ask her daughter if she would spare her a few moments! That she had a daughter for a start, and that she asked if you could *spare her a few moments*. That was another first. Madame don't ask, she tells. This Alexandra Brent, I says to myself, is someone to be reckoned with. But never a word since. Did you have a falling out?' Jonesy asked, ostensibly with sympathy but greedy with curiosity.

'We have never really got on,' Alex answered neutrally.

'Well, you're a brain-box, ain't yer? Madame don't have much time for clever women, which is queer seeing as she's as clever as a barrel load of monkeys herself.' He paused. 'Lived with yer dad, did yer?'

'Until he died.'

'I thought it was something like that. But you must have come here from time to time seeing as how Jacques knew you and a couple of the other servants.'

'Yes. I spent some time here.'

'Well, I'm only glad you had the gumption to let Chris go. She couldn't bring herself to do it, see. Too – final. She set great store by young Chris, great store . . .'

'I know.'

'Still, like I said, she's got you now, and that's a mercy because she ain't got nobody else – family, I mean. Oh, there's me and Mister Max – he's a laugh, that one, handles Madame like nobody else, even me – but we're not family.'

'And as *I* said, you're closer to my mother than I am.'

'Well, this'll probably do the trick; bring you together, like, once this is all over and done with and she's herself again.'

'It's nice to think so,' Alex said. She pushed her chair back, rose to her feet. 'I think I'll go for a walk,' she said.

'You do that; get some colour into those pale cheeks.' He caught her sleeve as she passed him. 'On the other hand . . . a little bit of rouge, high up on the cheekbones – make a world of difference.' He regarded her critically. 'First Blush should do it . . . lovely colour that is, looks dead natural – oops, pardon me.'

'I'll remember that,' Alex said gravely. 'Thank you.'

For the first time that day, as she left the house, there was a smile on her face.

Left alone, Jonesy picked up the cups, washed, dried and replaced them in the cupboard. He was compulsively tidy. Nice enough, but not a looker like her ma, he thought, as he neatly folded the tea-towel. And bones like a dinosaur . . . Still, it's obvious she don't care . . . that suit had Marks & Spencer all over it . . .

He went back upstairs, through Eve's sitting-room and into her dressing-room, its walls of mirrors concealing the big cupboards where her clothes were kept. Her furs were in cold storage in a room beyond. With the deft economy of years of practice he slid back the doors of the lingerie cupboard, took out a one-piece teddy of pale-grey satin trimmed with black lace; an unopened packet of sheer black stockings; pursed his lips over the rows of shoes, finally chose plain black glove-suede pumps with three inch heels – Madame liked a bit of height – picked a shiny black calf handbag, small, just enough to hold a mirror and a handkerchief – two, he thought, placing them inside. Then he went to another cupboard, reached unerringly for a simple black dress, cunningly cut to cling to the body yet flare from the hips for ease of walking, matched it with the de Givenchy *redingote* with its single row of black pearl buttons. Yes, he thought, just the thing . . .

'Now then . . . the hat . . .' Reaching up with the long pole always left standing in the corner, he slid back smaller cupboards fitted just under the ceiling, revealing dozens of hats, each one on its special stand, and carefully took down one that was small, round and utterly unadorned, its elegance in its shape which was cut in one piece, something in the fashion of the jaunty white hats worn by American sailors but worn over the forehead. 'Yes . . .' he said to himself. 'If I take her hair right back, coil it behind, this will sit just right, and I can drape the veil over it . . .' This he took from the island of lucite boxes in the centre of the room. A sheer square of finest silk organza with a two-inch border of black crêpe. 'Now then,' he pondered, 'the pearls or a brooch . . . we can decide that when she's dressed.'

Leaving everything ready, he went back into the sitting-room, tiptoed across to the bedroom door and put an ear to it. Silence. Then he sniffed. There was a smell of burning . . . He sniffed again. Yes, definitely something burning . . . Alarmed, he turned the ornate handle of the door. It turned but the door did not open. He pushed it. It still did not move. He tapped on the door. 'Madame!' No answer. He rapped harder. 'Madame . . .' He rattled the handle. No response. He darted to the little *bureau de jour*, jerked open a small drawer and took out a key. But when he inserted it in the handle it would not turn. 'She's locked it from the inside!' he exclaimed. He was so shocked that for a moment he was petrified. Then he turned and ran.

Max came out of sleep with a jerk to find Jonesy shaking him violently. 'What the hell . . .'

'I can't get into Madame's room. She's locked it from the inside and there's a definite smell of burning coming from it.'

Max was out of bed in an instant. He slept raw, but he snatched up the robe that lay on a nearby chair and struggled into it. Mora, who slept heavily, made a complaining noise deep in her throat and squirmed more deeply under the covers.

'Sorry,' Jonesy apologized, 'but I didn't know who else to call. I only wanted to get her jewellery box. I was laying out her things and I wasn't sure whether a brooch or the pearls –' He talked as he followed Max down the corridor. At the locked door Max rattled the knob before banging on it and shouting: 'Eve! Open the door . . . Eve!' He sniffed. 'You're right. There is something burning in there . . . stand back.' Jonesy retreated as Max took several steps back and then hurled himself at the door. It did not budge.

'No use in that,' Jones told him. 'Those doors came from a church. Thick as my arm, they are.'

'What about her window?'

'I always leave one open last thing.'

Max strode to the sitting-room windows, went out on to the balcony and peered across to the bedroom windows. 'They're shut now.' The two men looked at each other. 'Christ!' Max exclaimed. 'A ladder,' he called as he ran, 'find one, bring it round to her windows – go on, man, hurry!'

By the time Jonesy, helped by one of the gardeners, came running back with a ladder, Max was halfway up the big old magnolia which grew between the windows of Eve's bedroom and sitting-room, its branches trimmed back so as not to cut off the light. 'I'm stuck,' he called down. 'There's at least five feet between the nearest branch and her balcony. Can you place the ladder within reach?'

They did so and Max inched himself along the branch. 'Talk about Tarzan,' Jonesy tittered, but his eyes widened as Max stripped off his impeding robe and, stark naked, made a lunge for the ladder. It swayed dangerously but Jonesy and the gardener hung on grimly as Max pulled himself on to it. Then he was up the rungs and swinging his legs over the balcony.

'I'll have to break the glass,' he shouted down. 'Somebody bring my robe so I can wrap it around my hand . . .'

With alacrity Jonesy bent to scoop it up and then was away up the ladder to hand it over. Max wrapped it round his hand and forearm, right up to the elbow and then jabbed the pane by the lock. It fractured and at once the burglar alarm went off.

'Somebody go and switch that thing off!' Jonesy yelled above the din. The gardener went off at a run and Jonesy followed Max over the balcony. 'Talk about Casey's Court . . .' He trotted into the bedroom only to stop again. 'Oh . . . my . . . God . . .' The room was ablaze with candles, dozens of them, placed on every surface. 'No wonder I smelled burning . . .' Max was bending over the big bed, haloed by light, on which Eve, exquisitely made up, not a hair out of place, freshly manicured nails gleaming, the huge emerald that had been her engagement ring from Christopher Bingham glowing in the light, lay on her back, her arms folded protectively over the photograph she held to her breast. She was wearing a sumptuous nightdress and matching negligée of heavy apricot slipper satin and blonde lace, and she had heel-less moroccan slippers on her feet.

'Is she dead?' Jonesy gulped.

'No . . . there's a pulse but it's awful slow . . .'

Jonesy pounced on the empty brown bottle standing on the silk-draped bedside table. He shook it, sniffed it. 'Chloral hydrate or I've never taken it in my life! Now where did she get that from . . .' His eye fell on the empty glass. Picking that up he sniffed again. 'Vodka! She must have had a second bottle squirrelled away . . .'

'Call the clinic,' Max said. 'Go on – quickly! Tell them to stand by to handle a drug overdose . . . get whatshisname . . . that Frenchman.'

'Delours?'

'Yes, him. He's a fully fledged doctor isn't he?'

'They all are!' Jonesy snapped affrontedly, dialling the number.

Max picked up the cashmere throw lying over the foot of the bed and wrapped Eve's deeply unconscious body in it before lifting her in his arms. 'Will somebody for God's sake shut that alarm off . . .' he bellowed. The words were hardly uttered before somebody did. 'Thank God for that . . . right . . . open the door, Jonesy . . . we've got to get her to the clinic as fast as we can.'

Alex was pacing the edge of the lake when she heard the strident wail of the alarm. She stopped, swung round then took off at a run. As she entered the hall she saw Max, stark naked, coming with great care down the curve of the stairs carrying the unconscious figure of her mother, wrapped in a blanket, which fortunately trailed in front of him, thus covering his shortcomings.

'A combination of chloral hydrate and vodka,' he said briefly. 'I've got to get her to the clinic as fast as I can.'

'Not like that, you're not,' Alex said over her shoulder as she made for the little room where the coats were hung. She seized the nearest one, and coming back with it saw Jonesy running down to join them. 'They're setting up the emergency room for her,' he said breathlessly, 'and I've told them to bring the Rolls around.'

'Good man . . . Here . . . help me to put her in this chair while I put a coat on . . .'

'You'll catch your death,' Jonesy scolded, but he helped Max lower Eve into the big leather footman's chair. Keeping his back to Alex, Max shrugged into the coat. It was tight at the shoulders, short in the sleeves. One of Chris's he thought, buttoning it up as best he could. Ah well, needs must. He bent to pick up Eve again.

'You're in your bare feet,' Alex warned.

'I'm not walking there . . . is the car outside?'

Alex went to the front door. 'Just drawing up . . .'

'Right – get the door open . . .'

Alex held it wide so as to allow him to place Eve on the back seat. When she made to get in too Max said, 'No. You stay here and hold the fort. Jonesy will come with me.'

'Call me as soon as you can,' Alex shouted as the car moved off. Turning to go back into the house she saw that the hall had filled with people; all the servants, plus Mora and Pamela.

'Madame has taken an overdose,' Alex said evenly. 'Max and Jonesy are taking her to the clinic. All we can do is wait.'

'Oh my God . . .' Mora said, shocked. Pamela said nothing; she looked very pale, very strained.

'Why did the alarm go off?' Mora asked, as the servants began to disappear behind the screen that led to the kitchens.

'Max must have had to break a window to get into her room; they all have sensors, don't they?'

Alex made for the stairs and the two women followed her. 'What did she take?' Mora asked.

'Chloral hydrate and vodka.'

Alex went into Eve's sitting-room and through to the bedroom. She stopped so dead that Mora ran into her. 'Oh, my God . . .'

Mora echoed Jonesy. 'Will you look at that . . . it's like a shrine . . .'

Some of the candles had been blown out by the breeze through the broken window, the rest were fluttering. Alex went round extinguishing them, but as she went to draw the curtains her feet crunched on glass. Getting to her knees she began to pick it up.

'This was planned,' Mora said, looking round. 'Where did she get all these candles from? There are dozens of them . . .'

'Then put them out . . . I want to get rid of this glass.'

'How can you be so calm?' Mora asked accusingly. 'Your mother has just tried to kill herself!'

'Would you rather I had hysterics?'

'Of course not, but – well – I think I'm more shocked than you are.'

Alex made no reply as she dropped the glass into a wastebasket, then she noticed Mora was pawing amongst the objects on the bedside table. 'What are you doing?' she asked sharply.

'Looking for a letter, of course. Suicides always leave a letter . . .'

'She isn't dead yet!'

'There is this . . .' Alex turned to Pamela who had picked up the photograph Max had found Eve clutching. It was one of Chris.

Mora turned eagerly. 'Oh . . .' Her face fell. Clearly she had been hoping for something more dramatic. She lifted the silk sheets, delved under pillows. 'No letter . . .' she said, sounding disappointed. 'Perhaps she didn't mean it after all . . .' She let go an exasperated sigh. 'I suppose the funeral will have to be postponed . . .' Really, her tone said, some people have no consideration.

Pamela put a hand up to cover her eyes.

'Why don't you go and see if you can get some coffee,' Alex suggested to Mora. 'I think we could all do with a cup.'

'Oh, God, yes . . . I'm never fit to be spoken to before I've had my coffee.' When she'd gone Alex pushed Pamela down onto the bed. 'Don't let her upset you. Tact was never her strong point.'

'Do *you* think Eve meant to die?' Pamela asked.

'I don't know what she meant. She's done it too many times for it to *mean* anything.'

'But chloral hydrate is pretty powerful stuff, isn't it?'

'I think so, but it would depend on how much she took, surely.'

'Did you see her?'

'Briefly. She was deeply unconscious.'

'She was in church one morning, you know. I've been going every day and this particular morning so was she . . . she made way for me to kneel beside her. For the first time I felt sorry for her; her being there somehow brought us together, I felt we both shared the same sense of loss, felt the same pain . . . Her face was veiled but I could see her eyes and they were like black holes . . . We didn't speak, but in some strange way we each felt better for the other being there . . . And then, today of all days, she does something like this. She hasn't changed at all . . . selfish to the last . . .'

'The thought of the funeral may have been too much for her.'

'How does she think *I* feel?' Pamela asked savagely. 'If she wanted to die why didn't she do it earlier, not today, of all days. On the morning of her son's funeral she makes a suicide attempt.'

'She's made them before,' Alex said unemotionally, feeling as though her emotions had been amputated.

'She always has to make the grandstand play,' Pamela, who had lived for many years in the United States, said. 'She couldn't even let her son have his last day. What kind of a woman does that, for God's sake?'

'I don't think this was an impulse,' Alex said, looking round at the candles. 'This was planned and prepared for.'

'I'll never forgive her for this,' Pamela said, her lovely face contorted by rage and grief. 'When people talk about Chris it will be on the lines of: "Do you remember the day of his funeral when his mother tried to kill herself?"' She burst into shattering tears. Alex was sitting by her on the bed, awkwardly trying to comfort her, not knowing what to say to this normally composed and controlled woman, when Mora came back carrying a tray. Alex jerked her head.

'But I've brought the coffee.'

'So take it away again. I'm going to get Pamela to bed and give her a sedative.'

'I'm not surprised she's upset. Today, of all days. I will never understand that woman as long as I live. Do you need any help?'

'You could give me a hand to get her upstairs to her room.'

Between them they got the distraught woman up to her room, and while Mora got her into bed Alex went into the bathroom to see if she could find anything to help Pamela sleep. In the cabinet she found a small bottle. Mogadon 5g. it said on the label. Taking it back to Mora, she asked, 'How many should she take?'

'Let's have a look . . . oh, half of one, no more. You'll never get her up for the funeral otherwise and then *she'd* be ready to kill somebody. Here . . .' Mora took the small tablet, cracked it with her thumbnail, inserted half into Pamela's mouth, took the glass from Alex and made her drink the tablet down.

'I'll stay until she goes to sleep,' Alex said.

Mora shook her head disgustedly. 'Why does everything Eve Czerny does have to be over the top?'

When Max finally called, by which time Alex was expecting the worst, he said, 'She's alive. They got to her just in time. Another hour or so – if Jonesey hadn't called her until ten, as instructed, it would have been too late.'

Alex's breath of relief sounded like a gale to Max, on the other end.

'You and me both,' he said. 'I'll just tie things up here then I'll come back. Make the biggest pot of the blackest coffee. I need it.'

'The funeral is still on, then?'

Max sounded surprised. 'Of course it is.'

Mora was with Alex when Max walked in. She took one look and screamed, 'You've not been into Geneva like that?'

'No, I thought I'd liven things up a bit, that's all.' He turned to Alex. 'I'll issue a statement that Eve is too distressed to attend the funeral.'

'Where's Jonesy?'

'He says his place is with Madame.'

'This is going to be the smallest funeral I've ever attended,' Mora said, both affronted and disapproving.

'Then you'll have to put on an even bigger show, won't you?' Alex looked at Max in surprise; he sounded positively vicious. 'Go on,' he said to Mora. 'I know how much time it takes . . .'

She stalked off in high dudgeon.

'Steady on, Max,' Alex said quietly.

'Steady! What the hell is steady around here? Jesus, nine-thirty in the morning and we've already had an attempted suicide; come twelve o'clock we've got a funeral!'

Alex said nothing. He had every right to be feeling the strain.

'I shouldn't have let her hole herself up,' he said, raking a hand through dishevelled hair. His face looked more lined than she had ever seen it and he hadn't shaved. 'She's not the solitary type. But I thought – well, circumstances alter cases, leave her alone to handle her grief in her own way.' His laugh was a bark. 'And what a way! Did you see that bedroom? I've seen fewer candles in St Patrick's Cathedral!'

'You're not her keeper,' Alex pointed out.

'Who else is there that gives a damn?'

Alex flinched and Max said instantly, 'Sorry, that was uncalled for. Bear with me, kid, if I act like I have a sore head.'

'I'm thirty years old,' Alex said in a way that had him looking at her in surprise. 'Don't you think it's time you stopped calling me "kid"? I've known for a long time now that you aren't Humphrey Bogart.'

'Gee . . .' Max said in his Bogart voice, 'you shoulda told me . . .'

Alex bit her lip but the laugh would not be restrained.

'That's better. Don't you fold on me,' Max warned. He tipped her chin with one big hand. 'You look like I feel,' he said. 'What do you say after all this is over we get drunk together?'

Alex nodded.

'It's a date. Hold the fort while I go shower, shave and get into some clothes. And order me a big breakfast . . . things like this always go to my stomach.'

After the events of the morning the funeral could only be an anticlimax. Eve dominated the proceedings by her absence and the reason for it.

The little church echoed to the few voices that made the responses, said the prayers. Only Pamela, whose emotions got the better of her as the service progressed, was thinking of Chris. Max, who had taken one look and feared the worse, had suggested gently that it might all be too much for her, and, when she insisted on going, put her between himself and Alex. In the absence of Eve, the chief mourners were Chris's aunts, the Bingham sisters, very New York in their understated Old Guard mourning. They spoke only to Max, and as Pamela's sobs intensified, one of them turned to look at her with absolutely no sign of grief on a face that was utterly expressionless, but Alex felt the unspoken condemnation. She put an arm through Pamela's and stared back coldly.

When the time came for the coffin to be taken to the crematorium, Pamela watched it with the fixed gaze of a rabbit under the eye of a stoat, and when it had passed by, she crumpled like a falling leaf.

'I'll get her back to the house,' Alex said to Max. She felt him press a hand to her shoulder then he followed the Bingham sisters out of the pew.

By the time she got Pamela back to the villa – and once Pamela had regained consciousness Alex had made her sit quietly for at least ten minutes – Alex was exhausted, but she saw Pamela into the hands of her maid before climbing the stairs to her room. Kicking off her shoes she lay down on her bed, one arm across her eyes. After a while, a sob erupted from her throat, and she turned her face into the pillow and wept.

It was dark when she awoke and her clock told her it was ten minutes past eight, which meant she had slept for almost seven hours. She felt rested; she also felt hungry. She took off her crumpled clothes, showered, changed, brushed her hair and went downstairs.

Nobody was about; the big rooms were unlit and empty. It was not until she made her way to the kitchen, hoping to find someone preparing dinner and if not, to raid the fridge, that she found light, warmth and Max at the big hotel-sized range, stirring something that smelled delicious.

'Hi!' he said, turning to smile at her. 'Feel better for your sleep?'

'It was *you* who covered me with the quilt!'

'Only doing my lady-with-the-lamp bit.'

'Where is everybody? The house is deserted.'

'I gave the servants the night off; told them to go and drown their sorrows. Pamela is sound asleep, Jonesy is camping at the clinic, Mora has gone, which leaves but thee and me . . .' He gave her a mock leer: 'Alone at last.'

But she did not rise to the bait. There was no swift return, no instant entering into the light-hearted banter he had earlier decided, after taking in the sleeping, tear-stained face, that she needed. He knew his Alex. Today would have had that analytical brain of hers sifting and examining every pertinent word, act and fact of the previous week which had culminated in this morning's events. Now, he saw her smile was mechanical and did not reach her eyes.

'What are you cooking?' she asked.

'Spaghetti Bolognese. Hungry?'

'That's why I came here; looking for food.'

'Look no further. Sit yourself down, pour yourself a glass of wine. I'm one ahead of you.'

Alex did so. Sipping her wine she asked, 'Any news from the clinic?'

'Jonesy called earlier. He hasn't seen Eve – no visitors – but he says the doctors are satisfied that with the right care and a spell of R and R she will make a full recovery.'

He saw Alex release a breath too tightly held, saw her eyes close momentarily as though in prayer, heard the understatement in her voice when she said, 'I'm glad.'

'You and me both.'

Max had been too busy to give much thought to anything but the immediate concern of the funeral. It was in the church, he on one side of Pamela, Alex on the other, that he became aware of not only her strain, but shock. He had deliberately loaded Pamela onto her, not just because compassion wasn't one of Mora's virtues – and he was coming to appreciate her faults more and more lately – but to give her something to do, rather than do nothing but think. Only he and the Bingham sisters, Mora tagging along stubbornly, were present when the mortal remains of Christopher Bingham Czerny were consumed to the ashes mentioned in the funeral service.

His first act, on getting back to the house, had been to check on Alex, which had brought ominous rumblings from Mora.

'For God's sake!' He was in no mood for this. 'This is Alex. Don't tell me you are jealous of Alex! We're friends; old and good and close friends.'

'Men and women aren't supposed to be "friends". You spend more time with and on her than you do me. It's not natural.'

'Natural!' Max lost his temper. 'You should talk natural. Your hair isn't for a start, and your nose was bobbed at Eve's clinic when you became the Czerny Woman –' He knew he was hitting low but somehow he didn't care. Mora had been losing ground for some time now and this was the bottom of the hole. 'You're not affected by this one whit! You thought Chris was a spoiled brat and your only interest as far as his mother is concerned is your own obsession with what she pays you.' Now, he thought, was not the time to tell her that her career was about to end.

'At least I'm not a hypocrite! Alex and her mother have been at odds for years so why is she acting like the bereaved daughter all of a sudden?'

'Because, unlike you, she does have feelings!'

And one thing had led to another, which meant certain thoughts were pithily expressed – it was a relief, Max found to his surprise – and by the time they had finished throwing words around, the relationship was in ruins. Mora informed him that they were through and if she ever saw him again it would be too soon. She had put up with enough but no more. He was a selfish bastard and he was welcome to his Little Girl Lost because she, Mora, was leaving. Standard end of the affair dialogue.

But when he finally got upstairs he had found Alex asleep, her face tear-stained – which made him frown, for Alex never cried – and looking both vulnerable and defenceless. Shit! he had thought. Five will get you ten she thinks all this is her fault for telling her mother what to do with her plea for forgiveness . . .

He covered her with a quilt, went downstairs and poured himself a double Jack Daniel's on the rocks. What am I going to do with that girl? he thought. This morning's little earthquake would probably send her back into herself; Alex Brent would disappear inside Dr Alexandra Brent D.Litt., which was the persona she usually adopted to cope with crises. Except it had been Alex Brent who had cried, the little girl who had always been told not to, who had learned far too early to control her emotions until now it was hell's own job to get her to show them. That damned *alter ego* of hers is growing too big for her boots, he thought. I've been watching her muscle in for years now, and if I don't do something she'll be stuck with her – worse, so will I. I think, he thought, pouring himself another double, which hit his empty stomach and exploded, that it is time for a little heart to heart . . .

Now, eyeing her from beneath his long lashes he saw that although Alex had donned her hood and gown, there were tears in the fabric and the stitching had begun to fray at the edges. All he had to do was find the central thread and pull . . .

'You want to set the table?' he asked.

'All right.' She did so, and he saw she moved sluggishly, as though with effort, that her normal, sombre expression when she was deep in thought had intensified into brooding. And will she want to talk about it? He thought in exasperation. Will she hell! Which means I have to make her.

'I thought a nice cosy dinner for two,' he said.

That prodded her to say: 'Where has Mora gone, then?'

'For good.'

'Oh.' Then, obviously feeling something more was called for she said a polite, 'I'm sorry.'

'Why? You never liked her.'

Alex lifted a shoulder. 'It was mutual,' she said absently.

'So I thought a nice little dinner *à deux*.' A doleful sigh. 'You will appreciate I need a little feminine company.'

'It has been a somewhat fraught day.'

Fraught! He could see Dr Brent hovering in the wings. It *is* guilt, he thought. She thinks all this is her fault. Jesus, Eve, if you hadn't tried suicide I would have murdered you! There and then he made his decision. One way or another he was going to get rid of that stiff-rumped academic, Dr Alexandra Brent, D.Litt. That pain in the ass has been top of my shit list for a long time, he realized with something like shock.

He turned to check his pan of boiling water, saw it was ready and began to feed in the spaghetti, carefully separating the strands with a fork. 'I will not deny that today, I earned every penny of the exorbitant salary your mother pays me.'

'You held it all together.' For the first time there was warmth.

'And let it all hang out?' When he turned back to her his eyes were alight with teasing laughter, but there was no self-conscious flush, no scolding retort. She smiled faintly, that was all. 'Thank you for covering my confusion,' he persisted.

Another shrug. 'You've come to my rescue often enough.'

She wasn't with him. Her mind was still coming to grips with what she saw as her responsibility, her fault, her lack of compassion. Where her mother was concerned, she had never been able to be objective. He turned back to his spaghetti, let a moment elapse then tried again. 'I've not been sparing with the garlic. There seemed no point since we shall both be sleeping alone . . .' He let that trail off suggestively and it fell with a dull thud.

'That's all right, I like garlic.'

What's the treatment for shock? he wondered. Hot tea and a warm blanket? A sharp slap? This is probably delayed reaction, but whatever it is I don't like this almost catatonic state, and in the absence of an electric prod I shall just have to use my tongue.

'I'm sorry I had to offload Pamela on to you this morning,' he said, sitting down at the table opposite where she had lowered herself into a chair as though every bone ached. 'Compassion isn't one of Mora's strongpoints and it was obvious Pamela wasn't going to make it through the final stages. I thought she held up pretty well until then.'

'Was it bad – the cremation, I mean?'

'Bad enough, what with the Binghams' chilly disapproval and the slow processes of Swiss bureaucracy. Binghams are never cremated, it seems, only buried in the family plot with their ancestors. Their main concern was to know whether or not Chris had left a will.'

That hit. Disapproval mixed with distaste. 'That's horrible.'

'So was what your mother did. I've been trying to figure out why.' He waited.

'I don't think it was a spur of the moment thing this time,' Alex said finally, giving him a clue as to her feelings. 'I saw her when you carried her down. She had prepared herself; done her hair, her face, her nails, and all those candles must have taken a long time to set and light. It was as though she had made a ceremony of it; a deliberate offering of herself.'

'To punish herself, you mean? Out of guilt?'

'You told me you thought she was baptized a Catholic.'

'So was I, and we know all about guilt.'

'She also had a week to think about it.'

'But we both know that Eve is capable of extreme behaviour.'

'Like the ones she went to with me, you mean.' Pause. 'And the one I went to with her.'

Ah, thought Max. Finally. 'You had good reason not to take her at face value. She chooses them to fit the occasion, and this was one she was having trouble handling.'

'So was I.'

'But you didn't try to kill yourself.' He leaned forward. 'Look Alex, there are a dozen reasons why your mother could choose to

309

end it all. Like the fact that she had that final, catalytic row with Chris –'

'Pamela told you?'

'Yes. She believes that Eve was the cause of Chris's death, and though it's not normal for your mother to accept blame for anything, in this case there may have been no avoiding it. Then there's the fact that with Chris – and therefore her hopes – gone, she may have thought it wasn't worthwhile going on. He was her heir, to have taken over the company – yes, I know it wasn't what he wanted but when did what he wanted ever matter? Third, Jonesy said she'd been going over her life. Maybe she added it all up and the answer she got wasn't the one she wanted. Maybe she couldn't face the thought of growing old, of losing her beauty. For a woman who has lived by and for it, that's very, very hard to take, and what other resources had your mother to fall back on? The one reason I don't accept is your refusal to forgive her. That was out of character in the first place; the action of a woman who didn't know what else to do. Why should a woman who has denied you for thirty years suddenly try to take her life because you wouldn't accept her?' Max shook his head. 'No. That's not logical.'

'But she's an illogical person.'

'Even so.' Max got up to check his spaghetti and give his sauce a stir. 'But if you really want to know, ask her.'

'Easier said than done.'

'Not for Dr Brent, surely.'

He turned to meet her frown. 'What do you mean?' All cold affront.

'I mean that your mother may have a dozen faces but you yourself wear two. Alex Brent and Dr Alexandra Brent. Right now you're trying to decide which one to put in control of this particular situation. On the one hand, it was Alex whom her mother asked for forgiveness, but it was Dr Brent who refused it, and Dr Brent who is no doubt right now formulating a hypothesis which will explain this whole thing in those rational terms so dear to her heart.' Max let loose. 'Hypothesis–schmothesis! If you want the truth from your mother it's Alex she will tell it to, not Dr Brent.'

'But I am Dr Brent.'

'Not to her. What she did today shocked you rigid. Not spur of the moment, not hysterical reaction, but planned, methodical; as coldly rational as even you could wish for. *That's* what you can't handle as Alex, and why you will summon Dr Brent.'

'Why do you resent my being Dr Brent?'

'I don't. I merely deplore the way you use her as protection.'

'I most certainly do not!'

Max looked at her. Alex looked away. He got up to get the wine, poured them both another glass. *In vino veritas*, he thought.

'I can't help what I am,' Alex said, as if that explained everything. 'What is my nature.' She took a long pull at her wine.

Max drank his own wine. 'Ever hear the story of the frog and the scorpion?'

'What has that to do with anything?'

'A scorpion once asked a frog to carry him across a wide and deep river. No way, said the frog. You'll only sting me. That would be stupid, said the scorpion, for we would both drown. The frog thought then said, OK, hop on. Halfway across, the scorpion sank his sting deep into the frog's back. Why? asked the frog as they were going down for the last time. Because it is my nature, replied the scorpion.'

Alex was frowning down at the tabletop.

'We *can* help our natures because we have the power to change them,' Max said. 'All we need is the will.'

'And the desire.'

'And what would you know about desire?' Max asked silkily. He saw the expected flush colour Alex's cheeks and breathed an inward sigh of relief. Not totally out of whack, he thought.

'I was using the word in the context of expressing a wish.'

'Oh, that kind of desire.'

From between her teeth: 'I'm in no mood for teasing, Max.'

'What a pity. I am. This has been a hell of a day and I'm in need of a little – diversion.'

'Then you should have gone with Mora.'

'Oh, she told me where to go, but it's not a place I ever wanted to see.' He saw the corners of Alex's mouth twitch. 'You can laugh if you like,' he invited. 'I won't mind . . .' He checked the clock, saw that the spaghetti was almost ready, got up to get the plates out of the warming oven. 'God knows we could do with a little laughter around here.'

'I'll go along with that, but not if it's to be at my expense.'

311

'You think I'm laughing at you?'

'Aren't you?'

'Of course I'm not. I've always teased you but I've never laughed at you. Why so defensive all of a sudden?'

'I've a lot on my mind,' Alex said.

'Don't you always?' Max asked drily. But he knew when not to press.

'You've also got an empty stomach,' he said. 'I'll dish up and you can grate the Parmesan.'

Alex picked up the big block of cheese and began to grate it, but she was so distracted that she had grated her knuckles before she realized it. 'Ow!' She dropped the grater with a clatter and shook her fingers.

'Here . . . let me see . . .' Max took her hand and before she had a chance to resist he had her fingers in his mouth and was sucking away the blood. A jolt ran through her. Instantly she jerked her hand away and turned to the sink, where she turned the cold tap full on and put her hand in the water.

'I'll go find a Bandaid,' Max said.

Alex took the opportunity to splash her heated face. Calm, she thought. Deep breaths. The hand under the tap was trembling. This will do you no good, she told herself. You have enough on your mind without having to cope with – with what? she asked herself, knowing full well. This new awareness of Max as a man; no longer dear, familiar, unthreatening Max, but a man; a physical presence, worse – a sexual presence. Why, oh why has all this come about? she despaired. It's all quite useless, you know. Just so much wasted effort. You know damned well he isn't attracted to you as a woman, no matter how much he encourages you to act like one. He's not doing this for himself. He's doing it for you. He's fond of you, regards you as his best friend. He has your welfare at heart at all times. But it's not my *welfare* I want there; it's me. Steady on, she cautioned. You're not yourself.

The blood was no longer welling, merely seeping, and by the time Max came back with the Bandaids it was beginning to congeal. She controlled her inner disquiet as he took her hand, inspected the fingers. 'You've scraped the skin away,' he said, 'nothing serious.' He wrapped plasters around her first and middle fingers. 'This is just not your day, is it?' he asked tenderly, and raising the fingers, he kissed them. 'I used to do that when you were a little girl, remember? I always had to kiss you better.'

I'm not a little girl! Alex wanted to shout. Not physically, not literally. I'm a woman. Why won't you see and recognize me?

'A good dinner, a few glasses of wine and an early night. Tomorrow you'll be back to normal,' he said.

Chance would be a fine thing, thought Alex. She sat down again, reached for her glass, watched Max dish up; deftly, with an economy of movement that denoted an experienced kitchen stylist.

'Right, start on that,' he said, dumping a heaped plateful in front of her. 'There's seconds if you want them.'

'I'm probably light-headed from lack of food,' Alex said, as much to herself as to him.

They ate in silence. Both hungry, they cleared their plates. 'More?' Max asked.

'Yes, please. It's awfully good.'

'My father's recipe. They come from as far afield as the plains of Jersey for my old man's cooking. During the war he used to cook up great cauldrons of pasta and sauce for the aircrews when they came back from a mission.'

'He was in the Air Force?'

'From 1942 to 1945. A Sergeant-Cook. He was stationed at Steeple Morden with the 355th Fighter Group; the Steeple Morden Strafers. They did for eight hundred German planes.'

'But – Steeple Morden is only just down the road from Cambridge!'

'I know.'

'But – you never said anything.'

Max shrugged. 'Ancient history. I went back the first time I came to Cambridge to see you and gave my father a full report. No need to go back again.'

'You *are* a sly dog.' Alex shook her head at him but her smile was affectionate. It was also her first that evening.

'That's better,' Max approved. 'You should smile more often. It makes all the difference to your face.'

He saw it wiped away as by an invisible hand. 'I'm aware that I have a naturally downcast expression,' she said, 'but it happens to be the way my features are arranged, and short of plastic surgery I'm afraid there's not much I can do about it.'

'OK, OK . . . I wasn't criticizing or complaining. I was just saying that when you smile your face changes – for the better. You have a nice smile: makes your mouth turn up at the corners and your eyes crinkle. And that is intended as a compliment.'

Touchy, he thought. It wasn't like Alex to flare up over something he said about her looks; she usually forestalled that by making a derogatory comment herself. Usually wry, usually bitter but sugar-coated with wit. She might have minded like hell being missed in the beauty stakes but he had never known her not be able to laugh about it. Her sense of humour – and the ridiculous – was one of her best features. It was yet another area where she differed from her mother, who had no sense of humour at all. But then, he thought, she has deliberately created a persona diametrically opposed to Eve's.

'Why are you looking at me like that?' Alex asked irritably. She was very conscious of Max studying her, deliberately and at some length, and her new consciousness of him made it hurt, because it was so dispassionate. She had seen the way Max eyed women who were worth it, and it wasn't the way he was looking at her.

'I was thinking about you,' Max answered.

'Don't worry. If – and it is a big if – my mother does want to see me I will go as Alex Brent.'

'I knew you'd see reason, you always do,' Max said, 'but I wasn't thinking about you in that context. I was thinking about *you*.'

Alex said with forced lightness, 'What's to think about?'

'There you go again.'

'Where?'

'Down the road to self-denigration. Is it so hard to believe that there might be a great deal to think about where you're concerned?'

'I should have thought by now I'm a well-read book to you.'

'It's the blank pages I'm curious about. Like why they *are* blank.'

Alex made herself shrug. 'Nothing to write about.'

'Says who?'

When Alex did not reply, Max did it for her. 'Because you say so. Are you so lacking in self-esteem? Why is it you can come on like a steamroller as Dr Brent yet act like the poor relation as Alex Brent? I thought your researches had finally disproved the thesis that it was your so-called lack of looks which made your mother turn her back on you?'

'I'd hardly say the thesis can be discounted.'

'By me it can. So why do you still doubt? Is it because it's safer that way? What do you know about men? Have you ever been on a date? Held hands at a movie? Necked in the back of a car? And that's just for openers . . .' He glanced at Alex's tight, smouldering face. 'And you're supposed to be educated . . .'

'Mine was an unsentimental education,' Alex snapped.

Max grinned. 'Nice one . . . but we're not talking about Flaubert, we're talking about you. Why your education is sadly lacking in certain respects.'

'Spare me the bit about the University of Life.'

'I went to Columbia,' Max said blandly.

'And I choose my own subjects! I see no point in learning what can be of no use to me.'

'How do you know?'

'I know what suits me.'

'So do I, and that colour isn't one of them. Why do you always wear grey or black or brown? Are you trying to blend in with the woodwork or trying to minimize your size?' Alex's eyes blazed warningly. 'My mother is a big woman,' Max went on, 'and my father still takes her upstairs and locks the bedroom door every Sunday afternoon. Nor does she hide her light under a bushel. She wears colours: red and blue and green . . . At my youngest sister's wedding she was a knockout in navy and scarlet. If you would just let your mother's magicians take you in hand –'

'Never! I am what I am and if you don't like it that's just too bad!'

'Oh, God, not the "beauty is a snare and a delusion" bit.'

'It is, and nothing you can say or do will convince me otherwise. You and my mother con stupid women into paying twenty pounds for something that costs probably twenty pence to make, because you wrap it up to make it seem worth every penny. Well I happen to come in a plain brown-paper wrapping, and what you see is what you get!'

'People buy what appeals to the eye so it's no wonder you're having some marketing problems. You'd better do something soon or you'll find it's too late, you'll have passed your sell-by date!'

Alex's chair went over as she jumped to her feet. 'Don't you patronize me!' She was conscious of being very near to tears and her one thought was to get away before she made a fool of herself.

'I wouldn't pat you anything. You'd have my arm off at the shoulder before I could say "good girl"!'

Alex was almost speechless with rage and despair. My God, Max thought, once she gets her dander up she catches fire! But he was aware that the glitter in the now bright green eyes was more than just anger. It was moisture. He pushed his own chair back. 'Look, I didn't mean —'

'Oh, yes you did! You've had your hatchet out ever since I came into this kitchen!' She forced her trembling voice to steadiness. She wouldn't give him the satisfaction of letting him see just how deeply he had penetrated her defences. It would only serve to confirm his impression of her as a thirty-year-old teenager. As though I like having ten years' inexperience over the rest of the female population, or being so top-heavy with the feelings he arouses that I'm terrified I'll overbalance and spill the lot!

'I am not my mother!' she shouted at him. 'I repudiate everything she stands for. I am me, and I don't tell lies with my appearance. I happen to believe that it is what you *are* that matters, not how you look!'

'But it's how you look that makes people want to find out what you are!'

Alex clenched her fists and gritted her teeth, from between which issued a sound that was pure frustration.

'What is wrong in doing something about yourself?' Max persisted. 'Women have been doing it since the original Eve. Isn't it natural to want to make the best of yourself? In the battle of the sexes you use the weapons that will wreak the most damage.'

Not when you're so far behind the lines that you never get to fight, Alex thought, but she said, 'Damage is right! Look at the havoc my mother has created through her beauty. Five husbands, God knows how many lovers. What about beauty of the spirit, of the soul!' I might have a chance there, she thought, feeling her throat ache as her emotions, which had already undergone a Code Blue trauma, threatened to overwhelm her once more. What is the *matter* with me? she thought, panic rising. Why am I saying one thing and thinking another? It's not as though I haven't accepted what I am for a long time now. Ever since Fairy Beauty and her crony, Fairy Physical Attraction, had torn up their invitations to her christening. The Brains Fairy had been delighted to attend and brought a generous gift, so had her cousins Kindness, Understanding and Compassion, and their good friends Efficiency, Capability and Organization. Even Fairies Sweetness and Light had attended. But Fairy Sexuality had had a previous engagement.

'Is it that you still have hang-ups because of what happened with that bastard Stevens?' Max asked. 'I know you said you didn't, but –'

'No.' Alex could be truthful there. Max had explained it all in such a way that reduced it to proportions her thirteen-year-old mind could understand and accept, and gone out of his way afterwards to reassure and confirm.

'Then why do you consider yourself beyond the pale? I wonder if it's because you never had anyone to guide you; show you what being a woman means. Patsy was a great teacher and she's a fine woman, but there were things she couldn't teach you because I don't think she ever learned them.'

'Patsy told me all she thought I needed to know.'

'No. She taught you all she could, and from her you went to a single-sex school and a women's college.'

'Because we both thought that I would benefit from the attention given to women in an institution of higher learning that had no men, who invariably expect it for themselves.'

'That's feminist talk. I didn't know you'd joined the sisterhood.'

'I haven't. I just happen to believe that I'm the equal of any man. If that's feminist then so be it.'

'But you haven't had the experiences – well – just that one all those years ago – which turned them off men. You've been protected all your life –'

'Protected!'

'That's what I said. In spite of your mother's rejection there was always someone to look out for you. Think on that. You know nothing of the world outside; you've never lived in it. What I'm saying is that it's high time you did. You may come with academic prizes, but in one respect you're ignorant. You're a sexual illiterate.'

Alex gasped and Max saw her reel from the blow, but she hung on.

'To the Greeks, the word virgin meant being one's own person, not merely being without sexual experience.'

'Typical,' Max commented. 'I'm trying to get to the root of your personal hang-ups and you bring in Ancient Greece.'

'Nobody asked you to start digging into my psyche. You've got some kind of mood on you tonight. Don't take your sexual frustration out on me.'

Max threw back his head and roared with laughter. 'My what?'

'Mora's gone, hasn't she? And I caught that bit about us both sleeping alone.'

Max glanced up at the clock on the wall. 'Mora has been gone all of six hours; a bit early even for me to be feeling sexually frustrated. That's something I'm sure *you* know all about.'

'I'm not putting up with this!' Alex made to go but Max stood up to face her.

'That's right. Retreat. Am I getting too near the heart of the matter?'

Alex felt her flesh crisp. 'You're in an argumentative mood – for whatever reason – and I don't see why I should let you use me as your punch bag.' Or want to, she thought despairingly.

'We've argued before, many times, and I never knew you reluctant to pitch in and give as good as you got – better, sometimes.'

'You know very well why. This has been enough of a day without you lecturing me on the way I live my life.'

'I'm not. I'm lecturing you on the way you don't live it.' He came round the table to stand beside her. Alex forced herself not to turn towards him. 'Your trouble,' he said thoughtfully, 'is that you don't know what you're missing. Patsy may have been at fault there, but on the other hand, maybe it would be better coming from me. Patsy should have told you, but I can show you.' Before she could move he had pulled her into an embrace that brought her right up against him, breast to chest, hip to hip, thigh to thigh.

'What are you doing?' Alex demanded, horrified.

'Preparing to give you a lesson.'

'This is ridiculous,' Alex said, in the tone of voice of one reasoning with a madman. 'Let me go, Max. Don't do something we'll both regret.'

'You won't regret it, I promise. I know whereof I teach. Relax,' he soothed, as she struggled uselessly. 'This is a preliminary demonstration, not a full-scale initiation,' and before she knew what he was about he put his mouth to one of her ears, running his tongue around its convolutions. Alex bucked like a spooked colt.

'That's an erogenous zone,' Max said helpfully.

'I know what they are.' Alex made her voice as cold as possible, which was difficult considering the heat Max was generating.

'Which book was that?'

'You *are* making fun of me!'

'But this *is* fun. That's what I'm trying to impress on you.'

'I won't be used as a demonstration model.'

'You talk too much,' Max said, and prevented her from saying anything more by covering her mouth with his own.

He had kissed her many times, but never like this. Always, before, they had been affectionate but dispassionate kisses, in no way disturbing. This was something else again, and it induced in Alex a whole new range of uncontrollable feelings. Her eyes, wide open and startled to begin with, slowly fluttered closed and she ceased to struggle. All she was conscious of was Max's mouth and what he was doing with it.

She had always found the thought of someone's tongue in her mouth akin to using their toothbrush, distastefully unhygienic, but her reading of Krafft-Ebing, Havelock Ellis and Masters and Johnson had not prepared her for the sheer physicality of it all. They had not explained how the mouth felt when it was being kissed with commanding strength and passion, how it became sensitized, an antenna capable of receiving and sending the most subtle of signals which travelled to every nerve ending. When he ran his mouth down her throat, where a little pulse was fluttering with all the wild panic of a trapped butterfly, then over her eyelids, then back to her ear, biting it in a way that sent an electric jolt right down into her groin, she felt deprived, put up her hands to his face to return it to her own avid lips. She had no thoughts, only feelings, and they filled her with such a sense of languorous pleasure that she seemed to be weightless. Max's mouth was the only reality and she wanted this to go on for ever. It was something she had thought a great deal about, of late, but her imaginings had fallen far short of the reality.

It was not until she became aware of the change in Max's body, of his penis stirring and hardening and pressing against her, that she came back to full awareness, of her surroundings, what she was doing and with whom. She made a sound that was a cry of mingled shock and fright and pushed him away with all her strength, to stand, scarlet-faced, wide-eyed and trembling like a jelly.

'Normal physiological reaction in the male,' Max said, before clearing his clogged throat, but he looked as taken aback as she was. They stared at each other. 'Alex –' Max put out a hand, took a step towards her.

'No.' She shook her head. Then violently: 'No!' She whirled and ran from the kitchen. He heard her feet clattering up the wooden treads of the backstairs, fading as they reached the upper floors. There was the faint slam of a door being hurled shut, then silence.

He let out a deep breath. 'Shit!' he said explosively. He picked up his glass, drained it, set it down. 'Well, Stanley,' he said out loud, 'that's another fine mess you've got us into.'

17

Switzerland and New York, 1988

'How about some tea?' Patsy asked, as they came to the little *salon de thé*.

'Yes, all right,' Alex agreed listlessly.

'After an afternoon's shopping I'm always dying for a cup of tea,' Patsy said, 'but I don't think I could have done better than this blue crêpe, do you? And very reasonable since it was the last few metres on the bolt.'

'Yes, very reasonable,' Alex said.

They were shown to a table by the wall, and Patsy unloaded her packages with a sigh onto a vacant chair. 'Such a relief to have got everything in one fell swoop. That was a bit of luck finding those shoes . . . and I still have the blue straw I bought the last time I was in Cambridge; all it needs is some fresh trimming, and that lovely blue calf bag you bought will add the finishing touch.'

'How long will you stay in Harrow?' Alex asked.

'Only for the week. The house isn't very big, what with my niece and her husband, and the three children running about; the new baby was a late bonus, you might say. I don't think Sheila had planned on having any more, but it's nice to be asked to be godmother again. Now then, tea, I think, and perhaps some of those delicious cream cakes.'

'Nothing for me, thank you,' Alex said.

'But you ate practically nothing at lunchtime.'

'I'm not hungry.'

'It's not like you to be off your food.'

Patsy's concern changed to sympathetic understanding. 'But then, you've had a time of it, haven't you, what with one thing and another . . .'

'Yes,' Alex said. 'It's been quite a week.'

'Well, it's probably done you good to get away for a few hours.

It was a bit of luck you deciding to come over today. I do hate shopping alone; it takes all the fun out of it.'

'Oh, I'm all for fun,' Alex said.

Patsy glanced up from the menu, caught by the edge to Alex's voice, but there was nothing to be gleaned from her face, except for the distracted look it had been wearing all day. When she had arrived, out of the blue, and early at half-past nine, Patsy had been delighted. 'I was going into Thonon to do some shopping; now we can go together. I want to get some material for a dress for the christening, and there's a nice shop just off the square. We can have lunch and a browse around the shops.'

'We can go into Geneva if you like.'

'Oh, no, I can't afford their prices. Thonon always does me nicely, and it's market day today.'

But it had not been as pleasurable as usual. Alex was unwontedly quiet, for a start. When Patsy asked her advice, as she always did, for shopping was the only time when she required a second opinion, Alex gave it but without any real interest. Something was on her mind, but considering what had been going on at the villa it wasn't surprising. No wonder she had, as she had said, wanted to get away from it all for a while.

Patsy ordered tea and cakes. 'It's so nice to sit and have tea with the comfortable sense that you've achieved all you set out for,' she said, 'and all at very reasonable prices.'

'I told you to buy that silk, I would have made a present of it to you. It's not as though I can't afford it.'

'Oh, I couldn't do that! You're always buying me this and that, like the handbag. I only ever use that on high days and holidays so it's as good as new. No, the crêpe will do very well.' Taking an éclair and sinking her fork into it, she said briskly, 'Come on, out with it. You've had a sour-apple face ever since you turned up this morning. Something's eating away at you, I can tell. You always lose your appetite when you're worried. What is it? Your mother? I thought you told me she was out of danger.'

'She is.'

'Then what?'

'Nothing,' Alex said. 'Everything . . .' She made a visible effort to shake her blues. 'I'm sorry if I've been a wet blanket. I came to you for a bit of soothing calm and end up spoiling your day out.

Tell me all about your niece and this christening.'

Patsy was only too happy to do so, but it soon became apparent that Alex was miles away. Her features had taken on that downward curve which Patsy knew of old. Now what? she thought. That woman and her operatics, I suppose. Enough to depress anyone.

'. . . so I thought one of those adorable hand-embroidered dresses the French do so well,' she said. 'I didn't get the smallest size because Sheila says the baby's already eleven pounds. I suppose she'll be big, like her father.'

'She has my sympathy,' Alex said.

'Had you been living eighty years ago you'd have been bang to rights, my girl,' Patsy said sharply. 'The Edwardians went for big-bosomed, lavishly built women. It's only these past fifty years that females have regarded themselves as freaks unless they can see their ribs. I never could see mine.'

'I'd still like to be a size twelve instead of a size sixteen,' Alex said.

'That wouldn't suit you at all,' Patsy said decidedly. 'You'd look emaciated. Anyway, I don't think you're fat. You have a lot to cover, that's all.' What, or who, has brought this on? she thought. It had been a long time since Alex had brought up the subject on which she lacked a top skin. 'So, are you staying on at the villa until your mother returns?' Patsy asked, trying to coax her to talk.

'Yes. We still have our unfinished business.'

'Is that what's worrying you?'

'Well, it's not something I look forward to.'

'I've never known you to back away from a challenge.'

'There's always a first time,' Alex said, and something in her voice had Patsy frowning. She changed the subject.

'And how is Max?'

Alex bent her head over her tea. 'Fine,' she said. She could feel the blood rushing to her cheeks, but fortunately Patsy was engaged in deciding whether or not to have another cake, and by the time she had made up her mind the flush had ebbed. This is ridiculous, she thought, furious with herself. If I'm going to blush every time his name is mentioned I'm really going to be in trouble.

She had been fighting a battle between common sense and fantasy all day and most of last night, which had been another sleepless one. She had finally dozed off just before dawn, only to wake before eight, when she had decided that there was no way, feeling as she did right now, that she could look him in the eye. She had been up and dressed and out of the house by eight-thirty and had driven over to Thonon, where she had killed time in a café over several cups of coffee before taking the road to Patsy's little house. But all day he had been on her mind; she had gone over what had happened dozens of times, each time with the same reaction: her stomach taking the express lift to the basement. For God's sake, she had told herself scathingly, all he did was kiss you. He was only having fun . . . he told you so, didn't he? Fun, she thought. Why aren't I laughing? Why don't I find it as amusing as he obviously did. She kept seeing his smile when he said on a shrug: 'normal physiological reaction in the male'. While I acted like Little Bo-Peep confronted by the Big Bad Wolf.

I should have stayed, she thought. I should have let him see that it didn't mean anything to me either. That I was angry because he teased me, that's all. Except it hadn't been him she'd been angry with. It had been herself. Jumping like a scared *ingénue* at what was no more than he had said it was: a normal reaction . . . It's me who's not normal, she thought, still feeling shamefaced. All I did was prove him right: I *am* a sexual illiterate. God, how he must have laughed . . .

The thought of seeing the amusement in those brown eyes was unbearable; something she wasn't yet up to facing.

'I thought,' she said casually to Patsy, 'I might stay over a couple of days. There's nothing going on at the villa. Would that be all right?'

'But of course. You know I always love to have you and I don't leave for England until next Thursday. Stay as long as you like.'

Alex's look of relief was such that Patsy thought shrewdly: Something is driving her away from there, and it can't be her mother because she's elsewhere. And then she thought: But of course. Max is no doubt devoting his time to his ladyfriend and Alex doesn't want to play gooseberry.

'Stay as long as you want to,' she said. 'You can call the villa when we get back and tell them where you are.'

'No,' Alex said quickly. 'I want a few days right away from it all.'

'As you wish,' Patsy agreed tranquilly. I wonder, she thought, if Alex is just a little jealous?

It was eight o'clock when Max finally left the Czerny building, after a day spent in meetings, calming the panic and drawing up contingency plans to combat the latest threat by Eve's most bitter rival, a woman who, like H. Rider Haggard's She, was never referred to by name, but only as That Woman. For years she and Eve had conducted a war of attrition, referred to – but never in Eve's hearing – as Czerny's Vietnam, using every trick in the book to achieve a temporary triumph until the rival counter-attacked. Now, the grapevine was bending heavily under a load of very ripe rumours that That Woman was about to launch a new and revolutionary fragrance which would, unless countered, make a bulge in the Czerny market the like of which had not been seen even in the Ardennes.

Eve, he thought wearily, what the hell are you playing at? You picked a fine time to leave me high and dry. I'm no ideas man. All I can do is order up as many sandbags as the levee can hold.

His car drew up and he got into it.

'Where to, Mr Fabian?'

'Home, I guess – no – take me down to Little Italy.'

'The trattoria?'

'You got it.'

Suddenly the thought of returning to his empty duplex gave him the shivers. What he needed right now was warmth, lights, and the comfortable bosom of his family. It had been a long, hard day. Not only the threat from That Woman, but the threatened clamp-down by the Food and Drugs Administration on the claims currently being made by the cosmetics industry concerning their new anti-ageing products. On top of that, there was Professor Albert Kligman and his blockbusting invention Retin A, which, if its trials proved successful, was Armageddon for the industry because it really did what the cosmetic creams only claimed to do: actually did banish signs of ageing, and not just temporarily but for good. Kligman's Miracle – once officially confirmed as one – could well be the hottest thing since the invention of the lipstick.

He had read the published reports, and if they were right, Retin A was the breakthrough the industry had been searching for since the discovery of the moisturizer, because its effect on the dermis layer of the skin– hitherto entirely unreceptive to any sort of cream since it allowed nothing, especially the oil and water on which all current skincare products were based, to permeate it – was revolutionary. Retin A acted on the dermis – harmlessly and effectively according to the good Professor Kligman – to reduce its distortions, caused by natural ageing and the perpetual movement of the skin.

And there will go our unlicensed freedom to claim that our products do the same thing, Max speculated slowly. Since the FDA maintains that our claims must not only be proved but licensed, there goes the ballgame, too. If we do have to license our products then we'll have to sell them as drugs. The thought of what this would cost had been the cause of many anguished yelps at today's meetings. He sat back and closed his eyes. He could feel a headache coming on. The steady thrumming of the rain was soothing, that and the swish of the tyres lulled him into a light doze. When the car finally stopped, his driver had to tap on the glass and say, 'We're here, Mr Fabian. You want I should wait?'

'No,' Max said. 'I won't need you any more tonight.'

Peering through the café curtains Max saw that as usual, the restaurant was full; not a single empty table. Pushing open the door he went in, and at once the warmth, the noise, the smell of good Italian food, were like a cool hand on a fevered forehead. His mother was at the cash desk, his sister Ella – short for Graziella – was behind the bar, which was full of people waiting for tables, and as the swing-doors to the kitchens opened to allow a waiter with a loaded tray to come through, he could see the big, portly figure of his father presiding over frantic activity.

Max had grown up in the classic happy family. He was the youngest. The oldest was Graziella, now fifty, then came Aldo, a CPA with his own business; after him came Rosina, married to a wine grower in the Nappa Valley who supplied the restaurant with some of its wine, and her twin Susanna, who had moved to Philadelphia with her husband, a dentist; and then Bruno, a lieutenant with the 13th Precinct. His parents were third-generation Italian Americans, both sets of great-grandparents having come to America some hundred and twenty years before. His father, now seventy-two, had inherited the restaurant from his father and from being small it was now big, occupying a whole corner on Mulberry Street.

Max had grown up in the ambience of Little Italy; Italian music from tenement windows, old men playing *bocce*, old women dressed in black from head to foot picking judiciously over the vegetables in the markets, store windows filled with religious pictures and statues of the Virgin, pasta factories, and overall, the constant odour of Italian cooking. His first language had been Italian, and now, as he entered the familiar big room, heard the noise, smelled the smells, he instantly fell back into his *alter ego*, Massimo Fabiani, who thought, spoke, slept, dreamed in Italian. The tightness at the back of his neck eased, the weight slid from his shoulders, and a feeling of deep reassurance took its place.

Coming home was something he did often; every time he was in New York; and though he had his own duplex above the Museum of Modern Art, it was here, where he was born and spent the first years of his life, that he spent as much time as he could. It was everything that his life as Executive Vice-President of Eve Czerny Incorporated was not: solid, stable, secure and, above all, happy. There were dramas, sure – they were Italian – but never the grandstand plays, the vicious infighting that was par for the course around a woman who thrived on other people's unease and confusion. His mother, deep-bosomed, wide-hipped, was the rock; his father, tall, heavy-bellied now, was the calm sea in which it was anchored. He stood for a moment and let it all wash over him.

'Massimo!' His mother's voice boomed, every bit as deep as her bosom, and filled with delighted surprise.

'Hi, Ma.'

She came from behind her high perch to hug and kiss him. 'Back so soon?'

'You want I should go away again?'

'*Stupido!* Ella!' she bawled across the room. 'Jack Daniel's on the rocks for your brother.'

Ella, dark, handsome, every bit as big as her mother, poured him a double. 'Slumming again?' she asked, but teasingly. 'The Quilted Giraffe and the Four Seasons fully booked?' She leaned across the bar to hug and kiss him as his mother had. When her husband Gino had dropped dead of a massive coronary while carving the Thanksgiving turkey three years ago, she had sold up the Jersey print shop and come back home. Her two sons and one daughter were all married and had their own homes and she had found it impossible to go on with a life that did not include the man she had married at eighteen. Now, she worked in the restaurant as she had before she married, and slept in the room she had shared with her sisters.

'Right now I'm in need of a little filial affection,' Max said. 'I've had a long, hard day.'

'Go see Papa. You'll make his.'

Max said hello to various familiar faces as he made his way in the direction of the kitchen, answered some good-natured badinage about big-shots in Little Italy and finally went through into the kitchen. His father was at the big table, carefully slicing veal for tonight's speciality, Veal Parmigiana, and put down his knife to embrace his son.

'Why didn't you tell us you were in town?' he chided. 'You don't have a telephone in that big office of yours?'

'I only got here this morning and I was in meetings all day. I grabbed a sandwich at my desk and now my stomach thinks my throat is cut.'

Max said hello to the rest of the kitchen staff, most of whom he had known for years; as the restaurant had grown, so had its staff. Everyone in the family had worked there as soon as they were old enough to learn, and Max had done his stint in a long white apron and could juggle plates and glasses with the best of them. He investigated the various pots and pans. 'How about a nice big plateful of minestrone to start off?' he asked.

'Sit . . . Carlo, clear a space for my son,' Mario Fabiani ordered, turning to take down a warmed soup bowl and fill it with fragrant, vegetable- and pasta-filled soup, so thick you could stand the spoon in it.

'I see business is good,' Max said, tucking a red and white napkin into his shirt collar.

'Every night the same,' his father shrugged. He went on with his work, wielding the knife with the swift skill of the expert. 'So?' he asked. 'What brings you back this time?'

'Well, with Madame out of circulation somebody has to keep the wheels turning.'

'Too bad about her boy. To lose a child is hard, very hard.'

Max knew he was thinking of his youngest daughter Maria, born two years after Max but dead of spinal meningitis at the age of six.

'That's exactly how she's taken it,' Max said, covering a multitude of sins with that one, brief statement. 'But how's things with the family, Pa?'

'Good. Your brother Bruno has just been promoted. He's now Captain Fabiani of the Thirteenth Precinct.'

'He finally took the exam? Good for him. I told him he should do it.'

'You should have been here Thursday night; we had a big celebration.'

'I wish I could have been,' Max said truthfully.

Mario eyed his son from under his bushy eyebrows. 'So how's things with you?' he asked. 'How long you here for this time?'

'A few days; depends on how soon I can clear up certain matters.'

'It still seems queer to me that a lawyer as good as you should work for a woman. That's not the Italian way.'

'No, but it's the American,' Max said. 'How's your blood pressure?'

'I feel fine. I could work much longer than your mama allows me. Now I only come in at six and work till midnight. I got good help, so things go on pretty much the same.'

'You've lost weight,' Max said, eyeing what had been bulging and was now almost flat.

'Your mama watches what I eat.'

They chatted about this and that while Max ate his minestrone and drank a glass of wine, then his father said, 'You run along and see Mama now. You staying here tonight?'

'I thought I might.'

'Good, good . . . I want to talk to you about a couple of things.'

Max went back into the restaurant where his mother had kept the table-for-two next to her desk free for him. It was always the same; first his father in the kitchen, then his mother, who was the invigilator to watch for. She always wanted to know *everything*, and could talk to him at the same time as checking bills and making change. Now, she snapped her fingers at one of the waiters: 'Franco, some *polpette alla Siciliana* for my son.'

'Meatballs in tomato sauce!' Max exclaimed happily. 'Just what the doctor ordered.'

'You sick?' his mother asked.

'Do I look it?'

'No . . . but you look tired. You work too hard.'

'And you don't?'

Max eyed his mother lovingly. The black hair was now grey, but it still curled where it escaped from its pins, and her smooth olive skin was remarkably unlined, while the jet earrings she had worn as long as he could remember swung from her pierced ears. She had been very pretty, now she was handsome and had undeniable presence.

'I brought you something,' Max said, and delving into the pocket of the Burberry he had laid on the other chair, brought out a white and gold box. 'It's our latest fragrance,' he said. '*Enchanté*.' His mother took it, eyes sparkling, as though, upstairs on the big dressing-table in the matrimonial bedroom, she did not already have every single fragrance in the Czerny series, as well as the complete range from every Czerny line, all of them unused, although now and then, for special occasions she would dab a little *Essence of Eve* behind her ears and in the cleft of her enormous bosom. She was inordinately proud of Max; all her children had done well, but Max had done better than any of them. She referred as much as possible to 'my son, the Executive Vice President of the Czerny Corporation'.

'So, tell me all your news,' she said, settling down for a comfortable gossip. She was endlessly curious about his life, and most of all about Eve Czerny.

Max knew she meant the funeral, so he gave her an edited account. She shook her head, pursed her lips. 'I don't hold with this burning: a body should be decently buried so that there is somewhere you can go to, feel they're still there.' For years, Max had accompanied his mother to Queens where his sister was buried, helped her weed the grave, replace the wilting flowers, say a few prayers. She did not go so often now, but she still paid the occasional visit.

'And Madame? She is taking it badly?'

'Very badly.'

'An only son . . .' Rosa Fabiani shook her head. 'Too fragile to stand up to all that love . . . She should have had other children, and I can't think why she didn't because she certainly had enough husbands to father them.'

Most of what Rosa Fabiani knew about Eve Czerny came from

330

Max – who had never even begun to tell the half of it – and the gossip columns made up the rest. She was endlessly fascinated by the woman Max worked for, though, like her husband, she disapproved of what was to her an unnatural arrangement. Men ran things; that was the way God had ordained it and that was the way it should be. There was something both shocking and frightening about a woman who lived like a man, without recourse to either their permission or protection, making her own decisions, running her own life and making a damned good job of it, picking up and discarding husbands as the fancy took her. That was all right for men – they were men – but not for women. Rosa Fabiani had been born in the United States, and her parents before her, but her origins lay in Tuscany and so did her basic beliefs, based on the bedrock of the Catholic Church. When Max had first begun to work for Madame, Rosa had worried constantly about his immortal soul, a good Catholic boy exposed to all that was anathema to it, but now whenever she talked about him – which was constantly – it was with pride and confidence.

'So where is that fancy girl-friend of yours?' she now asked, disapprovingly. Mora was beautiful but she was a widow with two children. She was also a Protestant.

'That's over and done with.'

Rosa clicked her tongue but she was not displeased. 'And your little friend Alex, do you see her?'

'Yes, I see her and she isn't little – either in years or size. She's a Juno, like you.'

'I should like to meet her. How come you've never brought her here?'

'You know why. She lives in England and her world is very different from mine.' You can say that again, Max thought.

'But you are her godfather! And that isn't something to be treated lightly!'

I know, Max thought, that's where I made my mistake last night. I stepped out of character and changed the whole nature of our relationship. Good Old Uncle Max went right out of the window. You've got fences to mend, he told himself. And sooner not later.

He had gone up to the top floor just before he left, wanting to say something to restore what he had known, the moment he saw

331

her face, that he had put the boot to, but she had not answered his knock. Normally he would have gone in, but this time he had hesitated – he still didn't know why – then decided it would have to wait. He had other, more urgent problems to deal with. Now, unconsciously, he sighed.

'What's the matter? Lost your appetite?'

He came back from his thoughts to find that he had pushed his plate away. 'I guess I ate too much minestrone,' he said.

'You're worried about something?'

'I'm worried about lots of things. I'm paid to worry, remember?'

I'll fix things when I get back, he thought; one thing Alex is always open to is reason. But for the life of him he couldn't figure out the reason for his behaviour last night. He knew how touchy she was on a certain subject, so why the hell had he stomped all over it? Something had made him push her and push her, until he had finally gone too far, way beyond the light-hearted, affectionate teasing that was part of their rock-solid friendship. Why then, did he have the feeling that the rock was now rubble? All he had done was kiss her, for God's sake. He'd done that often enough. But not like last night. Somehow he had lost control of the situation, and in so doing had lost Alex. He had overstepped the bounds of familiarity, and found himself in unfamiliar territory. Oh, shit, he thought, I should have put things right before I left. But maybe it's not too late . . .

'I have to make a phone-call, Ma.'

'Help yourself.'

'No, not here. I'll do it upstairs.'

But when he got through to the villa Jacques told him that Alex had left that morning and called later to say she wouldn't be back for a few days. No, he didn't know where she had gone.

Max replaced the receiver, sat looking at it for a few moments then, as if giving himself a mental shake, reached out for it once more, dialled a number he knew by heart.

'Hi . . . how are you? Fine . . . yes, I know, but I'm here now if you've nothing better to do . . . I'll tell you when I see you. Put out the welcome mat . . . thirty minutes? Fine . . . see you then.'

He hung up. That will do the trick, he thought. God knows she's up to every one of them.

*

Alex stayed away three days, by which time she had reduced the mountain to a small pile of dust which she disposed of in her usual fashion. But when she arrived back at the villa she knew at once, by the atmosphere, that there had been developments in her absence, and as soon as she saw Jonesy hastening down the stairs with a case and a suitbag, she knew what it was.

'She's leaving the clinic?' she asked.

'Well, I've been sent to collect these, so I think we may assume she intends to.'

'What happened?'

'Something she read in one of the papers I took her. Her nearest and anything but dearest rival is about to pull a fast one and Madame is steaming . . . I swear I could see smoke.'

'Oh,' Alex said.

'It was just the thing to bounce her back into the world again,' Jonesy said. 'She was on the phone to New York before you could say long-distance, but fortunately Max was already there.'

'Max is in New York!'

'Where else would he be than where the action is?'

'Of course,' Alex said. 'Where else?'

'Well, I can't stand here gossiping. See you later.'

'Wait!' At the door he turned. 'Did she ask about me?'

'She didn't ask about anybody.'

Well, Alex thought, as she headed for the stairs. That puts me in my place all right. Max went off to New York without so much as a word and after all that forgiveness stuff my mother hasn't a thought to spare for me either. Business as usual, she thought bitterly; in which case, it's time I got back to mine.

18

Switzerland, 1988

'You understand,' Eve said, over the long-distance telephone – the hush-phone into which nobody could tap – 'that it's a matter of the utmost discretion.'

'Yes,' Max said.

'You are to do whatever is necessary, go wherever you must.'

'And if and when I have what you want?'

'You bring it to me.'

'At the villa?'

'Yes. I'm returning there today. I'm relying on you, Max. This is very important to me.'

'I'll do my best.'

'Of course you will,' said Eve, accepting no less than her due.

'But what about the rest of it. I told you –'

'Not now, Max. I will think about it, of course, and steps will be taken, but this comes first just now.'

'OK,' Max said. 'If that's what you want,' his curiosity at fever pitch even as he knew better than to probe.

'As to the other matters we discussed, you will have all the information you can get hold of ready for me when I next call.'

'I already have it,' Max said.

'Good. And it will do no harm to keep your eyes and ears open while you're about this other business. You know what I mean.'

Not this time I don't, Max thought. What are you playing at now, Eve? 'Are you fully recovered?' he asked, wanting to be sure.

'I am. The past is over and done with – or will be when you've brought me what I want; my concern now is for the future. It's been made plain to me that I still have one and there are things I must do.'

Jesus, it's the destiny bit again, Max thought. Either that or she's still got a load of barbiturate in her veins. 'OK, I'll do my best. I'll be in touch.'

'Good.' He heard the click as the receiver went down then the dialling tone. Well, he thought resignedly. Ours not to reason why . . .

Alex arrived back in Cambridge with relief. Now to get back to normal. No more high dramas and low opinions; no more unsettling confrontations, unforgivable conversations or unforeseen developments. Here, she knew what was going to happen because she had designed the pattern of her days a long time ago; each one flowed into the next without haste, as tranquil as the Cam which flowed between its grassy meadows. Here she could so order her time as to make best possible use of it, instead of hanging around, waiting, wondering and getting nowhere. Here she could talk on the subjects she loved; teach, instruct, enlighten, discuss, even argue, and feel satisfied, at the end of each unruffled day, that she had accomplished something.

But it was dismaying to find that some people did not even know she had been away; that apart from certain undergraduates, she had not been missed. One or two vague remarks such as 'Did you have a nice time in Switzerland?' or 'Oh, hello Alex, I see you're back, then' were all that came her way. Of course, it was still not generally known that she was a candidate for the Revesby Prize; the names had not yet been announced. Worst of all was the fact that her comfortable rut did not seem so comfortable any more; or that so deep had she been ensconced in it she had somehow failed to make her presence felt. Now, she was conscious that no matter how many times she turned round, she could not settle comfortably.

In the evenings, sitting listening to Mozart or Erroll Garner, she found herself wondering what was going on back at the villa, how her mother was, what developments there had been. She was even tempted to ring and see, but as nobody called her, the old sense of invisibility returned in full force. She would not allow herself to think about Max. That was a dead end. But an opening had been made into her quiet backwater which had allowed all sorts of muddy water to flood in. She kept going over the events of her stay, as if she needed to get them in the right kind of order to enable them to be put away. No matter how she tried she could not get past one incontrovertible fact. Nothing would be the same any more.

She had been back a week when her phone rang one morning as she was reading an essay on *Daniel Deronda* by her most promising student.

It was her mother. 'I would like you to return to the villa as soon as possible,' she said without preamble.

'Why?'

'You once asked me certain questions. I am now prepared to answer them.'

'What has brought this on?'

'I will tell you when I see you.'

'You're assuming I still want answers to my questions.'

'Then tell me you do not.'

Alex hesitated that much too long.

'It is time to tell you now. It wasn't the right time before.'

'I have only just got back.'

'You weren't asked to leave.'

'Nobody asked me to stay, either.'

'The circumstances were unusual.'

'You're out of the clinic, then?'

'Yes. And fully recovered. Will you come?'

Alex made up her mind. 'All right.'

'Good. I'll send the plane for you. It will arrive at the airport near you, I forget its name . . .'

'Stansted.'

'Yes. It will be there at two o'clock. I will have a car meet you at Geneva. You are wise to come. Believe me when I say it can only be to your advantage.' She rang off.

Now what? Alex thought. Why the sudden *volte-face*? Her brush with death? She sounded – dramatic. There was something in her voice . . . Well, she thought. Here it is. Your chance to hear the answers to all your questions. Especially if Max is there . . .

When she arrived at the villa Jacques met her, took her case and told her that she was to go straight up to her mother, who was in her sitting-room.

'Is she alone?' Alex asked. 'I mean, is Mr Fabian here?'

'He was, but he went back to New York the day before yesterday.'

'I see.' An unaccountable sense of disappointment hit her as she went up the stairs.

336

Eve was sitting at her desk. She was in black, neat as a pin and looking none the worse for her ordeal. She rose when Alex entered, and for the first time, the mask was missing. She smiled when she saw her daughter, but it was one of satisfaction.

'Come, sit down,' she said, indicating one of two chairs drawn up by the bright fire.

Alex did as she was told. Eve took the other chair, sitting very erect, spine not touching the back, ankles and hands crossed.

'You wanted to know about me,' she said, 'so I will tell you.'

'Why?' asked Alex. 'Why now?'

'All will be explained once I have told you my story. Max has told me that you are of the belief that there is a reason for everything. I am of the same persuasion. I will tell you of a great many reasons, but always, only one mattered.'

'Your destiny?'

'Three times I have tried to escape it; three times I have been brought back.' Alex knew she was referring to her suicide attempts. 'Things go in threes,' Eve said. 'There will not be a fourth. I have learned my lesson. Perhaps, when you have learned what I have to tell you, your – view – of things will not be the same. That is up to you.'

'I take it you no longer care about my forgiveness.'

'That was a plea made under great emotional duress, before I learned that what must be must be, and that if a thing is, it is. But to get back to what you want to know . . . In the beginning,' she said, 'I was Anna Farkas, born a peasant of peasants, living a life of much harshness and great deprivation. I hated it. I hated the drudgery, the lack of things I did not then know of but I felt existed somewhere. I knew that I had to have those things. I wanted – oh, how I wanted, and I made up my mind to have. No matter what the cost.'

Slowly, with frequent pauses to collect her thoughts and marshal her facts, Eve recounted the story of her missing years, those never quoted in the many profiles and feature articles on her 'life'. Placing this version beside what she had learned from her own researches, Alex found that Eve's story tallied in all respects, with one difference; beyond the plain statement of facts Eve built up a picture of an ambitious young girl, greedy with a hunger that devoured, who was determined to use what God had given her to pull herself out of the

337

mire of poverty and to the very top of that ladder whose topmost rung ended, as had the beanstalk, in a land of magic and endless possibilities. She pulled no punches; she described her life with her Russian and Hungarian protectors, she told how she had used all her cunning, all her wiles, to get what she wanted; she described how she had met Laszlo Kovacs, how she had stolen his formulas, used them to found the one-woman enterprise that grew into the mighty Czerny Corporation, of which she was sole owner. She told of her pregnancy, how she manipulated John Brent into marriage, how she left him and her child, how she had erased her former life so completely that she had, perforce, to erase her own flesh and blood.

'Eve Czerny had to have no connection with Anna Farkas, no connection at all. I created a new woman, a new life, and in order to do that I had to destroy the old one.'

'Including me,' Alex said.

'Everything had to go.'

'So I was sacrificed to ambition,' Alex said.

'I believed in my destiny, and that to fulfil it I had to do whatever was necessary.'

'Then why did you take me in?'

'I had no choice. John's mother brought you.'

'I remember.'

Eve met her daughter's eyes calmly. 'She threatened to expose me unless I accepted you, to create as much unpleasant publicity as she could. I was only just established, I had a great deal yet to do. Furthermore, I had married Christopher Bingham as a single woman. It would have been disastrous.'

'For Eve Czerny or Mrs Christopher Bingham?'

'Both. I loved being Eve Czerny – I still do; but I also loved being Mrs Christopher Bingham. He made me into Somebody. I couldn't allow the truth to be known; I had fought too hard, done too much. I was not prepared to let anyone take my new life from me. But I had no choice when my husband was taken.'

'I remember that day . . . I was watching from the windows. I saw you run out of the house, screaming and tearing at your clothes . . .'

'He was the love of my life,' Eve said simply. 'I have no recollection of what I did, but it was not meant to be. I had not fulfilled my destiny.'

'So you transferred your love from your husband to your son?'

'Yes. And he was taken too. Destiny has been kind to me, but it has also been cruel. I am not meant to be as other women are. A wife, a mother. I am Eve Czerny, and the two constants in my life are the person and the company I created. That is the lesson I have learned. I have much yet to do and I am meant to do it. I will do it. But alone.'

'Take what you want, said God, but pay for it?'

Eve nodded, almost approvingly. 'Exactly. There is a price, and I have paid it.'

Alex perceived that to her mother, what she had received in exchange had been worth every penny. 'No . . .' she said slowly, 'you are not as other women are.' Her mother obviously took it as a compliment.

'One final question,' Alex said. 'You have explained *why* you rejected me. What I would like to know is *how* you could.'

'You were not in my plans. I was angry. A child was the last thing I wanted.'

'And still is.'

Eve let her silence be her answer.

'Well,' Alex said, almost to herself, 'I wanted answers.'

'I loved my son because he was the issue of a man I loved. I did not love Laszlo Kovacs.'

'And all those other men?'

Eve shrugged. 'I wanted them.'

'Including Rik Stevens?'

Eve regarded her immaculate nails. 'That was a mistake,' she admitted. 'One I regret.'

'You got your revenge.'

Eve smiled. 'That was Max,' she said. 'I had turned down the idea of investing in a Hollywood studio. I hadn't bothered to find out who owned it. Max reminded me and explained how I could use it if I did. So I bought it.' Eve regarded her daughter with frank curiosity. 'Max has gone to extraordinary lengths for you,' she said, obviously at a loss to understand it. Her smile deepened. 'But then, Max is an extraordinary man.'

Alex said nothing.

'I did ask him if you had suffered any – ill effects,' Eve said after a moment. 'He assured me you had not, but I thought it wiser to

339

send you away to school. You have done well, but then, Laszlo was a brilliant man.'

'So,' Alex said, after some thought during which her mother waited composedly. 'Why are you telling me all this now? What has happened to make you change your mind?'

Eve rose to her feet. 'Come with me.'

Alex followed her out of the room and down the corridor where Eve tapped on a door before opening it. It was a bedroom, curtains drawn, dimly lit by only one lamp placed by the bed. On it, a figure lay, and beside it, a nurse sat, reading. She looked up before standing up.

'How is he?' Eve asked.

'Still sleeping. Physically he is exhausted.'

Eve nodded. 'Would you leave us for a while, please.'

The nurse went out. Eve went to the bed, bent over the figure. 'Come here,' she said to Alex. Frowning, puzzled, Alex went forward. The figure on the bed was an old man, with close-cropped white hair and a thin, fleshless face which seemed no more than an arrangement of bones; gaunt from years of suffering.

'This is Laszlo Kovacs,' Eve said. 'Your father.'

Alex turned a stunned face from the bed to her mother and back again.

'But – he's dead,' she said stupidly.

'So it was thought. He has been in Russia for the past thirty years, in a labour camp. Since Mr Gorbachev took over, there have been many unexpected changes; one of them has been the release of thousands of political prisoners. There was an item in the London *Times* a couple of weeks ago about a trainload of released prisoners who had been transported after the Hungarian Revolution, most of whom had been presumed dead since 1956. I had Max make enquiries. He found your father in a reception camp just outside Budapest and brought him here, to me.'

Alex clutched at a bedpost – the bed was a fourposter. She could not speak, so absolute was her shock.

'Come . . .' Eve took hold of her arm and led her, unresisting, back to her sitting-room. She pushed Alex into her chair, went to a lacquered cabinet, opened it and took out a decanter of brandy. Pouring a double she took it across to her speechless daughter. 'Here,' she said.

Alex took it, tossed it back and coughed splutteringly.

'Now do you see why I wasn't allowed to die?' Eve asked.

Alex stared. 'You think all this is part of that Fate you believe in?'

'But of course it is.' Her mother sounded as if she was explaining to an idiot. 'The wheel has turned full circle. I began to build what I am through Laszlo; now, all these years later, he's been brought to me again. I can never be a mother to you, but I can give you your father, since it seems to be so important to you that you have someone.'

Alex's jaw dropped. 'Give me a father?' She began to laugh. 'Oh, my God . . .' she groaned, 'you are unbelievable, you really are . . .'

'For thirty years I thought him dead.'

'And I'll bet you hoped he was! Everything you have is based on his original formulas.'

'For which Fate is allowing me a chance to repay him.'

'For God's sake, stop going on about Fate,' Alex shouted. 'What about *you*? What do *you* want?'

'It's not a question of what *I* want,' Eve said, with the infuriating calm of conviction. 'It is what must be.'

Alex fell back in her chair. 'I don't believe any of this,' she said helplessly. 'It goes beyond the bounds of credulity. You think that whatever appalling thing you do is justified on the grounds of a Manifest Destiny?' She shook her head as if to clear it. 'You're suffering from a case of galloping megalomania!'

'I have told you my life. Think about it. Then you will see.' Nothing could shake Eve's certainty.

'So what am I supposed to do with my "father"?' Alex asked presently. 'Gather him to my bosom and take him back to Cambridge where we'll live happily ever after?'

'Once he is restored to health – and I have given orders that he is to remain here until that is accomplished – if it is possible – you may do with him as you wish.'

'He's a man, an old man who has suffered enormously over the past thirty years, not a soulless obligation!'

'It was my hope, in bringing you together, that you might find, from or in or with him, the love you seem to want so much.'

'Love! What would you know about love? You haven't got it in you to love anything beyond yourself! Love is a giving of that self, and you've never given one particle of yourself to any living soul — no, not even your beloved Christopher Bingham.'

'Who is to say what love is? I loved Christopher for what he did for me, gave to me, brought me to. I made him happy, we made a son. But they were not part of my eventual destiny. I had to lose them both before I understood.' Still with that maddening calm: 'I am what I am,' she said.

Armoured in self-esteem, Alex thought hopelessly. Convinced she has been 'chosen'. Well, who is to say she wasn't? Perhaps there is somebody up there pulling strings, for she certainly has come far; from nothing to everything — or what she believes is everything.

'I can see I have given you much to think about,' Eve said, confident of the end result. 'Take your time. Stay as long as you wish. I myself must leave for New York. I have much to do. Things have been — neglected, and while Max is my right arm, it is my brain that controls everything. Pamela is still here. I have asked her to stay as well, for as long as she wishes.'

'Another loose end tied up?'

Eve ignored that. 'I am arranging to set up a trust fund for Laszlo; he will not want for the rest of his life.'

'Another pension like Jean Vernier?'

'You know of him?' Eve smiled. 'Yes, he too was a creator . . . I pay my debts,' she said.

'What if I decide to publicize all this?' Alex asked. 'Like Mary Brent?'

Eve met her daughter's eyes and smiled. 'But you won't, will you. She was a spiteful old bigot, a religious fanatic. You are not. Max tells me you adhere to reason and fair play — so very English — and I have been honest with you. I have told you how I am, what I am. I cannot be different.'

Alex contemplated her mother. 'Did you ever hear the story of the frog and the scorpion?' she asked.

Eve stared. Alex told her.

'Of course,' Eve shrugged. 'The frog had only himself to blame. The scorpion obeyed his nature, whatever the cost. I must obey mine.'

Alex rose to her feet. She was wasting her time.

'Shall I tell Max I have seen you?' Eve asked.

'No,' Alex answered. 'I don't want you to tell him anything.'

She left Eve's sitting-room and went downstairs and out of the house as if to escape what she had learned, but really to think about it. She set out at a great pace, which gradually slowed as she argued herself into some sort of calm. She realized she was approaching the big chestnut where Chris's ashes were buried, and rounding it she saw that the headstone was in place above an eternal flame which was embedded in a mass of flowers. A woman was kneeling there, taking out those that were wilting and replacing them with fresh ones; roses, lilac, big white daisies, yellow jonquils, pink carnations, all from the vast greenhouse at the back of the house. As she drew near she saw it was Pamela.

'Hello,' she said awkwardly, feeling guilty. She had forgotten all about Pamela, whose suffering was so much greater than her own.

Pamela looked up. 'Alex!' she said with pleasure.

'I'm sorry I left so abruptly. I –'

'That's all right,' Pamela said, rising to her feet. 'There was nothing to keep you here. I'm just surprised to see you back.'

'My mother asked me to come.'

'Oh?'

'We finally had our – talk.'

'Not a very satisfactory one by the looks of you.'

'She told me she has asked you to stay.'

'Yes . . . she came back from the clinic a new woman. More – I can't explain it exactly, but as though she'd learned something that changed everything. It was most peculiar. No explanation, of course. Did she give one to you?'

'Of a sort.'

Something had happened, Pamela thought, for Alex too seemed different. 'What do you think of the stone?' she asked, indicating it.

It gleamed, white and perfect, for all the world like one of Eve's famous jars, but the words proclaimed CHRISTOPHER BINGHAM CZERNY, and underneath, BELOVED SON 1962–1988. For all her sorrow about Chris, Alex felt a sudden stab of pain. Mine would read Unloved Daughter, she thought. But swiftly the pain was followed by a strange and new sensation. It didn't matter any more. Eve didn't matter any more. I know who

343

I am, Alex thought. What I have always been. What was wrong was that I couldn't – wouldn't – accept it.

'Oh, Pamela . . .' she said regretfully, 'what a fool I've been.'

When they reached the gravel sweep, on their return to the house, they saw that the big new-penny coloured Rolls-Royce Corniche was drawn up, luggage being loaded, Jonesy supervising.

'She's off then,' Pamela said. 'Max told me all hell was breaking loose.'

'You saw him?' Alex asked casually.

'Only briefly. He came and went in a day. Something to do with That Woman stealing a march. Eve is off to line up the troops and prepare a battle plan. God help That Woman, is all I can say, and she's as tough as they come. Another self-made miracle. Born Rosele Katzenschwantz or some such name in Brooklyn but now Eve's most dangerous rival. I've never dared let Eve know that I knew Rosele long before I met Chris. Any friend of hers is an enemy of Eve's. I managed that all on my own.'

Jonesy caught sight of them. 'More haste less speed,' he trilled, as they came up, 'but you've no idea how good it is to be back to normal. No – not in the boot, stupid, that always travels with Madame. Here, give it to me . . .' He wrested the alligator vanity case from the chauffeur. 'Now then, the furs . . . there should be the sable and the black mink . . . ah, there they are. Right, just let me check . . .' He was counting cases when Eve appeared through the open front doors, dressed for travelling in a simple but undoubtedly hideously expensive black suit under a short mink jacket, a tiny, jet and crystal trimmed pill-box on her gleaming red-gold hair.

'Check the hat,' murmured Pamela. 'That means she means business.'

With an all-encompassing smile and a little wave Eve climbed into the car. Jonesy shut the boot, hopped in beside her, and they were off.

'Well, that's that,' Pamela began, then stopped as she saw Alex take off at a run, bending down in mid-stride to scoop up a handful of gravel which she flung after the car with a shout of: 'And good riddance to you too!' The stones spattered harmlessly because by then the car had turned a bend in the drive. Pamela was open-mouthed.

'Do you know,' Alex remarked conversationally, as she walked back, dusting her hands, 'that is something I have wanted to do for years and only just realized it.' She heaved a satisfied sigh. 'And I must say I feel a hell of a sight better for it.' She grinned at Pamela. 'Suddenly I've regained my appetite. Let's go and eat Eve out of house and home.'

'So what are we celebrating?' Pamela asked later, as they both sat cross-legged on the wide window seat of what had been Alex's childhood home. She was watching Alex pour foaming champagne into two glasses.

'My freedom.'

'From your mother?'

'Yes. I finally got the truth from her this afternoon. No more illusions, delusions, or self-hatred. I know why she rejected me, and it wasn't because of the way I looked – or did look – which was what I always believed. She rejected me because as far as she was concerned, I didn't exist. I was part of a past she had deliberately destroyed; an inconvenient and irritating reminder of a life left behind. Anna Farkas – her original identity – had to be eliminated, which meant that everything connected with her had to be got rid of, too.'

'Anna Farkas?'

'The name she was born with.' Alex told Pamela her mother's history.

'Wow!' Pamela breathed, utterly fascinated. 'What a story! No wonder she buried it in an unmarked grave. So that old man Max brought to the villa is your father!' She shook her head with awe. 'Talk about chutzpah!'

'Not to her. To her it's all perfectly natural. It disposes of several problems in one fell swoop.'

'But does it? I mean – what are you going to do about him – your father.'

'That depends on him, and when he's fit enough to be told. He's a physical wreck. God knows what sort of an existence he has led for the past thirty years. But it must be what *he* wants – for a change.'

'Alex, *you* have changed. I knew, as soon as I saw you down by the tree that something had happened. You looked like someone who has just been told that they aren't, after all, suffering from a terminal disease.'

'Which is how I feel. It's not what I am, you see. It's *that* I am. A living reminder of things she doesn't want to remember. She never wanted me from the start – or any child. I was a mistake, no more.'

'And you can cope with that?'

'A hell of a sight easier than thinking it was *me*; how *I* looked, what *I* was. She thought she was rid of me, along with Laszlo Kovacs. She had used her pregnancy as a means of marrying John Brent and claiming British citizenship and she was delighted to leave me with him. Can you imagine how she must have felt when Mary Brent turned up with me in tow? That was most certainly not part of her Grand Design, but there was nothing she could do because that horrible old woman blackmailed her into keeping me. All I knew was that she didn't want me, and being too young to understand why, I naturally assumed it was because, as I had been told so many times, I was a Child of Satan: wicked, unlovable, unwanted.'

'How absolutely *awful*,' Pamela said in distress. 'No wonder you were the way you were. How you ever grew up even remotely normal is beyond me.'

'I wouldn't have, had it not been for Patsy and Max. From them I received the only love I knew – and craved. Patsy so steadfast, so calm, so – normal; and Max so strong, so protective – and so light-hearted. But I couldn't rid myself of the feelings I had where my mother was concerned. In spite of everything I *still* wanted her to love me. Final proof, I suppose, that I wasn't what I believed I was. When it was never forthcoming – well, it was like the oyster. That irritant grain of sand you ease as best you can; in my case by covering myself with degrees – all to show her that if I wasn't beautiful I was at least clever. And it still didn't matter a damn. Until the night I confronted her and she confirmed every single one of my worst fears. But the strange thing is, that once I had that confirmation I really started to think about it, and without the longing – which had blurred everything else – I realized there was more to it than that. Hadn't she left me behind when I was far too young to show what I would become? There had to be some other, deeper reason, and that I finally understood earlier today.'

'But why did she want your forgiveness, then?'

'She thought she had somehow lost Chris because of what she had done to me; that the guiding hand which had brought her so far was punishing her for it. That was why she tried to kill herself. She thought she'd been abandoned. It was only when her third attempt failed that she came to believe that where she had offended – failed, if you like – wasn't with me or with Chris, but with that same destiny. She had allowed other things to interfere. That was why she lost Chris's father. She was – and I'm telling you now what she told me – not as other women. Her course was set and no deviations were allowed. From now on, she will follow it and only it. That's why all this tidying up, so to speak. So she can go on absolutely unencumbered.'

Alex met Pamela's dumbfounded expression. 'She is the perfect dictionary definition of megalomania.'

'Which is?'

'Excessive overestimation of one's own importance. It's a form of insanity.'

'You mean she's nuts?'

'Not in the strait-jacket way, but not entirely normal either.'

Pamela shook her head. 'Wow!' she said again. 'So that's why she's like she is.'

'It's why I think she is as she is; a psychiatrist might not agree.'

'You didn't tell her that!'

Alex looked askance. 'I may have been a fool, but not that much of a one.'

Pamela sipped pensively at her champagne. 'Well, as a rational explanation it certainly makes sense.' She smiled. 'You haven't changed all that much, then.'

Alex laughed. 'That is *my* nature.'

Pamela looked admiring. 'I'd never have worked all that out in a million years. No wonder you're a D.Litt.'

'It's quite simple,' Alex said, 'when you think about it.'

'And when you know how to think about it. You have her sussed out to the last full stop. You should write a book about it. You analysed Charlotte Brontë and George Eliot – why not Eve Czerny? And here's another piece for your jigsaw. She's offered me a job.'

But Alex was not surprised. 'Of course. Galloping megalomania, just as I said. All that ever matters to her are her own concerns. She no longer has any reason to fear and hate you, so why not use you. What sort of a job has she offered?'

'Directrice of her New York salon. The present one is taking early retirement because of ill health. She said – and I quote: "It would give you something to do with your life".'

'Will you take it?'

'I haven't decided yet.'

'It would be some sort of connection – even if indirect – with Chris.'

'Yes, I'd thought of that, and if I accept it will be for that reason; until I've come to terms with his death, anyway.'

'It's funny, but I never saw Chris growing old,' Alex said after a moment. 'He lived life with such – fervour, as though he knew he wouldn't have it for long.'

Pamela nodded. 'Didn't he, though.'

'I wish I had. I've wasted so many years, Pamela. If only I'd understood all this before, but my emotions always clouded the issue.'

'Is that why you distanced yourself from them?'

'Yes. All they had ever brought me was grief.'

'But now that you do understand – why not change all that? If I take this job and go to New York – a city I know and love – you could come and stay with me for a while. It is *the* most marvellous city. Anything is possible there. You could shed the old Alex and I'd take you in hand and create an entirely new one. New clothes, a new face –'

Alex shook her head. 'No. Now that I know the one I've got is not what I thought it was, I'm quite happy with it. You know my views on the cosmetics industry; the con of all time. I don't need all that because, at last, I know who and what I am and that there's no need to be ashamed of it. That is what matters to me. I've finally got some confidence in myself.'

Alex went to pour more champagne, found the bottle empty. 'Let's have another bottle,' she said. She rang the bell that had now been fixed up to connect with the butler's pantry.

When Jacques came upstairs Alex said: 'Another bottle of champagne please, Jacques, and could we have some sandwiches? Smoked salmon, I think. Lots of them. We're both starving.'

'At once, Miss Alex.'

'I think even he approves of the New You,' Pamela commented on a giggle. 'Oh, Alex, you just *have* to come to New York!'

'You sound as if you've made up your mind.'

'I have. The chance to do Madame down is one I can't resist. Oh, do let me make you over, Alex – clotheswise at least. Those suits you wear do you no favours, you know. I promise I won't interfere with your face – though the judicious application of a little eye-shadow and blusher would work wonders – but in the right clothes you could be very striking.'

'I'll think about it,' was all Alex would say. Then as if to make up for her refusal: 'It's obvious you believe in happy endings.'

'Don't you?'

'I've only known them in books.'

'Oh, but it would be so satisfying to turn you around, make Eve eat her words.'

'That happy an ending is too much to expect.'

'That's what I did, you know, when Fritz dumped me. Went to New York and had a retread. My ego needed it. I bought a whole new wardrobe, made myself as beautiful as I knew how and launched myself into a life of one damned man after another.'

'Did it hurt – being dumped, I mean?'

'Yes, but it was only my pride, as I came to realize later. I'd not really been happy for some time. My job was to reflect Fritzie's light. To wear gorgeous clothes, fabulous jewels, look stunning – and make all the men he knew madly envious. He had his art collection, his horses, his houses, his yacht, and me – all possessions. Whenever he got tired of one of them he traded it in for another. And after five years, it was my turn.'

'Why did you marry him?'

'I was dazzled, and I was young. Twenty-one. To be pursued – and oh, how he pursued me – by the fifth richest man in the world was quite something, let me tell you.'

'I believe you. I've never been pursued by any man, rich or poor.'

'Well, that's not really surprising, is it . . .' Pamela paused. 'You can come across as very intimidating, you know.'

Alex looked uncomfortable.

'Oh, yes you can. Before I got to know you I thought you were very aloof and distant; frightfully "superior". It wasn't until I met you a few times that I realized it was shyness and lack of self-confidence. And now you know you have no need to feel like that, I shall make it my business to introduce you to some of the most attractive men I know.'

'You're ahead of me,' Alex warned.

'You have a lot of catching up to do.'

'Which I'll do in my own good time.'

'Oh, but New York is *the* place to do it! I lost my virginity there, in a suite at the Plaza Hotel.' Pamela sighed nostalgically. 'He was gorgeous; a professional lady-killer and at that time way beyond my means. But he fancied me and I think now and then he allowed himself the occasional affair purely for pleasure instead of gain.' Dreamily: 'He seduced me the way I'd always wanted it to be: all celestial harmonies and floating spheres. It was only the once, and when we met afterwards he was always no more than polite – and working on his latest meal-ticket. But it was the most marvellous initiation.' Pamela sighed again. 'I thought I might die of pleasure . . .'

Something in Alex's silence made her ask, 'You haven't the slightest idea what I am talking about, have you?'

Alex shook her head. In her head she could hear Max's taunting voice: 'Have you ever gone out on a date? Held hands at a movie? Necked in the back of a car?' No, she thought now, and sadly, nobody ever asked me.

Just then, Jacques came back with a second bottle of Krug and a plateful of sandwiches; smoked salmon and pâté de foie gras.

'Jacques, you angel!' Pamela said warmly. 'Just what we need.'

He bowed as he uncorked the champagne, refilled both their glasses. 'Will there be anything else?'

'If there is, we'll let you know.' He bowed himself out.

They fell on the sandwiches with alacrity, and for a while they ate in silence, then Alex asked: 'Do you really think something could be done with me – my appearance, I mean.'

'Of course it could! You should see some of today's acknowledged beauties without their "faces" on. You wouldn't recognize them.' Craftily: 'Am I to take it you're interested, then?'

'No. I just wanted to know, that's all. I haven't changed my opinion about face values and what they mean; the lies they tell. Look at my mother – who's well worth looking at. Yet what is she but a living lie. Her face value is counterfeit. I don't want to be like that. I am what I look, and that's all there is to it.'

'I had a dog once, called Beauty, a Sealyham. He was as bad-tempered a brute as ever there was but I loved him.'

Alex raised her glass. 'To Truth.'

'To Beauty,' Pamela said. They drank.

'I'm truth and you're beauty,' Alex said, the champagne getting to her, 'so be careful; "Beauty provoketh thieves sooner than gold".'

'Says who?'

'Shakespeare.'

'Alex! No wonder you scare men off!'

'What's wrong with poetry?'

'Nothing – in the right place.' Sounding disbelieving: 'Haven't you *ever* had a man in your life?'

'No.'

'But what about your mother's men? She had dozens.'

'I never knew any of them but one. Rik Stevens.'

'The film star? I always thought he was rather dishy but he's old, now.'

'Another example of the lie. He was a pervert.'

'You have got a jaundiced eye,' Pamela cautioned, wagging her glass. 'Not all men are rotten, you know.'

'I didn't say they were.' Pause. 'How many have you had, anyway?'

'Well . . . after New York there was a photographer, then a ski-instructor, and after him a divine Frenchman. Then I married Fritz and after him – well, let's just say I stopped keeping count. Then there was Chris . . . and only Chris.'

Alex put her nose in her glass once more. 'What happened between Max and Mora? I thought that was more or less permanent.'

'No; she only wanted it that way. I don't think Max did. Did you know she was jealous of you, by the way?'

'Now you *are* drunk.'

'No, seriously. She was. She was convinced there was more to your platonic friendship than met the eye.'

'Well there isn't.' Alex was short. 'Max doesn't see me that way.' It was like biting on a bad tooth. 'Max's taste runs to sexy, beautiful creatures with more curves than a scenic railway. He's told me more than once that working in the cosmetics industry was a bonus because it gave him access to so many, and in the years I've known him he's had more of them than I've had hot dinners.'

Ah . . . Pamela thought, conscious of the bitterness. So that's it.

'Max and I have always been the best of friends,' Alex said, over-emphasizing like mad. 'No more, no less.'

But you would like to change that, thought Pamela. 'Well,' she shrugged, 'I'm only telling you how it seemed to me. She was forever sniping at you.'

'That's because she's stupid. All she has to commend her are her looks, which are considerable, but otherwise she's shallow, vain and silly.'

Pamela raised her glass. 'To Mora. Good riddance to more bad rubbish.' She giggled. 'Do you know, I think I'm rather drunk.'

'That's the object of this particular exercise,' Alex said. 'I've only been drunk once, and I made a right mess of things, but today rectified all that so I intend to get drunk again.'

'I'll drink to that.' They did.

When Jacques returned, an hour later, it was to find them both asleep in their chairs. He noiselessly cleared away the bottle, glasses and empty plates then left them to it.

19

New York, 1988

New York City was having one of its sparkling mornings, when it seems as if a crystal bowl has been inverted over Manhattan, and the sharp, clear light of the sun is refracted through it into a million glittering shards, making the skyline stand out like black cardboard cut-outs. The young gofer stationed just outside the plate-glass doors of the Czerny Building gazed up at the cloudless, zinging blue of the sky and thought happily that it was good to be alive. Except for her nerves, that was. She glanced at her watch again. Any minute now, she thought. She screwed up her eyes, peered up the street, went a little further out onto the pavement because it was difficult to see through people, thought she saw what she sought, hesitated then confirmed that it was indeed the car, and raised the little handset she carried. 'The car is approaching the building – repeat – the car is approaching the building.' Sixty floors up, there was a mad scramble as windows were flung open, cigarette smoke frantically fanned out, desks tidied, skirts straightened, nail-polish checked, lipstick renewed, gossiping groups scattered to their stations.

Max Fabian sauntered into the big conference room, around which stood a group of assorted Vice-Presidents of one thing or another, smiled round at them affably and said, 'All right, gentlemen. Fix bayonets. Madame is in the building.'

One nervous executive fumbled for a small box of pills, gulped two and washed them down with water. The others smoothed hair, straightened ties, shot cuffs.

'Jesus, I'm not looking forward to this,' one of them muttered. 'She's not going to be pleased, not going to be pleased at all.'

'Relax,' Max said lazily, 'all she can do is fire you.'

The buzzer on the intercom sounded. Max rose. 'Right,' he said. 'Once more into the breach, dear friends . . .'

He was waiting when the elevator doors opened and Eve swept out. 'Madame.' He swept her a courtly if exaggerated bow.

'Max. Are they ready?'

'And waiting.'

'Good. Come into my office.'

It occupied a whole corner of the building, two walls composed entirely of windows: Eve always examined colours in daylight. The other walls were hung with framed pictures, every one a cover on which she had appeared. *Time*, *Life*, *Newsweek*, *People*, *Paris-Match*, *Oggi*, *Hola!*, *Vogue*, *Harpers*, *W* – just about every magazine that had a decent circulation. There were no mirrors. They were in her private dressing-room next door, where, if she was working late and going out straight from the office, she would change into the clothes Jonesy would bring. Her desk was a big square of lucite with eighteen-carat-gold trim – Eve had seen it in a shop window in Rome. On it stood three telephones. There were no drawers; she kept no papers on her desk. Whatever she wanted her secretary would bring. There were no filing cabinets, nothing office-like about it. The carpet was a soft silvery pink, matching the big sofa and four deep chairs grouped around a lucite coffee table. The chair behind her desk was an ordinary hardbacked affair; one which offered no temptation to slouch. There was no central light, only a scattering of lamps with rock crystal bases and silk shades the same colour as the carpet. The room always smelled of her latest fragrance. When Eve was in New York it was her secretary's first job each morning to spray the room.

Now, dropping her fur onto a chair, she went behind the desk, picked up a thin blue folder. 'This is it?' She hefted it disbelievingly.

'All I could get that is factual. The rest is rumour and conjecture.'

'And the FDA?' She picked up a green folder.

'No actual move but they're making sounds like somebody getting ready to.'

Eve threw it down. 'That is something we can't do anything about as yet and anyway isn't just our problem. It concerns the whole industry. This,' she waved the blue folder, 'is what we must deal with now.'

'I still think we should be ready for Kligman and his wonder product. That is the danger.'

'If and when it arrives. This –' she brandished the folder at him, 'is here now.'

She sat down, motioned to Max to follow suit, opened the folder and rapidly read the single sheet of paper.

'Have you confirmed the use of this soap opera queen?'

'I've tried. All I get is no comment or some line about her being committed to other things. But the rumour is strong and she's been wined and dined by certain people in plain sight. Old friends, is the given reason.'

Eve picked up the photograph lying beneath the paper, examined it closely. 'Retouched?' she asked.

Max shrugged. 'She has her own photographer and his lips are sealed with very generous bonuses.'

Eve picked up a magnifying glass, the one she used to examine variations in shade, and went over the exquisite face with care. 'Hmm . . . Remarkable for her age.'

Max forbore to say that the lady was at least five years younger than Eve.

'And the fragrance?'

'Again nobody outside the company knows a thing, but by all accounts it is another *Charlie* or *Giorgio*. Distinctive, instantly recognizable and sexy as hell.'

'Its name?'

'Absolutely secret, as is the launch date.'

Eve tapped her perfectly shaped fingernails on the photograph. 'This isn't a double bluff? Scare tactics? How do you say it – putting the frighteners on?'

'If they don't launch they'll be sitting there with egg all over their faces.'

'So . . .' Her fingers drummed like an execution roll. 'We have to counter.'

'Our own fragrance is ready. I've held the launch date. Everything is on hold, but we have to decide. Do we go first or do we wait and see what we're up against?'

'I will not launch without more information than this!' Eve wielded the blue folder like a weapon. 'What about your spies?'

'All I know is that the budget is their biggest ever. They're putting their money where their mouth is. The millions they're going to spend on world TV, press and promotion will total more than they've spent on all their other fragrances put together.'

'Do you know who they're using?'

'Word is – though he won't say yea or nay – that it's Jerry Stein.'

'Then they do indeed mean business. He is the best; the very best.'

'To go back to the name . . . I've been told that it will be a derivative of the soap queen's own name. She will be the image that sells the product. That means limitless sales potential. The woman is a legend.'

'Then we must find our own legend! But who . . . who . . . ?' Eve left her desk to pace to and fro in front of the windows. 'Garbo old, Dietrich old, Taylor is about to produce her own fragrance . . .' She whirled. 'What about Jacqueline Onassis?'

'What about her?' Max's voice had Eve scowling irritably.

She went back to the folder, studied the paper again. 'Not only the very expensive, ultra-prestigious fragrance but an accompanying range of cleansers, moisturizers, bases, blushers, glossers – pah!' She flung it down. 'That Woman has been spying on me!' she screeched.

She swung round on Max. 'She's doing what I was about to do to her in six short weeks! How did she know? Who told her?' Her voice had risen.

'I've checked and double checked. Our security is tight, but just as we have our sources she has hers, and you know this business thrives on rumour. You can never keep a launch as big as ours completely under wraps.'

'Oh, I know her . . . she thought that I was out of the way, too grief-stricken to do anything but mourn. Ha! How little she knows me! Does she think I would let something – anything – deflect me from my chosen course?' Eve's voice rang with scorn. 'I'll show her.' She paced back and forth, each step placed squarely on That Woman's face. 'I want to know everything, Max. Whatever you can find out. You have your ways, so use them! Any means to find out exactly what I'm up against.' She stopped, fixed him with one of her Looks. 'I have to know about that fragrance. I must know what I have to do to top it. I want to know where it will launch, how many "doors" she has, what is being offered in the way of mark-ups and special promotions. Information, that's what I need, every last little bit of information, but most of all I need a sample of that fragrance. You understand?'

'Doors' was the industry name for an exclusive outlet. Eve was telling him to beg, borrow, even steal, and giving him anything he needed in order to do it.

'I'll do my best,' Max told her.

'Good, good . . .' She patted his arm. 'I know I can count on you.'

She was back, Max thought, with a vengeance. No mention of the events of the last fortnight; they had happened, they had been dealt with, they were behind her. No explanations, not that he had expected any. No reasons why, no justifications for, only concern for the one thing that mattered to her: who she was, what she was, why she was. She would never say what had made her make her last suicide attempt, but it was obvious that its failure had been transformed, by her own tortuous reasoning, into a pointer to the future.

'Now,' she said briskly, 'let us go and hear the various feeble excuses my "experts" have prepared for me.'

As she swept into the conference room, there was an immediate chorus of 'Good morning, Madame', and then her Comptroller, Edward Gates, made a little speech, carefully composed and diligently rehearsed.

'Yes, yes . . . thank you,' Eve said, on an impatient movement of a hand. 'But let's get down to what really matters, gentlemen. I want some explanations for what has been going on in my absence.'

Already in place on the table in front of her chair was a pile of layouts, bottles, jars, colour swatches, and one box. She started with the layouts. 'Who is responsible for this?'

Her art director stood up. 'I am, Madame.'

Eve tore it across, dropped the pieces on the floor. 'That would not draw a first glance, never mind a second.' Of the next one on the pile she grimaced, shuddered and said, 'You call these colours? Mud and sludge, that's what they are. We're selling illusions, you cretin, and the colours must be dreamlike, evocative.' Again she tore the sketch across. 'You will start again from scratch, and this is your last chance. Do I make myself clear?'

'Yes, Madame.'

'Then I suggest you go and get started – and take your rubbish with you.' The hapless man came round to her chair, got down on his hands and knees to pick up the torn fragments, then retreated as quickly as he could without taking to his heels.

'Now . . . this full-page colour spread. Why is the name smaller than the bottle?' She picked up a red pencil from the pile lying in front of her, scrawled the name in letters six inches high. 'That is how it should be. A woman asks for a perfume by its name, not the shape of the bottle. Which brings me to this.' She picked up the elegant ovoid jar. 'Since when have I ever marketed round jars?'

The man responsible cleared his throat. 'We thought a new approach, Madame? Something different . . . a balanced, elegant shape to ornament a woman's dressing-table – and it isn't round, it's ovoid.' He ducked as the jar went sailing by his head.

'I'm not selling eggs!' she screamed at him. 'My bottles and jars are square. Don't you know that most women keep their cosmetics on a shelf in the bathroom? My bottles are square because that way they line up much more easily.'

She then rejected out of hand a particularly vivid scarlet intended as an addition to her Princess di Marchesi line. 'The only fit name for this is Bloody Mary! Does nobody listen to a word I say, or study the market for which this is supposedly intended? Hard reds are ageing on hands that are no longer young; the skin tone changes once you're past forty and my Marchesi line is intended for older women. God in heaven, why am I surrounded by idiots!' Then, in a calmer, approving voice: 'But it will do nicely for the Young Eve line.'

Next she picked up an eyebrow pencil. 'The woman who uses this is going to paint her brows, not a picture.' She snapped the pencil in two. 'There . . . that is the length. Easy to hold, balances nicely against the fingers and we can sell twice as many at the same price.'

One by one she went through the pile, demolishing, diminishing, denigrating. Now and again she would approve: 'Nice, I like that,' or 'Not bad, but needs more work.'

Finally, the only thing left was the box, her white and gold presentation box for the Easter promotion. Eve placed it in front of her, took off the lid with its thick gold tassel, examined the contents. Finally, she looked up.

'And who is responsible for this?' There was nothing to be discovered from her voice. It was merely enquiring.

'I am,' Max said.

Eve raised her eyebrows.

'The production line was screaming, the promotion had to be got under way, the contents chosen. You were not available so I asked around, got some opinions and finally went ahead with this.'

'Whose opinions?'

'All people you know, and who themselves are knowledgeable – except one, and hers was the suggestion I acted upon.'

'And who was that?' There was still nothing in her voice but a question.

'Her name is Alex Brent.'

Eve's head came up. Her eyes bored into his. Max withstood their onslaught.

'She came up with this?'

'Yes.'

Eve looked down at the box again, took out each sample, examined it before replacing it. 'I presume you have the costs?'

Max opened the folder in front of him, slid a single sheet of paper across the table towards her. 'Orders are up forty per cent. Our "doors" are very enthusiastic. They are convinced it is a lead seller.'

Eve studied the figures carefully. Again there was nothing to be discovered from her face. Finally she closed the box again. 'Approved,' was all she said.

Max released the breath he had been holding, slowly and silently, though he was aware he had not heard the last of this particular item. Sure enough, once Any Other Business had been dealt with and everybody rose to go, Eve said, 'Stay a moment, Max.' He sat down again.

When they were alone, Eve tapped the box with one long, vividly pink fingernail. 'Tell me about this.'

'I happened to mention my difficulty to Alex, told her what was wanted and once I told her the whys and wherefores, she came up with this.'

'Came up? A woman who uses nothing but soap and water "came up" with this? How do you explain it?'

'Alex is the one who has inherited your – instinct, I suppose you could call it – for what is "right", except she does it by a reasoned examination of the facts. I was every bit as surprised as you are.'

Eve was silent then she said: 'Tell me how she did it – everything.'

Max did so. There was another silence. Max waited. Eve used silences as weapons. But all she said, finally, was 'All right, Max. That's all for now.'

He left.

A week later Max laid a minute phial in front of Eve. She looked up at him, eyes kindling, then down at it again. 'This is it?' she asked.

'If it isn't then I've lost my touch.'

Able to afford it, now, Eve wrinkled her nose at him affectionately. 'Not you,' she said. 'I knew what I was doing when I took you on.' She lifted the phial between thumb and forefinger. 'This confirms it.'

'You haven't sniffed it yet.'

'But you have. Give me your opinion.'

'A blockbuster.'

Eve's breath hissed between her teeth.

'It will sell like there's no tomorrow. It's the best thing she's ever done.'

'Is it now . . .' Eve prised loose the plug, ran the phial past her nostrils. Max saw her close her eyes, inhaling as the scent drifted about her. 'It does have a certain – something.'

'It has everything and you know it. We have got a fight on our hands, Eve. Our biggest yet.'

'It's different.'

'Try it on the skin.'

Eve tipped the phial against first one wrist, then the other, waved them in the air to help the fragrance dry. Then she sniffed again. 'Tuberoses . . . bergamot . . . a touch of ylang-ylang . . . just a hint of jasmine . . . and something else . . . I cannot name it . . . but I will have it analysed.' She sniffed, then breathed deeply. 'Yes,' she said, 'That Woman has come up with something against which my *Toutes les Fleurs* won't stand a chance. This is –'

'Sexy,' Max said.

'Yes, very . . . it promises all sorts of things . . . Clever, very clever.'

'She's a clever woman.'

'So am I,' Eve said. 'And I will top this. I must. This, my dear Max, is a fight to the death.'

'Just the kind you like,' Max said.

'I'm at my best when I have a fight on my hands.'

'So how do you propose to go about it?'

'Analysis first. I want to know exactly what this comprises, the proportional blending. Then I shall create a fragrance that will obliterate it. But first I must think about what kind of a fragrance; who it's intended for. Leave me, Max. I must think about this. Get this sample to the laboratory. It takes priority over everything else.'

'Even the *Toutes Fleurs* launch?'

'That is cancelled. Put it on hold for a later date – spring, I think. It's a light-hearted, youthful fragrance, in no way powerful enough to stand up against this.'

'But the stores – the promotion – the cost!'

'Absorb it!' At his expression: 'Are you telling me we can't?'

'No, we can, but it means tying up a hell of a lot of money.'

'I will untie it when I think the time is right. Now do as I say. There's no time to be lost.' But Eve's glorious eyes were brilliant in the way they always were when she saw a challenge to be surmounted, a rival to be destroyed. 'I want that analysis as quickly as possible. See to it.'

He was dismissed. Typical, he thought, as he went back to his own office. She didn't bother to ask how I got it. All that matters to her is that I did.

Later that day, at his table, by the door, naturally, at Le Cirque, he rose to his feet as he saw Pamela Bradley enter the restaurant, eyes following her, filled with speculation and surmise. It would be all over the place in no time, he knew. More grist to the gossip mill.

'But I thought Pamela Bradley was *persona non grata* where anything to do with Eve Czerny was concerned?'

'They're up to something, mark my words.'

'Already? Chris Bingham has only just cashed in his chips.'

'Max Fabian always was a fast worker.'

And so on. Now, as he kissed Pamela's fragrant cheek, complimented her on her suit – 'Armani?' – he added on a murmur, 'The cat is scattering the pigeons left, right and centre.'

'More to the point, was your cat pleased?'

'To know what she's up against, yes. To find it's a hell of a sight more than she bargained for – no. I owe you one, Pamela. Thanks.'

'It was – shall we say, fortuitous, that I should be invited to a weekend at That Woman's. Every bit as fortuitous as my running into you just as I was about to make my way there.'

'OK, so I was lying in wait. I knew about the weekend and I managed to find out who would be there. Once I knew you would be – well, I was desperate. Besides, That Woman is no real friend of yours, is she?'

'No, it's only because she thinks I'm out of favour with Eve that makes me worth cultivating. I think she hopes to get a little lucrative spite out of me.'

'So you felt no guilt for what you did?'

'None.'

'Then tell me how you did it.'

'I waited until the Saturday night party was in full swing; then I slipped upstairs to her bedroom. The bottle was on her dressing-table – unlabelled, but I recognized its smell because she was wearing it. Talk about the cat and the canary . . . Everybody wanted to know what it was but naturally she wouldn't say. Anyway, I filled the eyedropper you gave me and decanted it into the phial. Then I ran. It was wildly nerve-racking but at the same time unbelievably exciting. It only took minutes, but during every one of them I expected her to come barging in for a respray.'

'You did well, very well. When ours hits the street you shall have the biggest bottle I can find.'

'I'll be expected to wear it anyway – as part of my job.'

'And when do you start?' Max had ordered them both a Martini and now he sipped his.

'One week from today, as ever is.' Pamela looked about her, saw several faces turn hastily away. 'You're right; we're causing minor ructions.'

'Do you mind?'

'Not in the least. It's nothing new, you know.'

'I guess not.'

Pamela laughed. 'You watch, they'll be coming to the salon like lemmings, dying to know what's going on. That should do me no harm.'

Max frowned. 'I wouldn't want any of that to come your way. That Woman has a lot of influence and a vicious tongue.'

'I'm used to that, too. Tongues never ceased to wag all the time Chris and I were together.'

'Just so long as you understand that you have entered a cut-throat business.'

'I'll back you and your knife any time. Alex says you would have made a good butcher.'

Max sipped his Martini. 'How is Alex?' he asked.

'Well, there have been ructions there, too.'

'Oh?' Max was instantly alert. 'Like what?'

Pamela recounted the stone-throwing incident.

'Well, hallelujah!' Max sounded as if prayers had been answered. 'It's been a long time coming but better late than never. Did she tell you what happened with her mother?'

'Yes, and that she finally realized it wasn't just her, Alex, her mother didn't want, it was her whole history. Once she saw that, it didn't seem to hurt her any more.'

Max's grin flashed. 'That's my girl!'

Is she? Pamela wanted to ask, some inner caution preventing her. She had known Max for some years now, but he was still pretty much an unknown quantity. Behind the natural charm, the easy confidence, the flippant wit, was a very different man of whom she had always been somewhat wary, and not because he was a power source at the Czerny Corporation. While Eve was always the star attraction with her God-given talent for attracting publicity – always in the right place at the right time – and her flair for dominating any milieu, Max worked behind the scenes. Chris had told her seriously, 'It's his planning that has made the company what it is today, you know. He's got things scheduled for a whole year ahead; stores tied up, launch dates arranged, who will get what and how much. My mother is entrepreneurial, he is systematic. She's the one you watch, but Max is the one to keep an eye on.' So she said nothing, for though she had the confidence that goes with beauty, it was not the kind of confidence Alex had, being, Pamela finally understood now, unafraid of him.

'We celebrated by getting drunk,' she told him.

'Alex – drunk?'

'I told you – ructions.'

363

'So it would seem,' Max said thoughtfully, 'so it would seem.'

Yes, think about it, Pamela told him silently, because unless I'm very much mistaken, Alex Brent thinks an awful lot about you.

The letter had obviously been following Alex about; it had been originally addressed to Cambridge and sent on. The paper was thick, expensive, the heading – a firm of lawyers in Geneva – unknown to her. She opened the envelope, read the single sheet of paper, frowned, read it again. 'Now what?' she said to herself, as she went to the telephone.

An hour later, when she came out of the building overlooking the River Rhône, she knew. She went straight back to her car, but did not drive off. Instead she sat for a long time, staring out at the river and thinking hard. Only when she had thought herself into some kind of calm did she start the engine, turn the car in the direction of the villa.

Jacques met her in the hall. 'Miss Bradley called from New York. Would you return her call as soon as you can, please.'

'Thank you, Jacques. Could I have a cup of coffee, please? Black, no sugar.'

'Very good, Miss.'

The phone rang once before being snatched up. 'Alex?'

'Yes. You know, then.'

'I'm still at the lawyers'. I called you at once.'

'I've just come back from Geneva.'

There was a silence then Pamela said: 'I know . . . I can't quite take it in either.'

'Did you know that Chris was so inordinately rich?'

'Yes. He told me once the lawyers told him.'

'Did he ever give you any idea that he intended to do this?'

'No, but I don't think I'm altogether as shocked as you are.'

'That,' Alex said drily, 'is the understatement of this or any year.'

'But you *are* glad, aren't you?'

'I don't know what I feel except utterly taken aback. It's something I never expected.'

'Chris liked giving surprises, remember?'

'As long as he wasn't on the receiving end.'

There was another silence then Pamela said decidedly, 'We have to discuss this.'

'Yes, we do.'

'Why don't you come over here? It's the perfect excuse, and we can sit down and talk the whole thing out. I can tell you're not altogether happy about it.'

'No, I'm not.'

'Typical,' Pamela said.

'What do you mean?' Alex bridled at the shortness of Pamela's tone.

'I mean that you take your suspicion of face values to alarming lengths. You think there's a catch, don't you?'

'Don't you?'

'I don't need to,' Pamela said. 'It's obvious that the sooner you get over here the better, otherwise you're liable to do something we'll both regret.'

'I've got a nasty feeling that this whole thing could lead to a lot of things we would both regret.'

'Nobody in their right mind regrets money!'

'There's more to this than just money.'

'Then you'd better come over here and you can tell me just exactly what.'

'Haven't you asked yourself why Chris has done this?'

'I don't need to,' Pamela repeated. 'I know.'

'Then perhaps you'll tell me.'

'With pleasure – when I see you. This isn't something to be discussed over an open transatlantic line. Get yourself on the first plane and we can discuss it to smithereens, if that's what you want.'

'Why can't you come over here?'

'I'm a working girl now, remember? And one thing we both seem to agree on is that we keep what has happened between ourselves for the time being. It would look odd if I suddenly decamped from a job I've only just taken up.'

'I have a job too, you know.'

'From which you're on leave of absence! It will occasion no surprise if you turn up in New York for a few days. You can stay with me and nobody will be any the wiser, if that's the way you want to play it.'

'This isn't a game!' Alex said angrily.

Pamela let an exasperated breath escape. 'Then why are you making it seem so complicated? Honestly, Alex, if you can't see why

Chris has done this then you need more than your eyes opening. Now don't let's argue. Come over here on the double and we'll talk it through.'

'I don't have an American visa.' Alex sounded as if she had trumped Pamela's ace.

'That's easily arranged. I'll get Max –'

'No!' Alex lowered her voice as she went on, 'I don't want *anybody* to know about this until I've decided what to do.'

'Suit yourself. I have other strings I can pull. Stay by the phone. I'll get back to you as quickly as I can.' Pamela cut the connection, leaving Alex feeling both frustrated and uneasy. But she did as she was told. She sat and drank her coffee and tried not to keep checking the time. It's ridiculous, she thought. I can't go trotting off to New York at the drop of a hat. She thought of a dozen good reasons why, and marshalled them in rank order, but when Pamela rang back – within the half-hour – she got no chance to parade them.

'It's all fixed,' Pamela said without preamble. 'All you have to do is present yourself at the American Consulate in Geneva – that's the nearest place seeing as time is of the essence – with your passport. They're expecting you at two o'clock. Once you've got your visa continue on to the airport. There's a London flight leaving at five to four your time. That will connect you with time to spare for the seven o'clock Concorde. Your tickets are bought and paid for; all you have to do is pick them up at the British Airways desk. When you get to JFK I'll be waiting. Now, have you got all that?'

'Pamela, I –'

'*Have you got that?*'

'Yes, but –'

'No buts. You can tell them to me personally when you get here. We can talk all night if you want, but get here first. This is important, Alex. I know that just as much as you do.'

Feeling – as she had done ever since her visit to Geneva – that things had been taken out of her hands, Alex found herself answering meekly, 'All right,' and perceiving what it was that had enabled Pamela Bradley to perform such radical character-surgery on Christopher Bingham Junior. Under the Madonna-like serenity there was a strong-minded woman. And I thought that was supposed to be me, Alex thought.

*

Before she left she called in to see Laszlo Kovacs. 'He was awake a little earlier and took a bowl of beef broth, but he's still not fully aware of his surroundings,' his nurse reported. 'It's going to be a long slow process of recovery.'

'I have to go away for a few days but I'll call you every evening.'

'He's not going anywhere,' the nurse said on a shrug. 'Not for some time yet.'

At the Consulate they were prepared for her. She filled in the necessary forms, answered the requisite questions, after which her passport was duly stamped. Alex did not know whose strings Pamela had pulled, but it was obvious they were attached to some Very Important People.

She made the London plane with time to spare and her transfer at Heathrow went without a hitch. The Concorde seats were somewhat narrow for her comfort, but by that time she was past caring. If this is life in the fast lane, she thought, I don't wonder that Chris went in for speed . . . She had brought a book – a feminist critique of Victorian lady novelists – but it lay unread on her lap as she stared out at the deep cobalt blue curve of the sky. She drank her champagne but couldn't eat anything. She felt like a stone in a catapult; Concorde was hurling her, at the speed of sound, into a new world, and she felt powerless, weightless and utterly ineffectual. Something Arnold Bennett had once said floated into her mind: 'Always behave as if nothing had happened no matter what has happened.' Well, she thought, all I can do is try.

Pamela was waiting for her, hugged and kissed her. 'Well?' she asked.

'I feel like I've just been dropped down one,' Alex answered pithily.

'This is just the beginning. Come on, I've got a car outside.'

It was a chauffeur-driven limousine, and in no time, after a quick flash through Immigration and Customs, they were on the Van Wyck Expressway heading for Manhattan.

'Right,' Pamela said, leading Alex into the low-key luxury of her Sutton Place house, 'just the two of us. I've given Consuelo the night off, the answering machine is on, the champagne is cooling and I went to Zabar's this afternoon and got us a bagful of delicious goodies. Sit down, put your feet up – that couch is long enough.'

She went into her state-of-the-art kitchen and got out one of the two bottles of Roederer Cristal she had earlier put to chill, uncovered the tray she had set in the cool box. Lox – always better in New York than smoked salmon – a bowl of dill sauce to accompany it, quails' eggs, five kinds of olives, taco chips and a tangy blue-cheese dip, an assortment of cold cuts, including pastrami, and a loaf of garlic bread ready for the oven. 'Seven minutes,' she said, as she set the electric oven. 'Time for at least one glass of champagne.' She had known the moment she set eyes on Alex that she was in for a hard time; her face was set and severe; her Dr Brent face, the one Chris had always called her 'D.Litt. Negativity' face. Negativity my ass, Pamela thought – a week in the salon and she was already thinking American. I'm damned if I'll let her turn what Chris has done into some sort of ego-trip. Just because she hasn't got an ego is no reason to expect me to dump mine.

She went back into the living-room bearing tray and glasses and a grim expression.

'Right,' she said, pouring champagne into two crystal flutes as delicate as spun sugar. 'Get this down you and then tell me why you're wearing a Friday Face instead of a Sunny Sunday one.'

'Have you thought about what Chris has done – I mean really thought?'

'No, but I'm sure you have – into the ground. You probably wrote a paper on it during your flight. From where I sit it's all perfectly straightforward. Chris has made us his sole heirs; between us we share all he had to leave, and since we were the only two people for whom he cared in this world, I fail to see why you aren't down on your knees and being thankful.' Pamela drained her glass and refilled it. 'Strike that last remark. I'll tell you why you're not. You don't think you deserve it, right?'

'Right is what I don't feel about it.'

'Why? In God's name why?'

'I can't help feeling that what Chris has left is Bingham money. It only went to him because our mother married his father for it – that and his name. It was made by the Binghams, increased by the Binghams, belonged to the Binghams until my mother came along and manipulated things differently.'

'I knew it! Your bloody mother! Sooner or later everything, every goddam thing, comes back to your mother. You're paranoid about

368

that woman, do you know that? She's got you as conditioned as Pavlov's dog. The only emotional response you ever make is to things that concern her. I thought you said you'd seen the light?'

'I have. *She* doesn't frighten me any more, if that's what you think. There's nothing she can do about Chris's will, anyway – or rather, nothing she will do. A, because the last thing she wants made public is my existence, and B, because the publicity of challenging the will would be disastrous for her image; that of the woman who is always on top of every situation. To have it generally known that her adored son left his millions to an unknown half-sister and the woman he loved is just not on. But if I take this money I'm aiding and abetting a scheme she set in motion years ago, and if I'm to cut myself free of her I have to cut away everything.'

'Are you saying that Chris had no right to his own father's money?' Pamela was so incredulous that her voice cracked.

'No. I'm saying that *I* have no right to it.'

'What's so different about me, then?'

'Chris loved you, would have married you had he lived. You lived together for six years and in my eyes were as good as married. It should go to you, what he left. All of it.'

Pamela was so astounded she was speechless. But not for long. 'That,' she said, 'is the biggest load of rubbish I ever heard. To begin with, I don't give a damn about why your mother married Chris's father; what matters here is that she did, and that when he died he left everything to his son, who has now left it to us, as was his right. I don't give a damn about the Binghams either; there are no more of them anyway. Chris was the last. If you mean those three wax-flower aunts of his, then let me remind you that they haven't been Binghams these many years. They shared what old Mrs Bingham left, and that, by all accounts, was a not inconsiderable sum; they have absolutely no right – no right whatsoever to what was left to Chris, who had every right to leave it to us. Why do you think he made his will in Switzerland, as a Swiss citizen, even though he had dual nationality? Because it puts those three witches right out of court, that's why. He knew what he was doing. Did the lawyers explain how he converted everything into money – gold? What was Bingham & Company no longer exists because he sold it to a multinational conglomerate. He got rid of the Bank, the real estate, the shipping line – everything that came under American law – and he put it all into a Swiss bank; and before the market collapsed last October. I used to wonder why he read the financial pages so thoroughly. Now we both know.'

Pamela paused then went on more calmly. 'It has occurred to me that maybe Chris knew his would be a short life; God knows he used to laugh about it often enough, at least I thought he was laughing. Now I wonder . . .' Pamela rose to her feet, went over to where she had laid down her black calf Hermès handbag. 'He even knew how you would react,' she said, 'which is why he wrote this. It was with the will.' She held out a letter to Alex, who shook her head. 'I have no right to read something that is private to you and Chris.'

'It was addressed to me but it concerns us both.'

'Then you read it.'

'Very well.' Pamela drew a steadying breath.

'"My dearest love" –' here Pamela swallowed. '"I know you always said you didn't love me for my money, and you proved that fact so many times during our life together. What I have done is the only way I know to say thank you. It's all I have to give, but it's given with love. To both of you, because I am making Alex co-beneficiary. She is the only other person I give a damn about, but I never was able to tell her because our mother did such a good job on her she wouldn't believe it anyway. Maybe she will believe this, though knowing her, she will find it difficult since rejection is all she thinks she knows. This gift is because she never rejected me." The rest is personal,' Pamela said.

Alex was sitting with her face averted. 'I never knew . . .' she whispered when she could.

'That Chris loved you? That's because you never expected him to, did you?' Alex was silent. 'Did you?' Pamela repeated mercilessly.

Alex's silence was her answer.

'He knew you much better than you realize. What he said about your mother doing a good job on you is right. She did. You had no self-esteem because she put the boot to it when you were far too young to know what she was doing, and by the time you did it was too late. Chris has left you his money for one reason only. Because he loved you. Now tell me you don't feel you have a right to it.'

Alex shook her head.

'Then drink your champagne.' Pamela went over to pick up her own glass. 'To Chris,' she said, raising it.

Alex raised her head. Her eyes were full in a face that wore an expression Pamela had never seen before, and for a moment could not identify until she realized it was pride.

'To Chris,' Alex said softly.

'No, no, no . . .' Eve flipped the eight by fours like a pack of cards. 'None of these is right . . .'

'That's every girl the studio has under either option or contract,' Max said. 'You won't find any better. Every one of them is a beauty.'

'Fine for pictures; not for the face in an Eve Czerny layout.'

'You've been through all the models, where else do you suggest we look?'

'Everywhere! What about television?'

'What about an unknown? Someone new and fresh.'

'Bring her to me and I will decide!'

'If you could be more specific,' the man from the advertising agency ventured. 'As to colouring, personality –'

'Colouring is not important, she will be made over to my design. As to personality – cool, distant, unattainable. The kind of face other women would kill for!'

The man from the agency looked at Max and shrugged.

'I am launching an entirely new and revolutionary fragrance,' Eve proclaimed. ('When she can find it,' the ad man murmured *sotto voce*.) 'So the face must fit the perfume. These girls are all too young, too – available. My face must be sophisticated, soignée, aware . . . she must personify the fragrance.'

'If we had some idea of what that is . . .' the adman said plaintively.

Eve glared. 'Are you deaf? Have you not heard me describe it to you – in detail – time and time again?'

'With respect, Madame, a description is one thing; the actuality is another. How can we fit a face to a product which exists only in your imagination? We're working in the dark.'

Which incited her to further rage that she should be surrounded by such morons, cretins and certifiable mental deficients. Why could they not see what she could see? Why could they not close their eyes, think of her accurate description and *realize* it?

She had been in this white-hot state for days now, ever since her return to New York. The laboratories were working round the clock, they had submitted a dozen fragrances, all of which she had rejected out of hand. With the second dozen, once she had played around with the bottles: a drop of this, two drops of that, a mere suggestion of the other, they came up with a second batch, which again she mixed, remixed, blended and refined. Finally, there were three which, she said, contained the essential 'idea' of her fragrance. 'Go away and see what you can do with these,' she had commanded. 'And quickly! We have much to do and little time to do it in. I want to cap That Woman's launch just as it's settling on its perch. Mine must knock it off into oblivion!'

She exhorted, she threatened, she cajoled, she soothed fevered brows, but it always ended up the same way; she lost her patience with these 'little' people who could not even begin to comprehend her Grand Design.

Nobody understands, she would think. Nobody. And then she would remember who she was and smile to herself and think: but how can they? There is only one Eve Czerny. Calm, Eve, calm. It will happen. Has that not been proved to you? You have stripped yourself of everything supernumerary; there is only you, obedient and willing to accept what *will* be.

I must go and inspire them, she thought now, reaching for her bag and gloves, for this is the apogee of my career. With this fragrance I will be crowned as Empress of Beauty. After this, when women think beauty they will think Eve Czerny.

As she waited for her car to be brought round she stood at her office window, staring out at the city, which was coming to life as darkness fell, the buildings first losing form and shape and then reappearing clothed in stars of light. Down on Madison Avenue, underneath the canopies of expensive apartment blocks, waited elegant men and exquisitely dressed women, their hair and their faces immaculate, eager to go out and taste the joys and excitement of this fabulous city. A new opening, a concert, a cocktail party, a theatre, the latest 'in' restaurant, so-and-so's party, the XYZ's ball, all of them honed and polished to the nth degree, courtesy of Eve Czerny Cosmetics, for Eve allowed her rivals no importance.

This is my destiny, she thought exultantly. This is what I have been working towards. To dominate this, of all cities; to bring the illusion of beauty to its plainest women and give them the confidence that only beauty can bring. This is my gift to the world. This is why I have been singled out. Chosen. It is I who have recreated these women, even as I recreated myself. Mine is the passport that will allow them to travel to the far reaches of success. She spread her arms wide, as if to gather the mightiest city on earth to her bosom, clasping it as she would the ultimate in prizes.

The buzzer sounded, indicating that her car was waiting. With one, last, infinitely satisfied smile, she went downstairs.

20

New York, 1988

'After all this family has done for Bertie Ransom,' Charlotte Bingham Ormonde complained bitterly. 'It was Daddy who got him into the Knickerbocker, who saw to it that Hughie Ransom was accepted at Choate, and Mother who took that dreary Lil Ransom under her wing: now he repays us with this stab in the back.'

'It is nothing to do with Bertie,' her sister Susan said for the umpteenth time. 'Can't you get that through your head? Sloane, Ransom are no longer Chris's lawyers; he fired them when he reached twenty-five and took his business to some Swiss firm. Bertie knows nothing but that, so how on earth can you expect him to tell you the contents of Chris's will? He doesn't know himself.'

'He should have told us what Chris was doing, given us some hint of what he was up to. The Binghams made Sloane, Ransom. We should have been told.'

'There is such a thing as client confidentiality,' Susan reminded.

'He told Mother when Laddie put the house in his wife's name.'

'He was his lawyer at that time. And Mama got the right to live in it until she died, didn't she?'

'And then that greedy bitch sold it! Actually went and sold the last great private house in New York! Now what stands there? Some awful vulgar bronze monstrosity, a Trump Tower pup. And now this; *our* money, for which that Hungarian slut mesmerized Laddie in the first place, all spirited away God knows where by her brat of a son.'

'But it isn't *our* money, is it?' Hester, the youngest asked innocently. 'Papa left it to our brother; it always goes to the male heir, you know that. And he had already settled the Trust for Mama, which came to us when she died. You talk as though we had been left penniless, Charlotte.'

'Compared to what Chris got we are! There must be some way to alter things, to get back what is ours.'

'Well there isn't,' Susan snapped. 'I've already talked to Bertie Ransom and he says there's nothing we can do. Christopher was perfectly within his rights to do what he did; it was his money, no strings.' She fixed her sister with a beady eye. 'Do you intend to sue for it? Have the name Bingham dragged through the courts in a front-page fight? You know Mother bent over backwards to avoid that at all times. We are Binghams, Charlotte, and that is more important than all the money there is!'

Charlotte glowered and Susan knew that she was thinking: Not to me. The older Charlotte got, the more money-fixated she became. A highly unsatisfactory marriage, a philandering husband and two children who had put at least a dozen states between them and their mother had turned her to money. She was bitter, greedy and a positive skinflint. Now, the thought of the Bingham fortune going who knows where had her climbing the wall.

'I don't like it either,' Susan said in calmer tones, 'but if Mother could put up with that impossible woman as her son's wife, then we can put up with his son doing what he chooses with his own money. Sooner or later we will know what that is; then, and only then, can we decide what to do.'

'As long as we do something,' Charlotte agreed grudgingly.

'I expect it has all gone to Pamela Bradley,' Hester said placidly. 'They lived together for some years, you know.'

'She doesn't need it either! She gouged a fortune out of Fritz Bahlsen!'

'Are you saying you need it?' Susan asked.

'I'm saying it's the principle of the thing,' Charlotte sidestepped her neatly. 'That money was made by Binghams for Binghams, and if it's the last thing I do I'll see that it comes back to the Binghams!' She nodded fiercely. 'So there!'

'Well, at least we no longer have any connection with our former sister-in-law,' Hester said encouragingly. 'That's something to be thankful for, isn't it?'

Max was leaving the Czerny building and getting into his car when he saw, across the street, a familiar head and shoulders. He straightened, stared, but it was gone. For a moment he almost ran across to find it. I'm imagining things, he told himself as he settled back in his seat. If Alex was in New York she'd have been in touch by now, wouldn't she?

All the same, he wished it had been. He could do with Alex right now. It had been long practice to go up to Cambridge and spend a couple of relaxing hours with her whenever he had a seemingly insoluble problem. Her analytical mind could always sort out the pieces and put them together in an order that produced a sigh of relief. And right now, Eve was draining him dry.

This bloody fragrance, he thought, is turning out to be the kiss of death. Everything, the entire resources of the Czerny Corporation, had been concentrated on finding the ultimate blend of rare essences, natural oils and hideously expensive flowers. Nothing suited. The laboratory had become a gulag; Eve cracking the whip and standing over her *parfumeurs*, exhorting and driving them on. Late last night she had called him, summoned him to Queens.

'I have got it, Max!' she had announced in thrilled tones. 'I've found what will establish my name for ever, as Gabrielle Chanel did with her *No. 5*. I want you to be the first to know what it is. Hurry, Max, hurry . . . this is a great day.'

So he had gone, found her in a state of vibrating excitement, almost gibbering with triumph. And he had to admit that what she had come up with was indeed a market knockout. Worthy of inclusion in the Perfume Hall of Fame. He had congratulated her, and the weary, red-eyed laboratory staff, who had not left their benches for days and days now; eating, sleeping where they worked. Eve had called for champagne, made a celebration and a little speech thanking them for their efforts on her behalf, stirring the bone-weary men with her own sense of accomplishment, for she had been the one who had taken the last three distillations and judiciously mixed, tested, blended, altered and then, finally, produced the winner.

He had thought that would be it for a while but no; Eve had swept them all back to the Czerny Building for a planning and strategy conference. Step one had been accomplished, now for steps two and three. A Name and a Face. Only when it finally penetrated her still working-on-all-cylinders brain that she was flogging a dead horse did she dismiss them contemptuously, tell them all to go and get some sleep and then return, bright-eyed and bushy-tailed, for some real work.

Now, he told his driver to take him home, where he fell into bed and exhausted sleep like a felled tree.

The phone woke him. Blearily he blinked at the digital clock. Almost four o'clock in the afternoon, and all he'd had was eight hours' sleep when what he needed was eighteen. Naturally, it was Eve. She had set up a meeting for six o'clock, and instead of a working lunch it would be a working dinner.

'Time's a-wasting, Max,' she carolled, 'and so am I.'

Wearily he dragged himself into the shower, mixed a warm flow and gradually reduced it to needles of ice, which stung his flesh into protest and his brain into action. Let no one ever say I don't earn my living the hard way, he thought.

Eve had gone to the salon, where, in her own exclusive treatment room, she had had a steam bath, followed by a relaxing massage which sent her off into four blissful hours of deep, satisfied sleep. After that she had spent thirty minutes in the jacuzzi being pummelled and invigorated, then dressed in the change of clothes Jonesy had brought.

'Another long night, then?' he asked her, as he hung the clothes she had discarded on their hangers.

'As long as needs be.'

'But you've got your scent?'

Eve smiled. 'Oh, yes . . . I've got it.' She made a slow twirl in front of the triple mirror, angled so as to give her a hundred-degree view of herself, devastatingly elegant as usual in sugar-pink Yves St Laurent.

Jonesy clicked his tongue. 'You're a bleedin' marvel and no mistake. Any other woman'd be wilting like a dead flower, but not you. Work's your drug, make no mistake. It beats heroin and cocaine any day.'

Satisfied with her appearance, Eve turned to him. 'I'm going to wipe the floor with That Woman,' she promised him, turquoise eyes gleeful with anticipation. 'She won't try to upstage me again. What I've got is another *Essence of Eve*, only more so. It's not perfect yet, but it will be by the time I've finished. Now, I need the right Name, and the Face to go with it – and the right flacon, of course.' Fragrance containers were *never* referred to as bottles. 'And the Name and the shape must go together like – like –'

'You and beauty?' suggested Jonesy.

'Exactly! It must be every bit as flawless a work of art as I am.' She faced him proudly. 'And am I not a work of art?'

Jonesy nodded reverently. 'If you was to be auctioned at Sotheby's you'd fetch a fortune.'

Which made Eve frown. 'That reminds me . . . I have heard nothing from Sloane, Ransom, which is strange. Remind me to give them a call once this meeting is over and done with. I don't have time to deal with it now.'

'Will do.' Jonesy was the repository of her private affairs; her other secretaries only ever dealt with business matters. He held her magnificent Russian sable coat at the ready, helped her on with it, held out her black suede pochette.

'What time tonight?' he asked.

'Expect me when you see me.'

'Right. Car's waitin'.'

She swept out, and on her way down the corridor glanced through the open door into the office of her Directrice, saw Pamela Bradley sitting at her desk going over the day's figures.

'Well, Pamela,' Eve enquired, her tone indulgent in the way it always was when she had achieved a victory. 'You are settling in all right?'

Pamela rose to her feet. 'Yes, thank you, Madame,' she answered politely.

'Good, good . . . as are the reports I have had about you. Keep up the good work.' She nodded, swept on.

Pamela was smiling as she tidied her papers, put them away, locked her desk. 'Oh, I will, Madame, I will,' she promised.

When she got home Alex was in the kitchen.

'Something smells good,' Pamela said, sniffing appreciatively.

'Chinese,' Alex said, turning to smile at her. 'I've always wanted to eat out of those boxes.'

Pamela laughed. 'So where did you go today?' she called from the living-room, where she made them both a large gin and tonic.

'Uptown. I walked through Central Park and then down the West Side.'

'Which museums?'

'I went to the Lincoln Center, the Museum of Natural History and the Hayden Planetarium.'

'Only you would spend your first time in New York visiting art galleries and museums,' Pamela said affectionately, returning to the kitchen to hand Alex her drink.

'I find them interesting.'

'Other women would go to Bloomingdales, Bergdorf's, Saks and other such places.'

'I'm not other women.'

You will be by the time I'm through with you, Pamela thought. 'So you didn't buy anything?'

'Just some more books and records. Compact discs here are much cheaper than they are back home.'

'Don't tell me; you bought in a discount store?'

'Of course! I was brought up to know the value of money.'

Pamela leaned against a worktop. 'Five million dollars a year and she spends it in discount stores.'

'I'm still not used to that.'

'I can't wait to see the day.' Pamela changed the subject. 'I saw your mother just as I was about to leave the salon.'

'That must have been a thrill.'

'She did look particularly radiant. The grapevine has it that she's come up with a new fragrance that is to die, destined to sweep That Woman's latest right out of the ballpark.'

She hadn't told Alex of her own small but vital part in its creation, because she would have had to mention Max, and not once, since her arrival, had Alex uttered his name. Pamela read that for the sign it was, but she was tired of eating in every night, solely, she knew, because Alex was afraid that if they went to the restaurants Pamela frequented, there was the possibility of running into him. Now, Pamela made up her mind.

'Let's eat out tonight,' she said. 'I'm tired of eating off trays in front of the television. I know just the thing. Small, quiet, off the beaten track, the last place we're likely to meet anyone I know.'

Alex looked doubtful. 'I enjoy eating in, and American television fascinates me. There's so little of it between the commercials.'

'There are eight million people in this city, and thousands of restaurants. The place I have in mind is way up on the West side; small and discreet. The sort of people who go there go to eat, not to be seen. It is in no way fashionable.' She put all she had into persuasion.

'You are out all day, aren't you? God knows how many miles you've walked in the past few days. And it isn't as though you know a soul here – except your mother and Max. Since they will both be occupied by a high-powered meeting tonight I see no reason why we shouldn't eat out for once.'

Alex didn't reply. Pamela decided to go for broke.

'Look, Alex. The non-mention of a certain name only makes it all the more obvious that it's the one you're thinking about. We have been tiptoeing around Max Fabian ever since you got here, which makes it pretty clear to me that something has gone wrong between you. Normally, he would have been the very first person you called.'

Alex did not answer for a moment then said tonelessly, 'We had a rather sharp difference of opinion.'

'So? You've had them before as I recall. Once, when Chris and I came to Cambridge and he was there, you did nothing but argue all night. They're the stuff of life to your relationship since you're both so strong-minded. What's so different about this one?'

Alex did not turn. 'I'll tell Max in my own good time.'

'Which sounds like never from your tone of voice.'

Alex whirled on Pamela, who saw that her face was flushed. 'Max Fabian is not my keeper, you know! I don't have to ask his permission to do what I think fit.'

Ah, thought Pamela, as enlightenment struck. So that's it . . . But of course, what else could it be? Hard words mean tender feelings in my experience. 'All right, but we won't run into him tonight, so can we please go out?'

'But I've bought all this Chinese . . .'

'Dump it.'

Alex looked outraged at the thought of such waste.

'Then put it in the fridge.' And I'll dump it, she thought.

They took a cab, and as Pamela had said, the restaurant was small, not more than a dozen tables; and each one was occupied by a couple who obviously had the same idea as Alex.

'Yes,' Pamela said, noting her instant assessment. 'It's that kind of place.'

Alex tactfully refrained from further comment. Any other woman would have wanted to know the ins and outs, who with, how long, etc., but one of the things Pamela appreciated about a woman she was coming to like more and more – even if she did need a good shake-up in certain other areas – was her total disinterest in gossip.

The speciality that night was Osso Bucco; Alex had eaten it many times, and after grilling the waiter on how it had been prepared, recommended it to Pamela.

'How come you know so much about Italian food?' Pamela asked curiously.

'Max.'

'Of course . . . It's a pity we couldn't have gone to his father's place down in Little Italy. The food is superb.'

'You've been, then?'

'Oh, yes. Chris and I always went when we were in New York. Max took us the first time, introduced us to his parents, since when we were always welcomed like royalty.'

'What are they like?' Alex asked presently, achingly conscious of all she had been missing.

'Very Italian, even though they're third-generation Americans. His mother is big and jolly, his father is big and quiet. Nice. A close, loving family. It's no wonder Max has all the confidence in the world. They all think he sits on the right hand of God.'

Alex said no more, and over dinner they talked of other things. It was still early when they left; Pamela marvelled to see it was only nine o'clock. Normally, she would have just finished the first course. When Alex suggested they walk across town, Pamela, who usually took a cab across the street, agreed unflinchingly. It was as they were waiting for the lights to change on Seventh Avenue that a woman sitting in the back of a yellow cab which was heading for the restaurant they had just left, leaned forward, stared hard and then exclaimed, 'I don't believe it!'

'What?' asked her companion.

'Alex Brent and Pamela Bradley, arm in arm like a couple of longtime friends. Now what has made them so buddy-buddy all of a sudden? And what is Alex Brent doing in New York anyway?' As the cab drew up she was lost in thought.

'Come on, Mora, we're here,' said the man she was with.

'Coming . . .' This, she thought, bears investigation. I wonder if

381

Max knows? The fact that he isn't with them tells me he doesn't. I wonder, she thought, and decided there and then to put her mind at rest first thing in the morning. She smiled at the man who was holding out his hand. Pleasure before business . . .

When her phone rang, Pamela, her mind busy juggling schedules, reached out an absentminded hand. 'Pamela Bradley.'

'Hi,' said Max. 'I have a bone to pick with you.'

'It was the wrong perfume?'

'Nothing to do with that – which was as right as you can get. No, I want to know why neither you nor Alex has bothered to tell me that she's here in New York.'

Pamela's instincts leapt firmly to the defence. 'I didn't know she was,' she replied coolly.

'Then how come you were seen standing with her on the corner of Seventh and Seventy-Fourth at around nine o'clock last night?'

'Says who?' Pamela protested, trying to hide her dismay.

'Mora. She saw you.'

'She can't have been wearing her glasses.' That was a nasty dig since Mora, who was indeed short-sighted, loathed wearing them, but as her eyes were intolerant of contact lenses, she had no choice.

'She's quite positive. You were under a street light.'

'And she must have been under the influence.' That they should have been spotted by Mora Haynes, of all people, had Pamela burning all her boats. 'Alex is in Switzerland.'

'No she's not. I checked.'

'Cambridge, then.'

'Not there either.'

'Then give me one good reason why she should be with me.'

'You and she are all of a sudden such good friends.'

'True, but what has that to do with anything?'

'I thought you might have invited her over.'

'I did. She refused.' It was the truth; Alex had refused the first invitation.

'So it wasn't you and her, arm in arm against the cold winter night?' Which was exactly how they had been standing, because the wind had cut like a knife.

'No.' Pamela made her voice utterly convincing. 'It was not. Come now, Max. Would Alex come to New York without telling you, of all people? You know she always tells you everything.'

'I always thought so,' Max said, sounding puzzled and, Pamela thought in satisfaction as it proved her theory, despondent. No longer friends, she thought. That relationship has obviously undergone some kind of revolution. No wonder Alex is so uptight.

'Have you tried Margaret Patterson? Alex spends a lot of time with her.'

'She doesn't answer her phone.' Better and better, Pamela thought happily. He's chasing Alex. I'll bet a large chunk of my newly acquired wealth that it's to say he's sorry.

'Oh, well,' Max sighed, sounding even more downhearted. 'We all make mistakes.'

'Especially when we're not wearing our glasses.'

Max laughed. 'Sheathe your claws.'

'She should have done that before she started wielding her long spoon. She was jealous of Alex for some unknown reason.' She paused. 'Do you know why?'

There was a silence then Max said lightly, 'I never gave her any reason.'

'Why are you so het up, anyway?' Pamela pursued, enjoying this. 'Alex is old enough to do as she likes, surely. I know you're close but you're not her keeper, are you?' She quoted Alex deliberately.

'Alex is a habit I've had for too long to be able to break,' Max said at last. Then, slowly, 'Not that I'd want to.'

'Then if I hear from her I'll tell her of your concern and ask her to get in touch.'

'Now that we're in touch, how about dinner tonight? I always eat better when there's a lovely face looking at me from across the table.' And that itch at the back of my neck tells me yours isn't being straight with me, he thought. Mora was absolutely positive. Vindictively so. Bitch! What the hell did I ever see in her?

'That would be nice,' he heard Pamela say.

'Good. Eight o'clock, at the Lutèce.'

'Perfect,' purred Pamela. 'See you tonight. 'Bye . . .'

When she told Alex, she added, 'This little cover-up of yours is turning into another Watergate. Now I'm lying on your behalf. That being so, I think you owe me an explanation.'

Alex knew she had gone – was stubbornly going – too far, but somehow she couldn't seem to stop. 'I didn't mean to involve you, Pamela, but if you remember I didn't want to come. I'm sorry you had to lie, but you'll just have to take my word for it that I don't want to see Max.'

'It must have been some quarrel.'

'It was. It was our bad luck that it should have been Mora, of all people, who saw us, but she's a mischief maker, a fact Max is well aware of. If we – if you – will just maintain the fiction for tonight, I promise you that'll be the end of it.'

Pamela sighed. 'All right.'

No more was said, and while Pamela was changing, Alex made sure that there was no trace of her presence downstairs, clearing away the books and magazines she had bought – not the kind usually found in Pamela's living-room. Then she went upstairs to her bedroom, where she didn't turn on the lights, because it overlooked the street.

She heard Max arrive; the slam of his car door, the faint peal of the bell chime, but she only went to the window, concealing herself behind the heavy, felt-lined, draped and swagged curtains, when she heard them leave; saw Max hand Pamela, exquisitely dressed in a short black dress and a swathe of mink-lined black jersey, into the car before going round to the driver's side. As he put his hand on the door he raked the house with his eyes, and though she knew he could not see her she instinctively shrank back. She watched until the red tail-lights had disappeared then went to get her case from the closet.

It was late when Max brought Pamela back, and being absolutely confident now that he no longer suspected Alex was in New York, she had no qualms about inviting him in for a nightcap.

'Why not?' he agreed.

'Jack Daniel's?'

'How well you know me.'

No, thought Pamela, as she poured his drink. I don't really. But it's obvious that Alex does, which is why she's running scared. Max had picked up that morning's *New York Times*, laid it down as Pamela held out his glass. He took it, thanked her, sipped and then said affably, 'Right. Now suppose we put a stop to this stupid game Alex is playing and you go and tell her I would like to talk to her.' The ice in Pamela's glass rattled at her convulsive jerk. Max nodded at the paper. 'The crossword. Not only completed but in her own inimitable hand.' His voice hardened. 'What's going on here? Why this childish game of hide and seek?'

Pamela rose. 'I'm not getting any deeper in whatever it is you two are fighting over. The best thing you can do is ask her yourself.'

She went upstairs. Alex's room was dark and empty. Checking the closet Pamela saw that her clothes and her case were gone. Which was when she realized that this was no game to Alex.

'She's gone,' she told him when she went back downstairs. 'Probably left just after we did.'

Max's glass went down with a crack. 'Of all the stupid –' he checked himself. 'All right. You tell me.'

'I don't know much.'

'You know why she came in the first place.'

'I invited her.'

'I've done that myself, countless times. She always refused. What made this time so special?'

He's going to find out eventually, Pamela thought, so what difference does it make. She told him.

Max was silent for so long that Pamela thought she had done the wrong thing. Then he asked, 'And when did all this happen?'

'Monday. I called her as soon as she came back from the lawyers and I could tell straightaway she wasn't happy about it. She had the most peculiar idea that Chris had done it to spite his mother, that it wasn't really his money but Bingham money, which his mother had more or less stolen from them when she married Laddie Bingham – oh, a whole lot of self-lacerating rubbish. I had to invent a letter of Chris's to get her to change her mind – I knew she would never dream of reading it herself so I read it to her.'

'You *what*?'

'I wrote a letter supposedly from Chris explaining why he had done what he did. I had to do *something*,' she protested to Max's look. 'You know what Alex is like; she never expects anything from anybody and always looks for the catch. Chris told me ages ago what he intended to do and I approved wholeheartedly.'

'So what did your invented letter say?'

'That he had left her half his fortune because he loved her, even if she still believed she was unlovable. That she and I were the only two people who meant anything to him – which was absolutely true – and that he was grateful to her for being there when he needed her. Also true. He didn't see an awful lot of Alex once he had me, but they kept in touch always. All he had to give her was money but it was given with love.'

'And just how much money is that?'

Pamela looked him straight in the eye. 'Five million dollars a year.'

Max was silent again.

Pamela leaned forward, spoke bluntly. 'I don't know what has happened between you and Alex, but knowing you both it must have been something she found hard to take, because, quite frankly, your name is mud. I always had the impression that you could do no wrong in her eyes, so you must have done something very wrong for her to be acting like this.'

Max shrugged. 'I made a pass at her.'

Pamela's reaction showed final and complete comprehension. 'I see . . . you stepped out of your frame.'

'And said some things in the heat of the moment –' Max stopped, an arrested expression on his face.

'Now I understand . . .' Pamela breathed. 'You shattered your image. The statue did a Pygmalion. But why, after all this time, did you decide to take your friendship a stage further?'

Max cocked an eyebrow. 'Do we have time for this?'

'As long as you like.'

Max glanced at his watch. 'Well . . . I can always get a plane in the morning. I know where she's gone.'

'You're going after her?'

He seemed surprised. 'Of course I am.'

Pamela's smile was slow but it had Max squirming.

'Why, Max Fabian . . .' Pamela sat back against the cushions. 'So that's it!'

'Nobody was more surprised than me,' Max admitted, still sounding as if he was having trouble.

'Well I'm not. No wonder Mora rang you – she knew too. Why else was she jealous? We women have a sixth sense for these things, you know, and I must say I always thought you an unusually intuitive man, but then, we all have our blind spots. It took me some time to see through Chris's camouflage. I'd known him for ages before I realized that I was no longer thinking of him as a friend, though from the start he made it plain what he wanted from me.' Pamela shook her head. 'Well,' she said. 'Who would have thought it?'

'Not me,' Max agreed. 'I'm still having trouble. I mean – after twenty years!'

'I think,' Pamela said, making herself comfortable, 'that you had better tell me all about it.'

When she got to JFK, Alex found that all flights were delayed. An outgoing jet had lost an engine just before it reached stick-speed and was blocking a runway. The other four were congested therefore certain flights had been rescheduled for Newark. Passengers were either at liberty to transfer or wait until the plane had been towed away.

'How long will it take to get to Newark?' Alex asked a harassed British Airways counter clerk.

'At this time of night, a couple of hours or so. If you will wait outside the terminal there will be buses along to take you.'

Alex hefted her case. This trip is doomed, she thought, doomed . . . Her sense of humour got the better of her and she began to laugh. She stood there in the middle of the busy concourse and laughed until the tears ran. Other passengers gave her a wide berth. She wiped her eyes, blew her nose, picked up her case and went outside. A lot of people were milling about but there was no sign of any buses. There was, however, a long line of taxis, and just as long a line of people waiting to use them. I'm fated, Alex thought. Somebody, somewhere doesn't want me to leave this city tonight. She set down her case again. She had bought so many books it weighed a ton.

What if it's Fate? she thought. That same Fate my mother absolutely believes in? Am I being told something here? Like you can run as far and as fast as you can but you can't escape your destiny? That, she told herself, is irrational and illogical. People make their own lives. Exactly, her inner self told her. Just look at the mess you're making of yours. Max won't let it rest here. He'll come after you. You deep down damned well *know* he will. Oh, God, she thought wearily. What have I done? What am I *doing*? The very thing he told you you were doing, that's what. Acting like a child – the sexual illiterate he said you were. Refusing to grow up, hiding in your nice, safe ivory tower, missing out. Not living, existing. If you do this you're stretching the most important relationship in your life to breaking point. Earning even more of his contempt. Do you want that? Face facts, Alex. God knows you've amassed enough of them, but only one matters. Life with Max in it is not to be compared to life without. If it wasn't for him . . . Make up your mind, Alex, but understand, once and for all, what you are doing when you do . . . more important – *why* you are doing it.

'So it was you who told her she was a sexual illiterate,' Pamela said, when Max had finished describing the night in question.

Max winced. 'She told you?'

'Only that it had been said to her. That must have hurt like hell.'

'I was trying to galvanize her into some sort of life.'

'Alex needs encouragement, not criticism. You know she has absolutely no confidence in herself as a woman, hence the *alter ego*. Until recently that's how *I* thought of Alex, because that's the only side of her she ever showed to me. Formidable, cutting, aloof. Chris kept telling me she wasn't really like that but I couldn't see it. Since he died, I've seen it in full measure. Of course she thought you were only having a little fun at her expense, because she's seen and known the women you've been involved with, every one of them everything she isn't. Naturally she would never have the confidence to believe that a man like you could ever feel anything more than friendship for a woman like her.'

'But I've always teased her,' Max protested, if uncomfortably. 'She was such a solemn little thing . . .'

'Who touched your heart.'

Max nodded, obviously still not wholly at ease with a knowledge newly and shockingly acquired and not yet explained to his satisfaction.

'You've got a new image to make,' Pamela advised him. 'You did for the old one when you broke it. Any normal woman on the receiving end of a pass from you would frame it and put it on her mantelpiece; but although she's coming along nicely, Alex isn't yet a normal woman. That bitch her mother did her work only too well, and it takes time, patience and a good deal of encouragement to coax a beaten dog to eat out of your hand.' She smiled. 'But if anyone can do it, you can. You start off with certain advantages.'

'Which I have every intention of using.' But nevertheless he still asked: 'You're sure she can be coaxed? I haven't smashed everything into pieces so small they can't be put together again?'

'But you don't want to put those particular pieces together again, do you? You want a new pattern, surely?'

'I don't want Alex changed; whatever she is is fine by me. That's why –'

'You love her?'

Max released a gusty breath. 'Yes. Have done for a long time now but either didn't or wouldn't realize it. In thinking about it since – and I've done a lot of that – I now see that it was because I was tired of waiting that I decided to force things, and that because she was already off-balance; I wanted to tilt her my way.'

Pamela shook her head. 'Max, my dear, blind, love-sick idiot – she has a tilt like the Tower of Pisa in your direction. If she hadn't, would what you did matter so much? She'd either have told you off in no uncertain terms or joined in the joke. That she took it so hard, so painfully, means very tender feelings. Alex has always loved you; now she is *in love* with you.'

Max came round the table, bent down to pull Pamela to her feet. 'I always thought Chris struck gold when he found you, but right now you're a fucking marvel.' He kissed her soundly on the cheek. 'I owe you one.'

As she saw him to the door, she observed, 'I can't think why you are so surprised. I'm not. I always knew that what you two had was special.'

'It seems Mora did too, which means I must have given her cause . . . I guess I knew, deep down. That's really why I went and asked her to come to Switzerland. I could have handled Eve. But I see now that I wanted Alex dynamited out of her hiding place and brought right up against life – and me. I sort of hoped if she couldn't cope she'd turn to me and –' he shrugged.

'But she did cope,' Pamela said. She smiled. 'Oh, you *are* in love. Alex is one of life's copers in most respects; her Achilles heel was always her mother, but that doesn't show any more. She knows now why she was ignored, as I told you. It wouldn't have mattered if she'd looked like Elizabeth Taylor in her prime; it was her very existence that her mother couldn't stand. Once Alex knew that, she was free. Except where you're concerned, of course.'

'I hope so,' Max said fervently. 'Life without Alex doesn't bear thinking about.'

Pamela laughed. 'She'll do more than enough of that for both of you. Go after her, make it up – you have the necessary equipment and know-how. I'm worn out with all this toing and froing.'

She opened the front door and there was Alex, in the very act of raising her hand to the bell.

Ignoring their open mouths she said to Max calmly, 'Would you pay the taxi please, Max? I'm afraid I don't have enough dollars and he won't take a traveller's cheque.'

When Pamela had closed the living-room door behind them, Max, who was so relieved he was euphoric, glared furiously at Alex. 'What the hell did you think you were playing at? You finally come to New York, and when you do you don't tell the one person who should have been the first to know!'

Alex met his sound and fury with equanimity and his roar rebounded like an echo, sounding hollow and empty. He saw that she was looking at him frankly, openly, and with a dispassion so chilling it froze his tongue. His euphoria went down the drain, and the hollow it left refilled with a fear so profound, so hideous, that he felt sick. He had told himself again and again that she was only proving every word he had said: that she was indeed the child not the woman – and what the hell do I want with an emotional retard? he had asked himself furiously. Now, he knew. Whatever Alex is – and it isn't all sweetness and light, God knows, he thought – I still want her. I want her logical mind, her quick tongue, her steadfast loyalty, her sense of humour, her kindness, her patience, oh, you name it and I want it, he thought. She's as complex a bundle – and a big one at that – as ever drew breath, but she's become so inextricably entwined around every cell in my body that I need her to breathe.

Now, he felt he was on the edge of an abyss; one false move and he was done for; that he had gone too far to be forgiven. And then he remembered what Pamela had told him. Ah, he thought with relish, it's to be fun and games, is it? He felt his chest swell. Hell, I invented most of them, he thought. Then, suspiciously: but how come she knows about them?

Alex saw the expressive face, its control undermined by the

violence of his emotions, go through a whole range of fast-forward frames, and in her new-found ease with herself, acquired in the course of what seemed like an endless drive back to the city and confirmed at once by the look on Max's face when he saw her, she finally understood the inexplicable anguish she had been through. But for the time being she decided to stay in character.

'I owe you an apology, Max,' she said earnestly. 'It was wrong of me not to have told you I was coming to New York, but – well, something utterly incredible has happened to me . . . I don't quite know how to tell you . . .' She hesitated. He smiled encouragingly. 'My brother has left me half his fortune! Would you believe it! I'm rich, Max! Indecently, unbelievably rich!'

Max kept his face straight. Why, you little witch! he thought happily. Play games with me, would you? Think you can pull the wool over these old eyes? He blessed Pamela for clueing him in. Otherwise, he thought, by God I would have been taken in! This is Alex, remember, and didn't she always learn fast?

'Oh,' he said, sounding both taken aback and crestfallen at the same time.

'That's why I came over here, to discuss it with Pamela – she gets the other half.' Her laugh was perfectly shamefaced. 'I had all sorts of qualms and reservations – you know me.'

'Indeed I do,' Max said promptly, and saw the suspicion in her eyes which he banished by adopting an expression of surprised regret.

'But Chris did it because he loved me. Oh, Max, if you only knew how that feels . . . to know you are loved in such a way that someone is willing to give you half of all he had. I had to think it out, of course, but in the end I saw there was nothing to think about. Chris has given me my true independence and you have no idea the difference it has made . . . to me, to my life – to everything!'

'Oh, I think I can appreciate that,' Max said bitterly, playing his role to the hilt.

Alex's smile was a dazzler. 'At last I can really start to live!' Her face sobered. 'You were right in all you said to me that night, and I'm going to do what you said: come out from my cosy, protected little world and live in the real one. I'm sorry I took it all far too seriously . . .' Now her smile was warm, tender. 'As though you and

I could ever let anything change our friendship.' She went forward, let her lips graze his cheek. 'Friends again?'

She turned away, needing to hide the grin she could no longer control; covered it by saying, 'I'm dying for a cup of coffee. I seem to have spent hours and hours travelling to no destination. Will you have one too?'

'No, thank you,' Max said.

He sounded subdued. Let's see how he manages to get control of this situation, Alex thought gleefully. He gave the whole thing away when he looked at me. She felt her heart do a handspring at that remembered look; blazing, heartfelt, filled with a staggering relief and an almost threatening promise. She had felt his whole being surge towards her, though he had not moved. It had been a revelation in more ways than one. Her whole laboriously built house of cards – every one of them an ace of Spades – had, like the cards in *Alice*, been transformed into Hearts, and all the picture cards were an illustration of her own blind self-hatred. I had it all wrong, she had realized as she fell, with belated insight, into the country of her dreams. Yet that had been followed, without a break, by an instinctive knowledge that whispered to her not to lose control of the situation; not to let him see how far matters had progressed or how much that which had hitherto been clouded by her own stupidity was now revealed so clearly it hurt the eyes. For once you have the upper hand, it hissed; keep it for a while longer.

'So,' Max said, 'you went all the way to JFK just so as not to have to tell me you had inherited five million dollars a year, but when you got there you underwent some sort of *volte-face* – God knows what they're putting into the air in Queens – which made you turn right round and come all the way back again. Have I got it right so far?'

Alex turned a disappointed face to him. 'Pamela told you!' Again she deliberately misunderstood.

'Oh, yes, Pamela told me. It's old news. Moreover,' he said, and his voice rose to a roar, 'it's a load of flim-flam!'

'You think five million dollars is a load of flim-flam?' Alex asked incredulously. Oh, the games we are going to play, she thought, hugging the knowledge to herself.

'Money, *per se*, has never meant a damn to you. Change your life? It'll take more than money to do that, my girl. The kind of changes you need to make can't be bought!' Max was also thoroughly enjoying himself. This new Alex was an adversary indeed. The ball hadn't hit the ground once so far.

'So we're back to that again, are we?' Alex made her tone bored, impatient with his persistence in harking back to what no longer mattered. She bestowed a kindly, tolerant smile. 'I know you only had my best interests at heart, but then, you always have, haven't you? I shall always be grateful to you for what you have done for me, but now – why now, Max, the possibilities are unlimited.' Then, crisply, coldly: 'Just don't assume any more where I'm concerned, all right? I'm not your property, you know.'

Max smiled and Alex's heart did a somersault this time. 'Oh, yes you are,' he said in a voice that had her breaking out in goosepimples. 'You've belonged to me since I saw you sprawled on the rug in front of the fire, reading aloud from *Alice in Wonderland*. You belong to me and I've waited long enough for you to grow up and realize that fact.' His smile changed, his voice deepened. 'Which, my game-playing whizzkid, you very well know because that's why you changed your mind.' Very softly: 'Correct me if I'm wrong.'

Alex hung on his eyes. He moved towards her. 'It wasn't the salubrious air of Queens or a lightning bolt on the Long Island Expressway; it was me. You finally realized what it took me far too long to understand: that I wasn't teasing. That I had never been more serious in my life. My body knew even if my mind kept telling me it was lying through its teeth.'

'I see . . .' Alex said, as though considering a moot point. 'You were forcing me – like early rhubarb?'

Max threw back his head and roared with laughter, before reaching out a leisurely hand to draw her to him. 'I've thought a lot about that night and its game of truth or consequences.' He had her in his arms, tight against him. 'Let's have another game . . .'

A long time later: 'Am I?' Alex asked dreamily, her fingers tracing the outlines of the mouth that had just won hands down.

'Are you what?'

'Your girl.'

'No. But you *are* my woman.'

'No longer "kid".'

'I only ever call children that.'

393

Alex sighed, made herself more comfortable in his arms. 'I'm sorry you had to wait so long for me to grow up.'

'You had the longest puberty in history,' Max agreed, 'but like everything else you do, when you do it, you do it properly.'

Pamela was in bed, but had left her door open so that she would hear Alex when – and if? she thought – she came to bed. When she did, Pamela called out, 'Put me out of my misery. Is it on or off?'

Alex put her head round the door. 'On.'

'Thank God for that. I don't think I could have taken much more of this particular farce.'

'A regular little Comedy of Errors,' Alex agreed, coming in. 'Most of them mine.'

'You haven't been down there all this time discussing Shakespeare!'

'Max took me to my first play – *Romeo and Juliet*.'

'What hasn't Max taken you to? What matters is what he's now taking you *for*.'

'Better or worse,' Alex said flippantly, but deeply pleased. 'And tomorrow, being Sunday, he is taking me to meet his parents.'

'Just like a nice Italian boy.'

Pamela laid aside her copy of *Vogue*. 'Well, since you started it, All's Well That Ends Well.'

Alex laughed. 'As Max would say, I owe you one, Pamela. Thank you for everything. Making me come across here, making me see things I was too tiresome either to face or to handle properly.'

'Just tell me one thing: why did you come back?'

'Fate.'

'Fate! Since when did you believe in Fate?'

Alex explained.

'But in the end the decision was still yours,' Pamela pointed out.

'True, but it seemed to me that somebody or something was using a cattle prod.'

'Did Max tell you about the crossword?'

'Yes. And I thought I'd removed everything. That paper was on top of a pile but I left it there.'

'That could have been accidentally on purpose.'

'Exactly. All my life I believed that there was a reason for everything; more, a logical, rational reason. Now I know that for some things there are no explanations; you either have to accept them or not. I decided it was time I said yes, please, instead of no, thank you.'

Alex got up, yawned. 'Heavens but I'm tired. I've been falling asleep late and waking early recently, but not tonight.'

'What time is Max coming?'

'Eleven. We'll be out all day, but we'd like you to have dinner with us tomorrow night.'

'With pleasure.'

Alex was not the demonstrative type, but she bent down, hugged Pamela hard. 'Thanks again.'

Pamela smiled, but it was tinged with a sadness Alex was too happy to notice. Sadness, and envy.

That's your good deed for the year, Pamela thought, as she switched off her lamp. Oh, Chris, it's at times like this that I miss you so. But she was too sensible not to be quite sure that somewhere out there was a man; the right man for the rest of her life. Chris had not been the kind to expect her to end her life as a woman just because his own life had been wiped out. And he had left her enough money to ensure that she could be choosy. I'm only thirty-five, she thought, and I know enough now not to be dazzled, as I was at twenty-one by Fritz. No more flash and filigree. She thumped her pillow, settled her rose-strewn Porthault sheets more comfortably. Yes, she thought, he's out there, somewhere. This year, next year, but not, very definitely not, never.

'So, the city is yours,' Max told Alex expansively. 'Where shall it be first?'

'What time are we due at Fabiani's?'

'Around three; my brother comes off duty then, and by three-thirty the last customers are leaving. Once they've gone we'll have our family get-together.'

'Then could we do some shopping first? I really think I ought to make a better first impression than this.'

She indicated her serviceable, wraparound navy-blue coat, under which she was wearing one of her 'academic' suits.

'Yes . . .' Max agreed feelingly 'It's high time you came out from under the burlap wrap. Bloomingdales it is, then.'

Left to herself, for she had never taken any interest in clothes, believing there was nothing to be done to flatter her broad shoulders and ample hips, Alex would probably have chosen another of the same, but Max waved away the clerical greys and navy blues, fingering through the rails with knowledgeable expertise. Finally, he beckoned a saleslady, conferred with her, indicating Alex who stood there wondering if she had bitten off more than she could comfortably chew. They were ushered into a small room where Max sat down and Alex was taken behind a concealing curtain where she undressed down to her slip. Then she was transformed, piece by piece. First a superbly cut skirt of heavy pure wool flannel, in a subtle shade of taupe, which swirled in full folds to just below the calf. It was worn with a wide chestnut leather belt which fastened with a big, circular gold buckle, and a heavy white silk shirt which the saleslady tied at the neck like a stock, fixing it with a single gold stud to match the gold cuff-links. On top of that went a check wool jacket in taupe, apricot, pale grey and cream, its hunt-type collar facings of apricot velvet. The whole outfit was finished off with a pair of glossy, chestnut leather boots and matching handbag. As an afterthought, a pair of gold earrings in the shape of snail shells completed the transformation.

Alex was so utterly astounded that for a moment she was speechless. For the first time in her life she gazed at her reflection with pleasure, for hitherto, confrontation with her image had been something she had learned to avoid. Not for her the sidelong checking in plate-glass windows or accidental sightings in unsuspected mirrors. Now, she gazed long and incredulously, turning this way and that, now quickly, so that the skirt swirled around her boot tops, now slowly so that she could examine every inch of an undiscovered self. She was so overcome that she felt tears pricking; and when she went out, somewhat shyly, to present herself to Max, the way he looked at her had her eyes welling again.

'What hath God wrought?' she asked tremulously.

'Sundays, somebody else takes over,' Max said lightly, himself overcome by this handsome, compelling stranger. Her height, her superb shoulders, her long legs were set off perfectly by clothes chosen by someone infinitely more knowledgeable than her and the result was a metamorphosis. The colours were perfect for her matt, clotted-cream skin, and the hint of apricot allied to the gold brought out the green of her eyes. The whole effect was restrained, classical, and in the best possible taste. It was also devastatingly elegant.

Now, as they left the department, Max having paid what Alex, when she saw the amount on the sales slip, dumbfoundedly calculated to be two months' salary ('My first present,' he'd said, waving away her *sotto voce* protests), Alex sought every mirror she passed, as if seeking additional confirmation of her right to be this stunning stranger.

'One last stop,' Max said, as he led the way to the hairdresser. There, while he contentedly drank a cup of coffee and read the Sunday papers, Alex's hair was washed, tinted with blonde highlights, blow-dried to give extra volume and dressed in what the assistant informed her was a modified cottage-loaf style, with small inverted question marks wisping around the ears. Under the lights it gleamed as if it had just been well polished with a silk handkerchief.

'That's more like it,' Max approved, when Alex presented herself once more.

'All you seem to have done this morning is hang around waiting for me,' she apologized.

'It was worth it.' His eyes lingered over her, touching her like his fingers. 'Oh, yes, very much worth it.'

On their way through the cosmetics hall, Max said, 'I can get everything you need from the salon.'

'Hang on there,' Alex warned. 'I love my new image, but I have no intention of making it a false one.'

There were still, Max realized, small pockets of resistance to be overcome, and the one concerning her direct opposition to everything her mother stood for was very well dug in. Well, he thought. No hurry. One thing at a time.

Outside, on Lexington Avenue, he asked, 'Where to next? You want to be a tourist? Shall we rubberneck like two hicks from Hayseed, Iowa?'

'I should like to see where you work,' Alex said. 'Is that possible on a Sunday?'

'For you, anything.'

The Czerny building was a sixty-storey tower clad in bronze glass.

'I might have known,' Alex said drily, 'that it would be a matter of self-reflection.'

'I'll have you know this won a prize,' Max lectured severely.

'For what – best mirror of the year?'

He rang a bell and a guard, wearing a gun, Alex noted, came to let them in.

'Hi, Mr Fabian. Still working a seven-day week, I see.'

'This,' Max said, indicating Alex, 'is pleasure.'

They crossed a huge marble-floored hall to a bank of elevators, but Max opened one which stood on its own. It took them straight up to the executive floor, roofed in glass and carpeted in bronze. Around the walls were framed copies of Czerny advertising stills, mostly of Mora Haynes in her role as the Czerny Woman, standing or sitting among her Ming *cache-pots*, her out-of-season flowers, the ancestral portraits and the family silver; rich, impeccably bred, humblingly beautiful. Max saw the way Alex examined them, in silence and intently. He went to a door facing the elevator, opened it by dialling a code into the set of telephone-type letters set into its frame.

'Why the security?' Alex asked.

'Everything on this floor is top secret. That's the only way you can steal a march on your rivals. This is a cut-throat business, as you well know.'

His office was filled with light from a whole wall of windows. 'Oh . . .' Alex breathed. 'What a view! How do you ever get any work done?'

'I've been looking at it for a long time now, but go ahead, look your fill.'

He sat himself down on the big sofa against the opposite wall and watched her as she wandered around, touching things, familiarizing herself. 'I've often wondered where and how you worked,' she said, 'when you weren't travelling, that is.'

'Right here is where it's done.'

'Do you have a secretary?'

'I do. She's fifty, comfortably married to a man who works in our Comptroller's Department, and I don't know what I'd do without her.'

'Where do you keep your files?'

'I don't. She does.'

Next: '*Four* telephones?'

'One is a private line to your mother's office, the other is the internal system, the third is an outside line and the fourth is a hush-phone – it can be scrambled so nobody can listen in. If your mother is travelling and I'm not, that's the one we use.'

'Such complications,' marvelled Alex, acid coating the sweetness.

'All right, so it's frivolous and totally unnecessary, but try telling that to our customers. It also makes us a great deal of money.'

'Obviously,' Alex said. 'What are you working on now?' She held up a full-colour glossy she took from a pile to the right of Max's big desk. 'I can see how interesting it must be.'

'We're looking for a face to go with the name – when your mother comes up with one – for our new fragrance. They are all rejects.'

'What a pity Venus is dead.' Alex examined the lovely face before asking, 'What's wrong with this one?'

'Not classy enough.'

'And this?' She held up another.

'Too young.'

'Only in the cosmetics world could that be so,' Alex said with an ironic smile.

'Look, sweetheart, this is my job. I like it and I'm good at it. This is a billion-dollar industry and Czerny Cosmetics has a goodly share of it. It paid your way through college. This new fragrance –' Max rose to his feet to go across to his desk, '– will hopefully increase our share.' He unlocked a drawer with a key he took from a bunch he carried in his pocket. 'Once we get the right name and the face to go with it, that is.' He took a small phial from the drawer. 'Product X,' he said.

Alex went round the desk. 'Can I have a sniff?'

'Hold out your wrists.' Alex did so and Max tilted the opened bottle first against one, then the other. 'Now rub your wrists together . . . right, now try.'

Alex sniffed. 'Mmmmm . . . typical.'

'What do you mean?'

'It's my mother.'

Max fixed her with an intent gaze. 'Why do you say that?'

'It reminds me of her.'

'Tell me how.'

'Well . . .' Alex sniffed again. 'It's sharp, yet – sensuous. Distinctive, provocative . . .' Another sniff. 'Very – feminine in a come-hither way . . . makes a statement that's the ultimate in confidence.

You'd have to know what you were and who you were to wear this, otherwise it would wear you.' A shrug. 'It's Madame.'

Max fell into his chair. 'Out of the mouths of babes . . .' he said, in a voice of awe.

'I don't mind being called baby, but babes?'

'Madame,' Max said, savouring it like a fine old wine. 'Better still, *Madame!*' He shook his head. 'Why do I bother?' he asked helplessly. 'We've been through dozens and dozens of names, none of them "right", as your mother would say. You take one sniff and bingo! That's it! That's absolutely it! *Madame!* It says it all!' He was out of his chair, had her in his arms and was kissing her breathless. 'You did it once before so why the hell didn't I think of asking you again. Jesus, the answer was staring me in the face — like a lot of other things — but could I see it? My God,' he said reverently, 'but you are your mother's daughter, and once I tell her about this she'll have no option but to be proud of it.'

'But I know nothing about perfumes,' Alex protested. 'All I did was tell you what it made me think of.'

'Which is what the name of a fragrance is supposed to do, my adorable idiot.'

'If you say so,' Alex said, not caring one way or the other, just as long as he was happy.

'Don't you see? That business about the gift coffret was not just a one off; you *are* the one who has inherited your mother's instinct, not poor, dead, amiable Chris. You! It's God-given and absolutely invaluable, and you don't even realize you have it!' Max shook his head again. 'Talk about a turn-up for the books! Ours are going to be as black as sin once this gets on the market!' He dropped his arms, strode first this way, then that. 'And not only her name but her face! *Madame!* by Madame.' He frowned. 'Unfortunately there are already two fragrances — both long established classics — on the market right now: *Jolie Madame* and *Madame Rochas*, but if we use her face there can be no doubt as to which is which, and ours doesn't even remotely resemble either of them. Wait until I unload this on to her! She'll flip!'

'She may not agree.'

'Oh, she'll agree. *Her* title — by which she is internationally known — and *her* face spearheading a multi-million-dollar advertising campaign? She'll kill anyone who tries to stop her.'

'Aren't you going from the sublime to the ridiculous?' Alex asked.
Max frowned. 'In what way?'

'You said that one –' Alex nodded to the glossy she laid down on the desk – 'was too young. Isn't my mother too old?'

'Not with the right photographer, and this fragrance is intended for the older, more sophisticated woman anyway; the range to go with the fragrance is focused on the anti-ageing angle – as long as we can get away with it, and I intend to persuade Eve to delay that for a while until we see what the FDA are going to do in that direction. But they can't block us on the fragrance. If we're lucky, by the time that has made its impact, the rest of the campaign will meet with no opposition.'

He was ablaze with enthusiasm and confidence, but as he looked at Alex he saw that while she was pleased for him, she was also being tolerant. To her, all this was of earth-shattering unimportance. He reined himself in. If he went on like this he'd be on the phone, ravenous to get started, awash with ideas tumbling over themselves in their eagerness to form a pattern, impatient to the point of obsession to see his ideas brought to life, and Alex put firmly, even absently, aside. No, he told himself. This is her day. Had he been alone, he would have called the restaurant, spent the rest of the day at his desk. God knows he'd done it plenty of times before. Not this time, he counselled himself. You have time, plenty of time. It's Sunday. Tomorrow is Monday; the start of a working week. The days of thinking only of himself were over. At last you have more to fill your life with than work. But if I can get Alex to work with me, he thought. He felt excitement rise again. By God, they would make such a team . . .

He saw she was looking at him quizzically, but, and his heart soared, with both total acceptance and loving understanding.

'All right,' she said. 'It's only half-past one. I'll give you half an hour.'

'Angel!'

Alex retired to the big sofa, where she picked up one of the industry magazines, but it was more interesting to watch Max. How concise he was, how persuasive, how dominating. He made calls, he scrawled, sketched, calculated. His excitement was contagious. He loves this, she thought. The wheeling and the dealing, the cunning and the conning. Watching, she understood and accepted that she had a rival. It meant no less love for her, he had made that plain last night, but he had another passion, an old mistress of long standing, with the familiarity and unbreakable hold of one who knew she would always have a claim on him. Two o'clock came and went, as did two-thirty. Finally, she said, 'Max . . . Max.'

He looked up and she saw him come to awareness. 'Jesus, Alex! Why didn't you say something . . . God, I'm sorry . . . I had no idea . . . I lose track of time when I get going.'

'Which is what we had better be doing, don't you think?'

'I'm there, I'm there . . .' He tapped his papers into tidiness, hid them in a folder, locked that in the safe which formed the left-hand pedestal of his desk. 'This is all your doing, you know,' he accused her virtuously. 'If you hadn't lit my fire . . .' He drew her to her feet. 'In more ways than one.' He checked his watch. 'My God, it's a quarter of three. Never mind, we'll grab a cab. And I was going to show you New York . . .'

'I rather think I've just been watching it.'

'God, I was going to do so much! You must be starving. I know I am.'

Alex was feeling nervous, rather than hungry, but she said, 'Mmmm,' non-committally.

'Come on, then. Let's see what my old man is cooking up for us.'

While Max paid the cab-driver, Alex inspected Fabiani's. Big windows, café curtains in red and white check, plants in hanging baskets, advertisements for beer and cigarettes. When Max pushed open the door the smell of garlic hit her, that and good olive oil. The restaurant was emptying, people were leaving as they entered, people who obviously knew Max.

'Max? How are ya!'

'Hey, look who's slummin'.'

A big woman came from behind the cash desk to meet them. 'Massimo . . .'

'Here we are, Ma.' Max was embraced and kissed, then he took Alex by the hand. 'Ma, this is Alex.'

'*Little* Alex! Something wrong with your eyes?' Mama Fabiani surged towards Alex, who found herself enfolded, hugged and kissed. 'About time,' she scolded. Her eyes approved what she saw.

'Any old friend of my son is a new friend of ours,' she said. 'Come . . . the big table is all ready.'

Alex was introduced to Max's sister Ella, who was a younger version of her mother and the image of Max, then Max took her through to the kitchen to meet his father, who examined Alex carefully, finally nodded, smiled, kissed her cheek. 'You don't look like a professor,' he said approvingly.

'I'm not,' Alex laughed.

'She's a doctor, Pa. Of literature.'

His father shrugged. 'Whatever. She still doesn't look it.'

That afternoon, Alex discovered that Max speaking Italian was not the Max who spoke American. As they sat at the big table, eating olives and *paglierino* cheese – 'but not too much or you'll spoil your appetite,' Max cautioned – and drinking red wine, waiting for the restaurant to empty and Max's brother Bruno, together with his family, to arrive, Alex was bemused and enchanted. The fact that she spoke Italian – learned because it was Max's language – was received with such pleasure that she felt her eyes prick. Once, when Ella, who had now left the bar since the 'Closed' sign had gone up on the door, was talking to a couple on their way out but who had stopped, as old friends, to say hello, he turned to her, smiled into her eyes and asked softly, '*Ti piacio io?*'

'*Tu lo sai*,' responded Alex. Did he, had he, was he pleasing her! she thought dazedly.

Bruno was a shorter, leaner version of his brother, his wife small, dark and very pretty, his four children, exquisitely dressed in Italian Sunday best, well mannered and obviously worshippers of Max. He shook hands warmly, his glance assessing as only an Italian can assess a woman, and Alex saw the tiny movement of the mouth he made at his brother, as if to say: 'You sly dog . . . no wonder you've been keeping her to yourself.'

They ate once the restaurant was empty of all but themselves, great piles of *prosciutto*, with the faint flavour of peaches and the texture of chiffon, followed by piles of *risotto al salto*; simple, but perfect. Alex had eaten the dish many times, but never one like this; sizzling hot, crusted, delicious.

Her nervousness evaporated like the steam from the risotto; in no time she was at ease, comfortable, free of constraint. She answered the many questions they asked with the unconscious assumption that they had the right; and she for her part was surprised to find they knew so much about her, though Mario Fabiani's face was a study as he listened to Alex telling them what she did at Cambridge. But when he found she knew Steeple Morden he talked her head off his time there, and she found he remembered Cambridge very well. He then told her all about his Garibaldi grandfather, the one who had fled Italy for the United States.

It was six o'clock when they regretfully rose to go; the restaurant opened again at seven-thirty and there was work to be done. This time, Mario Fabiani did more than shake her hand. He kissed her while Max nodded approvingly.

'It's been wonderful,' Alex said, for once at a loss for words. 'I have enjoyed this so much.'

'But you will come again, and again. Do not be a stranger. Our house is your house.' It was more than the conventional Italian politeness; she knew she had been accepted.

'Let's walk,' she said, when they were out in the open air. 'I feel I need to walk off all that food and wine.'

'The normal thing would be an afternoon nap,' Max said.

Alex found her throat constricted. 'If that's what you want.'

Max stopped, looked deeply into her eyes. 'Today, we do what *you* want,' he said.

And I do want it, Alex thought, on a shiver of nervous anticipation. I do want it.

'All right, then. Let's walk for a while, and then I would like to see where you live when you're in New York.'

They walked in silence, arm in arm, hand in hand, yet never had Alex felt so close to anyone. His hand was warm, firm, confident. Wherever you want to take me, she thought, I'll go. She felt she was on the verge of a momentous discovery, one that would make the final change to a life that had, in so short a space of time, undergone so much change already. Chris's death had been the catalyst, she realized; he had given her so much more than money. She resolved there and then to do something that would enshrine it in memory. A scholarship, she thought. Yes, I'll fund a scholarship, maybe two . . . She fell to planning.

They walked through Greenwich Village, under the arch in Washington Square, continued on uptown as far as Grammercy Park, with Max pointing out places that had hitherto only been names, like the little houses near the corner of Grove and Bedford Streets, where O. Henry once lived, and the narrow house, only nine feet wide, where Edna St Vincent Millay once wrote her poetry. He showed her the Chelsea Hotel, where Thomas Wolfe, Dylan Thomas and Arthur Miller had slept and written in its rooms.

Finally, at Thirty-fourth Street, Alex said, 'No more, Max. My mind is full to bursting . . . I've got enough to think about for weeks.'

Without a word he hailed a cab. They sat in silence, each aware of what the other was thinking. When the cab stopped: 'You live in a Museum?' Alex asked jokingly, to relieve the tension.

'Above it. Handy when I feel I can't do without thirty minutes' contemplation of Picasso or Van Gogh.'

Max had a duplex in the apartment block above the Museum of Modern Art, forty-four floors of high-security, state-of-the-art apartments which afforded the ultimate in privacy without the unnecessary clutter of shops, health club, restaurant and pool. Museum Tower gave unrivalled views of the city, and its ceilings were reasonably high for a New York tower block. When Max ushered Alex through the front door she caught her breath. Through the sixteen feet of uncurtained glass lay the lights of the city. 'Oh . . .' she said on a caught breath. 'Don't switch the lights on . . . not yet . . .' She went across, placed her hands flat on the glass. 'This is fairyland,' she exclaimed.

'No, that's San Francisco.' What am I saying? he thought, unaccustomed to the nervousness he was feeling. I've done this more times than I can remember, but this time it's different. Because Alex hasn't. And there I go making lousy jokes.

'I love your home town,' Alex breathed, dazzled by the prospect of not only what she was seeing, but what she was about to feel. Pamela was right, she thought. New York *is* the perfect place.

She felt Max come up behind her, wrap his arms about her. 'You have a lot of love inside you,' he said, 'but I'm greedy. I want it all.'

She turned to face him. 'I never could deny you anything.' Her eyes were suffused, and there was colour in her face, a glow that had nothing to do with the reflected lights.

'What a lot of time we've wasted,' Max said.

'No; it wasn't right, before. *I* wasn't right. I had to undergo a change not only of mind but of heart, of outlook, of – life. Every word you said to me that night was right –'

'You've already made that clear.'

'And tonight will complete the process. What I said about the Greeks and virginity meaning a whole person, wasn't right in my case; I wasn't whole, but I wasn't willing either to accept the fact or change it. Now I am. Now I want to. Oh, Max, how I want to . . .'

He drew her away from the windows, and with hands that trembled began to take off her brand-new clothes, laying them carefully over the back of a chair. Finally, when she was naked, he took the pins from her hair, spread it about her shoulders, then stood back and looked at her.

Alex had her eyes downcast, as if afraid to see the last of her fears revealed as unconquerable. There is so *much* of me, she thought in anguish. I want to be beautiful for him because he loves beauty so much, he taught me to appreciate it; not just women's faces and bodies but art, music, buildings, nature. I want him to look at me the way he looks when he looks at beauty, even though I'm not beautiful. She was afraid to open her eyes, to see the disappointment that even now, she expected.

He was silent so long that she knew she had to face it. But when she did look at him there was no disappointment in his expression; what she saw made her throat tighten and her eyes well.

'*Como sei bella,*' he said in a thick, awed voice. 'My God, Alex, you are magnificent; the very meaning of the word woman. Here . . .' his fingers brushed the slopes of her breasts, 'here . . .' his palms praised the indentation of her waist and the swell of her hips, 'and here,' his knuckles grazed the tight curls at the juncture of her thighs. 'Why did you hide such splendour away? What made you think no man would ever want you?'

Magnificent? Splendour? Alex felt the room reel.

'You were wrong, oh, Alex you were so wrong . . . Yes, you're big, but everything is in proportion . . . perfect proportion. An earth goddess. Demeter must have looked like you . . .'

He began to take off his own clothes, but impatiently, and those he let stay where they fell. Finally, he too was naked, and Alex let her eyes feast on him in turn; the beauty of hard flesh and muscles, the broad shoulders, the deep chest with only a fine sprinkling of hair, the narrow hips leading to long legs and his sex, hard and jutting from a bush of hair as black as that on his head, but without the grey.

'And Donatello once sculpted you . . .' She wanted to kneel and worship him, but he took her hands, drew her to him, breast to chest, thigh to thigh, his erection hot and hard as a stone between them.

Then he began to kiss her.

Alex opened her eyes, yawned, stretched till her muscles cracked. She felt boneless, replete, as totally relaxed as a cat, and alive. At last, she thought exultantly, I know what it means to be *alive*! Max had given her an initiation into the pleasures of the flesh: Pleasures! she thought. Ecstasies, more like. I *knew* about it all, but I understood nothing. I hadn't even the beginning of an idea . . . She ran her hands down her body; the one Max had adored, with his hands, with his mouth and finally, with that extraordinary organ which, when roused, turned into a creature with a life of its own. It had not only penetrated her body – and how extraordinarily well it had fitted, she thought now, as if it had been designed just for her – but she had absorbed it. It's not men who possess, she thought; that's only how they like to think of it. It's we who possess them; we who take them into us, we who allow them entry. No wonder they're so terrified of the power we wield; no wonder they fight so hard to limit it. Why didn't I realize this before? she pondered. She laughed. Why didn't I realize a lot of things. Like her own passionate nature. 'My God,' Max had said, after the first time, when he had fallen away and out of her, chest heaving, his body, like hers, slippery with the sheen of perspiration, 'you certainly are a quick study.'

She sat up, looked around as she realized he wasn't beside her. Throwing back the sheet which they had drawn over them before they had both fallen into a sleep as deep as dying, she went to find him. He was in the kitchen, and for a moment she stood and admired the neat, tight buttocks and the body she had explored – as he had explored hers – so thoroughly, with dedication and sensual pleasure. Her own nakedness she now gloried in, since Max had convinced her, by what he had done as much as by what he had said, that her voluptuous body was something to be proud of. 'These, for instance,' he'd said, cupping her breasts like melons, 'those god-awful clothes you wear always concealed these beauties.

Breasts are the most female thing about any woman and from now on you dress like a female; a little cleavage – but not too much. I want they should surmise but never know.'

But he had known, oh, how he had known . . . She felt heat rise. Once shown she had developed a talent for it; her shyness falling away as her clothes had, never to be worn again. There was nothing he had not done to her, brought her to, or she to him, and every minute had been a revelation. He had given her orgasms which ended at her toes.

Now she asked, 'Does sex always give you an appetite? I'm starving too, and after the lunch I ate!'

'It uses up a lot of energy,' Max said, turning to smile at her. 'I thought a nice fat juicy steak and a big baked potato.'

'Mmmm . . . yes, please.' Then she drew a shocked breath. 'We were supposed to be meeting Pamela!' Her eyes sought the clock on the wall. 'It's ten o'clock! Whatever will she think?'

'She knows,' Max said. 'I called her earlier.'

He had left the bed after her initiation, come back with a bottle of cold white wine and two glasses, so he must have called her then.

'I'm glad somebody still has his wits about him,' Alex said thankfully. 'I seem to have lost mine with my virginity.' Her arms stole about his waist. 'But I found something much better to replace it.' She kissed his shoulder. 'Thank you, my love.'

'Take a look at the potatoes, they should be ready.'

They were, and the steaks fell apart under the knife. Helping herself to more of the sour cream dressing, Alex said, 'If anyone had told me, a few short weeks ago, that I would be sitting in your kitchen, stark naked, putting away a steak as big as a dinner plate and feeling like I'd just been reborn, I would have told them to go and have their head examined.' Her smile was wicked. 'But I can't wait to be re-examined by you.' She chewed blissfully for a few moments then asked, 'Are first times always as good as this?'

'It depends on who's involved.'

'Well, it's probably because you've been involved so often that mine was so good, but the second and third times were even better.'

She laid her knife and fork together. 'Now I'm ready for a fourth.' She eyed him expectantly.

'Not on a full stomach,' Max said.

*

408

Later, after the fourth, truly sublime melding of minds, hearts and bodies, Alex lay in Max's arms, and asked, 'You're going to make an honest woman of me, I hope.'

'You've managed to do that all on your own.'

She shook him slightly. 'You know what I mean.'

When Max did not reply, Alex said uncertainly, 'I take it the idea doesn't appeal?'

'It appeals very much. I'd like nothing better than to marry you, Alex, and I would if I could, but I can't.'

Alex sat up slowly, as if someone had pulled her strings. 'You're not going to quote Samuel Butler at me again?'

'No. I can't marry you because I'm already married. Have been since I was nineteen years old.'

The sombre, yet bitter note in his voice penetrated the stunning blow of her shock and softened it. 'I think you had better tell me,' she said.

'I was going to anyway. My wife is in a private nursing home upstate where she has been for the past twenty-odd years. She's a manic-depressive and they had to put her away for her own good, but it was not, never will be, for mine.'

In the flat, hard tones of someone telling an unhappy story, he told Alex how it had come about.

He had met Lucia Manzini in his sophomore year at Columbia. She was best friends with his best friend's sister. She was very pretty, sensuously sexy, and he fell like the proverbial ton of bricks. She told him her parents were stuffy, old-fashioned Italians who kept her on a leash, which she hated, and she used to sneak away to meet him. She wanted them to elope, but Max, having been warned by his friend that Lucia's father was both very rich and very powerful, refused to be rushed into things. But she had been so tempting, so passionate, so desperate for him that he had not been able to resist her. They met wherever and whenever they could, and every time they made love. She was insatiable, demanding; if she did not get what she wanted, when she wanted, she would physically attack him, and he soon realized that there was much more here than the traditional spoiled little rich girl. He never knew what to expect, how she would be. She would either be way, way up or down, down, down; she would either adore him or flay him with verbal abuse.

Finally he couldn't take any more. He told her it was finished. She wept, she screamed, she threatened, she kicked, she bit, but he was adamant. She was too much for him, and what she was, once the first bright fire had died, he didn't want, for he finally understood she wasn't normal. When he got a message from her father asking him to go and see him at the big house in Scarsdale he thought she was trying to pressurize him, and went along filled with determination not to allow it. But Carlo Manzini was more sorrowful than angry. Max had been wrong in what he did. Yes, Lucia was headstrong, wild, but as a good Italian boy he should have known better. Now, he would have to accept his responsibilities. When Max, puzzled, asked what responsibilities, Carlo Manzini had told him that Lucia was pregnant, that he expected Max to marry her and that he would see to it that Max continued with his studies. He would buy them a nice house, Lucia would continue to live in the style to which he had accustomed her, and he would give them a traditional Italian wedding. But married they would be. Or else . . . He was affable, even indulgent; Lucia was Sicilian, and Sicilian women were, when young, a temptation to any man. Which was true, because to Max's bedazzled eyes, she had possessed the ripeness and bloom of a bunch of vintage grapes heavy on the vine; ripe to bursting and filled with heavy, sweet juice.

'It was when I discovered she was Sicilian, not from Calabria as she'd said, that I knew what I'd fallen into. A stupid, besotted nineteen-year-old kid who thought he knew everything but knew nothing. Her father was a Mafia Don; that's where the money, the big house, the cars came from. It was all behind the scenes, of course. He never had his name in the paper, they'd never got him to go and testify at the Kefauver hearings; he was a legitimate business man on the surface: a very successful wine importer, but to me he made it plain what his real business was. Not right out – he didn't have to. One look at the man who opened the front door and I knew. He also made it plain that I had a choice: I could marry Lucia or be a dead man. He would also see to it that my father's restaurant was "dealt with". What could I do? I was terrified my parents would find out; and it was my fault. Or so I thought until I discovered – again too late – that Lucia had been through the entire sophomore year. They told me – afterwards – that her sexual frenzies were all part of her illness.'

Max didn't speak for a while and Alex waited, sitting quietly, saying nothing, just holding the hand that was squeezing hers so tight it had lost all feeling. 'So we were married. A great big Italian wedding – and my funeral. He gave us a big house – across the street from his – and for a while Lucia calmed down. But it was only one of her "down" phases. It soon started up again. I'd have to go chasing after her, find her in sleazy bars and truck-stops picking up God knows who. Once or twice it was so bad I had no option but to call him and he'd send over a couple of his heavies, so she started going further and further afield. Finally, she grew too big and there was only me.' Alex felt Max shudder. 'I wouldn't wish that on anybody. I was falling apart. I wasn't getting any sleep, my studies were all to hell. When she went into hospital to have the baby I was relieved: at least I'd get some peace for a while.

'The baby was small but healthy – it was a girl, but they kept Lucia in hospital for a while, postnatal depression, they told me. Give her time; she'll come out of it with the proper treatment. But the baby was six weeks old before they let her home, and there *was* a difference. I'd find her sitting by the crib, staring at the baby. She was as quiet then as she had been frantic before. We had the baby christened – Angelina for her mother, who was dead, Rosa for mine – and Lucia seemed obsessed with it. Her father hired a nurse but she never got to do anything. Lucia insisted on doing everything. She used to sit and sing to it for hours, rocking it back and forth, back and forth. She moved out of our room and had a bed set up in the nursery. "See . . ." said her father, "she's happy now. It's what she needed. That's why I wanted it for her." And he seemed grateful. Whatever we wanted we could have. That I had been forced to accept something I didn't want wasn't important. Then, when the baby was three months old I came home one afternoon to find the house empty. I thought she'd taken Angelina out for an airing – it never occurred to me.' Max broke off, took a deep breath.

'When she didn't come home I called him and he instituted a search. It was dark by then and I still don't know what made me go out to the pool . . . she hadn't used it since the baby. But that's where she was, standing in the pool, rocking the baby, singing to it. Only it was dead. She'd drowned it.'

Alex bit her lip, her heart heavy and aching with pain and belated comprehension. After a while Max went on in a voice utterly devoid of expression. 'He managed it all, of course. A tragic accident was how it all seemed by the time he'd finished applying pressure in the right places. But Lucia was admitted to a private nursing home "for her own safety" and that's where she's been ever since. She doesn't know me, she doesn't know anybody. She managed to escape, finally, into a world where nobody could follow. They gave her a doll and she plays with that; dressing it, playing with it, singing to it. I used to visit her at first, but it was – awful. And there was no point. She had the best of care; she'd always have the best of care, but she'd be there for the rest of her life. All I could do was get on with mine. I told him he could have his big house back and I went home to Mulberry Street. He understood, he told me.' Max fell silent again then roused himself to go on. 'Anyway, I got my law degree, and then I met a girl. So I went to Lucia's father and told him all about her; asked him if, things being the way they were, I could have my freedom. I remember how he looked at me; sorrowfully, pityingly but absolutely inflexible. Lucia and I had been married by Holy Mother Church and it had its laws. While she lived, Lucia would be the only wife I would ever have.'

Max's voice changed, became acid with hatred. 'The smiling, unctuous hypocrite! He made his millions from every kind of vice: prostitution, drugs, gambling – but my marriage, my non-existent travesty of a marriage, was sacred. He said he understood my "needs" and that being so he would look the other way. But Lucia would either be a wife or a widow.' Max drew a deep breath. 'And that's how it is. He's still alive – he's only sixty-seven, and Lucia's only forty-two. I'm trapped, Alex. For the foreseeable future – maybe longer – I'm trapped.' He looked at her for the first time and his eyes were black holes. 'I'd marry you tomorrow if I could. I'm forty-three, I want some kind of settled life, one woman instead of one after another. I want *you*. But I can't marry you.' He paused. 'You have to know what you're getting into.'

'Oh, Max . . . I already have so much more than I ever expected. Do you think a piece of paper is going to make any difference to the way I feel? Yes, I would like to be Mrs Max Fabian, but if that can't be, then so be it.' She put her arms about him, drew him to her, held him close. 'We can still be together, that's all that matters. Never mind the benefit of clergy. I need no priest to say words that aren't necessary.' She smiled down at him, brushed back the silvered black hair, damp under her fingers.

'But he checks on me. He knows what I do, where I am all the time. He's pleased for me, he says. But he won't ever change his mind. And he's unpredictable. He's always looked the other way because I guess he knew there was no threat, no danger of me asking again. Once he knows about you . . . I don't know what he'll do. Even when I went to Italy all those years ago – and that was a form of escape – he had me checked on. He knew all about Eve, my job – everything – when I got back home because he sent for me. Told me so. He was kind – benevolent, even – but he jerked on the leash nevertheless. He'll make it his business to find out about you. He has power, influence –'

Alex laid a hand across his mouth. 'I'm a rich woman, Max. Let him try. I've learned through my mother the power of money and if he does try anything then I shall use it.' Alex's eyes were vividly green. 'I've only just found you, Max, after my own years in the wilderness. I'm not going to lose you. And maybe he'll think I'm just the latest number on your list. After all, you spent a long time with Mora.'

'It's just that I never worried before because – well, because I was only ever interested in short leases. After that once, I never let myself get deeply involved again. It wasn't worth the pain. But you – this is for the rest of my life. He'll know that and maybe feel Lucia is being threatened . . .' Alex saw Max's face firm into resolve.

'You're not going to ask him a second time?' Alex's voice sharpened.

'Well . . . it's more than twenty years now. Lucia is still the same. There will never be any change there, but maybe *he* has changed. It's worth a try. I *want* to be free, Alex, for you. Anything is worth it for you.'

Alex cupped his face with her hands. 'You would do that for me?'

'There is nothing I wouldn't do for you.'

'Then there's no need. We will live as millions of other couples live nowadays. What's a bit of legal paper? Did it ever do my mother any good no matter how many she collected? I don't need somebody to say words over us. We belong together – are together – and that's all that matters.'

413

Max wrapped her in his arms and for a while they lay in silence, then Alex raised herself so that she could look down at him. 'Come live with me, and be my love?' she asked softly.

'Try and stop me,' Max answered unsteadily.

21

New York, 1988

In the house at Oyster Bay that Christopher Bingham had left her, Eve had spent the weekend alone, or what passed for alone in her circle. Jonesy was there, and the Filipino couple who looked after the house when she wasn't in residence, and the Japanese houseman and the gardeners, but they were all there to look after her and her alone, so in her eyes, that was how she was.

She arrived on the Friday night, and her first action was to change into a favourite lounging robe; a treasured Balenciaga of tangerine velvet lined with taffeta that matched her eyes, with big cuffs like those of a mid-eighteenth-century gentleman. She ate a light supper and then went into her favourite room in the house; a small silk-hung treasure trove of furniture, hangings, porcelain and pictures that were a delight to the eye, all done in Chinese scarlet, celadon blue, jade green and sunshine yellow. It had a mullioned window overlooking Long Island Sound, with a wide window seat scattered with silk cushions she had bought in Hong Kong and a low, wide coffee table on which she placed the files and papers she was working on.

She piled up the cushions to form a soft wall against which she could lean, picked up her yellow lined pad and one of half a dozen very sharp pencils in various colours; red meant Immediate, blue stood for Rejection, green for Further Consideration and black for 'See me about this!' There was no telephone; when she was in 'retreat' it meant no interruptions unless it was a matter of life or death.

She settled herself comfortably, and then gave her mind over to her most pressing problem; the name for her new fragrance. She had sprayed herself all over with it when she had changed; now she closed her eyes, let it wreathe her in its potency and let her mind float on it, waiting for inspiration. But none came. It was eternally feminine, but Rochas had used *Femme* ages ago. It was sexy, but *Allure* was common, a drug-store name. It was chic, but *À la mode* sounded too much like a fashion magazine. It will come, she told herself, not worried – yet. It always does. There is no problem I cannot deal with.

She smiled to herself. Had she not just dealt with three in one fell swoop? The tiresome matter of her worst mistake was now settled to her satisfaction. It was highly unlikely that their paths would cross again. And if she took her father with her, so much the better. She scribbled a reminder – in ordinary pencil – to arrange the Trust Fund she would set up for him, wrote in a figure, pursed her lips, slashed through it and wrote another. Yes, that was enough. He was an old man, his health was ruined, what could he do with money? All he needed was enough to keep him in decent comfort, and after the deprivations of the past thirty years, that would seem like luxury. All that mattered was that he remain in obscurity. At this stage, when she was about to confirm, once and for all, her position as Empress of Beauty, she wanted no ripples from her past to disturb the flat calm of her future, because once she had her Name, and the Face to go with it, she would launch it in a way that had never been done before, with as much publicity as could be trumpeted, so loudly it would reach the furthest corners of her far-flung empire. It had to be absolutely *right*.

Of the five hundred perfumes on the market, only twenty of them dominated it by reason of the fact that they accounted for 80 per cent of sales that totalled 1.5 billion dollars a year. *Essence of Eve* was one. It had never had to fight for customers. Nor would this new one. It would be seen, tried, bought and become the ultimate conqueror. If I find a face first, she pondered, then fit the name to it . . . For a moment, Pamela Bradley's serene beauty hovered before her eyes. She had the necessary class, the well-bred distinction – but then, her father had been a Major-General and her mother was the daughter of an Earl – if somewhat impoverished. But there was always the miasma of old scandal there. First by her connection with Fritz Bahlsen, whose reputation was, by now, more than somewhat tarnished, and the later scandal of her connection with Eve Czerny's only son, which had brought so many unwanted headlines. No; leave her where she is, Eve thought. That was a brainwave of mine; it shows publicly that I am not a woman who bears grudges, and by all accounts she's just what the salon needs. The moment she ceases to be of real use that can be changed. I have made the gesture, and that is what people remember.

She frowned, as she now remembered that she had not yet heard from Sloane, Ransom. She scribbled another note to call them first thing Monday morning. Really, she thought irritably, I should not have to chase them. There is no one else to inherit all that Bingham money. Unless . . . of course, she told herself, Chris was not in the least organized. He probably hasn't left a will and they're trying to straighten everything out. Just like him, she thought fondly, and then sadly; he died so suddenly after all . . . She slammed the door on that particular vista. What was done was done and there was nothing she could do for him now. Nevertheless, she would still call them, find out what the situation was. It was fortunate in a way, she mused. Those millions would come at just the right time. She would really be able to splurge on this launch.

She scribbled yet another note: Talk to Max about launch. He was very good at publicity. Her mouth curved in a knowing smile. Max was very good at everything. I wonder, she mused. We work so well together, and that interlude we had was very pleasant. I don't intend to marry again and it would be 'in house', so to speak. Mora Haynes is out of the picture, and that would be another problem solved. He will have to end that ridiculous friendship, of course. I never liked it but he wouldn't be told. 'If you don't like it then you know what you can do,' he'd said flatly. Which was – then as now – the last thing she wanted to do. Max was too valuable. She had never understood what he saw in that great hulking creature anyway, for his taste in women was as sophisticated as everything else about him. Still, it was only a friendship. He felt sorry for her, I suppose, and aren't Italians sentimental? Yet he was anything sentimental in business. Well, he will just have to end it, she resolved. Once and for all. I will invite him here next weekend. To discuss the launch. Just the two of us. Her smile became hooded.

She poured herself a glass of Perrier water from the bottle in the ice bucket which Jonesy had left on a tray at her elbow, added a slice of fresh lemon, her mind going over her strategy. She had seduced him that first time; he was younger then – she did a little hop, skip and jump over the intervening years – this time she would let him make the running, once she wound him up, of course. All the way. Not that there would be much to wind; he had always protected her against herself where men were concerned. He had warned her about that miserable little pervert Rik Stevens, hadn't he? And he had shaken his head over her last, briefest of all marriage with Eduardo de Barranca. Why would he do that unless he felt a proprietory interest?

She swirled the ice-cold liquid around her mouth, let it trickle slowly down her throat. Yes, she thought. Max will do nicely . . . She let her thoughts drift, to be brought back to the present by the chiming of the little cupid clock. She shook herself mentally. That was a promised treat once she had everything else arranged to her satisfaction. For now, she had work to do.

'So, where are you going this morning?' Max asked Alex as they left his apartment at nine o'clock.

'I'm going to take a Circle Line cruise all the way around Manhattan Island.'

'I wish I could come with you, but I have to tackle Madame with your inspiration.'

'She won't go for it if you tell her it was my idea. I wouldn't do so if I were you.'

'Of course I'm going to tell her. It was your idea.'

'Then you take the credit. I don't mind.'

'But I do. I have a few points to make.'

'I hope you know what you're doing.'

'*Now* you complain.'

Alex kissed him. 'See you at one o'clock – or as near to then as I can make it. You're sure you can? Perhaps I'd better ring you. Give me your private number.'

Max scribbled it in the small notebook she handed him.

On 54th Street she was going West, he East. 'Have a nice day,' she said mischievously.

'It won't be for want of trying.'

When he got to the office he was told that Madame was coming in from Long Island and wouldn't be in until around ten, when she wanted to see him in her office. No more than I want to see you, Max thought. When he went in she was standing by her window, neat and trim in a Saint Laurent suit of French blue slashed with white, and when she turned to face him she had 'the look'. 'I've got it, Max,' she said. 'I went into the country for the weekend to think in peace and quiet and it came to me. What do you think of *Always*?'

'It's the title of a song, isn't it? By Irving Berlin?'

Eve frowned. 'Is it?' Eve knew nothing about music, it didn't interest her.

'I've got something better,' Max said.

'Better!' Eve fixed him with a look he ignored as he opened the folder he was carrying, laid on her desk a series of rough drawings. 'It's perfect,' he said, 'so perfect I can't for the life of me understand why you didn't think of it.'

Eve took three steps to her desk and bent over it. Max waited. Finally, she straightened, and by the way she spoke he knew she was miffed; for two reasons. One, the name was 'right', and two, she hadn't thought of it herself. She and she alone, had been responsible for the names of her fragrances up till now, and it maddened her to think that for this one, the most important one of all – the most important ever – somebody else had beaten her to it.

'There are two classic fragrances with the name Madame in them –'

'I know, the Balmain and the Rochas, but this is just one name – yours, well, your title anyway. And with your face – we'll get Bill Frazier to do the photography – it will be a sensation! Can't you see it? *Madame!* by Madame.'

He saw anger and resentment fight a losing battle with ego. Ego won. But she couldn't let him get his way that easily. 'You don't think it's a bit – much? I'm already accused of being on a constant ego-trip; this might be taken as evidence that I've reached the point of no return.' But her smile was a preen, and the look in her eyes was of one who was seeing visions. '*Madame!* by Madame.' Her voice caressed the words. Then, coolly: 'Yes, I think you have something there, Max. How clever of you to come up with it now, after all the time we've spent on it.' She couldn't let him have an untarnished glory.

'Oh, it wasn't me.'

Her eyes narrowed. 'Have you taken this out of the office?' Her voice was soft with menace.

'No. The name was suggested right here, in my office.'

Eve sniffed. 'I should hope so. Secrecy is *absolutely* essential. This must come as a bolt from the blue – a lightning bolt,' she added, with a smile that boded ill. 'So, who is the genius, then?' Now she was sardonic, and Max knew what she was thinking. Whoever it was would bear watching. Eve tolerated no rivals.

'It was Alex,' he said.

'Alex who?' Eve was frowning; it honestly didn't occur to her that it could be her own daughter, not even after the business of the gift box.

'Alex Brent.'

Eve stared at him. Max held her eyes. He could almost hear the wheels and ratchets whirring and clicking as she adjusted previously held opinions. Finally: 'Explain,' she commanded. He did so.

'All it took was one sniff. She had it dead to rights. This fragrance *is* you. You created it, you will personify it. It is sheer genius, Eve. Who would have thought that Alex, not Chris, would inherit your flair, your innate instinct for what is *right*? She wants nothing to do with it, by the way. You're welcome to the name, but she has no further interest in what you do with it. She believes that the beauty business is the biggest con of all time.'

Eve said nothing. She was still staring at him but not seeing him. Finally she asked, 'How long has she been in New York?'

'Since last Friday.'

'Did she come to see you?'

'No. Pamela Bradley.'

'Why?'

'That's something I am not at liberty to divulge.'

'Max . . .' It was a warning.

'I'm sorry, but it's nothing to do with you.' He let five seconds tick by. 'I can only tell you that it has to do with Chris.'

'My son!'

'He was Alex's brother,' Max reminded, 'and he was going to marry Pamela.'

He held Eve's extraordinary eyes, now hard and bright as the stones they matched, saw her devious mind unerringly make the connection and plug into a knowledge that had those eyes flaring like blue flames. Without taking her eyes from his she stretched out

420

a hand to the row of buttons set into her desk top, stabbed one of them viciously.

'Margaret, get me Bertram Ransom of Sloane, Ransom. You have their number.'

Neither spoke as they waited for the call to come through. Eve's face was a mask; the one she had always worn when faced with her daughter, but her eyes were alive in a way that spoke death. Her telephone buzzed and she snatched up the receiver. 'Mr Ransom? Yes, fine, thank you. About my son's will . . .' She listened, and Max saw her face tighten on its bones. 'What is their name?' She picked up a gold pencil, scribbled a name and a number. 'Is that a branch or an associate . . . ? I see, yes, thank you.' She replaced the receiver, once more stabbed buttons as she called the number she had been given. 'I should like to speak to a Mr Alain Bernard . . . my name is Eve Czerny.' She waited, then: 'Mr Bernard, about my son's will . . .' She listened and Max saw her face tighten still further. 'Of course I have a right to know, he was my son . . .' By now, there were scarlet temper patches on the cheekbones that threatened to split the taut skin stretched so tightly across them. 'Mr Bernard, I do not think you know with whom you are dealing . . .' She listened some more and Max saw her breasts heave as she failed to get the information she wanted. 'We shall see about that!' she shouted, before slamming the receiver down. Then she picked up the red one, pressed a button. 'Pamela? I want to see you in my office. Now.'

Max made to leave but Eve snapped, 'No. Since you know so much already there's no point in your leaving.'

Max shrugged, went to one of the deep, comfortable chairs and sat down. Eve had turned her back on him; her shoulders were square with outrage. Thank heavens he had warned Pamela. Alex had insisted on it once Max had told her he intended to reveal the source of the name *Madame!* 'One thing will lead to another as it always does with her, so Pamela ought to be prepared.'

The Czerny salon was a mere two blocks away so it didn't take Pamela long to arrive. When she came in she looked at Max, who shook his head warningly. She nodded and said politely, 'You sent for me, Madame?'

Eve did not turn. 'Tell me about my son's will.'

'Why should I?' Pamela asked. 'It doesn't concern you.'

421

Eve whirled, and Pamela took a step back even as Max rose to his feet. 'How dare you? It wasn't enough you should take my son from me, now you take my money!'

'It was never your money. It belonged to Chris.'

'It was mine!' Eve shrieked. 'It belonged to my husband and then my son and should come to me now! I demand to know what he has done with it!'

'You can demand all you like. It is still nothing to do with you.'

With deadly, precise clarity Pamela said, 'There is no mention of you in Chris's will, therefore you are not concerned in *any* way.'

'You dare tell me that? About my own son!'

'Whom you drove to his death!' Now Pamela's topaz eyes took fire. 'He took out that suicidally fast car because you had him in such a state he didn't know how else to release his anger but in speed, as he always did. You harangued him and tore him into strips so thin he was in pieces! Don't you demand of me. I owe you nothing – and that is what Chris has left you.' Pamela smiled. 'Not even the lickings of a dog.'

'You are fired!' Eve howled. 'Get out of my office, my building, my company! If you set foot in my salon again I'll have you arrested!'

'With pleasure. And you have no power over me, Madame. Chris has seen to that. *I* now have the power his money gave him. So does your daughter. And that is all I'm saying. Take this further and we will release certain pertinent facts which will blow you off the face of the earth! Go on, take it to the courts. I should like nothing better than to expose you for what you are.' She ducked as Eve threw one of her telephones after her, but caught by its cord it dropped short and fell with a musical crash.

'Out!' Eve screamed. 'Out, out, OUT!'

Pamela turned on her heel and went to the door. 'Coming, Max?' she asked.

'If you leave this office you need never come back,' Eve snarled at him.

'That was my intention,' Max informed her gravely. He shut the door behind them.

Eve fell into her chair. She was trembling with rage; her heart was banging, her head felt as if it would burst. With one sweep of her arm she swept her other three telephones to the floor. Her door opened and her secretary put a scared face round the door. 'Get out!' screamed Eve. She put her elbows on the desk top, sank her face into them. I must think, she thought. Calm, calm . . . think. She breathed deeply as she always did when she needed to get herself back under control. In-out, in-out, eyes closed, mind a deliberate blank. She did not open her eyes until her heart had quieted, when she raised her head, let her hands fall, sank back in her chair. Her eyes fell on the sketches Max had placed on her desk. She snatched them, crumpled them, tearing, screwing until they were shreds, then let them lie where they fell.

So . . . Her son had rejected her in favour of his sister and his mistress. Well, it was only money and she had plenty of that. It would have come in handy but she could still carry out her plans. She massaged her forehead with thumb and forefinger, as if trying to loosen skin which felt as if it was clamped by an iron band. There was a pain there which throbbed in time with her heart. Think, she told herself, think . . .

God, I can't think, she thought in a panic. How could he *do* this to me? After all I did for him! Well, it's done now. And there's nothing you can do to change it, because everything you have fought for all these years will be destroyed. It's only money. Let them think they have achieved some sort of – of what? she thought aggrievedly. Revenge? For what? I kept that girl, didn't I? I paid for her to go to a good school then a fine university. I gave Pamela Bradley a job. What have I done that I should be ashamed of? All I have ever done has been pre-ordained anyway. How could my own son *do* this to me? I tried to make him accept his heritage. I only ever wanted the best for him. All he wanted was to drive fast cars and tinker with engines. And he went against my strict orders – not to mention my wishes – by taking up first of all with the last person I wanted him connected with, and then with a woman ten years older and infinitely unsuitable. And now he does this.

Her face changed. It must *never* get out. If it did she would be a laughing-stock. As if she would contest Chris's will when that would mean losing something far more important than his few millions. Let them go, she thought, them, the money, everything. Leave them behind. It was your intention, after all. Go ahead with it. Your plans are made. Carry them out.

But Max. Max was a loss, a terrible loss. How could *he* do this to her? She had brought him from nothing, given him everything. What would he be if I hadn't taken him up? she thought balefully. A lawyer. In some small office – well, perhaps not so small. But he wouldn't be where he is today. *I* made him. And now he does this. Well, her next lawyer would be a very different man and she would see to it that he knew his place. No more Maxes.

Which brought her to her daughter, and what she had done. I knew she was clever, but this! Why did I not know about this? Max should have told me. He knew her well enough; deliberately going against my wishes and positively *dedicating* himself to her. It wasn't me he cared about, when that pervert showed his true colours, but her. He didn't actually do anything to her – well, nothing serious. But he was *my* husband; I, Eve Czerny, had actually married him. But it was her he worried about, not me. He must have known what she was, even then, and kept the knowledge to himself. Perhaps to use when the time was right. She sat up in alarm. Like now? No, no . . . he said she wasn't interested and that's obvious from the way she looks. But what a waste of talent. My talent. I gave her that. *Madame!* by Madame. Why didn't I think of that? It's perfect. It will crown me as Empress. Who would have believed it? Never Chris as I had planned, but that plain gawk of a girl who reminded me of things I wished to forget. Concealing behind that appalling exterior that she was indeed my daughter. *She* was my heir, not Chris.

She shot upright so suddenly that her chair almost went over. Her eyes widened and she drew in a sharp, shocked breath. Of course! Oh, she thought, almost faint with shock and a sense of triumph so exultant her face glowed as if lit by inspiration. It *was* all planned, she thought in awe, but not in the way I thought. The wheel has come full circle. *This* is what destiny had in store for me. This is why everything I *thought* was important was removed. So that the only thing that *is* important was waiting for me when the time came. Fool! She grimaced at her own blindness. Idiot! She struck her forehead with her palm. *This* is what it has all been for! No wonder I was punished! I was on the wrong track and had to be put back on the right one. *She* has inherited my talent, my flair. She is the one meant to carry on the dynasty!

She left her desk, paced first one way, then the other, her mind working furiously, thoughts, plans, ideas coming so fast they fell over each other.

I have to get her back. Somehow, some way, I have to get them *both* back. There is too much at stake. Why, she thought dazedly, this is only the beginning, not the culmination. There are things waiting to be achieved the like of which will make what I have already done seem as nothing! *This* is why Laszlo has been brought back into my life. So that I can marry him, acknowledge our daughter and found a dynasty! Oh, she thought, dazzled by the prospect. How simple it all is now that I finally understand. *This* is my destiny! To found a dynasty! The possibilities are limitless. Oh, yes, I have to get them both back. And I will. Oh, I will. I'll think of some way. I know how to persuade, to cajole, to encourage. I'll get them both back and together we will go on to do things such as have never been seen. She will have to be remade, of course, but that will be easy. Have I not been remaking women for the past thirty years? By the time I'm finished with her nobody will recognize her. She must be worthy of the name Czerny.

Once again she fell into her chair, visibly trembling from the violence of her vision. So much to do . . . by the time I launch my fragrance the dynasty must be established. *Madame!* by Madame, and Alex Czerny, also by Madame. It's perfect! I will think of a way to persuade her – and she will be persuaded, because this is meant to be. This is my destiny. *She* is my destiny. I had it all wrong! Oh, how wrong I was. Looking elsewhere when the truth was right under my nose. She smiled. But Destiny knew. Destiny would not let me go my own way; I had to be faced with the fact that in spite of everything, I do not control my own life. It does. I *am* fated, and what must be must be. She will come back. So will Max. I will think of a way to do it. Fate will help me as it has always helped me. Has it not led me right here, to this particular enlightenment?

She raised her arms like a champion acknowledging the roar of the crowd, then lowered them to clasp her hands and bite on her knuckles, so feverish, so raging was her excitement. Which was when she noticed that in her temper, when shredding the sketches, she had broken a nail. Normally a disaster. Now she laughed. Nothing that can't be fixed, she thought. I will fix it all. I will get them both back and what will we not do? And the money will come

Fortunes

The sudden death of Charles Despard –
creator of Despard's, the world's leading
auction house – was greeted by turmoil in
the international art world and furore when
his will was read.

He had set up a contest between his two
daughters: young, inexperienced Kate and
her French stepsister Dominque, a
powerful figure who thrived on intrigue. To
the winner would go the whole mighty
empire.

Blaise Chandler, referee in this unequal
conflict, was at a loss to understand the
reason for setting up the bitter rivalry.

Until the contest began . . .

FONTANA PAPERBACKS

Also by
VERA COWIE

The Bad
and the Beautiful

Julia Carey, interior designer to London's social élite, is used to keeping unwanted admirers at arm's length. But even she cannot resist the charms of fabulously wealthy Brad Bradford. Their whirlwind affair turns to love, and when Brad returns to America Julia goes too – as his wife.

In marrying Brad, Julia has unwittingly made a fearsome enemy: Brad's mother, the ice-cool Lady Hester. Head of the oldest, most powerful family in Boston and creator of a vast business empire, she has plans for her beloved son – and they do not include Julia . . .

FONTANA PAPERBACKS

The Rich and the Mighty

The news of billionaire Richard Temoest's death sends a ripple of unease through the world's financial markets – and a tremor of anticipation through his rapacious stepchildren.

But control of the Tempest fortune passes to a stranger. Elizabeth Sheridan, already a top model, has a cool head and an unexpected streak of ruthlessness. But are they enough to ensure her survival in the dangerous, decadent world of wealth and privilege to which she is suddenly heiress?

FONTANA PAPERBACKS

Hot Type
Kristy Daniels

When Tory Satterly starts at the second-rate afternoon paper, *The Sun*, she's just a lowly, overweight reporter, relegated to the women's pages and hopelessly in love with Russ Churchill, golden boy of the prestigious rival morning paper, *The Post*. But Tory is tenacious and she soon enters the hard news world of smouldering sex scandals and drug deals. As her career soars, Tory becomes a svelte and sexy woman equally at home at exclusive spas, Swiss resorts, and in the arms of multimillionaire Max Highsmith.

And when *The Post* and *The Sun* are merged, there's room for only one at the top. Russ Churchill becomes Tory's rival . . . as well as her lover. Which of them will get the plum job – the one they have both wanted all their lives?

FONTANA PAPERBACKS

Fontana Paperbacks: Fiction

Fontana is a leading paperback publisher of fiction.
Below are some recent titles.

- [ ] ULTIMATE PRIZES Susan Howarth £3.99
- [ ] THE CLONING OF JOANNA MAY Fay Weldon £3.50
- [ ] HOME RUN Gerald Seymour £3.99
- [ ] HOT TYPE Kristy Daniels £3.99
- [ ] BLACK RAIN Masuji Ibuse £3.99
- [ ] HOSTAGE TOWER John Denis £2.99
- [ ] PHOTO FINISH Ngaio Marsh £2.99

You can buy Fontana paperbacks at your local bookshop or
newsagent. Or you can order them from Fontana Paperbacks,
Cash Sales Department, Box 29, Douglas, Isle of Man. Please
send a cheque, postal or money order (not currency) worth the
purchase price plus 22p per book for postage (maximum postage
required is £3.00 for orders within the UK).

NAME (Block letters)_____

ADDRESS_____

_____